THE BRUJA

MICHAEL MOLISANI

authorHOUSE®

AuthorHouse™
1663 Liberty Drive
Bloomington, IN 47403
www.authorhouse.com
Phone: 1 (800) 839-8640

Published by AuthorHouse 12/29/2017

ISBN: 978-1-5462-2253-8 (sc)
ISBN: 978-1-5462-2252-1 (e)

Library of Congress Control Number: 2017919503

Print information available on the last page.

DEDICATION

Before you, my dear reader, embark on this journey of wonder and horror, I want to take a moment to thank those individuals who supported me tirelessly in seeing this work brought to fruition.

To my wife, **Kimberly Molisani** for always listening to my manic story development. For suffering long weekends where I sat at my desk for 12 hours at a time, writing. For always reading the next chapter; *and the next chapter after that.* I love you.

To my best friend, **Athena Driscoll** for *being* my best friend. For telling me what was garbage when it was garbage. For your endless honesty, loyalty and dedication. I would not have come this far as an author without you. I love you.

To my friend, **Kristen Walls Kearney.** You never had to support me as much as you did, yet you never hesitated, and you became someone I trusted implicitly. We wouldn't be here without you.

Lastly, to my friend **Jennifer Volk**. In the earliest stages of this work you were my first (and only fan.) You supported me when I wanted to quit, counseled me when I was confused, and always pressed me to be better.

Act 1

A WITCH NAMED MAGGI

RURAL PENNSYLVANIA. PRESENT.

I was hunched over the driver's seat of my pickup truck, a pocket flashlight protruding from my lips as I carefully assembled a gift in the darkness. A small, metal tin rested on the faded upholstery as I meticulously collected a series of contents. Buttons, three or four pairs of old and mismatched earrings, refrigerator magnets, some coins, a roofing nail, a glittering silver necklace, two hair ties, and a children's flip book. I picked out what belonged and added it thoughtfully, before depositing the remainder to my pockets, or dashing them across truck's cab.

Once satisfied with the small, square tin, I close the lid and discard the flashlight to the side. It provided enough ambient light to keep working. I removed a switchblade from one of my pockets. The tips of the handle were faux pearl and the metal was quality, not cheap Pakistani steel that broke on bone. It was, genuinely, one of my favorite knives. I flipped out the blade and slashed open the palm of my right hand with practiced ease. If you're quick, you don't leave blood on the blade.

I closed the knife, and reached for a length of sky blue silk, wrapped it around my palm, flexing my fingers, clenching a fist, to force yet more blood into the fabric. Once I was satisfied with the blood, I dropped the silk to the truck's seat and grabbed the roll of gauze bandages to wrap my hand. I glanced around, calming my heart, letting the bleeding slow. The forest around me was quiet and lit by the faintest of moonlight. A cracked, rural road next to my truck was barely visible from the turn-off.

After a few minutes passed, I reached for the small, tin box and started to truss it up like an ornate gift, using the bloody blue silk as a ribbon, complete with bow. Finally, I held the small box to my chest, directly below my breasts into the concave of ribs, and dug under the driver's seat for an old hunting knife. Dull and rusted, it was little more than a jagged piece of metal. I pocketed this dull knife, turned off my flashlight, and turned away from the truck, using my right foot to kick the cab door closed behind me. The sound was clamor and noise in the silent woods.

I began walking away from the truck, into darkness. Darkness was the *key*. I'd driven these roads for hours, looking for the right location, the right spot, *the right kind of darkness*. A place where trees were so thick that the moon couldn't penetrate, so deep that reflections from the road couldn't sneak in.

It went without saying that a few limbs bumped me. I tripped, and nearly fell on some roots, but this was part of the journey, an expected inconvenience. The deeper I went, the fewer obstructions were found. I finally stopped, mid-stride, withdrew the rusty knife, knelt, and began stabbing at the earth with my left hand, right hand still cradling the tin under my breasts.

This sort of digging needed to be rhythmic, pulsing, you must let your hindbrain take over and set your breathing in time with the movements. Despite the chill of the night, I broke a sweat before finishing, then drop the tin, with its neatly tied ribbon of bloody, blue silk, into the fresh hole. I raked loose soil back with my left hand, favoring the bloody right palm.

Finished, I stood, turned my back, and walked away slowly. Very slowly. I meandered, even whistled a little tune once or twice. I was waiting.

"*For me?*" The voice was feminine, distant, and muffled, as if it was being forced through water. "*I need not share?*" The voice moved around me, accompanied by a sound somewhere between a satisfied lover and an amused child.

I caught glimpses of motion and soft blue light, a blur of color in my periphery. For a moment, I could make out a skeletal form, bleached white bones wrapped in tattered clothes, that moved in a haphazard dance, somewhere between a skipping step and a meandering walk. There was pressure in my chest; the power of something like *this*, penetrating my world.

I spoke, smiling, with a laugh in my voice, as I welcomed her. "My Lady of the Dry Arms, I'd never ask you to share your treasure." We'd known each for many years, and the last several hours had been dedicated to finding *Her Lady of the Dry Arms*.

I heard her walking around me, bones grinding softly, veils writhing, caught in a wind that existed only for her. "*I know you,*" Her Lady of the Dry Arms said slowly.

"We've met, many times before."

"*Ah-ha! Yes.*" She drew out her syllables, as if she was talking in her sleep. "*You gave me the egg, the colorful little egg. So pretty. It's still my favorite.*"

"I'm sure you tell us all that, my Lady." I had, in fact, once given her a 'colorful little egg.' It was exceedingly difficult to find, made by the House of Fabergé.

"*No! I would never.*" She paused, thoughtful and serious. "*Oh. Yes, I would.*"

"I am seeking your favor once more." I felt her sidling up to me as icy breath brushed my ear. I felt her veils and shawls move around my coat and my hair brushed aside.

"*What was your name? Maria? No, you don't like that. Maggi? Yes, Maggi.*" I felt teeth touch my ear, the bones of her jaw moving as she spoke. Her Lady of the Dry Arms was in my mind. I could feel her digging, testing me, pushing and pulling at my defenses. I paused and pushed her back, gently but firmly, focusing my thoughts and avoiding distraction.

"I seek your boon. I seek power.," I replied.

"*Power? Is that all?*" She speaks as if this were a tiny thing, barely worth her attention. That was how she set the trap. If I wasn't careful, she'd offer more, and it would never seem as high a price as she'd ask for.

"That's all."

"*Do you want the flames on your fingers to kiss flesh? Melt the bone?*"

"Yes," I whispered.

"*Do you want to bite, to gnaw, to rip and rend with your mind?*"

"Yes," I whispered, again, pressing calm into my heart, afraid I would betray a degree of excitement, unseemly at a time like this.

"*So be it. But, I require a gift.*"

"I've given you a gift already," I answered hesitantly, unsure of where she was taking our negotiations.

"One day, this body, that which you wear, will die." Instead of flanking me, breathing on my neck, or playing with my hair, she wrapped around me and leaned in. I could almost see the outline of her skull, next to my cheek. "You will have two eyes when you die. One of these eyes will not see as the other. I want that eye, one last gift."

For much of my adult life, I have bargained and traded with *entities* like Her Lady of the Dry Arms. Ancient spirits, gods, or something in between. In all that time, this was a new request, and it set me on edge. My mind raced over her words and I wondered how could she benefit? More importantly, how could this *hurt* me?

I decided, after long minutes, that she had a deal.

Her Lady of the Dry Arms giggled, neither sinister nor mean. She sounded like a child who has been promised a day in the park. Her skeletal form wrapped around me, tugged at my clothes and armor, and pulled at my skin. It was hard to breathe, and just when I felt panic set in from the threat of suffocation, I was dropped to my knees, breathless. Her Lady of the Dry Arms was gone, exiting this world *through* me and leaving behind her gifts, *her boon.* For one like her to use my body as a doorway, it was considered *polite* to leave behind a gift. The actual value of the gift was unimportant, but in this case, she had left me exactly what I'd asked for.

The joints of my fingers burned, each a burning pulp of coal eating away at the sinew of my hands. My throat was raw, made worse by gasping at cold night air, the saturation of which felt like ice picks driven through my lungs. A strange kind of exhaustion set in, causing me to shiver, palms pressed against the forest floor, fingers clawing at the dirt beyond my will, in pain.

The power I requested, and now suffered from in consumption, was not something that just *anyone* could have bought. Her favor did not come quickly or easily. She punished those who brought her excessively extravagant gifts on their first visits. The first time I had met the Lady of the Dry Arms, I was much younger and far more arrogant. That night I had borrowed a small tin of mints from my teacher. That tin would end up containing a few rubber bands, some chocolates, two nickels, three pennies and a lock of my hair. My one advantage in dealing with Her Lady was that I had always known exactly what she would most enjoy.

Back then, of course, I'd never *seen* Her Lady of the Dry Arms. I had sensed her, and listened to my instincts, that blind knowing in the back of my head that hides somewhere between doubt and faith. It wasn't until the *Collapse*, it wasn't until the *Veil* faded, that I knew her with my own eyes. Heard her voice, felt her touch.

It took me perhaps a half hour to regain control and equilibrium, body and mind caught in the process of acclimating. Regulating my breathing, I calmed myself, and swallowed hard a few times. I shook cold hands until they became merely numb and once I felt like I could walk easily again, I continued back to the road. When I returned to the cab of the truck, I replaced my rusted knife under the seat, and searched for a pair of gloves.

The road I drove out on soon cut through grassy meadows, erupting like fountains from ruined corner stones and burnt foundations, ghosts of rolling suburbs. I crossed forests and hollowed structures, rusting cars, all abandoned. Time passed, and I became drowsy, as miles continued, one after another. It would be *hours* before I finally curved around a stretch of road to see lights sparkling on the horizon.

As I drove, I saw tank-traps in jagged lines all along what were once foundations; basements, dug out to form sharp and abrupt drops. They were intended to play havoc on an invading army and would force a bottleneck into the main road.

On the main road, I drove past people, one or two would become five or six, and quickly a river flowing, lanterns or torches held high. My headlights illuminated men, women, and children sporting backpacks, boots, overcoats, cloaks, while handling baby carriages, carts, and mules. Many of them were traders, bringing wares in their wake, selling goods or services, mercenaries and whores alike. Some sought a better life, others were simply passing through. I swept my mind over them, feeling the buzz of hope tinged with shades of greed, excitement, anticipation, and disgust.

I slowed when I saw the line of red tail lights waiting for entry. In front of me was a mix of vehicles, the smallest of which was a salvaged pickup truck bed, being pulled on wooden slings by two burly men, the bed filled with produce. The largest was a relic, old world remains of a tractor-trailer rig, complete with an armed escort.

Above the city gates hung a sign, stenciled neatly, tightly, reading "Crafton."

I was there, many years ago, when Crafton was born out of Pittsburgh. Much of that city had burned to the ground, late in the Collapse. We had arrived here from California, and had saved part of it by carving a desperate firebreak along old Crosstown Boulevard. That slice of land, at the confluence of the Allegheny and Monongahela rivers, had transformed into a city-state over next two decades. I'd been a resident of Crafton, on and off, for the better part of those decades.

When I finally arrived at the checkpoint, an enclosed station with several men and a set of radios, I was approached by a soldier half my age. His fatigues were gray, save for body armor, flak vest over a chainmail shirt. The rifle slung over his shoulder had a fixed bayonet, and one of his front teeth was missing when he tried to smile at me.

"Where are you from?" I didn't see him bristle, nor did I feel fear. The soldier didn't recognize me and that was just fine.

"Returning resident," I answered calmly.

"Cargo?"

"Nothing."

"Sounds like a waste of fuel, ma'am." The guard shook his head and waved me forward, stepping back a foot or so to let me pass.

The guard was right. Any normal citizen would be foolish to waste expensive petroleum on a joyride across Pennsylvania, late at night. However, I was neither a normal citizen, nor had I indulged in a joyride. I'd been doing my job.

* ——— ✳ —— *

LOS ANGELES, CALIFORNIA. LONG PAST.

I knew that I was dreaming because none of the tastes and smells were quite right. My throat wasn't abuzz with adrenaline; there was no scent of strong antiseptic in the air, no hum of traffic behind me.

Instead, I was stepping into the liquor store. The black and white tiles glistened, freshly mopped, cluttered with stacked boxes of cheap vodka or tequila. As I walked across the floor, I made a straight line for the register, a desk and alcove, covered with a thousand pieces of cheap garbage for sale. Fluorescent lights above buzzed, and everything was painted an unhealthy shade of *teal*.

I glanced over my shoulder, back at my friend Rosa. She was a year younger than me, looking less like a teenager and more like a child in thick red lipstick and painted eyebrows. Her frizzed hair glistened, and her big brown eyes darted around in terror. Rosa was *stupid*, and I knew it when I convinced her to help me rob this store. She was easy to manipulate, easy to convince, those big brown eyes had nothing behind them.

I flashed her a smile and a wink, then turned back to the register, pounding my hand down on a little bell and a scrawled note which read; *ring for service.*

The clock, over the door to the backroom, said it was after midnight. From that backroom emerged a middle-aged Chinese clerk with a thin head of hair, wearing an ugly red and blue polo shirt. He was smiling, or perhaps sneering, asking me what I want. My voice caught in my throat, I didn't reply as quickly as I'd have liked, my eyes darted up to the clock again, watching the seconds pass.

7

I felt Rosa's knuckles in my lower back, then I blinked. A minute had gone by, and the clerk was looking at me with a gaze between fear and annoyance.

My right hand pulled the gun out of my back pocket. It was a snub nose .38 revolver, too big for my hands, requiring me to use my left hand to cock the hammer. The Chinese clerk didn't answer, he just blinked.

"Pop the *fucking* register open, *chino!*" I shouted.

"*Hurry the fuck up!*" Rosa screamed behind me, her shrill voice drowning out mine.

The man, who'd spoke English to me moments before, stuttered back in Chinese before starting to yell. He was leaning over the counter, tugging back at his register, pointing at Rosa. I couldn't understand a word he was saying; it was a staccato storm of vowels and syllables.

"Give me the *goddamn money!*" I fired back at the man, shoving Rosa aside so I could be heard. I closed range, and moved up against the register, my gun a few inches from the Chinese clerk's head, his spittle moist on my face.

It was at this moment that I felt ice water in my spine, and I shivered. Something had changed and I willed the world to be silent so I could focus. Much to my surprise, this was exactly what happened.

The Chinese clerk was still *screaming* at me, still pointing, but no words erupted from his mouth. I turned slowly, and next to me Rosa was yelling, her face twisted into a snarl of fear and panic.

My eyes caught something by the door through which we'd entered, long yards away; the glass peppered with stickers and advertisements, but I could see a body, and a face, looking back at me. *It* was watching me, eyes locked on mine, tugging me *towards* it.

Little Maria Magdalena Lopez.

I could hear it. The words dribbled down the back of my throat like sour milk, thick and chunky; I was terrified. Then night enfolded the creature; gone were the flicker of lit streets. It stood stagnant against a monochrome world, tapped into the core of my soul, and a base fear spread through me. The creature gave me a look of pure malice, the brick and mortar of nightmares, tapping something in my mind that had lain

8

dormant in genetic code for ten thousand years. Some part of me knew that face, warped into a look of pure hatred.

I'll never fully understand what happened next.

This was a dream that I'd suffered through every night I slept, up until the Collapse. It was a replay of memories that had not blurred with time. In all the incarnations, I'd endured, I had never fully made sense of *why* I pulled that trigger on my snub nose .38 revolver.

It could have just been a knee-jerk reaction to primal terror. It could have been that I was responding in rage to something so unnatural that it needed to be *stopped*. I'd even considered that perhaps the creature had *made* me pull the trigger. *That* was a willful fantasy, and I knew it.

All that mattered was that I had pulled the trigger.

The *pop* spun my head back to the clerk, and I saw the manifestation of gore before me. The man was knocked backwards against the plastic wall of cigarettes, a spray of blood and brain across tobacco. Blood was *everywhere*, on my hand, my arm, the counter, on the plastic *take a dime, leave a dime*, the collection of lighters adorned in naked women and the novelty bottle openers.

I had licked my lower lip. *Blood.* The Chinese man's blood.

"You shot him." Rosa whispered, her voice quivering.

"*Shit. Shit!*" I was loud. I couldn't help it; my voice has always risen beyond my control.

"*You shot him!*" Rosa repeated. "You *fucking* shot a *chino* in the face!"

"*¡Chinga tu madre!*" *Fuck your mother!* "*¡Yo sé!*" *I know!*

"*You* killed him. *Not me!* You did it. This is *all you.*" I saw Rosa back away, shivering as her big, stupid, brown eyes turned feral. She was beyond her ability to reason, even on a good day. I didn't know how to answer her, didn't have any more words; so I simply watched her run away, nearly slipping on the freshly mopped floor.

I turned back. In life, he'd been a *clerk*; he'd taken money for beers and cigarettes, counted his cash drawer, and mopped the black and white tile. In death, he was a man. My mind slowly questioned who he had been, and how he'd lived his life. Did he have a wife? Or a child? How many children would never speak their father's name again because I shot that man in the face?

I'd been in knife fights, had beaten *bitches* to a bloody pulp, and I'd taken some hard hits. But I had never taken a life. I had never imagined something like this, never dreamed it possible.

After I had killed the Chinese man, I couldn't hear a single sound, but in these dreams, all I heard was the *ticking* of the clock above the backroom. In my dream, I counted down those long seconds as I stood, gun in hand, waiting for the police to arrive. This was a long time ago, I was only a child and the world hadn't yet begun to Collapse. I would be in my late twenties before I was released from prison.

Only in my dream, could I hear the creature's voice in my mind, whispering, crawling under my skin, laughing at me.

Little Maria Magdalena Lopez. How you've grown.

CRAFTON CITY-STATE. PRESENT.

My alarm clock was made of brass and copper, one of those that needed to be wound each night before bed. When it went off, it was undeniably the most annoying sound on the planet. Using my fist to end the *cling-clang* cacophony, I pulled myself up in bed almost immediately.

I was drenched in sweat, breathing hard, and coughing.

It'd been at least a year since *that* dream. The dream about the liquor store, the Chinese man, and his cigarette wall covered in blood and brains. Over thirty years had passed and I was still rattled today. Almost as punctuation to that disquietude, I hear a *rap-rap-rap* at my door, knuckles on aluminum.

"Yes?" I shouted, unwilling to get up, or dress, just yet.

"Ma'am!"

"Yes..." I repeated, picking crunchy, yellow sleep from my eyes.

"The General would like to see you in the boardroom."

"Yes." I replied, biting on my lower lip for a second, annoyed. I glanced around the room, observing compact wooden walls and aluminum plate, sparse furniture, piled with discarded clothes, armor, mementos, treasures, and guns. I could feel the man outside my door holding his breath, afraid. "Yes, I'll be along." I responded louder.

"Thank you, ma'am!"

"Don't call me *ma'am*." I whispered, mostly to myself, before kicking off the covers and standing. I grabbed an apple off my nightstand, and began biting into it while walking toward the bathroom. The water in my shower is low on both pressure and heat, but it was *running water*, and I've

11

never much felt the need to complain. After the Collapse, it was close to a decade before I had an opportunity to enjoy such opulence.

When I exited the shower, I began to dress, rummaging through various piles of clothing, figuring out what was clean, what was dirty, and what I should have thrown away years ago. I dress for perception, I dress for *power*. It was the oldest kind of magic, one that required no special talents.

I settled on a narrow dress made of brown leather and embroidered black linens. Heeled boots with little metal charms that *clicked* and *clacked* when I walked provided me with additional height. The boots were for show; but the finger bones that weaved through my laces were *not*. Neither were the daggers strapped to my boots. I didn't bother with a belt as I wouldn't need my sidearm or magazines, but I did wear a long sash made from black silk and dark, red lace. A relic of times past and a gift from my teacher. It always smelled like sage and coffee.

The dress had short sleeves as well as a low neckline so I wore a black mandarin collared shirt underneath. I typically also wore several necklaces; a few were for show, mainly silver ones. Simple wooden beads or snake vertebrae served me better. As did the polished stone skull that always slipped inside my shirt to rest, unseen, in my cleavage.

Satisfied, I returned to the bathroom to dab charcoal at my eyes, for shadowing, then pulled back my hair to braid it. I watched myself in the mirror, two cracks running vertically cutting through my image. I was not as young as I once was. Gray hair was more prevalent now and lines creased more thoroughly at my eyes and mouth. Tattoos that I had acquired in prison had faded and bled over time; professional ink wasn't as bright or clear as it used to be. The word *Lopez* was spelled in elaborate cursive, across the left side of my neck. On the right was a spider's web stretching from behind my ear all the way to my throat, ending with two crossed razor blades. Ink covered most of my body. After the Collapse, I learned that certain symbols, worn on the flesh, had properties that became effective to a skilled witch.

Last, but certainly not least, I put on my earrings. Large, gold hoops, the same ones I'd worn my entire life. I'd be buried in them, if I had anything to say about it.

I left my room, locking the door behind me. My abode was underground, near what had once been a series of light rail stations. Where I chose to stay was near the officers' quarters, larger suites, all of us enjoying running water. The "neighborhood" tended to be quiet most nights.

The "boardroom," was exactly that. Before the Collapse, it had been used as a meeting place for the public transit executives. There were wide double doors, and windows that looked out on what had once been a large rail station.

Two large men stood at watch outside of the boardroom as I turned a corner. They were burly, with heavy brows, serious mustaches, and eyes colder than the concrete floor. I didn't wish to engage them, to speak them. I didn't wish *anything* but to simply walk through those double doors, so I spun my consciousness out like a whip. My mind wrapped around theirs, penetrating their wishes and dreams, leaching into the hindbrain. I was their mother, coming to tuck them in, whispering in their ears, *"Hush, darlings. I'll keep your monsters at bay."* For a moment, their eyes softened and hardened jaws relaxed. In an instant, they *were* children again, safe, content. They made no move to stop me as I burst in, my palms firmly on each door.

The room was warm and brightly lit, the walls covered in paper, scrawled with notes and maps, pins and threads connecting various items. The original table, faux wood that had been scraped and scarred over the years, dominated the room.

Close to the door sat two men wearing relaxed city camouflage, mixed black and gray motley. "Good morning, Maggi." The oldest man nodded to me. He was in his late sixties, sporting a white goatee and hair trimmed short. His demeanor was calm; the hint of a smile at his lips, blue eyes familiar with me.

"Lorne." I approached him and leaned forward to place my hand on the back of his uniform, being careful to not touch flesh, accidentally peeking inside his mind. I kissed him on top of the head, my lips barely touching his hair. "Who the *fuck* is this guy?" I stood, pointing to the second man at the table. His brow was too big, his chin too narrow. I could feel fear seeping from his pores.

13

Laughing, Lorne gestured at the other man. "This is Colonel Chandless."

"Pleasure, ma'am." Colonel Chandless extended his hand to me.

Squinting at his hand, I replied, "*Most* soldiers salute me."

"*Uh,*" with a degree of panic, Chandless withdrew his hand and saluted.

"Be kind," Lorne laughed. "He doesn't know you by anything other than reputation." I withdrew from Lorne and seated myself two chairs down, so I could face them each uniquely. "Colonel Chandless is actually the commander of the Morgantown garrison, down the river."

"You're a frontiersman." I nodded at Chandless.

"Yes, ma'am." Chandless nods, starting to speak.

"Don't *fucking* call me 'ma'am.'" I didn't need to raise my voice. My response was low, level, and though not tinged with the slightest hint of *magic*, it was a voice that commanded people to unequivocally *do as they were told*.

"Yes, *Bruja*," Chandless corrects himself, using my title. "We're on the frontier. My men typically keep the locals in check, build alliances with independent townships, and discourage raider activity. We see mostly marauders, very little real military power."

"Until this week." Lorne corrected Chandless, nodding.

"Until *this* week," Chandless agreed. "One of our patrols ran into a Federal patrol, random happenstance, really."

"I don't believe in 'random happenstance.'" I rolled my eyes.

"Regardless, we were able to take the Federals by surprise. Our patrol brought their captured soldiers back to Morgantown for interrogation. We don't have any witches, so we needed to have *discussions* with them, the old-fashioned way." Chandless looked almost embarrassed to admit that his men tortured the Federals. Despite his oversized brow, Chandless was in fact a *dandy*, if I ever saw one.

"Go on." I brought my hand up to rest my chin on knuckles. I was becoming concerned with where this conversation was going, but I needed to maintain The Bruja's poker face.

"This patrol, it seems," Chandless cleared his throat, almost stalling, "was part of a much larger convoy, roughly two battalions. Heading north on Husky Highway."

"Not a big deal," Lorne shrugged. "There's a major base in Wheeling."

"That's what we thought," Chandless nodded. "Except that the patrol's commander told us that his units were on their way to rendezvous with *two regiments* of frontline troops at Wheeling for an assault operation."

"Assault operation?" I transferred my gaze from Chandless to Lorne, directing my question to him rather than the younger commander. "How large an army would that be?"

"That's close to ten-thousand troops," Lorne answered me calmly. "Enough to lay siege to a city-state, if they so desired."

"Crafton is *excellent* target," I leaned back. "Close enough to Wheeling that they're not stretching their supply lines. They can cut off and isolate the other city-states and townships to our south. Potentially deal a killing blow to us." I chewed on my last few words, my accent coming out stronger than I expected. Lorne merely nodded, and Chandless fell silent, as I leaned back to consider both my actions and my words.

Lorne finally interjected, "Crafton fields roughly one thousand as a standing garrison."

"Most of our frontline troops are with Alexander, to the north," I sighed, then glanced at Chandless. "How many men could you summon, Colonel?"

"Three hundred, and some armored cavalry." Chandless replied.

"Union Town, Eight-Four, and New Stanton could probably bring another three hundred on short notice. If we call up all the militias." Lorne followed.

"So," I leaned in, my fingers playing patterns across the table, "we could field about two thousand men to defend Crafton. Against more than two regiments?"

"We've managed worse odds." Lorne raised his eyebrows.

"*No*, we haven't. That's what we tell ourselves when we *fucking* drink together. No, those odds are *shit*, and you know it." I stood up needing to pace around the room in order to think clearly. After my teacher's death, Lorne and I had commanded the defense of Crafton and other city-states for nearly two decades. We'd laid siege to New Castle, and we'd broken the backs of many marauder bands. This was a *puzzle*, a puzzle we had to solve. "Colonel, you're dismissed. Don't go far." I shouted over my shoulder as I turned towards the man.

"Sir?" Chandless glanced from me to Lorne, who merely nodded.

15

He stood, pulling his camo blouse down, then saluted us both uniquely before departing.

"There's no reason we can't trust Colonel Chandless." Lorne leaned back, crossing his arms, letting out a deep, low, sigh.

"I trust *you*, my son, and perhaps Mayy. Chandless can *fuck off*."

"Have it your way." Lorne laughed aloud.

I threw my weight to the side, sitting on the table, and perching my left boot on a chair, favoring Lorne with my gaze at an angle. "We can't beat them."

"Maybe. If the Federals are truly serious about capturing Crafton, this will be the first in a long line of hard conversations."

"Why now?" I bit back a little rage. Whether I trusted Chandless was beside the point. I didn't want him to see The Bruja this shaken, *this* angry. "Twenty *fucking years*, we butt heads with them, take a few of their bases, they hit us, we hit them. The Federals *never* tried to be this bold."

"There *are* rumors." Lorne replied. "Rumors from the frontier. We hear stories of Federals, marching with *monsters*. Monsters in armor."

"They have *no witches*, so what could they possibly do?" I scoffed.

"You tell me, Maggi," Lorne seemed frustrated, "Rumors are rumors. We hear *crap* out there, but the bottom line is that we can't stop ten thousand Federal assault troops."

"Maybe we don't have to." I glanced around the room, my mind racing. "What did you used to say? Back in the day, back when I had to fight that other witch, *Vix?*"

"I said; 'No army should ever march without a witch at their side.'"

"Right," The fingers of my left-hand drummed over the table. "A witch can do much."

"A witch can get to the truth of a thing. Or obscure it. Ask Sun Tzu how he feels about that sometime."

I wrinkled my nose, then continued, ignoring Lorene's comment. "A witch can also *destroy*. What if I took Mayy, and maybe a company of our best, right down the throat of Highway 79?"

"To do *what*, specifically, get yourselves slaughtered?" Lorne seemed completely exasperated.

"*No!*" I smiled, leaning in, my palms on the table, "How many battles have we fought together? You've taught me *all* you know of tactics, and I've taught you all I know of magic. Mayy and I can delay the assault. Allow us more time to reinforce Crafton, turn them *back* to Wheeling for a month or three!" I was laughing, despite myself.

"You're talking about using magic as a *weapon*, not just fire support."

I snarled. "Why not? You have special forces, here at Crafton, right?" Lorne nodded to me, so I continued. "Magic, since the Collapse, has been this awkward thing that no one has known what to do with. What if we generate a new class of soldier, *no*, a class of *nobility*? Like *knights* and *shit*?" I grinned at Lorne.

"As a young man, I loved to read old stories of adventure. Good and evil, love and loss. You know the stories, *Jason and the Argonauts, King Arthur.*"

"I saw those on television when I was a kid." My smile only grew, but Lorne rolled his eyes at me.

"You're suggesting something new. A *battlewitch*, if you will."

"Yes, *yes, I am*, old friend. And I'm volunteering to be the first."

———✳———

CRAFTON CITY-STATE. PRESENT.

Although the city-state of Crafton was only about a quarter of what had once been Pittsburgh, it was still a sprawling maze of civilization. Parts of the city enjoyed running water, while others suffered through sewage-stiff streets. Same for electricity, certain areas enjoyed it, while others did not. I wasn't afraid to get a little dirty, but I avoided the streets that would put my boots ankle-deep in *shit*, from horses, livestock, and humans.

This meant I needed to take the long way around the city proper, following a narrow finger of *upper class* that ran south to north in Crafton. To the west were the apartments and tenants of Crafton's worker and trader classes; to the east was the river on which trade relied. Streets here were gravel, thoroughfares full of carts and horses, lined with low, squat buildings. Each was constructed from Pittsburgh's bones, the craftsmanship sound, solid, and uniquely attractive in its own way.

A few more blocks passed before I saw the large, two-story, stone building. Overgrown, and re-painted, it had once been a hotel. The Collapse had treated it well, and even today private guards stood outside with rifles slung on three-point harnesses. It's not that Crafton was a particularly dangerous place, it's that the people who lived here were mostly from the old world.

As I stepped into the lobby and proceeded back to the forward hallway to ascend a set of stairs I passed a man and woman, holding hands. They wore antique clothing, discolored with age, but clean, well kept. They were older than me, by perhaps a decade, and their eyes darted from me, to the floor, quickly, thoughts projected like loudspeakers. *Is she another witch?*

When I reached the second floor, I took a left and found the door I sought, just a dozen yards down the first hallway. A steel gate had been affixed over the frame, the previous occupant's doing. There was a faded number etched under the peephole, *twenty-eight*.

I rapped at the door with my knuckles, reaching through the gate.

"*Go away.*" I heard, muffled, behind the door. Reaching my mind through the door, pushing past the basic barriers and defenses a good witch would have placed around her apartment, I could feel, could *see* another. She was a flame of glowing red energy, sparking softly in a dark void of mediocrity. She was *asleep*, not paying attention, no proper barriers around her mind. It was no challenge to walk into her consciousness. No challenge to fit myself into her broken dreams.

It took a few minutes, but I could hear frantic screaming from within, followed by thumping, then gasping. I reached through the gate a second time, rapping my knuckles against the door.

The door *clicked* as it unlocked and a woman stood before me, eyes swollen from sleep, dried spittle across her cheek.

"*That shit is fucked up, Maggi.*" She growled.

Shrugging, I replied, "You're the one who's afraid of spiders."

Mayy opened the door for me, as well as the gate. Her name was *Margaret*, but she'd gone by the name *Mayy*, with two *y*'s, for years. She stepped away, walking to her bed and grabbing a pair of jeans to pull over white panties. I politely averted my eyes.

A bathroom was set off to the side, and a small kitchenette. This was once an extravagant hotel room, now dull from years of use, cluttered with Mayy's clothes, belongings, and her charcoal artwork etched across the walls. Above her bed is an intricate sketch of a man burning alive, charcoal smeared, to create the image.

"*Jerk.*" Mayy rummaged through a dresser and withdrew a crumpled package, "I even got you a gift."

I accepted the crumpled package she thrusted towards me. It's an old pack of cigarettes, or least it was. Only two remained inside, one broken near the filter, the other pristine. I pulled out the broken one and put it to my lips before passing the package to my left hand and snapping my middle finger, forefinger, and thumb in front of my face. Flame ignited out of thin air and the cigarette was lit. A parlor trick, nothing more. All I needed to do was reach out with my mind, borrow the flame, and ignite it in my fingers. "Thank you." I replied, inhaling the stale tobacco.

"Can you just wake me up like a normal person? Next time?" Mayy sunk down on the bed, rubbing at her eyes with the butt of her palms.

"You're not a *normal* person, you never will be. You need to learn how to barrier your mind, even when you're asleep."

"You're the *only* other witch in town." Mayy replied, hunching over, shoulders sloped down, as she watches me smoke.

"*Today* I am, tomorrow I may not be."

"What are the numbers, Maggi? Only one in a thousand people are witches?"

"Only one in one hundred witches are *dangerous*." I nodded, inhaling more smoke. "It's funny you should mention that, because I'm here to ask you for help. Being *dangerous*."

Mayy smirked, "Anything."

"No, you need to hear me out first."

"Maggi." Mayy sighed. "You're my teacher, and you're... *much more* than that. I've never forgotten why I'm here."

Mayy was young, though she had no idea her age, but older by nearly a decade than my son. Her auburn-red hair was cut in a short bob. Her dark eyes were *too big* for her face, her lips too narrow. She was smaller than *me*, a child of the Collapse, malnourished as a baby.

"Shut up about that *shit*." I shook my hand, walking to her bathroom to crush out the smoldering tobacco clutched in my fingers. She had an old comb and some charcoal on her sink, same as me, but also an array of antique earrings pinned to the wall with thumb tacks.

"*Fine*. What does The Bruja demand of her servant?" I watched myself in Mayy's mirror, the lines in my face, my eyes, my lips. Whatever happened to the young woman who used to stare back at me? When did she vanish? At this very moment, however, listening to my student chirp sarcastically, I realized I would not live forever. What an odd thing to consider.

"Someday, you'll be one of Alexander's Generals. Someday, you'll be me." Mayy doesn't reply to me, instead I heard her get off the bed and join me at the bathroom door, fingers wrapped around the frame, peering in at me, watching my reflection in the mirror.

"What are you talking about, Maggi?"

"I'm talking about *war*," I pursed my lips for a second, then turned away from our reflections to face her, a foot or two away. Her eyelashes were thick and she had two rings on her lower lip, each towards the corner, giving her the look of one possessing tiny fangs.

"With the East Board?"

"No, the Federals." I reached out, my right hand against the frame, bracing myself.

"*Shit*." It took her a second to respond, all her bubbly sarcasm has vanished.

"'*Shit*' is right. They're getting ready to attack Crafton; they've got a ten-thousand-man army coming up from Wheeling."

"Are we evacuating the city?" Mayy's voice was very quiet and it was a struggle to hear her.

"No. We're going to reinforce the city. But, before we do, I volunteered us to meet them in the field, with a company of troops."

"You want to break that attack. Shake 'em up." Mayy nodded.

"Lorne doesn't know me as well as he hopes." I chuckled softly.

"Lorne has never seen you *scrap*." I taught her the word, part of me was proud that she used it now. Part of me was proud, like a mother, anytime she swore like me. While I expected much more from my *son*, I was warmed every time my student mimicked me.

"We're both combat veterans," I shrugged, "we can fight *with* magic."

"I've seen you burn men. Burn men *alive*." I remembered the charcoal sketch over her bed now. Her voice was full of awe and respect.

"Together, with some rough & tumble gunner types..."

"We could *fuck some shit up*." Mayy finished my words as I trailed off.

"No one has ever done anything like it. Lorne called us battlewitches."

"I kinda' like that." Mayy licked her lips.

"One thing," I reached out with my left hand, placing it on her shoulder, thin cotton separating me from her flesh to prevent me from knowing her mind as well as I knew my own. "If this goes sideways, you don't stick in the *shit*, got me? You take the soldiers, pull out, get out, come back to Crafton. I'm not kidding Mayy. Someday, you'll be *me*."

"What is it with you today?" Mayy shook her head, an expression halfway between a sneer and a laugh crossing her face.

I don't reply because I don't have an answer for her. Maybe I felt a little drunk on the power I'd earned from Her Lady of the Dry Arms the night before, maybe I felt like I could conquer the world and now I was suffering the *hangover*. When I chose to meet Her Lady of the Dry Arms, I'd planned that meeting for *years*, I'd laid out the gifts, scheduled the visits. This was a natural progression in my relationship with that ancient spirit. I had no idea that I'd meet with Lorne that morning, no idea that I'd invite my student on a dangerous operation the next day.

I don't believe in 'random happenstance.'

"Do as you're told." I whispered, finally, in response. "Someone has to live on, to protect Crafton, and protect Alexander."

"*Oh.*" Mayy stood up straight suddenly, physically pulling away from me. "I forgot. Only your *flesh and blood son* matters to you."

———※———

REDWOOD CITY, CALIFORNIA. LONG PAST.

I found myself dreaming of the past again as I slept.

The world I had been born into was a glowing, vibrating, shouting holocaust of quick-cut ads, drinks made of liquid sugar, and the pounding bass rhythms of hyperbole. It made us numb to the struggle of the common person, a struggle not so different after the Collapse. It was inevitable that our system would break down; it exceeded its load-bearing weight. Too many people, too many conflicting ambitions. As an old woman now, I missed that above all else: the crush of humanity. So many of us had died in the Collapse, there were so few now.

My dream took me to Redwood City. I was living in the Bay Area, just south of San Francisco, halfway down the peninsula. In my twenties now, no older than Mayy, I'd been released from prison and I was staying with cousins. I was too ashamed to go home to *mi mamá y papá*, after the murder; I couldn't show them my face. I'd planned to get back on my feet, to make something of myself, before I returned home, earn their pride once more, their eldest daughter. Their *only* daughter.

In my dream, I sat on a bench at a bus stop on El Camino Real at midday. The sun was brighter than I remembered and the air slightly cooler. A smoldering cigarette was hanging from my mouth, and I was spreading my elbows back behind me on the back of the bench, watching the traffic whiz past through oversized, plastic sunglasses. Jeans and a white tank top cover my skin, while ashes from my cigarette fell and cinders burned my cleavage. *I don't care.*

I wasn't smoking back then because I *liked it*, it wasn't the indulgent luxury I considered it to be today, it was a *güero* thing. The American side of me that grew up watching movies and thought it looked *cool*. It looked *tough*, a cigarette hanging from your lips.

I remembered this scene as vividly as the night in the liquor store. I could *feel* the fear on people as they passed me, the *chola* with prison ink, letting cinders burn her tits. I reveled in it at this age, reveled in the power it gave a very powerless young woman.

"Afternoon!" A young woman sat down on the bench next to me, but I couldn't feel her weight impact the bench. In the dream, I could smell the bubble gum that she's *smacking*. I don't remember that part ever happening. I glanced at her, sideways, removing the cigarette from my mouth but not answering.

"I'm Mandy. What's your name?"

"Maggi." I replied, dully

"Mandy and Maggi! That's awesome!"

What the *fuck* was wrong with this bitch? I exhaled smoke and turned to the girl. She was just a kid, maybe fourteen. Her long blonde hair was *frizzed up* on her head, and her bangs were a bunch of curls at her forehead. Something was off; she looked as if she'd walked out of a garage sale, clothes a decade out of date. "I just rarely get to talk to someone like you!"

"Like *me*? What's that supposed to mean?" I responded, incredulous.

"You know," she leaned in slightly. "Someone who sees."

Someone who sees. The younger me questioned if she was crazy or high. The older me knew very well what she was talking about. The *eyes behind your eyes*, my teacher would say, that sense you got when you walked by an old house, or maybe the moment you questioned whether you should visit the store today, something terrible might happen.

"No. I don't know." It was all I said.

"What's your full name? *Please* tell me. I wanted to give my daughter a long, long name."

"What makes you think I have a long name?" I answered, suspicious.

"Well, you're..."

"*Mexican?* What if I'm *Salvadorian?*"

"You're not. Your family is from *Michoacán*." We locked eyes and

I dropped my cigarette I didn't want to answer her. Something was off, I felt a quiver in my stomach. My eyes darted around the streets, wondering what was really going on.

"*What the fuck is wrong with you?*" I finally whispered.

"I was raped and stabbed to death, right around here," Mandy gestured near a fast food parlor. "Over by those bushes, in fact. I never got to be a mother, I never got to do *anything*. The man who did it, I never saw him again. But, I keep watching, here."

Her voice was dead serious, there was no tone change, no visual tick, she rambled her words as if it was the most natural thing in the world to discuss *your own death with a stranger*. I remembered my heart skipping a beat. I knew, somehow, in my gut, that this girl wasn't lying. This was no trick.

I took my cheap sunglasses off, and when I gazed at the place she'd been sitting, no one was around. I was completely alone. The cool air turned freezing and I swallowed hard. This was the first time I'd *spoken* with the dead and this memory, as it stood, would change the flow of my life forever. I remembered that I sat there, for many long hours, before I resigned myself to visiting the local liquor store. I purchased a plastic bottle of tequila and proceeded to drink myself into a stupor outside of my cousin's apartment complex. It was the only way I could forget Mandy, who'd been raped and stabbed to death, right around there.

———※———

Crafton City-State. Present.

"My name is Captain Winslow, sir."

I was wearing flat-sole combat boots so I stood at barely *five feet tall*, while Captain Winslow looked down on me. She was lean, her bosom lost in her flak armor, and chest rig, lined with magazines and supplies, geared up in dark green camouflage, and scorched-black chain mail jerkin. One hand, clad in black padded gloves rested on her rifle, slung across her chest. She saluted me, like any good soldier.

"Lorne speaks very highly of you." I nodded, looking her over. Her short, black hair was pulled back in a knot of a ponytail. Her serious, gray eyes straddling a hawk's nose do not once glance down at me as she stands at attention. "At ease, *calm the fuck down.*"

"Yes, sir." I'm dressed similarly to her, outfitted for a combat operation in the field. The only exception was that I didn't share her affinity for a long sleeve camo blouse; instead I was wearing a flak vest and chest rig over a black tank top. My rig had magazines for the 9mm I had holstered at my hip, but it was mostly full of water and rations so that I wouldn't need a backpack or full kit. I needed my arms exposed, my hands exposed; I needed to be able to *feel* the world around me in ways that constrictive armor and clothing couldn't allow. "Blitz Company is at your command."

"No, Captain, Blitz Company is at *your* command." I shook my head, "It's been too many years since I went into the field and took charge of a raid. I'll leave that to you."

"As you wish, *Bruja*." Captain Winslow nodded, and turned away from me.

We were underground in what once been a parking structure, below a large steel and concrete office building. Three of the concrete levels had been utilized for a tertiary motor pool consisting primarily of light military vehicles as well as converted civilian cars and trucks that we used for reconnaissance, runners, and miscellaneous deliveries.

The walls echoed and resounded with idling engines, shouting mechanics, air tools, and metal parts or tools falling to the floor. It also smelled of gasoline and oil, something I'd been fond of since I was a little girl. That was how my father's hands had smelled.

In the center of the upper level was a large HMMWV. The vehicle was squat and flat, with a bulky grill, an array of lights, and a turreted gunner nest on the roof. A second one sat not far behind, the flag vehicles of Winslow's Blitz Company. They were prizes of war, captured trophies from engagements with the Federals in years past. Most of the combat vehicles that called Crafton home had been converted trucks, and 4x4's, modified with light armor, weapons, and added space to transport both soldiers and supplies. Our real prizes were a handful of light armored vehicles and one or two main-line battle tanks that we'd pilfered.

I climbed up the bulky grill onto the hood and perched myself there, watching the motor pool scene unfold, boots resting down on the steel bumper. Daylight poured in from the ramp leading up and out of the structure. This had been modified for large vehicle clearance, and a chain gate had been added to draw across the entrance. Winslow was waiting for the motor pool to release all the vehicles under her command, a little over a dozen. Her company was already geared up, sitting or relaxing on the concrete floor, waiting for the green light. I glanced across the group, a collection of men and women, all young. Some of them had been soldiers before the Collapse, others had joined our forces over the years. They were paid well and enjoyed the benefits of inheriting land after their service-an idea that my teacher had developed in the early days of the Collapse.

"Captain Winslow." I shouted to the woman. I had to shout it twice for her to hear me. When she glanced back to me, I pointed at the hood of the vehicle I'm sitting on. Winslow looked confused for a second, then trotted back over. I asked her to climb up onto the hood with me. At first, she refused, then I pulled rank and ordered her to sit with me. She was uncomfortable with it, I could tell, bracing herself and then sitting down on the HMMWV. It was not that she was physically unable to, she was simply not used to something so *casual*.

"Talk to me Captain. We're about to fight together. I'd like to know who you are."

"Sir?" Winslow responded.

"Don't call me 'sir,' when we're in private." I didn't look over at her, instead I continued to watch light pouring in through the motor pool's entrance. "I wasn't a soldier before the Collapse, I'm still not."

"*Okay*," Winslow drew both syllables out, "what shall I call you?"

"Maggi will do." I nodded with finality. "What shall I call you, Captain?"

"My name is Jennifer." Winslow said quietly, barely audible over the ruckus. "I guess you can call me *Jenn*."

"You're blocking me, *Jenn*. I can't sense a single emotion on you. I could push, of course, gouge into your mind, but I don't need to. You smell of talent."

"A little, sir," Winslow caught herself, grunted and corrected her words, "*Maggi*. My mother was gifted, she always seemed to know when people were lying. Or speaking true."

"Your father?" I replied.

"Army. Both my parents were US military, before the Collapse. My mother died in the New York riots, my dad served *you* for nearly a decade, an Antecedent soldier."

"Really?" I turned to look at Winslow and her gray eyes. A deep gray, both threatening and intrinsically beautiful, like storm clouds on the coast. "I don't remember a Winslow in my ranks."

"You wouldn't," Winslow smiled, creasing lines at her jaw and her neck. I realized she had a dusting of freckles across her cheeks. "My dad wasn't one of your officers; he was just a common ground pounder. He died at the siege of New Castle."

"Many men died at New Castle." I answered. "Now you're a Company commander."

"Blitz Company serves, *Bruja*." Winslow pulled herself off the hood and stood up on the bumper, looking down at me. "We serve General Lorne, you, and most importantly-*your son*." Before I could answer her, or even ask her to stay, Winslow jumped down from the vehicle, boots loud on the cement floor. I studied her from behind for many long moments, running her words through my mind, repeatedly. She *was* a witch, though not like me or Mayy. Untrained, not talented in ways that made her gifts an asset.

Her force of will projected out, and when she picked up her helmet from a backpack and supplies, she cracked it twice against her knee pad. Her soldiers, roughly eighty people, stood up from their positions gathered on the floor.

"Blitz Company, *can you hear me?*" I watched those soldiers, hands on rifles, holding helmets, or packs, snap back, "Sir, *yes sir*." She asked, again, "Can you *hear me?*" Again, her soldiers replied, "Sir, *yes sir*." She continued her speech, "Do you *ugly cocksuckers* see that woman?" Winslow pointed directly at me. Without thinking I stood up. "*Sir, yes sir*."

What was she doing?

"That woman is *The Bruja*, Maggi Lopez. You know her name. Your parents spoke to you about The Bruja. Your older brothers and sisters spoke to you about The Bruja. Maybe you've seen her walk the streets of Crafton. Maybe you've nodded a greeting once or twice."

"*Sir, yes sir*."

"I can promise you, *none* of you have marched with The Bruja into battle. Each and every one of you has heard the stories. How she saved an entire regiment at New Castle. How she met and butchered the whore *Vix*. She is the mother of *His Lord, Alexander*, and she is the true mother of the Antecedent States."

Blitz Company let out a quick, two-rhythm grunt, helmets cracking their knee pads.

"Today is your lucky *fucking* day, Blitz Company! Today we roll out with The Bruja. She will ride with us, she will watch over us, and when we engage our intended target, she will *unleash hell* the likes of which you will tell your grandchildren about."

When someone gets to be my age, they assume they've seen everything.

I always figured I'd seen *all* the sights, heard *all* the songs. I remembered commanders winding their men up like this before a fight, I'd known Lorne to do it, and my *teacher* was a genius at it. It was only when Winslow turned and nodded a wink to me, that I realized *this was her form of magic*.

Her troops surveyed me, and I stretched out my hand, a smirk spreading across my face. This Captain, this Jenn Winslow, *was* trained. She understood the basic principle of magic, the showmanship, to be the ringmaster, the *magician* who pulled a rabbit from his hat and distracted you while another hand grabbed your wallet.

I played the role of The Bruja for her, and her men. The role I cultivated, the role I let Winslow see *past*. My smile was hungry, my eyes promised death. I wrapped myself in my own unique, simple glamours. I snapped the fingers of my outstretched right hand, still wrapped in bandages from earlier in the week. Just as I had lit my cigarette earlier, I borrowed fire, but this time a torch, a *ball of flame* the size of a small animal ignited in my hand. Winslow's troops went crazy for a moment, and I bared my teeth a second before casting out the flame, dissipating it around me and letting the heat wash off and vanish.

"*Enough gawking*," Winslow shouted, "Give me final gear check, we roll out as soon as the motor pool Cap gives us a green light."

I jumped down from the HMMWV's hood, glancing up at the entrance to the underground structure. I saw Mayy heading down to join us. Winslow approached me again.

"Lorne is sending *three* witches, isn't he?" I smiled at her.

"I have no idea what you mean. *Sir*."

I nodded to her, accepting the respect.

* —— * —— *

BLITZ COMPANY, ON HIGHWAY 79. PRESENT.

I was riding in the backseat of the HMMWV on which I'd perched myself earlier. Mayy rode behind us in the second HMMWV. This one was Captain Winslow's personal vehicle. Above us was one of her men on the gun turret; in front were two Corporals, both young men. Riding shotgun was Corporal West, perched at the window with a scoped .308 rifle. Winslow's driver, Corporal Mohamed, was at the wheel. On my left was Winslow herself, studying a series of maps, folded out across her lap. We were all wearing our helmets, even *I'm* wearing a helmet, though I doubted that they would last long.

"If we're heading this far up Highway 79, I can't imagine we'll find much." Winslow shook her head after a few more minutes of study.

"Why's that, Captain?" I turned away from her and looked out the window. The highway had been cut through low, rolling hills, some of which were covered with line after line of geological record. I had no idea what it meant, but I considered it beautiful.

"Because we'll be close to Wheeling. There's no marauders who'd get that close, not with a Federal base there."

"You gave a good speech back there, Captain." I didn't look away from the window. An array of trees surrounded the road, along with abandoned vehicles. Hundreds, if not *thousands* of cars, trucks, and tractor-trailers, had been bulldozed to the side, rusting, covered in dust. We had the road to ourselves, for the most part. The lonely stretches filled me with a hollow sadness though, it always had. I remembered when these highways had *bustled*. "Now apply that logic. Why would The Bruja go out with a

31

Company of soldiers? An *elite* team, commanded by another *witch* who can motivate her soldiers through sheer force of will?"

"It's the Federals we're fighting." Winslow replied after a moment.

"Yes." I nodded, my eyes locked on the road, a spider web of weeds and tall grasses without constant traffic to keep it in check.

"*Oh.*"

"Don't worry, Captain," I looked away from the window and fished out the crushed pack of cigarettes which Mayy had given me. I withdrew the remaining, pristine, cigarette, and tossed the package out the window. "This isn't a suicide mission. At least, not for you, or your men."

"You think you could die?"

"I don't *know.*" I shrugged, then snapped my fingers, summoning flame to my cigarette, lighting it in a quick burst. "I've been having this strange feeling lately, this feeling that it's the end of the line for me. I keep dreaming of the past. *Shit* I saw, and did, thirty years ago."

"We all have dreams about the past." Winslow answers. She has a knack of speaking softly, yet clearly.

"Not like these, Captain. When I'm there, when I'm remembering the old days, I have this *sense* that my life is almost played *out*. I wouldn't mind, I guess." I inhaled the cigarette smoke deeply, "The world is moving on without me. My son seeks to take Cleveland, extending the peace of our Antecedent States for hundreds, *hundreds* of miles."

"Sir, *Maggi*, you talk like you're obsolete."

"Maybe I am. A relic of the old world. Just like all these wrecked cars." I gestured out the window, exhaling smoke as I did.

"Antecedent soldiers *and* citizens alike, look up to you Maggi."

"Oh, Captain," I laughed, turning to her, "don't *blow smoke up my ass.* They're afraid of me, and you know it. *You're afraid of me too.*" I smiled.

"How do you know?" Winslow tilted her head at me.

"Because, you've blocked your base emotions from me since we met. You want to hide something from me. Unless you plan to *murder* me in my sleep, smart money says you're *afraid.*" I glanced back out the window, watching trees and grass flow past us. Winslow didn't respond to me, and that was *okay.* I didn't blame her for being afraid. The Bruja was more myth than reality now, my exploits larger than life, my life exaggerated beyond reality.

What they had said, *all* of what they had said was true. I did save an entire regiment at New Castle, but I didn't mean to, it had been pure luck. I'd also defeated a powerful witch named *Vix*. Victoria had been her name, and no one remembered now that she'd beaten me within an inch of my life *before* I returned to put her down. The stories these kids had created around me would have me *slaying dragons* in a few centuries.

"I am afraid." Although I heard Winslow with my ears, she fell away and she was very distant. At that very moment something strange happened, something that felt like ice water pouring down my spine, a feeling I'd nearly forgotten.

There was a car on the side of the road, a black station wagon, with tinted windows. Decades of dust, snow, and rain had left it covered in a gray coating of dust and grime. It reminded me, quite suddenly, of the car that my teacher and I had fled California in, the car he'd driven across the country in the first weeks of the Collapse, me in the backseat holding our son, Alexander in my arms. Thousands of miles of groping, desperate *fear*. Not for me, or even him. It was the tiny, defenseless baby I'd clutched to my breasts. I'd done my best to forget about that trip. The things we *saw*, and what we did to *survive*. That journey had left me with a thousand scars no one would ever *see*.

Next to the car sat two dogs. No wild or feral dogs, no these were big, black, sleek dogs. They were *huge* like greyhounds with glistening coats of solid black that seemed to consume the morning light of an overcast day. One was slightly larger than the others, and they sat at attention, watching us, *watching me*, their eyes locked with my eyes. Eyes of *pure malice*, eyes I remembered from long ago, staring back at me from outside a glass door as I stood at the register of liquor store, gun in hand.

"Maybe you *should* be afraid." I gasped, turning my eyes away from the window, tossing the cigarette out as it burned at my fingers.

"What?" The moment was lost on Winslow, as I glanced at her. There was no sense of knowing in her eyes. *This* was the true loneliness of being a *witch*. Knowing a truth, witnessing a horror, and realizing that a window to your own nightmares existed *just for you*.

I opened my mouth once to speak, paused, and forced myself to regain my composure. The Bruja didn't get rattled like this. "Black dogs."

"Dogs that are black? Wait, *no. What?*" Winslow's confusion became palpable. Although I was quick to cover wounds from twenty years ago, quick to hide my own reaction, the sight of the car *and* the dogs left me shaken. I needed to share my mind with someone. I didn't *trust* Winslow, and she wasn't a witch in the same way that I was, but in the last several hours we'd formed the most basic of connections. Sharing these words with her now seemed natural. "There are stories of black dogs that protect lonely travelers along certain roads. I even grew up with stories, as a child, of the *Nahual*. A devil, a black dog."

At this point the driver turned to face us, eyes off the road for only a moment. He was just a boy, perhaps seventeen years old, at the oldest. His skin was very dark, with patchy stubble under his lip. "They're Djinn"

"*Yes*, they are. I'm sorry, who the *fuck* are you?" I inquired, somewhat shocked.

"Corporal Mohamed is a Muslim." Winslow interjected on the driver's behalf.

"A *monotheist*, in this day and age?" I raised my eyebrows, genuinely shocked, then turned away from the driver, and back to Captain Winslow. "*Regardless*, yes, your boy is correct. They're Djinn. A sort of demon, neither good nor evil, and often they appear as a black dog."

"You've had much experience, with these *Djinn*?" Winslow inquired.

"Not much, *thank the fucking gods*," I shivered, "Only twice. The first time I was just *fourteen fucking years old*. Before the Collapse, before I'd ever heard of magic, *real magic*. A very long time before anyone would call me 'The Bruja.'"

I pursed my lips, unwilling to say more. I didn't trust my emotions here and now, I didn't feel comfortable being this *open* with Winslow. I didn't feel comfortable being *this* open with anyone still alive. Not Mayy, not Lorne, *absolutely not my son*. I'd only ever told *one* person about what I saw in the liquor store. I'd discussed my *fear* of the *Djinn*, the black dogs, with the man I'd once called "teacher," the man who'd founded the Antecedent States.

My son's father.

REDWOOD CITY, CALIFORNIA. LONG PAST.

Had I fallen asleep? I must have, I was dreaming again.

"I'm a *fucking ninja* with this box cutter, *güero.*" I winked at the man standing next to me, a full foot taller than me. His shirt had long sleeves and buttons, and despite the black freight dust that covered him, he was *sharp*, put together well.

I was employed, a few blocks down from our apartment at a big-box retailer, working their night crew, stocking the store. My criminal record would have made it harder to find work *anywhere* else, but in Redwood City, during those years, it was easy. I had valid *social security number*, I had the advantage of being a citizen, and that was my golden ticket to earning *ten dollars an hour*. They even made me a little, plastic name badge. Misspelled of course, *"Maggie."*

"I can see that." He gestured with his chin to the cart of flattened cardboard next to me. "You're faster than anyone else on this team. You've worked here, what, *two weeks?*"

"A week and a *half.*" I smiled, flipping my box cutter closed, and moved the cart out of the aisle, bending over to grab debris off the ground in such a way that my *ass* faced the tall, white Supervisor. Had I been *flirting with him?* Had I just forgotten all these details in the years since his death?

"You should consider working on my team instead. We need *fast* people." He was a *güero, a white boy*, maybe a few years older than me, certainly not thirty yet. He kept his hair as crisp as his work uniform, yet hadn't shaved in half a week. His stubble was *red*. There was something about the man that made my stomach churn and my fingers go numb. A snap or *crackle* in his *black eyes*, something that looked right through me, pierced my secrets and found a part of me that I had never known was vulnerable.

"I've *seen* your team, *güero*," I laughed, "they're all *mamacitas, sexy ladies.*"

"Random happenstance." The tall, white boy laughed, a deep, *loud* laugh.

"I don't believe in 'random happenstance.'" I rolled my eyes.

Had I *really* said that to him? Back then? I couldn't remember, I was a bystander in my own dreams, watching them unfold beyond my control. I'd told Colonel Chandless the same thing, days ago, and never even considered my words.

"*Seriously*, Maggi, you're not like the rest of this team. I'd like you to come and work on my team. The hours are long, the work is tough, and the pay is the same."

"Hey, don't get into car sales, huh?"

It was then that something strange happened to me. My body faced away from him, and a tear fell down my check. Did I *actually* cry, suddenly, at work, or was this the old woman who sat asleep in an HMMWV, somewhere on Highway 79? *I missed him so much.* That stupid grin of his, and the way he had never shaved often enough. His stubble had hurt my face when we kissed.

I pulled myself back together, turning to face him.

"Are you okay?" His brow furrowed. This dream was beyond me to control. Those tears were a part of my memories, whether I remembered them or not. I didn't answer him, rather I walked away, taking my cart of cardboard with me, bound for the compactor. I wiped at my face with dirty hands, realizing that I was smearing freight dust across my cheeks. I didn't need everyone to see that, I didn't need to answer their questions, or fight with them over something that was none of their business.

I went to the bathroom, washing my hands under cold water at the sink, washing my face, running my fingers through my hair, and then tying it back into a ponytail. The younger Maggi was prettier than I was today, her lips were full and there were no lines creasing at her eyes, no gray streaking her black locks.

Assembled again, I left the bathroom and its harsh fluorescent lights. As I stepped out and used the water fountain I saw, at the side of my eye, the big white boy with his red stubble.

"What *fuck*, did you follow me to the bathroom?"

"I think I know what's wrong." His voice was serious now, a deep growl, and my heart skipped a beat. Partially because it resonated somewhere deep in my soul. Partially just because I liked the way he sounded. I'd never tell him of course.

"*Fuck you.*" I swear at my Supervisor. I swore at my supervisor?

"Hear me out. I know what's wrong."

I walked away from him, and there was a moment where my heart skipped a series of beats. I remembered this well, my back to the big man, grinding my teeth. What would have been the harm? He could have just assumed I was crazy, he could have just forgotten me, this would have all been over.

I was a coward back then, and I knew it. I told him in *Español*, not English.

"*Los muertos me persiguen. Creo que estoy maldito por mis crímenes.*"

I paused, waiting for an answer. Perhaps two, three, even four seconds I waited before I kept walking, grabbing my cart, heading to the backroom. My cardboard needed to be compacted. *The dead haunt me, I am cursed for my crimes.* Why was it that I had chosen to tell that man, at that time, in that store, in the middle of the night?

———✳·——

CLAYSVILLE, PENNSYLVANIA. PRESENT.

Dusk had come and gone by the time I woke in the backseat of Winslow's HMMWV. I didn't remember when sleep had overtaken me. I'd been tired this week, especially during the last few days spent readying this excursion to the south, low on sleep and running myself ragged.

Captain Winslow had pulled her Company into the abandoned town of Claysville. On the map, it was just a single dot and a name, no streets to speak of. Before the Collapse, less than a thousand people likely lived here, since then it had fallen into disrepair, the wilds of Pennsylvania overtaking it in a slow dance of entropy. An old Main Street sat, dusty, forgotten off a highway that few people still traveled; free of vandalism and damage, windows were intact and screen doors stood undamaged, the town had been frozen in time.

"How can we fight at night?" Captain Winslow's driver approached from behind me. He was my height, a small man, diminutive even in full gear. His crisp voice bore no accent, and he was clearly better educated than most kids his age.

"By firelight," Mayy answers, across from me. She was not wearing the same green and brown camouflage I was. Instead, she was in black pants and boots with a length of black linen wound around her chest, covering her breasts. She has smeared black grease across her pale skin, across her chest, stomach, forearms, and face. "You'll fight by Maggi's flame."

I didn't answer; instead I glanced over at Winslow, a map folded in her hands, deep in thought, ignoring all of us. The table was illuminated by several candles, casting a soft glow. Mayy and Mohamed continued

38

to banter as I reached into my chest rig, removing a flask of Crafton local brew. Winslow caught sight of me chugging and did a double take.

"You're *drinking?*"

"I always drink before a fight." I shrugged.

"How do you know we're fighting tonight?" Winslow responded, incredulous.

"I'm a witch, *remember?*" I winked at her, "Actually, I hope to be *fucking plowed* in another hour or so for this battle."

"The Federals have bunked down for the night. We'll need to wait," Winslow shook her head. "They'll come up Highway 79 in a day, maybe two, and we'll be waiting for them."

"Captain," I hit the flask again, the moonshine burns, and I just didn't care. "Lorne has a saying about witches. *I can't fucking remember* what he says, but it's something about courting the advice of wizards or some King Arthur *shit.*"

"You should listen to her." Mayy nodded at Winslow as she continued to smear the black grease across her face and eyelids.

"All right," Winslow set her map down to ask, "why would Federals want to continue a march at night time? They're cutting through a heavily forested area, they'd be prone to an ambush."

"Have you fought the Federals, before?" I asked Winslow, not intending to sound rude, but as I heard my own voice, I realized that I didn't sound kind.

"*No.*" She replied, a second later.

"Federals have *night vision.* They *own the night.* They're not afraid of an ambush like we would be. They're also marching more than two regiments up Highway 79, much of that is infantry, right? They can only move as fast as their slowest. Their slowest are on foot."

"Right, their armor, vehicles, all of it has to slow down." Winslow nodded.

"Now, if you're the Federal commander, would you like to get caught camping on a road in the middle of *fucked off nowhere*, or would you push your army through the night to reach the ruins of Washington, by morning?"

Winslow looked around, at Mayy covered in her black grease, then at Mohamed. I could feel her tension now. She was not concealing her emotions as well as she had been, tension and concern flows off her body; her attention was spread in too many directions.

"You're right." She said finally.

"I can also *feel* them approaching," I drank again from my flask.

"*Thousands* of men," Mayy looked at Winslow, now. "Each one has a beating heart, boots on the ground, with a *brazen lust*. It's a *taste* unlike anything else."

"*Fuck*," whispered Winslow, her voice nearly cracking.

"Captain, this is your *shit show* to command. I'm here to back you up. Don't be surprised that things aren't going as you planned. Nothing *ever* goes as you planned."

Without warning Winslow turned and walked away from the table, with its lit candles. Mohamed looked at me, then at Mayy, and stepped away. The two of us were left alone as Mayy painted her face with white now, fingers crossing down her lips like the teeth of skull. She wasn't using a mirror, only committing to the paint from memory.

"You're not going to commit valiant suicide, are you?" Mayy said, not meeting my gaze.

"*What?*" I offered the flask to her, and she declined.

"All this talk about your own mortality. You sound like a woman on the way to the grave, like someone just told you that you had weeks left to live."

"Maybe they did." I shrugged, happy to continue drinking the moonshine by my lonesome.

"*Do as you're told. Someone has to live on, to protect Crafton, and protect Alexander.*" I wished I could honestly say that Mayy's impression of me didn't sting, but it was hurtful. She mimicked my accent, over the top, chewing on her vowels far more than even my parents had when they learned English. I supposed that I had it coming, but it didn't make me less irritated.

"*Watch your mouth.*" I bite back.

"Sorry, I'll *do as I'm told.*" Mayy's response was every bit as venomous.

"Maybe I'm going senile," I shrugged, the moonshine starting to make me buzzed, "But I keep dreaming of the past. Things from my childhood. When I met my teacher, when I was a just a *kid*, a kid like you."

"Dreaming of your past doesn't mean you'll die *tonight*."

"I don't believe in random happenstance." My temper flared, and when it did, the candles on the table also rose in height and light. It'd been a decade or more since I'd done such a thing, beyond my control. "I taught you that."

"*You* taught me to read the world for patterns. To *look* and *listen*. You taught me that the world was one big riddle to solve. *Reach your mind out, feel that army like I did.*"

I tilted my head, fighting off the desire to remind her of her place, as my *student*. After a second I set aside my arrogance and closed my eyes, reaching southward down the highway. It was a simple thing, stretching your senses that far, listening, being quiet, watching the energies pulse and flow across the landscape. The army was closer than I'd expected, but not by much. I searched through them, the flame of internal combustion, and the soldiers themselves. It was a familiar sense; familiar, I realized, save for one detail.

"*They're not afraid.*" I said softly.

"Maybe you *are* going senile, *Bruja*, you should have corrected me earlier."

"I should have," I replied, blinking, then knocking the flask back again.

"Why aren't they afraid? They're marching at night, alone, through the forest." Mayy leaned forward, her hair falling across her black and white face, obscuring eyes that dig into me, accusing me, burning me. "What are they so confident in?"

I shushed her then, closing my eyes, and returned my mind to the army, searching with real intent now, digging, gouging into the truth of things, biting my lower lip hard. I could feel the soldiers, feel the tanks and trucks and other vehicles. They had no air support, not enough fuel in reserves, not even *that* many tanks, of course. What else? *What else* was I missing? It wasn't long before I noticed eyes *watching* my mind, my consciousness, explore the enemy. The eyes weren't human, they were like tiny spotlights, connected to dead things, animated amalgamations, things I'd *never* have noticed unless Mayy had warned me.

The Federals couldn't use magic, why would I have looked so close?

Throwing open my eyes, I glared at Mayy. "Did you see *them?*" She'd not moved an inch.

"*No.* You're still the master. I only knew something was wrong."

"We're facing — I don't know *what* we're facing."

"We'll find out soon though, huh?" Mayy sneered, showing me her white teeth, showing me a darker side, her more caustic nature. My skin prickled with her energy, she was spinning it up deep in her chest, she was rising to the challenge, hungry for the fight. Just like I had taught her since she was a child.

My own mind stretched out for Winslow's guarded thoughts. I could smell her scent, grimacing under helmet and tightly bunched hair. I pried open the simple barriers she kept. Simple images popped up, a sea of flowers, an older man in uniform, her father. Much to my surprise, I *recognized* him.

I ignored those images and spoke directly to her. *Come back to the table.*

"I'll see you in the fray." Mayy began walking backward, golden sparks snapping off her hands. It was pure energy, pulled from her heart, from the ground, the sky, manifested in the physical world. It was nothing more than a reaction, a seepage. As she backed away from the candle light, she vanished into the darkness of a dead Claysville.

Long minutes passed before Winslow returned, and when she did, I heard her voice stutter. She was not as certain of herself as she was before, she'd never experienced another speaking in her mind. Probably not even her mother could do that.

"That was *you?*"

"Your instincts already told you it was." I nodded, finishing my flask off and replacing it in my chest rig. There were two more hidden in there. "In about an hour the enemy will be upon us, we'll need to strike. Do you have a plan yet?"

"Sort of?" Winslow wasn't a soldier now, just a scared human in front of me. "There's no off ramps for the highway that passes by Claysville. We have some explosives we could plant on the overpass at the north end of town. Lure their troops to follow us under the highway the southern tip, and split Blitz Company. There road diverges down there."

"Me and Mayy would attack the center of their column?"

"That was my plan." Winslow sighed, exasperated.

"Good plan." I smiled, pulling out my second flask. "I need you to know something, however. That Federal column is hiding something we have *not* seen before. There's something in there, *unseen*, something born out of the Veil, or magic. Mayy and I will need to engage it together, and shatter their center. *You and your Company* need to flee south, regroup, and return to Crafton with this news."

"Those aren't my orders." Winslow shook her head, unstrapping her helmet at the chin and pulling it off to look at me. She was serious, intent, all her fear vanished in a second. "General Lorne ordered me to break apart this army *all costs*, including the lives of my men and I."

"I respect that, Captain, I do. *However*, when I *tapped* at your mind, I saw an image of your father." Winslow didn't answer me, but her eyes did not fall away either. "I was wrong. I'd seen him before, I saw him *die* at New Castle. There were *two* witches there. The second one hid until we were already committed. Your father was part of a fire squad that followed me into a trap. He was *no match* for the magic he witnessed that day. He went brave to his death. *You don't need to do the same.*"

I thought Winslow might cry, but she didn't. Her chin quivered, and she blinked hard several times, but not a single tear fell. When she spoke, it was in a crisp, cool tone. "Mayy is just a teenager, and you're an old woman."

"*I know.*" I nodded. "Leave us a truck, north of town. I don't plan to *fucking* die here either."

———— * ————

CLAYSVILLE, PENNSYLVANIA. PRESENT.

When Winslow's explosives shut down the highway ahead of the Federal regiments, their column stopped mid-march. The overpass toppled in a cloud of dust and smoke, debris rolling down the side streets, chunks of cement and rebar.

Soldiers responded in kind, running off the highway, taking positions, finding cover. Lighter vehicles cleared the path, and men dove behind some of the heavy tanks *in* column. Absolute darkness still favored the field, flames providing scant light from where I watched.

One minute passed, then two. Chaos calmed for a second before I saw headlights from Blitz Company ignite in Claysville. The Federals saw it immediately, chatter from small arms fire lit up the highway. Winslow's vehicles were on the move, and fast, racing through the streets for their lives. The town was dark, tight, and it'd be easy for a few trucks to get lost in the streets, take an RPG from the Federals, never make out alive. The Company was deftly handling the narrow streets to make an escape, however. Captain Winslow was a *witch*. Whether she knew it or not, her men stayed organized in those streets because of her, taking turns and corners, falling in behind her two lead HMMWV's. She was a kind of pied piper, weaving a trail of energy and focus for her mice to follow. Heavy turrets on her lead vehicles answered the Federal barrage, and her Company raced for south, to dive under the highway.

While Federal troops engaged Winslow's Company from cover, glued to the edges of the highway, they never perceived that this was only the start. They never noticed the barefoot girl climb up on their two lead tanks, big M1 Abrams, main line battle tanks. They didn't notice the turrets slowly turning, nor did they see the gun barrels aiming down the highway. They never expected those M1 tanks to *open fire on them*.

I expected it, of course, watching from my perch, across from Claysville and the main highway itself. Mayy had an ability to chisel into minds, grasp them in her hands, rend a cancerous madness, a parturition of paranoia and panic. It wasn't that she *controlled* other people, it was that she drove them mad with fear and terror. I could *feel* the M1 crews screaming, their words babbling, thrumming, nonsensical. They genuinely believed that *somehow*, the enemy had replaced their column in the march, and now they were under attack from the rear.

Parts of the highway exploded as 120mm shells registered with asphalt, grass, and dirt. Federal troops who'd clumped together for cover against an ambush from *beyond the road* never dreamed their own tanks would fire on them. They never scattered, never took cover. Their bodies flew in all directions. As years went on, into the Collapse, I had seen horror beyond imagination, and had even become insensitive to it. A deluge of *body parts and bloody precipitation* was enough now to churn my stomach, despite my years spent watching true ugliness unfold.

Mayy's range was limited, so she had to get in close. Close, like her teacher taught her, close like her teacher *favored*. I watched her small frame jump off the M1 Abrams and race directly down Highway 79 southward, arms spread wide. Behind her was a wake of madness, chaos, and paranoia. I felt her power as it twisted up my guts, chattered at the back of my head and whispered doubts in my own ears. She was projecting *harder* than I'd known her capable, and gambling that no one would see her.

She was right. Entire Companies turned on each other in her wake, weapons *popping* rapidly, men vomiting on themselves in panic, they fell on each other like mongrel dogs with firearms, knives, stones, *anything they had*.

The entire highway alongside Claysville was on fire now. The two lead M1s had shifted into gear, one plowing *forward*, directly into the underpass that had been detonated. Its long gun turret buried in the earth, stalled halfway down the incline. The second M1 had begun rolling *back* through the carnage of the Federal line, cutting a bloody swath *across their soldiers* locked in mortal combat.

"*Mayhem.*" I whispered. It was at this moment that my student had earned her own title, just like I once earned the name *Bruja*. A *Mexicano* soldier, I never knew his name, saw me covered in blood, on fire. He stood up from his trench, screaming, "*La Bruja! La Bruja!*"

It was my turn to join my student in the fray.

I jumped down from the old front porch where I was perched, only a few hundred yards off the highway, and I stalked up into the madness. The physical act of this was *nothing* to me right now. My age didn't matter, and my years weren't that long. I was *no one's abuela*, my chest was aglow with adrenaline.

I crossed up onto the highway from where Blitz Company's explosives had dropped debris up and over the damaged M1, and onto the assault. The gunfire was subsiding as the Federal column wiped themselves out. A second column would be advancing up front the center, and these men would not be as easily surprised.

The M1 that had rolled *across* the Federal lines had rolled off the highway, and I dropped to my knees, running my hands, arms, wrists and elbows through the gore. The *blood* was filled with power, and I whispered the old words *my* teacher had taught me, words in dead languages that summoned up the power from the blood, wrapping me in the weight of the slaughter. As I stood, some of the tattoos on my exposed arms glowed bright red.

I closed my eyes, whispering, *over and over and over*, the words a rhythm in my heart and soul, I was whipping the fire and ash of the melee into a powerful force stored around me. The wind gusted against my skin and then went silent.

I opened my eyes.

Four more broad, squat, HMMWV's like Winslow's slowly rolled up from the southern side of the Federal column. They were slow and monotonous. There will be lines of Federal fire squads behind each one of them, they were advancing to contain an unknown threat.

"*Burn.*" I closed my fists, hands stretched out before me. They burst into flames for a second. I sent my mind around the vehicles, telling the flame where to go, wrapping around, *inside their fuel tanks*. One, two, three, and then all four of the HMMWV's exploded.

The sound was deafening, and I could only hear a soft ringing after the initial burst. The highway grew silent, and I advanced southward toward the Federal lines. I used flames around me to swallow at the night air, to obscure me. I hid behind the heated curtains, my hands playing a marionette game across the road ahead, fingers jerking, twitching, as men ignited in flames, consumed by heat and fire. A second, larger, fireball erupted from deeper in the column lines. Ammunition ignited, explosives detonated.

I was smiling and breathing hard. I was the ringmaster, the disk jockey, the queen of all I survey, and the burning inevitability of death. How I had missed this power.

You're going to catch a bullet in the middle of the road. Mayy was in my mind. I could feel her moving around me, though I was not sure where. She was concealing her location. *Smart girl.*

You didn't. I snapped back, in her mind.

They're coming. Mayy vanished now, even her voice just an afterthought, something I was not even sure I'd heard. She was right, I knew, and I wouldn't conceal myself, not as she had done. I was here to lure out their secret, the Federal mystery they concealed in their center. Winslow and Blitz Company were on their way to safety, racing across the Pennsylvania countryside, Mayy was hidden in the shadows.

Only I stood in the wake of *thousands*. Perhaps a full fifth of the Federal army lay dead around me. I may as well have been in the center of spotlight.

I didn't feel them until they were close, and I expected that. They wore bulky suits of machinery formed into dull, metallic sheets of armor wrapped around a bubbling black soup, chunky with unidentified elements. They were humanoid in a way, or as humanoid as the suits forced them to be. Their eyes glowed yellow, burning bright, and I knew them.

Djinn.

They weren't smart, or dangerous Djinn, they were more like feral animals, clenching and biting at the air. They saw me, *smelled* me, big dumb creatures who were blind to fear, to the wisdom that came with magic. Yet, they were intrinsically manufactured from magic. My mind scurried over them, across them. There was no spark, those exo-suits they wore were *wearing* them, there was no electricity, no batteries, no fuel. They powered their armor.

"*Burn.*" I reached out, spinning up a raging inferno around one of them. From the ground, it burned white hot, *so hot* that I could feel it draining at me, *exhausting me.* I was summoning everything I could from the air, the earth around us, even from the rapine around me. I wasn't playing games here, *I hit that thing* with all the flame and heat I could muster.

The metal did *not* melt. The creature did *not* burn.

"Why did I think that would work?" I whispered to myself. It was foolish to waste that much power, I should have known better. There was no accelerant on them, nothing to *explode.*

The creatures in their suits held a kind of base intelligence that made them very dangerous. If they charged Blitz Company, or the walls of Crafton, the average soldier would likely turn and flee. When they charged me I dropped to one knee and prepared to fight them *hand to hand* if I had to. It was a ridiculous idea, but I was riding high on adrenaline, and Mayy knew I was a *scrap*; I'd fight the armor suit with my knuckles and brittle bones if needed.

The lead creature closed distance with me first, and a bolt of ingenuity struck me. If I couldn't burn the Djinn, and couldn't break their exo-suits, then I *maybe I could render them immobile.*

I glanced to my right and saw the broken wheel of a ruined HMMWV. I spun up a whirlwind of kinetic energy around it, hard enough to toss the heavy tire at the charging Djinn.

"*Burn.*" I whispered again, eyes on the tire. The thick rubber ignited, *white hot.* It melted midair and slammed into the powered exo-suit. The force from the kinetic blast and the liquid rubber dropped the beast to the ground, *cracking* the asphalt open behind it and rattling the highway under me. The Djinn-powered suit attempted to pry itself off the ground, coated in burning rubber. Joints failed, frozen or damaged. First, its clumsy arm gave out, then a leg, then finally the fame collapsed, unable to stand. One down, five more to go.

I smiled. I smiled *big*, and *sincere.*

It was at that moment that a third, massive, main line battle tank plowed out of the center of the Federal line, from the south. Another M1 Abrams, this one was on fire, its *entire* gun turret was gone, shorn off and belching black, sooty smoke that trailed it like a cartoon wake. I saw the small figure walking out of the wreckage and smoke along aside it. No armor, no kit, the silhouette was small, miniscule so far away. *Mayhem.*

The D*jinn* were nowhere near as clever as a living, breathing human could be. They were so focused on my demise that they never noticed the out of control armored vehicle plow through them at *full speed*. I couldn't melt the exo-suits with my fire, but a *fifty-fucking-ton* tank would easily crush the armor like eggshells in its path. As each one was pulled under the treads and torn apart, I saw blue flashes and old sigils, characters written across the air in dead languages, bright, then fading away. The suits themselves, in all their ingenuity, were *popped* like excrescence on the face of a teenage boy, oozing oil and fiber optics, wires and hydraulic liquid ruptured violently, only to lay dead, inert, on the highway.

The creatures had been captured *by* the suits, held against their will. Once released they no longer sought a fight with me, once released they evaporated into the night, or boiled at the asphalt, a whirlpool of soup and meat, pulled back into the earth whence they came.

The M1 tank rolled by me, barreling down the highway. It went off the side, almost flipping over, and continued off into the forest, a jangling cacophony of *mayhem*.

"I said, I'd see you in the fray." Mayy approached me, her face still coated in black grease and white paint, now running with sweat and caked in blood. The white of her eyes a stark contrast, peered back at me.

"Did you see those?" I pointed at the bent and broken pieces of technology scattered down the highway. "They've captured Djinn. Enslaved them as weapons. No witch, *no human* could do that."

"Let's talk later. An entire Federal regiment is following me up that highway."

"You don't want to see if we can take them *all?*" I grinned at Mayy, realizing that my heart was pounding in my chest, and her words were the first thing I'd heard within my own ears in many long minutes.

"You can keep fighting?" Mayy said, exasperated.

"*Respect your elders, girl. Let's go.*" I waved her to me. We still had a long run across much of Claysville to find the truck that Winslow had left for us. There was a chance that Mayy and I could have killed more Federal forces, but there was a better chance that those soldiers were now fanning out to encircle the carnage on the front of the column. When that happened, we would be dead, and our escape route would be captured. No matter how grim my sense of humor, I had taught Mayy well.

Redwood City, California. Long Past.

Previous dreams had confused, even confounded me, and now I welcomed this one. Here, in these dreams, my skin didn't burn hot from the battle, my bones didn't ache, and I wasn't exhausted. Here in my dreams I was *young again*, lost in my vices.

There was roughly a gram of cocaine on the mirror in front of me, not that much, *coca* was expensive, and I only made *ten dollars an hour*. I used a large, trapezoid razor, from my work blade to cut lines out of the white powder. As I chopped through it I could smell the pungent, anesthetic odor. I'd already *snorted* a line, and found myself fiending for a second.

My room was a small, curtained off section of my cousin's living room, behind the sofa, and in front of his big screen television. One long curtain ran from the ceiling to the next wall, directly across from the kitchen. There was just enough room for a narrow dresser, a mirror, a laundry basket, and a twin bed. It was dark out, I remembered, though I had no windows. I could hear my cousin cooking in the kitchen a few yards away, the smell of burning oil strong after the sharp intake of cocaine.

The second line hit like a train and *burned* my sinuses before the engulfing euphoria hit me. It wasn't a wild or crazy high, rather it was like a simmering pot, a burning ecstasy that I could just lean back and enjoy, my feet still on the floor, knees braced across my dresser.

This was a *good dream* for me. In my youth, before my son, I would have done *coca* two or three times a week. More if the money allowed, more if someone offered me a little. I wasn't an addict, I wouldn't have *fucked someone* for a baggie, but I might have lifted my shirt for a line if that opportunity had presented itself.

After long minutes on the bed, I sat up shaking my head and absorbing a giggle under my breath. I had never really giggled as a child, or as a young woman. As I looked over, through the eyes of my younger self, I saw the monochrome vestiges of Mandy, the dead girl, next to me. She was sitting cross-legged on my bed next to me, eyes hollow and dull, face sad. She wasn't even watching me, she was just looking off into nothing.

Oh, it was going to be this memory, I remembered. That was what I would get for assuming that the gods saw fit to remind me of a few *nice things* in life before I died.

Mandy rattled me, *hard,* and I jumped off the bed, yelling at nothing, kicking at the blankets, pulling myself against the wall. My heart raced and I fought to *forget* she was there. I closed my eyes, counted to ten in Spanish, then opened them again. Mandy was still next to me, on the bed, looking morose, only this time my cousin's shaved head peaked through the curtain.

"You okay in there, *cuz?*"

"*No.*" Angry, I stood up, grabbing my jacket off the narrow sweep of floor at my feet. "I'm going out. Don't wait up for me."

"You *gon'* leave that plate of *yay* out like that?"

"You can have it."

I couldn't look back at my bed, or the cocaine, and I wasn't high enough to miss the powder now. I pushed by my cousin, not rudely, just quickly, pulling my jacket on. It was heavy and black with a hood. I was only wearing a tank top under it, and I knew it would be chilly outside.

"*Fuck!*" I swore under my breath, digging out a pack of menthol cigarettes. I couldn't handle this curse, or this gift, or *whatever it was.* I didn't want to see, I just wanted to be left alone to do my mindless job, sleep in my tiny bed, and *snort my godforsaken cocaine.*

I needed to sleep somewhere else tonight, not in my bed, not with Mandy watching over me. I had few friends in Redwood City, most of them my co-workers, and none of us close enough that I could ask to crash on their couch. There was always that supervisor, the tall guy who'd cornered me, weeks earlier. What was his name? He was weird, but he was *cute*.

I pulled out my little, silver cell phone and dialed one of the girls who worked on his team. I shared lunch with her a few days before, we traded our numbers.

"*Bueno?*" She answered after a few rings, just in time for me to light my cigarette.

"*Oye*, Marcia, it's Maggi. Maggi, from work."

"Aren't you *at work?*"

"No," I shook my head, as if Marcia was standing right in front of me. "I'm off tonight. Your boss is too, right? Friday night?"

"*Yes…*" I hear Marcia's hesitation.

"Can you give me your boss's phone number?" I inhaled from my cigarette, and spoke again on the exhale, "We talked, we had a thing maybe planned, tonight."

"Why didn't *he* give you his number?" Marcia answered, her tone growing more suspicious.

"*Fine*, don't give me his number. Give him mine. Will you do that?"

Marcia responded to me after a long pause. "I guess. *I guess so.*" I only closed my phone after I heard her hang up, grinding my teeth, agitated.

"*Fucking whore*," I growled to myself, "you're *fucking* two guys on the backroom team and you're married to some big *vato motherfucker*, but you want to act like this *fucking Sunday school teacher* when I ask for your boss's number?" I was talking to myself as I began to pace, up and down the block, in front of my cousin's apartment building. I waited the entire length of the cigarette, compulsively checking my phone, and was lighting a second one before the phone rang with a number that I didn't recognize.

"Is this Maggi?" A man's voice asked me.

"Who the *fuck* do you think it is?" *That was too much*, I scolded myself. "Sorry, *sorry*, I'm having a bad night."

"Yeah, it's okay. Marcia said to call you. What's up?"

What's up? What the fuck is up? Is that all he has to say to me? I paused, considering my next few words, wondering how this would turn out. The pause lasted for a very long time before I finally replied to him. "Want to hang out?"

Now it was his turn to pause. When he finally answered, I was almost ready to throw my little plastic phone across the street. "Okay… one condition."

"Right. *What?*" I answered.

"'*Los muertos persiguen. Creo que estoy maldito por mis crímenes.*'" He didn't pronounce everything correctly, he rolled his rs at the wrong times and said certain vowels too flat, but he repeated my words back to me, ending in English. "You're cursed?"

"*Okay,*" I sighed, closing my eyes, "I'll explain."

I gave him my address and told him that I would be waiting outside for him, then I closed the phone and pulled out a *third* cigarette to smoke. What exactly was I hoping to accomplish here? Even in my memories, even looking back at this dream, I wasn't following any set path. The white boy *was* cute, and I liked his eyes, but why had I chosen to trust him with my secrets, and why would I call him out to Redwood City in the middle of the night? For company? I wasn't going to *fuck* him, I wasn't that kind of girl, I never had been.

I chain-smoked half my pack of cigarettes by the time he arrived. He was driving a small, two-seat sports car, cherry red but tinted a bright orange under magnesium street lights. I couldn't identify it, but it was neither new, nor particularly attractive. He didn't get out; instead he stopped in the middle of the street and leaned over to open the door for me. I bristled at first, somewhat annoyed at him, then I remembered; *this wasn't a date.*

I just *maybe* hoped it was a date.

The interior of his car was better looking than the exterior. Black leather seats, vinyl dashboard, red displays, all black. I felt like I belonged for a second, like this was the most important place I could have ever been tonight, in this stupid white boy's old sports car.

I glanced over at him, pulling on my seatbelt. He did the same.

"Buckled up?" He finally asked me.

"Yup." I nodded.

"I need to visit Santa Cruz tonight. You're down to come along?"

"*Yup.*" I nodded again, slapping at my knees with the palm of my hands then finally stretching out my legs as he put the car in gear and took off. Not only was the car unattractive, it wasn't that fast either.

For the time being I found myself momentarily content. I was out of the apartment, away from the dead girl Mandy, away from all my fears and paranoia. I realized, then, that here in the car, with the man who worked with me, I felt *safe*. I'd never really known that sense of safety in my life, up until I met him. I pondered that in my dream, wondering if perhaps that was what had won me over to him so fast.

"So…" He began after a few blocks, as we headed for the freeway, "you *see* the dead?"

"*Yup*." I responded, pursing my lips.

"It's a long drive, you know. May as well start talking. It *was* my condition to pick you up tonight. I'd wager, it's also the reason you wanted to '*hang out*."

I glanced over at him in the darkness, street and watched traffic lights play colors across his face while his eyes darted and drifted across different parts of the road. He wasn't wrong.

"*Yup*." was all I said.

ARVELLA, PENNSYLVANIA. PRESENT.

"Do you want me to drive?" I opened my eyes, blinking against the morning light, realizing that I'd fallen asleep in the passenger seat of the old 4x4 truck that Captain Winslow had left for us to escape in.

"I'm okay, get some rest." Mayy replied, watching the road. The road we'd needed to take north, out of Claysville, was a jumbled mess of twists and turns across miles of rolling hills and Pennsylvania forest. After decades those roads had been consumed by nature again, meaning it was slow going for the most part.

"Where are we?" I rubbed at my eyes, looking around, smelling the cold, fresh air outside.

"Arvella, I think. We didn't bother asking Winslow for a map."

"That's my fault." I groaned, attempting to pull my hair out of its braid. After a second of frustration that stemmed from my realization that I needed to comb it, I looked down at my hands and arms. They were covered in dried blood, soot, and dirt. My wrists hurt, the bones *inside* my wrists hurt, from the magic I'd used and the power I'd wielded that night. My fingernails had caramelized, though that wasn't new to me. It'd just been many years since I was in that deep, in the fight, *in the fire*.

Mayy glanced over, smiling. Her face was still a mess of grease, paint, and blood, "I still can't use kinetic energy, like you. I tried again, anyway."

"*Good*," I nodded, coughing smoke from the previous night out of my lungs. "Now if you'd just focus that much on *all* your studies."

"I *do*," Mayy sighed, pulling the truck out onto a larger road inside a mostly complete town. I glanced around with my eyes, seeing a few chimneys spitting smoke as well as a few people watching us. My mind spread out across this place, across Arvella, checking in the nooks and the crannies and wondering if it was safe. "I just don't *care* about all the *boring shit.*"

"When I was your age I hated the *boring shit* too," I nodded at her, straightening up in my seat, curious about the world around me now in the new daylight. "I wanted to know all about the monsters in the night. I was hungry to understand what I saw."

"What was *that* like?" Mayy questioned, her voice soft now.

"What was *what* like? *Oh*, what I saw? I could *always* see ghosts, maybe not gods or other spirits, but the ghosts I saw even before the Veil vanished. No one else could."

"So, you *always* had a gift that made you more powerful?" Mayy didn't seem resentful as she said it, she sounded genuinely curious.

"*Powerful?*" I chortled, "*My dear Mayy,* no. People just assumed I was mad." I continued my intense survey of the landscape as we turned northeast in the search for a road sign. I knew much of the areas around Crafton by heart after so many years, the original road names as well as the current ones. If this was the township of Arvella, then we were likely on Highway 50, sometimes called Arvella Road.

"You *are* mad, Maggi." Mayy chuckled, until I gave her a grimace.

"I'm not the one who ran down the center of a Federal line last night, barefoot." I snapped my tongue at her, more interested in giving her a *ration of shit,* than chiding her talents or her tactics.

"It's what *you would have done.*" Mayy clipped back, I believed that she knew I was teasing her, or at least I *hoped* she knew. "You didn't even take your helmet with you, it's still *back* in Winslow's *hum-vee.*"

"I get it, I get it." I sighed, not in the mood for my *student* to chide *me.*

"What's that you always told me? One good bullet, that's all it takes. No witch can take a gunshot to the skull."

"*We're all equal in the eyes of lead.*" I replied, whispering.

"Yeah, *that,* that's what you always say." Mayy laughed; her laugh not directed at me, but it cut to the bone easily enough. I reminded myself to be less curt with her, to be less *mean.* I knew that she saw me as far more than a mentor, a teacher.

"Just *drive*." It was all I said, and when I said it, it came out as a growl.

"As you command," Mayy looked over at me, shocked, and a little incredulous under her messy face. "It'll be noon before we're back in Crafton, try and nap a little more."

———*———

SANTA CRUZ, CALIFORNIA. LONG PAST.

What I didn't realize about that ugly, red, sports car was that it could handle the mountain road to Santa Cruz at unrealistically high speeds. While I slept next to Mayy as she drove us through the winding roads back to Crafton, my mind had no difficulty in recalling how much my stomach churned on that long-ago drive. I had gripped the door handle tightly, and whispered *Hail Mary's* under my breath. It wasn't until we had reached the bottom of the hill that I had pushed the electric switch and rolled down my passenger side window.

"*Yes*, you can smoke," He glanced at me, watching me pull my pack of cigarettes from my jacket.

"*May I please smoke in your ugly ass car?*" I balked at myself, in the dream, wrinkling up my nose, acting so caustic.

"Are you sure you're not a fighter pilot?" He turned, as we came up to a red light, a half grin spread across his face. I didn't answer, only squinted at him until he finally spoke. "Because you're *really* good at evasion."

"This *fucking comedian.*" I swore to myself as the light went green. The salt smell of the ocean was thick and the air was a few degrees cooler than Redwood City. "Look, I'm not telling you *everything* about that night in the liquor store. Maybe I will someday."

"I'm not asking you," He shrugged, "but that was over a decade ago. Something has you scared today. *Every day.* You had scared eyes at work, and when you got in my car."

"That's just because I'm scared to get in a car with some white boy I don't even know." I snapped back, my cigarette now lit. "You pick me up, drive me to Santa Cruz *like a fucking maniac.*"

"Oh, I can do better," He said, pulling off the main highway and down a series of side streets, "We're going to a cemetery, a very *old* cemetery."

"Are you *fucking out of your mind?*" I shouted, "I got in this car, I *called* you so I could get away from *fucking dead people.*"

"*Ha!*" It was his turn to shout, laughing at me.

"What. *What?*" I leaned forward, almost dropping my cigarette out the window.

"I got you to admit your curse, what you're so afraid of."

"*Fine.*" I hit the cigarette for one more drag, hard, before dropping it to the road. "You're right, that *shit* is hard to say. *Yes,* I've been seeing the dead since I got out of prison, all over the *fucking place,* and now in my bedroom. *In the bed with me.*" I hadn't even noticed that I'd let slip the words *since I got out of prison* in the heat of the moment. This was why I didn't like to talk much, *why* I never really talked. I never knew what might slip loose.

"Prison?" He didn't seem concerned, and I realized my error.

I tried to skip over it, as if I'd never spoken the words. "Before I called you up? *Fucking* dead girl, sitting next to me on my bed. I know her too, it's not the first time I've seen her."

"You *saw* her with your eyes? Not just a *creepy vibe* or chills?" He seemed shocked. "That's *very rare.*"

"It's *so* rare that I'm going crazy now." I sighed, letting myself fall back into the seat, resigned that I'd be traipsing through a dark cemetery in the middle of the night. I couldn't decide if that was genuinely terrifying, or simply ridiculous.

"Maggi," After rounding a corner, I saw the graveyard on our left. It *was* old, with huge headstones and obelisk grave markers, complete with an arched entryway that read *Evergreen Cemetery* in wrought iron. "I don't know what to tell you. If you think someone, *anyone,* can make them go away, they *can't.*"

"All right." I nodded once, "So what do I do?"

"You learn to control it. You have sight. It's a curse or a gift, depending on your point of view, but the better you control it, the less it can control you." He spoke as he parked across the street from the cemetery, next to what seemed like a baseball field. When he reached over to pull the parking break, I moved for his hand, putting my weight into it. Whether I wanted to admit it or not, I'd spent most of my formative years in prison. I was older now, and I couldn't hide behind secrets forever.

"*Wait.*" I said quietly, quieter than I had been this entire drive, "I want you to know that this is *retarded*, but I'm going with you. Don't think for a second that any ghost in my apartment is so scary that I'd run away to *spelunk a cemetery* in the middle of the night with some weird white guy." I was talking too much, *more than I usually did*, "You're *cute*. Maybe I want to see you more, but I'm no liar, understand?" I looked right at him now, jaw set.

"Understand, what?" He replied, just as quietly.

"I killed a man in that liquor store." I couldn't hold his gaze anymore, I had to look away to finish my words. "I was fourteen and I accidently shot the store clerk. So, if you decide you like *this*, and maybe want to see *me* again, you'd best know all the facts."

"So," He began hesitantly, "this your first... *date?*"

"*Yup.*" I opened the door to the passenger seat. It was heavy, and when I climbed out I was so close to the ground that I needed to almost kneel first before standing. When I closed the door, it briefly reminded me of my father and the old truck he drove when I was very young.

I was warmed, watching myself speak to him that way, back then. I was never as nice to him as I should have been, but at that moment I'd been honest and open. It was a rare, but in the memory, *in the dream,* I could reveal a little.

He gestured for me to follow him across the street, and I did, about two paces behind. The place was dark, open, and no one was around. The baseball field was closed, the trails to my right were chained and locked; all that was left was a cemetery that seemed to climb the side of Santa Cruz's hills as far as I could see.

I wasn't *stupid.* I liked the boy, and maybe he liked me. But I still quietly withdrew my work box cutter from my back pocket and opened it up. It was buried in my left palm. I was *not* afraid to cut him. He beckoned to me again. "Let's get off the street. Cops usually get curious when people stand around outside cemeteries at this time of the night."

"Like, they'd think we were Satanists or something?" We walked briskly up to the gates.

"I don't think Satanism is against the law," he said, chuckling softly. "Pretty sure they're more worried about vandals and drug dealers." I was additionally glad now that I had the knife buried in my palm.

"I guess now you can now say that *you saw the elephant.*"

"*What?* What does that even mean?" I balked, louder than I wanted, now confused.

"Back in the old days this farmer is going to town, *right?* He has his horse, his wagon, and the wagon is full of produce, for market. Unfortunately, there's also a traveling circus on the road. The circus has an elephant, and when the farmer's horse sees the elephant, he startles, breaks his reins, overturns the cart, and spills the farmer's produce."

"I bet he could have sued that circus." This was a stupid story, I decided.

"A newspaper man, a reporter, who was writing an article, *watches it all unfold.* He goes over, tries to help the farmer, and says, 'What a terrible disaster this must be!' The farmer just shrugs and replies, 'At least I saw the elephant.'" He finished, a big smile across his face.

"*What the fuck?* That still doesn't make sense, *güero.*" I'm now confused and slightly annoyed. Was he making fun of me?

"It means you did something, *saw something*, amazing and terrible. You saw it at great personal peril and you were glad for it. A little like your secret," he nodded, speaking quietly, "or coming to this cemetery in the middle of the night with me."

"You're such a dork," was my only reply. It was the first time I called him that.

The inside of Evergreen Cemetery was wet, overgrown, a thick canopy of trees blotted out the stars and dripped a soft rain on us we cross the paths, coursing into and up the hill. I could *feel* the place humming with activity, and even the slightest hint of whispers. It didn't scare me. Not the way it would have a day, or even a week ago, it wasn't because of my companion either; it was the words he'd shared. *The better you control it, the less it can control you.*

I closed my eyes. I could feel Evergreen watching me, so I watched it back. Slowly I became aware that a *small crowd* was gathered behind me, watching, quietly. There were no footsteps I could *hear with my own ears*, of course. They weren't *really* there, even if I could almost see them in my mind.

One of them stood out however, a brazen figure, taller than the others with a big set of white teeth, grinning at me. "What's up with *top hat guy?*"

"What's he wearing?" I could hear my companion lighting a cigarette of his own. It didn't smell like mine; it was rich and strong, like cloves, I heard it snap and crack as he inhales.

"A black tuxedo, I guess." My companion made a sound halfway between a grunt and an exclamation. I opened my eyes to meet his. "What the *fuck* does that mean?"

"I'm impressed." He nodded at me.

I stammered inside my head, but refused to show him. Instead I closed my eyes, dug harder, loosened myself up, and let my eyes drift, unfocused. I could *feel* more, much more. "There's a guy on my right. A foot away from me. He's got a jacket and vest on, and one of those little watch chains. He's holding the watch. Big mustache. Up ahead there's a lynched man hanging from the tree. *I can smell his blood all the way up the path.* There's a little girl next to you. She looks mad. Or pouty. *Maybe both.* And she doesn't like me very much." I was breathing faster now, letting myself absorb everything around me.

I could feel the man in the top hat coming for me, almost see him in my mind. He didn't fade into the cemetery background like the others, he made the cemetery itself fade into *him.* I thought I could feel his breath at my neck and maybe I could? When he talked to me, he spoke with the rumbling bass of an old black man.

Now, darlin', you don't care if I take a ride, do ya?

Maybe it was the act of an old *lwa,* an ancient spirit, stepping into me, that made my memories so blurry. My dream faded in and out as I fought to focus on the events as they had unfolded that night. This was my first time being *ridden* by something *else.* I couldn't move my head or my hands, I couldn't even blink. I became relegated to the back seat.

I was *terrified* now; I'd have soiled my jeans if I had not had control of my faculties.

I became aware of my mouth moving as my lips formed words. The voice belonged to me, but it was warm molasses soaked in brandy, drawn out and slowed down as if the syllables needed to be spun like taffy.

"*Ya' brought me a big tittied girl, didn't ya' son?*" I was now the passenger of a passenger in my dream, watching my hand grab the clove cigarette from my companion's mouth and inhale it hard.

"I didn't know she was coming." He answered, trying to hide a look of shock.

"*The way she was breathing, ya shoulda' known!*" My body cackled at the joke. I realized and accepted that I *couldn't* change whatever was happening to me. I did, however, have the overwhelming feeling that it would *be okay.*

"I brought chocolate."

"*And a bit o' rum?*"

"I didn't have time."

"*Damn it, boy!*" My voice dropped to a low growl, annoyed, angry, hitting the clove cigarette hard before casting it away. "*You're forgiven. But only this one time. On account of such a fleshy and amazing member of the female gender ya' brought me.*"

"Be careful. This is all new to her." My companion dug in his own jacket and offered me a bar of chocolate and a filterless cigarette, not a clove.

"*No, it ain't. This one's got eyes.*"

"Having the Baron Samedi step in, is a *new experience.*"

"*Everyone needs a little Baron inside them sometime!*"

"Little, eh? Sorry to hear that, man." My voice let out another chortling laugh at his joke. "*That's what I call style, son! Keep that up!*"

"Shall we discuss business?"

"*First, ya' better break a piece off that chocolate, and light me another cigarette.*"

This was all I was allowed to see.

From where my mind had rested in my own body, I was cradled in a deep, dark womb, a place that smelled of old bourbon and tobacco.

Whatever madness had overtaken me was something I *understood* on a core level. This wasn't a foreign world, even if it was a *new experience*.

Do you know who I am, dahlin'?

Unable to speak, I questioned in my mind if he could hear me.

Of course, dahlin'. Now I want to introduce myself to ya'. I am the one and the only Baron Samedi. I am the keeper of the cemetery gates. I hold the keys to the world of the dead. If you wish to walk through those gates, or back out, ya' talk to me, and me alone.

Was I dead? Am I dead? Was that what I'd been talked into?

Hell no, dahlin'! I'm just borrowing that little body of yours!

But, why? I didn't understand that.

I cannot walk in your world the same as mine. I exist somewhere in between. It makes it much easier to enjoy the finer things in life. Rum, chocolate, cigars, ya' understand.

I'd been possessed to smoke and eat chocolate? Is that what's happened?

Can ya' think of a better reason?

I thought that there were far worse things that could be done with my body.

I didn't ask permission an all that. I got caught up in the moment. Big ol' titties.

Should I thank him for that? Sure, why not? Thank you.

I cannot imagine any kinda' world that a lady of your, endowments, should ever live a single day without a lavish shower of compliments and kindness.

I realized, suddenly, that I didn't get such compliments.

Tell you what. I'll give you a gift. Repayment, you see, for allowing me this opportunity to not only examine every luscious inch of your personage, but also to delight in sweet tobacco and chocolate.

A gift? Was this a test or a trap of some kind? Is this a trap?

I'll give ya' privileged information. Privileged! It's the future. So, don't go around telling everyone about it. Fact is, don't tell a soul. See that boy? He fancies ya', and maybe ya' fancy him too. The two of ya' need to get it on, see, make a baby pop out.

What? I didn't want a damn baby!

Not now, but a day will come. Trust me, dahlin'. That baby will be important.

I didn't even know what to say about that.

'Thanks, Baron!' Now look, see here, dahlin', I gotta be in other places. I'll be seeing ya' around. Thanks for the ride!

There was a wave of vertigo, but it lasted for less time. I was confused, but at the same time I understood everything completely. My eyes focused on my companion and I reached for him with both hands, the sound of my box cutter hitting the cobbles loud in the air.

"Do you know what just happened?" He asked me, concern in his eyes, genuine and sorrowful. "I never expected *that to happen.*"

"He paid me." I laughed. "This is one *hell* of a first date" I raised my eyebrows, looking around, my hands on his arms to keep myself steady. I didn't feel afraid anymore, I wasn't sure I would ever feel afraid again.

"I *really* am sorry about that." He sighed, like a forlorn puppy.

"Stop being such a gentleman." I stepped forward, my mind a jumble of words and feelings and without thinking I said, "Do you want to kiss me, or not?"

"I've wanted to kiss you since the night I met you." He replied.

"Ladies don't kiss on the first date. You okay with that, *güero?*"

He kissed me. I didn't stop him.

It was not my first kiss, but it *was* the first time I had kissed a man. His stubble was rough against my lips, my chin, my face. I liked it. I liked the way he smelled and I liked his hands on me. The Baron was right, we did '*fancy*' each other, but he also had a world of things to teach me.

Although he would be my son's father, although we would spend many years together, I would always call him, simply, *my teacher.*

———✳———

CRAFTON, PENNSYLVANIA. PRESENT.

There was a *rap, rap, rap* at the door of my room.

I exited the bathroom, brush in hand, so that I had a line of sight to jerk the door open with a quick burst of kinetic energy. I couldn't do anything complex, like work the latch on a lock, but the door was already open. I was just being *lazy*.

Shocked, for just a moment, Lorne's expression faded to a smile and he stepped in. He wore his black and grey jumbled camouflage, and eye glasses framing blue eyes. I returned the smile and moved in to hug him, keeping my fingers off skin as always.

"I already spoke with Mayy when you returned." He withdrew.

"I needed the sleep, I'm *sorry*," I showed my teeth, apologizing.

"*Don't*, there's nothing to speak 'sorry' for."

"I'd offer you a seat, but…" I looked around my room, piles of clothes on the bed, the floors, the furniture. The only place that *wasn't* was mess was my actual closet.

"*No, no*," Lorne shook his head, palms up, "I only stopped by for a moment before we all meet later. I wanted to thank you, privately. Again, you acquitted yourself with valor."

"I don't know about all that," I shrugged, tossing my boar bristle brush to the bed, "we *fucked some shit up*, is all I know." I searched for my necklaces, the wooden beads I'd worn before, the silver ones as well.

"Winslow's people came back this morning; her scouts reported a full Federal retreat back to Wheeling."

"I'm not surprised," this time I laughed, finding one of my necklaces, "it was a massacre. Do you know I've given Mayy her own title now?"

"*Mayhem?*" Lorne nodded, showing me a yellow, toothy grin, "She told me."

"*C'mon*, that's a *badass* title. Better than *Bruja*. I get called 'The Witch.'" The rest of my necklaces had been discarded with the leather dress I'd worn a week earlier. I had worn another dress today, similar, made from black and green linens, though I had declined to wear a shirt *under* the dress. This time my chest, shoulders, and neck were visible along with all the ink across me.

"You'll be leaving us then?"

I paused, necklaces in hand. "How did you know?"

"Mayy talks too much," Lorne shrugged, turning to close my door behind him so we had some privacy. "She told me you suspected high-level Djinn had worked with Federals to create the exo-suits you saw in Claysville."

"Mayy *does* talk too much." I stood, then turned to sit down on the bed, "*C'mere.*" I patted at the bed next to me. Lorne seemed uncomfortable then resigned himself to sit next to me. I extended my free hand, taking one of his hands in mine. Our skin touched and I get flashes of his mind, Lorne eating breakfast, walking to my apartment, standing at my door for long minutes before he knocked.

"You'll need to hunt them down." Lorne nodded.

"Djinn can't be commanded like other creatures, or spirits. No witch, *no Federal witch*, could have bound them to those suits. They're better than any engine, any battery. They never get old, *they run forever.*"

"So, what *kind* of 'high-level Djinn' are you talking about?" Lorne kept his voice level and spoke clearly, but I could feel sadness seep from his pores and could see his eyes dim. He was not happy that I was leaving, and I knew why.

"*Ifrit,*" I guessed, "maybe even one of the seven Djinn kings."

"Let me understand this," Lorne chuckled, "the Federals can't command magic like us, so they manipulate a Djinn king to enslave their own kind in pre-Collapse powered suits? Is that, about right?"

"No." I pursed my lips and considered my next words carefully. "No, the worst of the Djinn *cannot* be manipulated. This is *their game*; the Federals are just tools."

Lorne turned and watched me. I studied him. Lines creased his face now more than ever, and he'd gone bald at his temples. The old commander had been my friend, my confidant, and some ways a surrogate father for my son. He'd also been in love with me for as many years.

"I'm no witch, Maggi, but I don't like how any of this feels."

"*Ohh*," I raised my eyebrows and squeezed his hand, "this *feels* like something *nasty*. I saw a vision of *black dogs*, Djinn, on the way to Claysville. Not to mention my dreams."

"Take Mayy with you then," Lorne wouldn't plead, he was too much of a General to ever do such a thing. Rather he attempted to reason with me. "You two were *nigh unstoppable* at Claysville if she's even telling me half the truth."

"She's telling you the full truth. She'll be *much* more powerful than me one day; she'll be one of your *battlewitches*." I stood up and stepped over to the dresser, looking for a belt. "That's why she'll *stay here* with you."

Lorne didn't answer.

After the Collapse, in this new world, I had not become a "battlewitch" overnight. When my teacher was still alive, I had served almost exclusively as nothing more than my son's mother, caring for him, scavenging food, milk, clean napkins. The two of them, Lorne and my teacher, had been the architects of Antecedent States. After my teacher's death, I had been pulled into his role, falling into a fierce power vacuum. The demands that fell on me were merciless, unrelenting. I was a thirty-year old woman with a baby and a broken heart, suddenly required to lead soldiers, summon ancient magic, and fight more experienced witches like Vix. In all these years, Lorne had never demanded anything of me. I had never been kind enough to do the same.

"I *am* sorry," I didn't turn around right away, "I was never quite what you needed."

"Like I said, Maggi," I heard Lorne chuckle, "nothing to speak 'sorry' for. You were always, *you still are* exactly what *we* needed. Antecedent is real because of you, and Alexander commands an army to the west, *because of you*." I didn't feel proud. The road from California was one paved in regrets. I merely did what was required of me, I survived so that my son would survive, and I fought so that my boy would have a better world. The power at my command was inconsequential, it always had been.

"Do you want me to lie to you Lorne?" I turned, jaw set, facing him in earnest. "Do you want me to tell you all the sweet lies? Or do you want cold, unkind, truth?"

"*You* should know me better than that." Lorne answered.

"*I probably won't be back.* I think, *I suspect* I may die on this hunt, and I have no idea why. I pursue dangerous prey, and I'm not so young anymore. When I leave Crafton, you'll never see me again."

"I know." Lorne nodded. He didn't betray any emotion, didn't grovel or act like a fool. He had seen worse unfold in his life than an old witch leaving his side.

"I want you to speak the words to me - *now, before* I leave."

"What words?" Lorne's head tilted, looking up at me.

"The words you've *whispered* with your mind for nearly *twenty fucking years*. The words that I can smell on your breath and hear in your laughter every second of every day. The words that you think are such an amazing secret, hidden from a woman they call *The Bruja*." I smiled at the last part, not out of arrogance or pride, but to soften my statement, to remind him that I'm being neither cruel, nor capricious. He *didn't* answer me, only stared, a look like anger at the edge of his eyes, but not quite. I sighed at him, letting my voice soften; "It's not a *game*. If you don't tell me now, you'll regret it for the rest of your life. I owe you too much, *care* for you too much, to ever allow such regret."

I had to kneel, in front of Lorne, before he'd answer. He didn't seem angry at me anymore, but it seemed like a challenge to force the words out. I didn't blame him; I'd never *really* spoken those words to anyone in my life, not even my son.

"I love you, Maggi." Lorne finally spat out, nodding.

He stood, then, and I stood with him. In my boots, with heals, our heights were less unbalanced. I went up on my tip toes to kiss him on the cheek. The contact with skin was enough to show me an emporium of sorrow spreading in his soul. I understood and related to him better at this moment than ever before.

"I'll see you at the meeting. Make sure Captain Winslow is there, *mm?*" I chirped.

"Of course," Lorne nodded at me and then turned to reach for the door, letting himself out. I watched the man leave, quietly, and then let my eyes wander across the room. I didn't quite know what to feel just then, maybe sadness, maybe regret, but I could summon neither. The truth was, sincerely, I'd felt very little, since the *only* man I had ever loved was killed.

CRAFTON, PENNSYLVANIA. PRESENT.

"*N*o *ordinary weapon may penetrate the divinity of the Ifrit, they are smokeless fire and ancient magic. No sword cast in steel, no axe in iron, they are susceptible only to the ways of sorcery. They are portents and dream eaters in the form of Black Dogs, they watch in the shadows of night and stand tall in the noon light, and know no allegiance to good nor evil.*"

I snapped the book closed, rubbing at my eyes momentarily. I'd never *liked* reading, not as a young woman, and not now. For all the homework, I'd forced Mayy to do over the years, I myself had cracked only a few books in my day. This particular book belonged to my teacher, and I'd mostly kept it *because* I could remember him pouring over it, late at night. Sometimes he read aloud to me, other times in silence.

This book was over a century old, bound in faded brown leather, and written in Arabic. Someone, perhaps my teacher's *teacher* had carefully translated it and written between the lines in pencil. The text was so small now, so faded, that I could barely make it out. It was also, more likely than not, that my eyes were beginning to grow weak with age.

I wasn't sure I could read more, I wasn't sure I *wanted* to read more. Although I had a cursory understanding about Djinn, their hierarchy, their strengths, and weaknesses, it had served me little over the years and I'd forgotten most of what I knew.

I sighed, blinking back tears from the eye strain, and looked around my room. I was laying in my bed, knees pulled up close to my chest, a single flickering, fluorescent light overhead. It had been a long day: my awkward goodbye to Lorne and the meeting with Lorne, Chandless,

Mayy, and Captain Winslow. Winslow hadn't absorbed the news that I planned to take her along with me on my hunt as well as I'd liked. I respected her reasons, honestly, it wasn't that she was afraid, or she considered this a waste. It was simply that *she* was a commander, and *she* wanted to be with her Company. Unfortunately, I held as much authority as Lorne, and he supported my choice to bring her with me.

"And *Mayy*, dear Mayy, what do I say to you?" I spoke to myself, not even a whisper; the words erupted from my mouth as if the stacks of old clothes in my room would respond back. I bit at my lower lip for a few minutes. Mayy was the *challenge*, and I wasn't quite sure how to handle this.

She'd screamed at her mentor, her commanding officers, and stormed out of a meeting with some of the most powerful people in the Antecedent States. I admired her, and *hated* her for it, because I knew there was no way she would learn the discipline she needed. I wouldn't be able to save her the suffering I'd endured. I paused, running my tongue across the back of my mouth, to where empty gums once seated four of my teeth. Teeth knocked out of my skull, fighting Vix. Mayy would lose a few of her own teeth to learn those lessons.

Frustrated, I leaned across the bed and started digging through my dresser, searching inside the drawer. I found tools, screwdrivers, knives, nuts, bolts, some old polaroids of people I'd never met, and finally a pencil. The pencil was older than me and still mostly sharp. I'd written with it perhaps once, ever. If I hated to read, I hated *writing* even more.

I sat back up, braced the leather-bound book in Arabic across my legs, and opened to the first page. It was blank, so I began to scrawl on the old parchment. My penmanship was terrible, though I did *try* to keep it clean and neat.

Margaret,

This book is for you. It belonged to my teacher, and his teacher before him. It contains old magic, words, rites, and symbols. I've taught you some of it. It also explains the Djinn. If I do not return, if I fail, you need to protect the Antecedent States without me.

I'm sorry I've always been such shit at talking to you. You were an angry little girl and I never knew what to say. For all my faults, you always looked up to me, always wanted to be me, always called me "brave." I hated that. I'm such a coward I won't even tell you goodbye because I don't want to see what your eyes will say. Be a better woman than me, be a better witch.

I'll always be proud of you, Margaret.

I scrawled my initials, MML, and closed the book, tossing it to the side of the bed.

I was rarely ashamed of myself, but tonight, my last night in Crafton, I loathed myself. That note was a joke, I knew it, and Mayy would know it. She'd toss that book across the room and not pick it up for years. She'd also never throw it away, she'd never let anyone but her touch it. I knew how she thought, and I accepted it years ago.

I crossed my hands over my chest, eyes growing heavy. It wasn't hard for me to walk away from Crafton, from Lorne, or Mayy. As much as I may have loved this place, as much as I may have cared for them, it was nothing without my son. If Alexander were to face an army of Djinn powered exo-suits, our witches, like me or Mayy, would be useless. Our troops would be ineffective. All that would remain would be a half-remembered dream, and a broken gift that his father and I had wished for him.

I cared for Lorne, and Mayy, deeply. But I loved Alexander.

* — ❋ — *

SAN JOSE, CALIFORNIA. TIME: PAST.

I was *trying* to not dress like a *chola* today.

My teacher was driving us to San Jose that morning, Saturday morning, on no sleep. We'd been seeing each other for nearly a month by that point, long enough that I'd grown accustomed to his ridiculous, ugly, sports car.

That I'm dreaming was no surprise, I had *hoped* that I'd be dreaming tonight, a taste of the past to make me forget the bitter present. I was not disappointed.

I looked down and saw that I was wearing a long sleeve sweater that hid most of my ink and jeans. The sweater was something I'd picked out, used, and hoped it would make me more presentable. He'd only laughed at me when he saw it, and I'd slapped at him for that laughter. He dodged of course, grinning like a maniac, and then I too began to laugh.

"Relax. *Relax*," He said, as we got off the freeway, smoking one of his clove cigarettes, "you don't need to hide your tattoos, she has ink also."

"Yeah, right," I nodded, "tattoo from a *tattoo parlor*, real ink."

"Are you jealous?" He glanced over at me. I didn't reply. Instead I forced myself to *not* smoke, fearful of getting ashes on my new sweater. I sat stiffly in the car, drumming my fingers on the knees of my jeans, wandering through every possible outcome for today. I wanted a cigarette, I wanted an entire *pack of cigarettes*, but I was trying to be on my best behavior.

When we pulled up to the house, it was the end of a cul-de-sac, facing a huge wall that obscured the freeway behind us. The neighborhood was quiet around us and it was quite honestly a beautiful day.

My teacher liked being a gentleman, and I liked being treated like a lady, so I sat in the car and waited for him to open the door for me. It made me feel *good* that he did that, it made me feel like the most valuable thing in the universe.

"Check my teeth." I told him, as he closed the door.

"You don't have lipstick on your teeth." He answered, not looking.

"How the *fuck do you know?*" I barked at him and then I heard the screen door open from the house ahead of us. My heart dropped for a second, and I wondered if the woman at the door heard me.

"Because there's no lipstick on your teeth." He answered calmly.

"Okay. *Okay.*"

The woman who'd stepped from the screen door after our arrival approached. She was short, but not as short as me. She had larger hips, a fuller figure, and better proportioned bosom than I did, not to mention a thick and wild mane of curly, red hair. However, her attitude belied the feminine attributes. She walked like a *man* and kept her fingers in her pockets.

She hugged my teacher, tightly, for a second longer than I liked.

Then she turned to me. The hug was awkward, I had my arms extended too long, I wasn't sure how to react and I didn't *like* her that close to me.

"Maggi, meet Aubree." My teacher gestured from me to the red-haired woman. She was pretty, easily beautiful, with a small nose and mouth, but her eyes were crawling all over me like a predator. I was instantly on edge.

"Call me Aubriana," the woman replied, leaning in, examining me. Her perfume was musky, thick, without being oppressive. It made me want to *sniff* at her, outside of my own control. "May I?" She gestured at me.

"May you *what?*" I looked from Aubree, to my teacher, and back again.

"Give me your hand." Aubree commanded. Much to my surprise, I obliged her. That made me angry. My teacher didn't even give me such orders. Aubree gently took my wrist, turned my palm to face the sky and pressed her palm against mine. Her expression was stone. I couldn't read her, her expressions, or her emotions, the way I'd been learning. "He's right, you have a great deal of talent."

My teacher nodded, his lips pursed.

Aubree was my teacher's *teacher*. She looked younger than either of us but she moved like a much older woman. When she spoke, she was clear, concise, her words well chosen.

"It's good to meet you." I nodded along with my teacher, attempting some level of polite decorum. This wasn't my strength.

"It's a pleasure, Maggi," Aubree didn't nod back; instead she withdrew her hands and reached for a pack of cigarettes in her pocket. I was relieved, *beyond relieved*, and thrust my hands into the pockets of my jeans, searching for my own menthols. I was even further surprised when she leaned forward to light my cigarette, something my teacher had also done.

"So, you're *fucking* your student." Aubree took her eyes off me, and settled them on my teacher. He was visibly taken aback, shock washed across his face.

"*Excuse me?*" I was too shocked to take a drag off my own cigarette.

"Don't act like I wouldn't notice." Aubree smiled, ignoring me completely. "You know better than that, *I taught* you better than that."

"Who makes these rules, anyway?" My teacher grimaced, laying a hand on my shoulder to calm me down. That, in turn, made me angrier, but I was trying to learn the restraint he was teaching me. "Who decided that a teacher and student can't *date?*"

"*Dating* may be worse than *fucking*." Aubree replied.

Almost as though he realized that it was making me angrier, he let go of my shoulder. "You know I respect you and I will take your advice in most things, but not this. We're together."

"As you wish." Aubree shrugged, a look of resignation crossing her face. A look I would have *hated* my teacher to *ever* give me. To some extent I realized what was going on here and that made me a little less upset. "And you, *little one? How does that make you feel?*"

"It makes me feel like you should mind your own *fucking business*." I snapped back, now taking a hit off my menthol. I was, again, shocked, when Aubree's face turned to one of pure glee. She was laughing, not *at* me, but *with me*.

"Fair enough, Maggi. I *like* you."

"*Okay.*" I responded to her, eyes shifting from her to my teacher again.

"No, genuinely. If you both want to make a future of this, *knowing the risks*, I'll support that. But make sure my *student* explains those risks."

"*Yeah,*" I was about to lie to her. I remembered this part well. It wasn't that I wouldn't rage on my teacher later, in private. It's simply that right here, *right now*, Aubree was trying to cut down *my man*. This was unacceptable, and I would not allow him to be embarrassed publicly. He'd never let it happen to me, I wasn't about to allow it now. "We've talked all about the *fucking* risks."

"Say no more, in that case."

I had always assumed that Aubree knew I was lying at that point, but I had also always assumed that she knew I was defending her student's honor. I believed she respected that.

Aubree turned and gestured us both to her house, we'd been invited her for breakfast and I was supposed to get to know her. I didn't know how well *that* would go, but we'd already managed to stand our ground with each other. In my dream, like in my memory, my teacher went first and I followed.

As he entered Aubree's home, I felt a sharp, violent stroke of cold wind hit me. I stopped this time, when I hadn't years back. I looked around and realized that a storm had rolled across the San Jose sky and the sun had been obscured.

This was *not* how the events had unfolded. I was in new dream territory.

I turned back to Aubree. Her eyes were solid spheres of darkness, reflecting nothing. Her red hair had turned black and something like thick, chalky oil emerged from her lips. When she spoke, it was in a rasping growl; "*Little Maria Magdalena Lopez. How you've grown.*"

"Aubree?" I knew this was *not* Aubree.

"*We remember what you did to Aubriana.*" Her face smiled, a cruel smile, her chin covered in viscous oil.

"I didn't do anything to her. She's dead." What else was there for me to say? I should have asked *who* I was talking to, but this abrupt change in the memory caught me off guard. The visage of Aubree grabbed me in the dream, by the back of my neck, and slammed my face into the wooden entryway, pressing hard against my skull.

"*Liar!*" I couldn't move, I couldn't move my hands or feet, I couldn't even speak. The thing that wore Aubree like a costume leaned in, close to my ear, throat bubbling and gurgling before it spoke again. "*If you wish to hunt us, you will suffer your past sins.*"

CRAFTON, PENNSYLVANIA. PRESENT.

The right side of my face was bruised, and there was a scrape under my right eye.

I stood in my bathroom, for the *last time*, looking at my face and smelled my own vomit in the sink. It had been there since I had woken up, rushed out of bed, and wretched my dinner up at the memory of Aubree and her oily smile and black eyes.

If you wish to hunt us, you will suffer your past sins.

I never had time to dig into the dream, into what had walked in and made puppets of my memories. It was a strange and invasive feeling, as though someone had just read my diary and *then* used the words against me.

"Fuck you all." I whispered back to my reflection.

I walked away from the mirror and began to grab the final accoutrements for my trip. There was an old 9mm pistol I kept next to my bed that I withdrew. I checked to make sure that a round was chambered then I holstered it on my utility belt. My big carbide combat knives were on the side of my boots already, so I began picking through a dresser for my other blades. I pocketed the switchblade that I had used to cut my right palm open a week earlier, as well as two or three expandable gravity knives. The last two I grabbed are stainless steel balisongs, *butterfly knives*, my preferred knife ever since I was a child. Each one was clipped in a back pocket on either side of my buttocks.

I already had two additional magazines for the 9mm, more necklaces than I needed by a long shot and my red and black sash. I grabbed a green and black shemagh and tied it under my chin like a scarf, draped down across the olive drab flack armor.

Finally, I reached for the heavy jacket on the back of my door. It had belonged to my teacher long ago, and was far too large for me. The black milspec fabric had faded to grey over the decades and I'd left his various pins and buttons along the collar. All I'd really done was install a chainmail interior, making me impervious to arrows and knives. It was warm, had a hood I could pull out of the collar, and served as a windbreak if I took the metal and lining out.

I was as dressed as I would ever be, as ready as I would ever be.

I stopped and looked back at the room, holding the door open with one foot on the concrete outside. I'd lived here for years, I'd chosen the bed for myself, as well as the furniture. Mayy had drinks with me, sitting on the floor in my endless piles of mess. I'd wept into those pillows on the occasion that I dreamt of my teacher, or more specifically the night he died. In the bathroom mirror I'd watched myself grow old.

After a minute or so I decided I wanted the room to burn, if only so that I could cleanse that site of my memories. I'd have burned it all *myself* if it wasn't for the fact that many others shared this space with my room.

So, instead, I simply turned to walk away. I left the door unlocked. No one would come here but Mayy, simply out of fear, and she could take whatever she wanted.

I met Captain Winslow in the same motor pool that we'd waited days before. She looked tired with dark circles under her eyes and dry lips.

"Looking sharp, Captain," I laughed, approaching her. "No sleep?"

"You look like you *mouthed off* to the wrong Captain, Maggi." Winslow didn't smile, and I didn't think she shared my amusement at the situation.

"*That* was very casual of you, calling me Maggi," I tossed my jacket down onto a pile of gear next to her, two or three backpacks and duffels.

"You're the one who gave me permission to call you 'Maggi.'" Winslow leaned in, just then, examining my face. She reached forward with fingers, as if to touch my face, but I pulled away. "What happened to you?"

"Too *much* sleep." I didn't smile, and neither did she, so I let the joke fall to the wayside and answered her in earnest. "Remember how I talked about Djinn helping the Federals enslave the baser types of Djinn?"

"I remember Mayy screaming at us all, as well." She nodded at me.

"This was a warning," I pointed to my face, "from such a Djinn, to not pursue." Winslow favored me, then, with a look I'd not seen in her before. She didn't study me with anything like fear, or trepidation. I wasn't in a hurry to know what was on her mind, so instead I allowed her eyes to remind me of a storm crackling on the sea near Santa Cruz.

"Your Djinn kings are real." Winslow finally said to me.

"Kings or Ifrit, I don't know. But there's one, maybe two, out there. They're playing the Federals like a cheap harmonica, *blowing hot air up their asses*. They don't want me near them."

Winslow licked her lips and then placed her hands on her hips. "I asked my driver to come with us, *mostly* to drive. He's also a good soldier."

"The Muslim kid?" I answered.

"Yeah, his name is Rizwan. He doesn't much like you, but he'll follow orders."

"How about you, *Jenn*, how do you like me?"

"I don't know you Maggi." Winslow took her hands off her hips and gestured at me. Her voice cracked and I couldn't tell if she was upset or exhausted. "But I know this is never what I dreamed of, playing bodyguard to a hunter, pursuing *demons* across the country."

"No, you're a soldier," I reached forward, pointing at Winslow's forehead. It was now her turn to flinch away from me, "I don't have to be a witch to know what you dream of. A chance to command large units, maybe serve on the front. Take orders from Alexander himself."

"*Yes!*" She half smiled, half cried the word, "That's *exactly* what I dream of. I never imagined I'd be signing up for a suicide mission with Alexander's *mother*."

I didn't have a response for her just then. Winslow was too smart for her own good and possessed too much sight into the truth of a thing. Rather than betray her honesty with hollow words of condescending sweetness, I simply turned away. Locking my thumbs in my belt loops, I wandered over to a large concrete pylon and watched the motor pool move and bustle with activity. I watched Winslow also, as she paced away from me and walked into one of the offices across the concrete berths.

This didn't *need* to be a suicide mission. I had fought other demons in years past. I had fought other witches as well and, no matter how bad of a beating I had taken, I had always stood victorious. I *was* a scrapper, I was *ruthless*. More than just a need to survive, I was powered and driven by a burning fire to see my son *safe* and on the throne his father dreamt for him.

My teacher had taught me cunning manipulations; I had taught him the meaning of brutality. Together we agreed on what we wanted for Alexander and his future.

Twenty, perhaps thirty, minutes passed. I saw the Muslim boy arrive, dropping an oversized duffle and backpack down next Winslow's gear. His rifle was shouldered, and his helmet was clipped to the gear. His black hair had been buzzcut and there was nowhere near enough stubble on his face to grow a proper beard.

"Rizwan?" I called over to him from my pylon. He looked around for a second and then saw me. He rushed over quickly, saluting. I nodded back, "I hear you're going to be our driver."

"Yes sir," he replied, coolly.

"*Don't* call me 'sir,' or 'ma'am,' or anything besides my name once we leave Crafton. Call me Maggi. Understood?" I returned, and he eased from attention. "Where are you from?"

"Massachusetts," Rizwan answered, crisply. I realized at that second that I was doing something to Rizwan which I *hated*: I was assuming he was the sum of his nationality. How many times had I answered that question tritely, "California?" However, I didn't *really* care.

"We're all strangers in America. What country did your family come from?"

"Pakistan," He replied, almost smiling, "My father taught at Harvard."

"Oh? That explains your English. You speak better than most kids; you speak more properly than *I* do." I wasn't all that impressed. Formal education had never intimidated or amazed me. People like Rizwan's dad could sleep safely in their ivory towers because an *uneducated dirt-eater* like me could burn an entire battalion of soldiers alive.

"I was born *here*." Rizwan seemed defensive.

"So was I," I raised my hand in a calming gesture, "My parents were immigrants also, but I won't get mad if you call me *Michoacána*." The boy calmed, realizing I wasn't trying to mock him. I *might* mock him later, but only because of his background. I *might* make friends with him even, but he'd need to relax a little more. His eyes told me he was ready to fight anyone and I wasn't surprised. A little man, my height, with a name like *Rizwan* had likely gotten his share of *shit* in his life. "Jennifer speaks highly of you."

"The Captain is a good officer," Rizwan nodded.

"Did *the Captain* tell you why you've been invited into this *shit show*?" I asked.

"No, sir. *Maggi*."

"You seem to know enough about Djinn, are you familiar with the Ifrit?" I continued, allowing him his mistake.

"I know that the Djinn came first, before man." Rizwan replied curtly.

"That's one story," I shrugged. "Regardless, the Ifrit are one of the most dangerous djinn in existence. I believe that we're going to hunt one." I paused, thinking, my eyes jumping around the room before I returned them to Rizwan and smiled. "Maybe two."

"You have no need to doubt my gun, or sword." Rizwan's voice was still that of a boy, but when he spoke, he spoke with a conviction I'd heard from few people in my life. Even Jennifer Winslow seemed to hesitate when faced with the possibility of hunting djinn. I could respect that in him, even if I held no respect for his father's career or the world he'd been born into.

Over Rizwan's shoulder I spotted Jennifer emerging from the offices. Rizwan noticed my distraction and turned to follow my eyes. Spotting his Captain, he saluted. Jennifer made a brief acknowledgement and dismissed him to the lower levels in order to retrieve our vehicle.

"Jennifer," I gestured her over. She came closer so we could speak, but she did not show any degree of warmth. "I like that boy you have, Rizwan. He's *sure of himself*."

"Yeah," Jennifer nodded, looking away, "He'll never care if he's going to get himself killed." I had considered for a while what I would say to Jennifer, about her concerns. Before I spoke, I asked her to look at me and I made sure I never took my eyes off hers.

"Jennifer, you will not die fighting for me like your father. I promise you, *here and now*, that I will allow no harm upon you or your Corporal."

"You *can't* promise that." Jennifer ground her teeth.

"*Yeah*," I drew my syllables out, "*I can*."

"Maggi, *really?*" Jennifer glanced away from me and chuckled to herself. "That's the first time you've lied to me."

"No," I answered, "I'd rather *not* die out there. I'd *like* to see my son again, I'd like to spend a few more years being an *angry old witch*. This isn't a suicide mission for *me* or *you*."

Jennifer studied me for a while, smiling a little, a smile that hints at no mirth. I didn't break our gaze until she did; a coming engine gets her attention. We both looked toward the ramp leading up to our level from the motor pool. Rizwan was driving a mid-size 4x4 truck with heavy tires, a skid plate under the hood, and a brush guard. It had a front and rear cab, four doors, and thin metal bars across the windshield.

"Just keep telling yourself that, Maggi." It was all Jennifer said before turning away from me to grab her gear. Rizwan jumped out of the driver's seat, grabbing as much as his small frame will allow. I watched them load the truck with equipment, packs, and rations. The truck looked like it had augmented fuel tanks, as well as red canisters tethered to the truck bed in the back with more provisions of gasoline.

As the two of them finished loading the truck, I grabbed my jacket off the concrete and headed toward the idling vehicle. Rizwan was in the driver's seat, adjusting his chair and checking various gauges. Jennifer had jumped in the back seat next to a pile of duffle bags and backpacks. She was giving me the front seat and I couldn't tell if it was an intentional sign of respect or if she was genuinely holding a grudge. I didn't *really* care.

I climbed up in the truck and closed the door behind me. As I shoved my jacket down onto the floor next to my boots, I took note of the roominess of my seat. Rizwan waved at the motor pool officers who gave him a green flag to depart as he slowly rolled us up from the underground garage and out into the daylight of midday Crafton.

The streets were busy with street stalls, merchants and their wares, families shopping, and small children running in the streets. We shared the roads with horses, carts, but no other gasoline-powered vehicles. The lighting rig at the back of our cab brushed the brightly dyed fabrics that hung across the street, drying in the cool, autumn air.

I watched the streets turn and zigzag, as we proceeded to the main entrance of Crafton. A few people met my gaze back, some of them children who smiled and waved. I met those waves with a smile, a smirking grin.

I didn't have an answer for Winslow's words. I didn't have answer for *myself*, or what I hoped to achieve on this adventure. I had *felt* like I'd never return to Crafton, but that didn't mean I would die out there fighting rogue demons. Every ending is the start of a new beginning; I'd learned that from my teacher as a much younger woman and I had never seen evidence to suggest it wasn't true.

I wasn't lying to Jennifer. More than anything in this world, I wanted to see my boy again. Pull him away from the public gaze of his officers and advisors and hold him against me. It was difficult now; he hadn't been a little baby in many years and he'd grown taller than his mother, *taller than his father*. That was my wish, if I was given a wish to make. I wasn't done living and I wasn't done protecting my son.

Once we left Crafton, Rizwan accelerated up to about forty miles an hour, covering clear highway without obstructions. We were heading west now, chasing the sun crossing the sky.

"We're seeking the elephant." I said, mostly to myself.

"*Pardon?*" Rizwan answered, at the wheel.

"Nothing. Nothing of consequence. Just a *stupid story*."

Act 2

SEEKING THE ELEPHANT

SALT LAKE CITY, UTAH. LONG PAST.

This time, as I found myself walking through my dreams, I was on guard, on edge; waiting for something to reach in to try and hurt me.

I was standing on a promenade overlooking the bulk of Salt Lake City, at the peak of sunset, orange and yellow light blinding me no matter which way I turned. The rays were sharp, unrelenting, and made me regret leaving my sunglasses in Aubree's car earlier that afternoon.

I glanced right and saw Aubree wandering away from me, on her cell phone, lighting a cigarette. It reminded me that I needed to call my teacher. I pulled my own cell out, the same little plastic flip phone I'd always had, and dialed him. As I listened to the ringing, I casually walked away from the promenade's overlook and into the sparse and moving crowds of people. The concrete steps descended downward, into neatly trimmed hedges and small fountains.

"*Hey*, babe." I heard his voice answer.

"*Bitch*." It's how I always answered the phone for him. I thought I was being so funny. Now, as I watched the scene unfold again, I was repulsed.

"How's Utah so far?" He continued, ignoring my greeting.

"This *shit* is *weird*," I pulled a cigarette out of the pack given to me by my teacher before we left; they were his cloves wrapped in black rolling paper with a gold filter. It tasted sweet on my lips, even before I lit it. "We drive around Utah and it's all *Mormonlicious*, then we come into Salt Lake City and its *fucking crazy*."

"Sounds about right," I heard him laughing at me, "You and Aubree playing nice?"

89

"Yeah." I lit the clove, while we were talking. "She took me to a movie."

"What did you see?"

"I *dunno*, some *shit* with Spartan guys. She keeps talking to me about the history and *shit*, she's as bad as you." The clove *snapped* and *popped* as I took a drag. It tasted sharp, exotic, and my lips went numb like I'd just licked cocaine. I was trying to be a *little* better behaved for my teacher, so I needed to find my thrills elsewhere. "You can get away with that *crap* though, you're cuter."

"*Be nice*," he answered, and I could barely understand him as static cut in and out of the call. "She's trying to make friends with you. Besides, she *can* teach you a thing or three. Everything that I know, I learned from her."

"Yeah, we're going to some abandoned *bullshit* tonight. She said she has something to show me, I guess." It wasn't that I disliked Aubree, or that she was unkind to me. Something bothered me about her and the way my teacher interacted with her. Although neither one had *said as such*, my gut told me they'd slept together. She was always just a little *too* protective of him, and he was always just a little *too* protective of her. For all the noise Aubree had made, about a teacher *fucking* his student, it was the only truth I knew about magic so far.

"Pay attention to her. You can show me what you've learned when you come back on Monday." I could barely make out the words and the call suddenly dropped. Out of habit I withdrew the phone from my ear and examined the signal strength; it was just fine.

I turned to start walking back toward Aubree and found my path blocked by two young boys. They were tall and scrawny, wearing plaid flannel and sporting long, bushy hair. They couldn't have been more than fifteen or sixteen years old, with huge protruding Adam's apples and sloped shoulders. One was holding a skateboard; the other had big aviator style sunglasses on, too big for his face. The sun was in my eyes, so I couldn't see much more.

"Is that a clove cigarette?" The one with a skateboard asked me.

"We love cloves," the second smiled behind his aviators.

"We can smell them a mile away," that time skateboard boy spoke.

"*We can smell them a mile away*," repeated his friend with the sunglasses.

"May we buy some off you?" Back to skateboard boy.

I had no idea how to react to this. I absolutely felt threatened, somewhere, deep in my spine, I felt like these two were *dangerous* to me. My eyes disagreed; they were just stupid stoner kids, like *all the other stupid stoner kids in Salt Lake City.* What could they possibly do to someone like me? I responded to them, but only after a moment. "Yeah, I guess, sure. I only have one pack, so one each, okay?"

"Awesome," replied the first boy, the one with a skateboard.

"*Awesome,*" repeated his friend.

They stepped closer to me and the hairs on the back of my arms stood up. There was something completely *off* about this. They weren't merely strange, and their body language itself was non-threatening, but every fiber of my being cried out that I needed to get away from them. Against my better judgment, and true to my word, I withdrew the black pack of clove cigarettes, took two out and offered it to them. They were smiling with closed lips, and their hands tittered.

"We owe you," said the one with sunglasses. He produced a coin and handed it to me. It didn't seem to come from any pockets; he simply thumbed it forward as though he'd kept it ready for me.

"You're *delicious,*" exclaimed the skateboard boy, followed by a violent shake of the head before he held up the clove, "I *mean* these are *delicious.*"

Dumbfounded, I accepted the coin and backed up a few steps. I couldn't take my eyes off the other kid's sunglasses. They were starting to melt. It wasn't that the aviators themselves were melting; it was as if the gold frames and dark lenses were running down his face and *his face was running too.* It was like a bad wax sculpture left too near the oven. I couldn't even blink, I was transfixed.

"Thank you, *Maggi,*" said the one melting boy. My heart stopped and I had not been so terrified since I was a child, standing in a liquor store, holding a gun.

"How the ever-loving *fuck* did you know my name?" My answer wasn't cool or calculated. I watched myself stutter, consumed by fear as I backed away from these two freaks.

"Thank you, *Maggi.*" I turned away and now looked at the boy with the skateboard. The flesh was running down his face like thick, creamy, oatmeal. I had no more words, I couldn't stand by. I turned and ran, sprinting across the promenade, narrowly avoiding couples locked hand in hand, and children at play. I made a long, circular pattern and came back to the theater, near the populated overlook where I'd stood moments earlier. I looked around for Aubree, but I didn't see her at first. My heart raced faster and I was on the verge of panic when a hand touched my shoulder.

I screamed like a child and spun around. I had my box cutter out, a gravity blade in my other hand, ready to draw blood.

"*Whoah!*" Aubree looked at me, serious, wide eyed, withdrawing her hand. "What the *hell* happened to you?" I didn't have an answer, so I didn't reply, simply looked around me. My head spun, allowing my eyes to dart behind me, behind Aubree, and through the crowds of people mingling across the concrete steps. I didn't see the boys with melting faces but that didn't make me feel any safer. I felt like I was being watched.

Aubree's look of concern only grew, but she didn't ask more questions. She was a smart woman and in some ways every bit the scrap I was. She tensed up and put her back to the railing so that she could watch, jaw set, eyes narrow.

"Did someone hurt you?" She asked quietly, calmly.

"*No,*" I followed her, learning something just then about keeping my back safe. I leaned against the railing next to her. "There were two boys, they asked me for a *fucking cigarette,* and they weren't right. They weren't *real like us.*"

"Okay," Aubree nodded, watching the promenade like a hawk, "Were they ghosts?"

"*No!*" I ground my teeth together, "They were worse. Their faces *fucking melted.*" Although I'd have felt safer with my teacher, that was only because I trusted him more. I'd seen Aubree spar, I'd seen her put men twice her size on the ground. She didn't fight like I did, but she *reveled* in violence and had no fear. No matter what differences Aubree and I shared, this very moment galvanized her in my eyes.

"*Melted?*" She replied, quietly. I didn't answer. "That's a new one."

I whispered, "Even for you?"

"Even for me, Maggi." Aubree looked over at me, pointing at the coin held in my right hand. I followed her eyes and examined it closer. It was silver, untarnished, and old. The face was covered with Arabic characters and unfamiliar symbols ran over the edges as I turned it over in my hand. "What is that?"

I didn't reply right away, instead my words trickled slowly from my lips as I realized what I had done. "One of the boys gave it to me." Much to my relief Aubree reached across me, pulling the coin from my fingers and tossed it out across the overlook. The coin was hot in my fingers when she removed it, I didn't try to stop her. Afterwards, I felt almost instantly calmer.

"Let's get out of here."

It was all Aubree said as she grabbed my hand in hers and pulled me away from the overlook. She reminded me of my mother then, bulldozing through the sporadic crowd, dragging me to safety, her face a stone, focused mask.

That afternoon in Utah, Aubriana became my friend.

———✳——

COLUMBUS, OHIO. PRESENT.

"Maggi, wake up."
Jennifer's hand was on my shoulder, her fingers heavy on me, pushing and pulling me awake. It startled me, my hand already at my 9mm, jaw set, my mind searching for flames that I could borrow. She saw how I reacted, twitched, and pulled away.

"Sorry." I shook my head, blinking away sleep. Jennifer said nothing, although when I glanced at her she was giving me an accepting look. "Where are we?"

She was standing next to me, the truck's passenger door open and night had almost fallen, the sky a deep, intimidating beryl. Structures nearby silhouetted themselves against it, yellow and orange hues in flickering gas lights. "Columbus," Jennifer responded.

Although Highway 70 was a straight shot across Ohio, we'd detoured around Wheeling, going northward toward Cleveland. This allowed us to travel many miles in friendly territory, crossing the Antecedent States unmolested. Over two hundred miles had to be crossed at varied speeds, meaning we'd taken much of a day to arrive here.

I jumped out of the truck cab, stretching. I imagined that I'd fallen asleep late in the afternoon, my eyes heavy against the setting sun. "Corporal Mohamed," Jennifer winced and closed her eyes, remembering my desire for familiar names, "*Rizwan*, I mean, is getting us some fuel. We can trade with Columbus; Alexander's name has weight here. *Your name* has weight here."

Columbus was a large exporter, a rich city-state, richer than Crafton by

94

far. They traded far and wide, with us, with their neighbors, even with *the Federals*. Columbus was one of the few places left that still manufactured vehicle parts, leaving them wealthy and *very* well defended. Alexander, Lorne, and I wouldn't dream of directly assaulting this city-state.

"So, call me *Maria* here," When Jennifer gave me a strange expression, I shrugged, stretching my back and shoulders, before explaining, "It's my first name."

"'Maggi' is a nickname?" She questioned.

"Maggi is short for *Magdalena*. I'm named for a whore."

"*Whore?*" Jennifer seemed genuinely confused. I glanced past her at a large, wide storefront sprawling across a cracked and rough parking lot. There was light from within, *electrical light*, judging by the skipping, dancing, fluorescent ambiance.

"Is that a *goddamned convenience store?*" I pointed, over Jennifer, to the structure that I had been eyeing a moment earlier.

"I suppose? It's where Rizwan is getting the fuel." I nodded to Jennifer, then to the building, before I finally lurched into a staggered step and approach the facade. My knees hurt, so did my lower back. The cold night did little to help me.

Entering the store was an experience I had not been prepared for. It was something like a cross between a *convenience store*, an antique emporium, and a pornography stand. Memories from the old items, ghosts and minds attached to them, flooded my mind the moment I was inside, flushing my face warm and skipping my heart a few beats. Jennifer was close behind me, and although she tried not to show it, I could see that she was also impacted by the raw history that fluttered around this place like a thick vapor of humanity, all wrapped up in the store's basement smell.

It had once been a supermarket, perhaps, wide aisle and empty shelves latched into pegboard and display slats. The walls were adorned with chairs. Some happened to be matching sets of two, or three, or four. Others were lonely, unique, hanging at a nervous angle over the floor. The shelves themselves were cluttered with *millions* of unique objects. Silver piggy banks, pool balls and racks, electrical cords, phone chargers, reading glasses, tea cups from a thousand collections. Rows upon rows of CDs with cracked and dusty jewel cases shared shelves with *fresh bread* and other foodstuffs. Along with that food was the *most* pornography that I'd seen since before the Collapse. Thousands of books and magazines were arranged in dozens of spinning racks. Some of it was antique, old, tattered and dog-eared. Some of it was *new*, collections of photographs appealing to every desire, whim, or fetish.

"I don't even know what to say." Jennifer spoke behind me.

"It's like an abstract disco," I chuckled, feeling a smile spread across my face. I wanted to touch it all, *I want to hear every voice and whisper in those memories.*

"I think I'm going to vomit," was all Jennifer had to reply with.

At the back of the store, on the walls behind the counter, were several old, flat-screen televisions. All of them were quietly cycling video, hiccupping, choppy video. I recognized old action films from my childhood, flashy and bright, mixed with vintage 1970s pornos.

The clerk who stood in the middle of this electro-sexual maelstrom of violence was tall, lanky, and balding. His face was groomed, his shirt and jacket neat and clean. "*Whacanni* do for you kids?" His speech was like a driver hitting the accelerator too hard, tires barking before they caught traction.

"What *can't* you do?" I laughed, more genuinely happy than I'd been for some time. Just because I'd never been a slave to *consumerism* before the Collapse, didn't mean I wouldn't take joy in it. Behind the clerk and around his desk, was a collection of the smaller, more precious items. Old picture boxes, brightly colored skirts, well-loved toy cars, signs, glasses, dishes, small knives, firearms, and more than I could not clearly make out. "Do you have cigarettes?" I asked.

"*Lemmeshow* you kids what I got." The clerk turned around slow, fishing through display cases, before producing a narrow box full of cigarette packs. Each had been separated into its own sub-section. "*Yuvgothem* old packs. Can't say how good they are. *Yuvgothem* new packs. They're all right. *They'remakin'* the tobacco again, down south.

"*Oh really!*" I shouted, looking over at Jennifer who seemed to be in her own world. I could feel her trying to block the place, resisting its caress, denying the dusty and obsolescent kisses. "Show me the best, *your best.*"

"*Don'tactully* know." The clerk shrugged. "I don't smoke."

I pursed my lips then and realized that I was enjoying this place alone. This boutique of bygone days was a flashback to my youth. It reminded me of *desire*, a thing that I had long ago distanced myself from, an old lover I never courted anymore.

Left to my own devices I chose a new pack, a *black and gold* pack of cigarettes. They promised to be a "subtle, bold flavor," farmed fresh in the *South Carolina Republic*. I had no idea what that meant, I simply chose them for the package. It reminded me of the cloves that my teacher once smoked and had summarily introduced me to. I withdrew Antecedent coins from my pockets, in growing order, until I had enough for the pack. I wasn't surprised that they accepted our currency here, but I was surprised that the clerk needed to make change.

While he did this, I turned to the small box of photos next to other displays and began to thumb through them. It made for a refreshing distraction, looking back at the old world. My world before it tore itself apart and was consumed by ghosts and gods.

I was, under no circumstance, expecting to find an old Polaroid of myself and Aubree. And yet, here it was. The picture was faded, but clean. I was standing next to Aubree, my left arm embracing her, my black hair pulled back in severe ponytail, looking *angry* at the world. My tattoo collection had begun to grow under my white, *wife-beater.* Aubree was wearing something that showed off her cleavage, and she was smiling. Not a posed smile, a real smile, as genuine as my grimace. I think we'd been drinking in San Francisco when that photo was taken.

Words and emotions boiled up in my throat. I felt my fingers quivering and my heart racing. The store no longer smelled musty and old, it smelled like *spices* and deep, rich incense. It almost made me gag. I turned to Jennifer then, wondering if she could *see* this, *feel* this, or if it was all in my imagination.

When I turned, Jennifer was holding her gun, pushing it against the clerk's head. The clerk who'd jumbled his words for me. She was serious, *dead* serious, eyes as hard as steel, jaw tight, a terror in her fatigues and armor.

"Give me the *goddamn money!*" She screamed at the clerk. I knew full well what I was watching. Jennifer was playing a role; this was *only* in my mind. "*This isn't real,*" I growled.

Jennifer turned to look at me. Her eyes were not her own, they were filled with fire, burning hatred and unapologetic malice. "*If you wish to hunt us, you will suffer your past sins.*"

I closed my eyes then, I closed them tight. A witch is only as good as her barriers and I'd let mine slip in this place. I'd made myself receptive to nostalgia; I'd opened myself up like a welcoming lover. I didn't regret that mistake, I was *too old* to ever regret joy, but I now needed to bring my barriers back. I bricked myself in, stacking my defenses with mortar and stone, surrounding myself with a wall to keep my mind private from the waking world. When I opened my eyes, I saw Jennifer leaning against the counter, reading an old magazine. My heart was still racing, so I controlled my breathing. I glanced quickly at the photos. The Polaroid wasn't me and *Aubree*, it was some college frat boy and his dog.

A black dog.

The clerk cleared his throat, his hand extended with my change. I accepted the coins, pocketing them, as well as my new cigarettes, and turned for the door.

"We're finished?" I heard Jennifer behind me.

"Yup." I answered through a clenched jaw.

"I thought you were *in love* with this place?" She spoke a second time.

"Yup." Is was all I said.

"So, we're *leaving?*"

"Yup."

MOUNTAIN VIEW, CALIFORNIA. LONG PAST.

It was now nearly two weeks since the dreams had started, and I had hoped, maybe even prayed that *this* dream would not be one of them.

When I blinked my eyes, they were *gummy*, and strained. My mouth was dry and I was so tired. That feeling, that *sleep deprivation* was left to me in these memories, wholly untouched. What I lost was the *smell* of the child in my arms, his clean blanket, fresh from the dryer and the coffee I had just set to brew for myself. I knew what it smelled like that morning, it smelled like some kind of foreign heaven ruled by benevolent gods who'd chosen to smile down on me. It smelled like a winning lottery ticket, the ambition of joy, and an unyielding sense of righteous contentment.

Alexander was just a month old, swaddled, at my breasts now. He'd finally fallen asleep after a long night of agonized screeching, his cries endless and maddening. My frustration was washed clean now by the hint of a smile at his tiny lips, and I bobbed my frame up and down rhythmically, humming a song to myself, a melody I must have heard from my mother long ago.

It hadn't even been two years that my teacher and I were together when I became pregnant with our son. There was no world where we *didn't* keep him, no world where we didn't *want* him so desperately in our lives, and no world that he didn't ignite with his laughter.

I'd left our job, perhaps six months earlier, and Alexander's father supported us both. Times were tough, to be sure, but there wasn't time for crazy adventures to Santa Cruz cemeteries nowadays or midnight movies in Santa Clara. These last six months I'd been at home on bed rest or taking care of my boy. The pregnancy had been difficult and the doctors had told me that attempting *another* child would kill me. That seemed so odd to me, but I was an only child as well, I wondered if my mother had suffered the same medical problems as me.

I brushed that thought off in the dream, but my older-self remembered that my mother and I never spoke after I was fourteen. I always meant to call her, to *tell her* I was okay, to say that I was *sorry* for the shame I visited on our family. I always meant to tell her that she had a grandson, a beautiful baby boy named *Alexander*.

In the distance, I could hear a soft *thump*. Soon, there was a second *thump*, this time a little louder, and finally a third. I paused, still, listening. The noise was curious, out of place, it set my mind ill at ease and my stomach turned over. I tried to dismiss it, forget it.

I placed Alexander in his crib, pulling a little quilted blanket up, and over him. I worried that he was too cold, I *also* worried that he was too hot. Motherhood, I had learned, was a constant state of furrowed concern.

I heard three more *thumps*, further away, now that Alexander is out of my hands. I worried for a second that the noise would wake him and decided to pour myself a mug of fresh coffee to calm my stomach. Maybe it would do the same for my nerves.

Our apartment was *tiny*, just a studio. The central living room had an adjoining kitchen only large enough for one person to stand within, a refrigerator built into the wall and a tiny window that looked over a community swimming pool. Our bed was at the other of the room and beyond was a closet and bathroom.

As I sipped the black coffee, bitter in my mouth, steam wafting in my face, I heard *three more thumps*, these perhaps a little louder I thought, maybe, I heard our dishes rattle in the cupboards. Or perhaps it was my imagination. I was so focused on that *rattle*, whether it existed, that when my cell phone rang I almost dropped the coffee mug.

"*Maldita sea, ¿qué?*" I answered, *damn it, what?*

"Are you awake?" It was Aubree on the other line. Her voice was cool, collected, almost to the point of excess. She was choosing her words with care, and *that* too set me on edge. Aubree was always a calculated woman, a trait I *tried* to learn from her, but right now she seemed different.

"Alexander kept me up all night. What's wrong?" I heard it again, as we're speaking. *Thump. Thump. Thump.* "What is *that*?"

"Turn your television on. You know I don't have one." Aubree answers. Looking back now, listening to Aubree's voice, I think she was afraid. She'd never *show* that, she'd never let it *impact* her, but I remembered all the times that *The Bruja* pretended to be calm and commanding when in fact, all I wanted to do was *piss my pants and run away.*

I did as Aubree said, holding the phone between my ear and shoulder as I found the remote. I flipped to a second channel, then a third, then through *all of them,* and they were all emergency news. I remembered now, so vividly, standing a few feet from the television, watching it unfold.

"Aubree," I sighed, "*fuck me running,* they're shelling us."

"I thought so."

As I scrolled through channels, I couldn't *listen.* It was a stern, rolling diatribe of words, telling me that I needed to *not be afraid* as I saw images of burning buildings, smoke rising from the streets, and panic as people reacted. I couldn't wrap my mind around this, young Maggi could barely grasp ghosts and ancient spirits, the idea that anyone would *launch artillery shells* at her home was so alien as to be unobtainable in perception. "They're actually *fucking doing it,* they're shelling the Peninsula. It's all south of us, down by Sunnyvale. *Fuck,* I don't believe what I'm seeing."

"Maggi." Aubree's voice never wavered. I wanted to *leech* off that calm, I wanted my eyes to stay dry, but tears were running down my face unbidden. "The cell networks will go down soon; we don't have much time. I need you to listen."

"Yeah. Yeah. I'm listening." I *wasn't.*

"Pack some clothes and food. Fill whatever you can with water, as much water as you can. Get Alexander, and get his father. Then come *here.* My car isn't working; I need you both to pick me up. We'll meet here in two hours, and then we need to head south, away from the occupational forces, out of the Bay Area."

"*Right.*" I said, but I was not focused on Aubree. The television jumped to a scene of a store in Sunnyvale, on fire. The camera shook, moved, and I saw a man in jeans and a white t-shirt dragging a woman from within a burning store. Her legs were gone, just glistening red stumps, bloody, and *so much like a raw steak*.

I shook myself out of it, forcing myself to breath, forcing myself to remember that I was still on the phone with Aubree. "Can you do that for me, Maggi?" She said.

"Yes. *Yes*, of course, I'll get Alexander." I wiped at my eyes, the tears were making it hard to see now, hard to focus. "*Wait*, what did you ask me? Where should I go?"

The line was silent.

Cursing, I tried to call Aubree back repeatedly. A recorded message told me about *busy circuits*, demanding that I *try my call again later*. The voice on the phone was shrill, condescending, acting as if this was something that could just *wait*. It was at that moment that I lost my temper, I *screamed*, and launched my old flip phone across the studio, smashing it on the wall of the kitchen. Parts exploded, landing in the sink, the ceramic counter top, the tile.

I'd woken Alexander up.

The *thumping* continued now, always coming in sets of three. I picked my son up and cradled him against my neck. I was apologizing to him, rocking him, and probably clutching him too tightly against me. No matter how hard I tried, I couldn't take my eyes of the television. I settled on one channel, then another, and watched. They just kept repeating the *same* thing, urging people to stay in their homes, telling them to stay off the roads. All they did was talk, *talk endlessly about* nothing. Men called on the phone and talked about *nothing*, they had experts in the studio who also talked about *nothing*. While they talked, an endless torrent of images unfolded. Burning stores, homes shredded into wooden bonfires, streets pockmarked.

Panic and fear groped my body, and I couldn't move. I remembered this part well. I wanted to run away, take my *baby and run away*, but I knew that was a fool's errand. So, I sat, waiting, listening. The *thumping* did not subside. The video did not cease.

My son was back in his crib, again asleep, when my teacher returned home. I realized I'd forgotten about him, my mind had never wandered to his safety; I was never gripped with that kind of fear. The sour taste of self-loathing filled my throat and I dove for his face, pulling his lips to mine, wishing to drown my anxiety in his mouth. We embraced for long seconds, or long minutes, his warmth, his strength, was the crucible by which I centered myself.

"Are you both okay?" He asked me.

"Of course," I laughed, wiping at my face with the back of my hand, "babies don't know what artillery shells are."

"We *need* to leave the Bay Area. I missed a call from Aubree, did she call you?"

"Yeah," I nodded, "earlier when it started. How long has it been?"

"*Hours*, Maggi. It's past noon now. Traffic was impossible."

"*Noon?*" I looked at him, agape, then turned back to my son. "I need to feed Alexander."

"*Maggi*, look at me." I snapped back, blinking. I remembered this conversation, I remembered it well. It felt like it was a dream. "What did Aubree say to you?"

I thought, my mind racing, trying to ward off the soft undercurrent of fear that had been eroding all that I was. How had *hours* passed by? I'd held Alexander when I woke him up, sang to him, before putting him to sleep. "I don't remember." I *didn't*, I remembered Aubree on the phone, remembered her calm voice, I knew that she was talking to me, words were ringing in my ears, I knew all this had *happened*, but I just couldn't remember.

"Maggi. This is important. We need to leave; do we need to get Aubree?"

"I don't think so," I shook my head. Why was my teacher so worried for her? His *woman* stood here in our apartment, with his *son*, his mentor be damned his family would come first. This thought served to crush my panic, focus my mind, I felt like I had my feet back under me again. The savage monomania of *our survival* took hold and I spat down onto the carpet before responding to him. "Aubree is fine, she called to say *she'd be fine.*"

"*Okay*," He nodded, "that's a relief. Then let's pack. Get Alexander some clothes, food, pack us both bags. I'll load the car."

"*Water*," I replied, hadn't Aubree mentioned water to me? "We'll need as much water as we can carry with us."

"Good idea, I'll start collecting water for us."

I moved like a woman possessed now, my mind clear, free to plot and plan. I moved around our apartment gathering up what I could. I pulled on the combat boots my teacher had gifted to me, on my birthday, the previous year. After a second I realized I'd forgotten socks, so I needed to take them off and lace them up again. We needed *jackets*, we needed *more socks*, we needed underwear. Alexander would need *all his diapers*, he'd need formula, his clothes, everything from his drawers in my dresser.

The same dresser I'd once snorted coke off, at my cousin's apartment.

I wondered why, at that moment, a younger Maggi would dwell on that? It wasn't shame, but perhaps a strange kind of disjointed madness. I kept a cooler mind now as I watched her pack frantically, and I was dismayed at how truly terrified she was. I wanted to step back in time and tell her to slow down, tell her it'd be okay. She didn't need to be afraid now, the *real* fear was yet to come, the *real* terror would be found in dark places and battlefields she'd never even imagined.

I wanted to tell her that she needed to go get Aubree.

By the time that I'd finished packing the car and gotten Alexander into the backseat in his carrier, darkness was falling. The afternoon sky was the color of broken pencil lead and bleached concrete. The air smelled of fires and the sound of sirens would not abate Half of the apartments in our complex were now abandoned, the other half were closed tight against the outside world.

By the time we were in the car, my teacher's all-wheel-drive station wagon, the lights in Mountain View had cut out. Street lights went dark, windows, porch lights, all of it, simply faded into the shadows. Only the lights from vehicles on the road illuminated the world.

My teacher had a plan, I recalled. He wanted to get us south, towards Milpitas, where we'd cross over the rolling hills, on or off road, and head east. We could cross Modesto, and make one of the passes through the Sierra Nevada, maybe via Yosemite. I would fall asleep on that route, I remembered, out cold until we hit the Nevada border.

Until then, until the Milpitas hills, I was awake and locked in a strange new hell.

Alexander, hungry, woke up at one point crying. Even with the windows rolled up the air was smoky and probably stung his eyes, as it did mine. I did my best to sooth him from the front seat, but I dared not get out. Rolling traffic jams plagued us at every corner, looters rushing down packed streets, arms full of electronics and jewelry. Men fought other men in the streets, baseball bats and crowbars in hand. Neighborhoods burned, unchecked, next the road where we spent long minutes waiting. My teacher entered full contact driving, pushing unoccupied cars off the road, taking scrapes and dings from others too close. I saw a police officer shoot a man in the head, I saw a fire truck hit by an artillery shell. Children ran by us, screaming, *begging*, and a three-story parking structure collapsed, blocking our access at one point.

I had no more words for this devastation. I didn't then, and as an old woman, I still didn't. This was the first day of the Collapse, this was ground zero, and I'd signed up for a front row ticket to the apocalypse.

This experience I had never relived in my dreams until *now*. I would rarely speak of this, I would rarely think of this. Those survivors, from my generation, shared a mutual denial pact over the events that lead to our new world.

It was midnight, maybe later, when we reached the Milpitas hills. I had asked my teacher to let us stop so I could breastfeed Alexander, relieve myself, and claw the wretched memories off my skin. Memories burned onto my eyeballs forever, a kind of visual tattoo, inked in soot and blood.

The Bay Area was burning, a deep, dark red haze of smoke, a pyre of dreams dashed asunder. After nearly twenty-four hours my panic and my fear were gone, I felt nothing but a cold and simmering lust to *sleep*.

It was then, at that second, I heard a voice in my mind.

Maggi! Can you hear me?

Confused, I spun around. It was a woman's voice, and as much as I swore it was *inside* me, I also felt it was *behind me*. The peculiarity of this didn't weigh on me, that very second. As I looked back now, this was only possible due to the fading Veil.

"What? *What* did you hear?" My teacher asked me.

Maggi, do you know who this is? Do you know who I am?

Was that Aubree? It didn't *sound* like Aubree, but it smelled of her musty perfume, it felt like her, the unique weight of her tone, the direct voice. It *felt* like Aubree. "No. No! I can hear you." I locked my eyes somewhere, on the horizon, where the voice seemed to originate from.

"Who are you talking to?" My teacher repeated, confused. How could he *not* hear her? Her voice was clear and unbroken. He was her student, they'd known her for *far longer* than he'd known me. Jealously gouged into my heart, *he'd fucked her long before me too.*

Maggi, please. It's Aubriana, I need you. I'm in one of the hospitals, I may be in a coma. The words were shaky now, and for the first time I heard Aubree speaking with *fear.* Whether she knew it or not, her words, her energy, vibrated with desperation and terror.

"No! We aren't going back." I growled bitterly. Just the *idea* of falling back into the boiling, churning pit of depredation and havoc made me retch bile into my mouth.

"We aren't going back where? Maggi who are you talking to?" I wanted to tell my teacher to *shut up*, he didn't need to know, he didn't need to put me or our *son* in danger so we could fetch his old flame. We were a family now; we looked out for *each other.*

Only you need to come Maggi, please, you don't have to risk your son. I don't know where my body is, I can't open my eyes, I can't move. I need you. Leave my boy here? On a mountaintop with his father and a jar of formula? When it was *my* breasts swollen with milk, when it was *my* voice that soothed him, when it was *my* arms he slept in? Leave my boy here, and descend into the foul spoliation we'd endured for *hours*?

"I'm sorry." I closed my eyes. I knew what I was about to do and I resigned myself at this moment to being a monster.

There was very little difference between killing a man accidentally and leaving a woman to die. If Aubree *was* hurt, in a coma, she didn't stand a chance. What would we do? Load her dead weight into the trunk and hope she woke up one day? The power was dying in the Bay Area and when it did all the machines in all the hospitals would go dead. When all those machines failed, anyone on life support, or in a coma, would also die.

No! There's no one else. Please. I've never begged in my life, but this I will beg you for.

"That's because they're all dead. They're all dead." I laughed at the carnage, at Aubree for being so foolish, and most of all, at myself. Her words wrenched out my guts, pulled my organs out one by one and left me hollow.

"Who's all dead?" My teacher asked me, his voice angry and frustrated.

"Everyone. *Everyone* we knew," I turned away from the voice that cried out across the long miles of burning cities. "Aubree is dead."

You fucking bitch. That's his name for me. How dare you lie to him and call me that. Aubree's rage was a tangible thing. The hairs on my neck rose, my bones chilled and my head pounded in rhythmic agony, in time with my pulse.

"She's dead, they're all dead." I repeated to him now, eyes on his dirty, sooty face. He'd spent more time outside, loading the car, than I had.

"What are you talking about? How do you know they're dead?" He reached for me and I felt his hands on my shoulders, but that too was hollow, like my insides. He owned my heart, that man; he saved me from a world that was never mine to inherit. For his love, for his kindness, and for the baby boy in the backseat of our car, I would save him now.

"I was talking to Aubree. She's dead. They're all dead." My voice was soft, as I watched a younger me lie to the man I loved. My eyes looked dead in reflection to that day, *I looked dead.*

Maggi, you unrepentant cunt, I will never forgive you for this.

I could feel Aubree clawing at my mind, for a second I imagined fingers on my back, pulling me away from the car. I locked my arm around my teacher's and spun him toward the car. I'd have cried, but no more tears remained, my eyes felt like bacon left to burn on the skillet. I didn't look back at Aubree, I didn't even acknowledge her again, and I absolutely did not tell her goodbye.

Maggi! I swear to every god on this world, I will end you for this, one day!

I hoped she would. At that moment, and twenty years later in my dreams, I hoped that Aubree *would* end me for my crime against her. It was my greatest regret, and my lowest moment. I *thought* I knew shame, when I accidentally killed the liquor store clerk as a child. This, however, was infamy and opprobrium beyond any imagining.

My teacher drove us away. Drove us far from the flame and smoke, far from the shelling and chaos. He drove us far from Aubree also. The woman who I *had* called my friend, who had taught me aspects of magic, who had protected me, who had watched over me when I was still small and weak. I was leaving her to die.

You'll be back, you fucking cunt. We'll settle this someday.

OUTSIDE OF OMAHA, NEBRASKA. PRESENT.

The bartender in this road house was a teenager with thick hair that looked like straw and two missing front teeth. He had the Nebraska accent I'd assumed that he would and even wore an old pair of blue coveralls. Every time he poured me a drink, I would greet him with another challenge, attempting to pick apart his cliché, trying to prove to myself that he was better than he seemed at first glance. He failed each challenge.

It had started badly; "Three fingers, tequila."

"What's tequila?" He answered me. I hadn't come here expecting anything fancy; the place had no name hanging outside. The front was packed with horses tied to the banister rail, and a trough of water in the shade of gnarled wooden porch.

"Are you *fucking* kidding me?" I replied to the boy, not even sure what else I could say. The boy shook his head at me, and I decided I would *explain* to him exactly *what* tequila was. Then, I realized, with a certain degree of surprise, that I had no idea either. "*Fine*, what do you serve?" I say after a moment.

"Beer. Some whiskey." He nodded, showing me what few teeth he has.

"*Fine*, three fingers. Whiskey."

"Three fingers?"

I didn't slap the boy, but I wanted to. I held my fist up, then counted to three, slowly. First my index finger, then my middle finger, and finally ring finger. "See *that*? That's three fingers. Put that much whiskey in a glass."

To his credit, the boy shrugged off my disdain, did as he was told, and slid the glass over to me. It wasn't a *bar* glass, it looked like something you'd drink orange juice out of in the morning if you lived in New Hampshire. Regardless, it was clean, and the warm alcohol wasn't rotgut. At least Nebraska knew how to make a beverage.

The roadhouse was as clean as it could be. It had been built sometime before the Collapse and was lovingly maintained despite the age. Cattlemen sat at tables behind me, joking, laughing, and occasionally throwing punches. Mostly they just drank and played cards. Merchants kept to themselves on the other side of the tavern, eating, joking loudly, and *also* occasionally throwing punches. In the center of this whole affair was a circular bar that my straw haired bartender worked behind.

I was the *only* woman at the bar. I made sure that I lit a cigarette with a snapped finger so I'd be left alone. I didn't want local conversation, I didn't want to be hassled, and I didn't want to explain *anything* to *anyone*.

I was watching Jennifer and Rizwan argue with each other.

They didn't *know* that I was watching them; they didn't *know* that I could see them or feel them. Jennifer was shaking her head and waving her hands in objection, while Rizwan is so worried that I could feel him bristling. *We're running low on coin, what happens when we also run low on fuel?* I could hear the numbers ticking repeatedly his mind. He was grinding his teeth and if I didn't know better I could hear the enamel wear down. Jennifer was a good compatriot and explained it. *It's not your job, or my job, to question her methods. We follow orders. Did you forget how to follow orders when we left Crafton?*

I chuckled to myself and replied, also to myself; "I don't know. *Did you forget?*"

I'd been at the bar for a few hours, and I'd had significantly more fingers to drink since when I had arrived. I was now genuinely *drunk*.

"Did you say something?" The bartender asked, turning, confused.

"How did you lose *yer* teeth, boy?" I slurred my words slightly, and remembered to keep my composure.

"My cousin punched me in the mouth." The bartender shrugged. "When I was a kid."

I withdrew a second cigarette, and I partially regretted that. Before the Collapse, I had been a heavy smoker, lack of supply had necessitated my cessation. I wondered, I *doubted*, that I could find another pack like this one. The tobacco burned slow, smooth, a rolling canticle of taste and hot smoke filling my mouth, my nose, my lungs.

"Did you *punch* him back, boy?" I smiled, nursing the cigarette lazily.

"No." He shrugged, and I decided I wanted to get a rise out of him, I decided I *was* bored, that I wanted entertainment.

"Why not?" I reached out delicately, my percipiency peering into the boy's memories, looking for sights, sounds or smells. "Your cousin was *bigger* than you? *Wasn't he?* He always liked to push you around. *Didn't he?*" The boy didn't reply so I searched deeper. His cousin was a ranch hand with sun tanned skin and big hands like boiled meat on a deer's thigh. "It was a game to him, searching you out as a child. Finding all 'yer sins.' Was the floor properly swept, Jacob?" I had already located his name.

"You're a witch." *Jacob* looked at my cigarette. He'd watched me light it, a snap of my fingers, a few sparks falling to his bar.

"Your father had a *baseball bat* that he kept next to the bed. Did you ever fantasize about taking that *slugger*, going to your cousin's room when he slept, and just *fucking crushing his skull?* You imagined it, didn't you? Did you wonder what it would sound like when a skull cracked? Or, how much blood there would be? Did you wonder if he'd wake up and stop you?"

"I think you've had enough to drink." Jacob only said in a deep voice that belied his transcendence to puberty as he finally wavered. He was rattled. I smiled at him, throwing back the rest of my drink.

"*Fine.* I'll stay out of your head. Pour me another."

"*Ma'am*," He started, and I cut him off with deep growl that I didn't expect. The roadhouse was lit by flame lamps, as I snapped back my reply they flared up, brighter for second.

"*Don't call me 'ma'am.'*"

The boy got the message, loud and clear. He sat the bottle next to my ornate glass, the glass from New Hampshire, and walked away. I could feel fear like pustules bubbling up from his pores, ripping at him painfully, and exploding in rancid presentiment all around me.

I could be a mean drunk. Most of all when I *hated* myself.

A man sat down next to me then. He was not much bigger than me, a small frame, small bones, but rough and scarred hands. The brown overcoat on his back smelled like crayons from waterproof waxing. His hair was dark, swept back with fresh water that dripped down his nose and chain. I didn't say anything to him right away, instead I poured myself a drink. Not three fingers, either, I filled the glass full, spilling some of the alcohol on the bar. The man with dark hair said nothing to me as I smoked or as I savored my drink for a moment. I finished it, and he still said nothing, he just sat next to me quietly.

My eyes were still watching Jennifer and Rizwan argue while my mind was *poking* and *prodding* at the man next to me, finding no opening in the smooth wall of reflective defenses. Every attempt I made to crawl inside his mind or read his feelings returned me to my own wretched emotions and self-loathing.

I started the conversation, since he wouldn't.

"Sitting next to *me* won't get you the bartender's eye." I spoke, carefully choosing my words, hiding how drunk I actually am.

"I do not drink." He nodded, without looking at me.

"That's the stupidest thing I ever heard," I sighed, considering how I'll make a play toy of this dark-haired fool.

"You will *not* make a play toy out of me." The man turned, slowly to face me, meeting my eyes. I smiled, as the lark grew less boring. "*Unless* you want to fight."

I finished my cigarette, crushing it out in the bar, "*Maybe* I do want to fight. And maybe I want to be amused."

"I seek neither pursuit." His eyes were as dark as his hair with no distinction between pupil and iris. His Sclera was yellow, *jaundiced*, as if he was sick. "I come only to help *you* in *your pursuit*."

"You're Djinn" I didn't bother pouring myself a drink. Instead, I pulled the cork off the bottle and drank straight from the neck. "Wearing that skin like a Halloween costume, all tricks, no treats. Eyes like that, a man ought to be *dead*."

"It is as you say."

"Muslim?" I asked, sitting the bottle down.

"It is as you say." He repeated himself. "*And there are among us some who have surrendered to Allah and there are among us some who are unjust. And whoso hath surrendered to Allah, such have taken the right path purposefully.'"*

"Yes," I laughed at him then, taking care not to lose my balance. "I've read the Quran. My teacher made me read it, and every other *boring, fucked off* holy text."

"You are a wretched creature, Maggi Lopez." He answered, quietly.

"I know." I winked at him. "But, not for the reasons you think."

"I *think* you are wretched because you left a woman you called *friend* to die." As much as I had played a game with the bartender, this Djinni now played a game with me. No matter how good, or *awful* they were, Djinn were manipulators above all else. Clever, with minds and magic that could easily walk through a skilled witch's defenses. This man, this *thing* next to me, knew more than my name. "It was your nightmare, a week ago, that lured me to this meeting."

"I haven't slept much this week." I replied, forcing myself to stay focused.

"You hunt very dangerous prey. They are an *Ifrit* couple, one male, one female. They are older than your entire race, and have walked this world since it was young." I didn't answer him, not wanting to play my hand yet, regardless of my intoxication. Though I did not feel particularly respectful, I felt like I wanted to know what he would tell me. "I know these Djinn you hunt. We were something like what *you would call friends*. If creatures such as we understood a concept like *friendship*."

"My *prey*," I took another drink of whiskey, slower this time, with care, "did they abandon you? Is that why my nightmare caught your attention? Did they abandon you, like I abandoned Aubree, twenty years ago?"

"You're *clever*, ever so *clever*. For an ape." The Djinni replied with something that could have been the hint of a smile at the corners of his lips.

"A good Muslim Djinni would *never* turn on his brothers and sisters to commit murder." I licked my lips, "But *me?* A heathen *sorceress*, a *heretic*. Damned by my past already. You *hate* me as much as Rizwan does." I nodded to where my driving companions stood arguing.

"I don't *hate* you Maggi." He maintained the smile, or the hint of it, "I feel sorry for you. But, in the eyes of Allah, all creatures are beautiful.

Your gray hair, angry lips, and sagging teats. Those eyes that burn like the fire on your fingers, and the seething hatred that eats your heart."

"I'm sorry," I grimaced at the creature, "did you just say *'sagging teets?'*"

"You can be the instrument of Allah's anger." He ignored my retort, "You seek Djinn as your prey. Why?"

"Three *reasons.*" I slurred, and extended my index finger. "They're teaching the Federals *magic*, they're enslaving *ghouls* to Federal technology, and," I extended my middle finger, "I believe that these particular Djinn have been *fucking with me* since I was a child."

"You believe correctly." The creature nodded.

I extended my ring finger. The finger that *still* held a *stupid* little promise ring my teacher had given me. "I think these Djinn want to *fuck with my son* after I am dead and *dust.* I think they're going to enslave *more* of you, more Djinn, more ghouls. They'll destroy Alexander and the Antecedent States." The man's dark eyes looked far off past me. The smile that threatened to spread across his lips vanished. He didn't answer me, rather he watched the event horizon for long minutes. In this time, I did not drink, I barely even breathed.

"How much would you pay for revenge?" He asked me, finally.

"*A lot.*" I answered.

"How much would you pay to protect your son? Alexander?"

"*Don't* speak his name, Djinni. You're not one of us. He's not your family. If you were speaking to him now, as you're speaking to me, I would burn this whole *fucking roadhouse* to the ground and make you eat the ashes." I growled the words, leaning in, so close that I could smell his skin beginning to turn, filling my nostrils with the scent of crayons and rot.

"How much would you pay to protect your son?" The Djinni repeated.

"*Everything.*" My words were claws, my lips were scimitars, my teeth were hammers, when I spoke my words become manifest, carving themselves into reality. "*I would pay with my life, I would pay with your life, I would pay with a million lives to protect him.*"

"You're such a wretched creature, Maggi Lopez." The Djinni answered, softly.

"*I don't care.*" I showed my teeth, and I was close enough to kiss him now.

"Would you pay with *eternity?*"

I simply nodded. He returned the gesture and reached for my left hand, the hand I had counted to him with. I balked for a second, but then allowed him to take me by the wrist and lay his palm on my own. As our skin made contact, I saw glimpses of the life lived once by the dark-haired man, the corpse that sat before me, animated and cold with sick yellow eyes. He was a rancher who died, far from here, *far from anyone,* due to liver failure. A reminder that no matter how dangerous our world was, no matter what ghosts or demons would roam free, humans could sometimes still die from simple biological failures.

My hand suddenly was, without warning, aflame with pain. It was an intense burning, the kind of pain I'd felt when I was younger, learning how to wield my power. I'd burned my fingers a hundred times.

"There is a place in Utah," the Djinni caught my eyes when the pain hit, "it's known as The Citadel, *very old ruins.* There dwells something you have never seen before, an entity wholly unique on this earth, the last of her kind. She is lonely, she is broken, and she will *feast on your love and rage.* In return she will offer you an orgy of power so sweet, so divisive, that a century will pass before you realize your mouth is full of maggots."

"*Mouth full of maggots* and *saggy teets.* You're a real lady killer, aren't *ya?*"

"Look at your hand." He ignored my response and I withdrew my burning palm from his. I was not surprised to see angry, red scars raised against my flesh. The lines of the palm were twisted, pulled, melted, and burned into a deep and complex topography.

"It's a map." I answered, wondering only to myself how much more that would have hurt if I had not been as drunk.

"You will find her here, in this place. Only with her power, *only* with her *love* will you be able to kill two *Ifrit.* We are made from smokeless fire, Maggi, we are broken stars ripped from the heavens and molded like clay. No simple *monkey magic* can harm us."

"Who do I tell her sent me?" I reached for the empty glass in front of me and wrapped my palm around it. It was slightly colder than room temperature, and felt like heaven against my flesh.

"*No one.* She considers herself a *god.*"

"Don't we all." I laughed and reached for the whiskey one more time. I drank it, *chugged* from it, in a very real attempt to make the pain in my hand more manageable.

"*Fi Amanullah.*" The creature said, standing up from the bar.

"*Hakuna matata.*" I answered, wryly. He simply turned and walked away. I sat there, watching him as he walked out of the bar. He had a limp, and his arms swung too widely. I wrapped my fingers around the bottle of whiskey and stood up. "*Fuck it,* I need to *piss.*" I whispered, only to myself, then pointed at the enameled, wooden bar with my fingers twitching slowly. Carefully, with burning flame I borrowed from all over the roadhouse, I etched three characters into the glossy wood and then turned to walk away.

I O U.

HIGHWAY 80, WESTBOUND, NEBRASKA. PRESENT.

"*Sangre, siento latir mi corazón, mi corazón, mi corazón.*"
Blood, I feel my heartbeat, my heart, my heart, my heart.

I was rapping in *Español*, singing mostly to myself, for myself. I was loud, and probably very obnoxious. I also *really* didn't care.

We were back on the road, Jennifer at the wheel this time, and Rizwan seated behind me. My right hand, my *unburnt* hand, was clutching the bottle which I'd all but stolen, a few swallows of whiskey left at the bottom. The boy with straw hair had never resisted, he'd never asked for payment when I returned from the bathroom. Instead of just *stealing* from him, I'd also *vandalized* his bar top. I didn't *really* care about that either.

I *was* a mean drunk. The more I hated myself, the meaner I was. The boy had made me angry with his sallow voice and lack of rage. I walked his memories, watched his cousin kick him, hit him, *punch his two front teeth out*, and even when I crawled under his skin and offered him a chance to confess how he hungered for blood, he'd refused. Meek, pathetic, power held no allure to him, even as a tool to accomplish a degree of payback. I couldn't wrap my mind around that, the very principle disgusted me.

"Jennifer, if I slapped you in the *fucking* face, would you slap me back?" My words were sloppy, and my vision blurred. We drove into the sunset across endless Nebraska horizons. The light was diffused by a wide layer of dust and turned into stark shades of orange and pink.

"No." Replied Jennifer, curtly.

"If I *wasn't* your boss? If I *wasn't* The Bruja? If I just slapped you in the

117

face. Would you slap me back, or would you *cry like a little bitch?*" I turned to look at her. She didn't favor me with her eyes, instead she favored the road, and held herself stiff. I was nearly certain that I was annoying her.

"In that circumstance," She answered, "yes. I'd hit you back. Harder."

"*That's what I'm talking about!*" Was I talking about it? Or was I singing? Or was I doing both? I was *very* drunk, and being this drunk I found it easy to talk. I found it easy to relate to people. More importantly, I found it easy to forget my nightmares. "That's what a *real* person does. That was me."

"I think that *is* you, today." Rizwan said, loudly, from the back. I could feel his frustration, it oozed from his words and violated my ears.

"I was a *runt* little girl." I laughed, ignoring Rizwan's sour mood, "I was smaller than the other kids, smaller than the other girls. They used to slap me in school, on the playground. The playground was *asphalt* and when they'd push me or shove me, I'd fall and skin my palms." I turned my left hand over to look at the new scars, a gift from a nameless Djinni. "They all laughed when I cried, holding my palms up, bloody and full of grit." Jennifer didn't reply, but I felt her relax slightly, maybe even Rizwan as well. I decided to favor Rizwan then, pulling myself around and looking behind me at his small frame, nestled in the backseat like a rodent surrounded by sticks and twigs.

"*What?*" Rizwan looked confused, after I held his gaze for maybe a minute. I was drunk, however, so that could have been ten minutes.

"You're an *awfully little man*, Rizwan. How about *you*," I caught myself slurring again, "did you get beat up a lot as a little kid?"

"Yes," He nodded, "of course."

"Made you *strong*, didn't it? Made you tougher, meaner, *didn't it?*"

"If you're asking me if I'd slap you back, if you weren't my boss, if you weren't a witch, the answer is *yes*. I learned how to fight as a kid, I was *quicker* than everyone else."

"*Me too!*" I shouted, realizing I was actually *very loud*, "I was quicker than all of them, I could move fast, I could dodge, I could twist, I could do everything but *hit back*. So, I brought a knife to school one day, and I learned some *shit* about people."

Rizwan gave me a look I couldn't understand, not in my current state. "You learned that the most fearful people are *bullies*."

"Well, *yes*," I nodded, "I was *gonna* say that adults *freak the fuck out* when little kids cut each other, but *yeah, totally*, bullies suck." I nodded to Rizwan then turned around, getting myself comfortable in the truck seat.

"How old were you?" Jennifer asked after a second.

"Eleven years old." I answered. "It was one of *papa's* knives. Just a little fold-out." I reached into my breeches and pulled out one of the two stainless steel balisongs I kept. It was almost certainly a terrible idea to start playing with it while we drove down the road, but, much to my surprise, the inebriation didn't prevent me from swinging the two handles and blade, end over end, as much an expert as I had always been.

"You cut a kid at *eleven years old*."

"She shoved me, and *laughed*." I replied, not looking at Jennifer, just studying the knife in my hands as it went through practiced motions. "No one laughs at me, Jenn Winslow."

"What did your parents say?" Jennifer sounded genuinely interested, and I wondered how much of this was her attempting to placate the *crazy witch in her truck with a knife* and how much of it was real concern.

"*Nothing good*." I closed the knife with a few wrist flicks, and leaned my head back to watch the sunset again. "My *papa*, I think he was proud of me. He took a lot of *shit*, from everyone. He took *shit jobs*, he took *shit pay*, and he smiled and said '*gracias, mi amigo.*' So, he could buy us meat and milk. So, he could pay the rent. I think he was proud of me."

"Your mom?" Jennifer questioned further.

"*Mi madre y yo somos dos bestias separadas,*" I answered in Spanish, then corrected myself, surprised that it slipped out, "My mother and I are two separate beasts. She *was* meek, she always worried what people would say, *or think*. Magic runs in the blood, maybe she was just a witch like me, maybe she *heard* whatever they said, what they thought. It was her obsession. She would humiliate herself, my father, *me*, if she thought other people would just *think well of us*." I laughed to myself, "What a *fucking joke*."

"I'm sorry," Jennifer's voice was so soft; I could barely hear her over the engine.

I shrugged, and then raised the neck of the whiskey bottle to my lips, lifting it high, and drinking the last few swallows. "People's genetics, their parents, their community and culture, all contribute to a person. You can live fifty miles from someone and they'll be alien to you."

I considered chucking the bottle out the window, just for the thrill of tossing it out and hearing the brief echo of a *pop* as it hit the ground, exploding at thirty or forty miles per hour. A bottle like that was valuable, however, and could store additional fresh water. I felt tears at the corner of my eyes as I considered that, remembering my nightmare, and Aubree's words. *Pack some clothes and food. Fill whatever you can with water, as much water as you can.*

I reached my left hand out, and placed it on Jennifer's thigh. Her fatigues were tight, across her skin, where she sat. I could feel the rough fabric under my fingertips, and if I tilted my hand up my nails would drag across those fatigues with promises of the taut and succulent flesh.

"Maggi?" Jennifer asked me. I ignored her.

"The Djinn we hunt, these *noble* Djinn, they're old friends of mine. I first saw them when I was only a girl. They've hunted, or *haunted*, me since. I never knew why until this very moment." I could hear Rizwan pull himself forward. They were both listening to me. My eyes were heavy now, the exhaustion of being awake was pulling me down into a sluggish enervation. "We're just *monkeys* to them, clever little apes who somehow left the desert. The idea that one of us would *resist* so hard, would fight *so hard*, is an insult. I *am* a wretched creature, but I am also proud, and that's vulgar to them."

"You're not wretched." I was surprised, above all else, that Rizwan spoke first, not Jennifer. I had assumed I had earned his ire, since he was a monotheist. I had pictured him judging me as harshly as my nameless Djinni friend, back in the roadhouse. If I'd been soberer, I'd have scolded myself.

"Rizwan, you dear, *sweet, tiny man*," I chuckled, opening my eyes and turning my neck just enough so that I could see him, craned forward and watching me. "I just drank an entire bottle of whiskey to help myself sleep. Because I have *one too many regrets* on my soul. If I say that I am wretched, it's not because I want you to *stroke my ego*, it's because I have actually done *fucked up shit to people I loved."*

The cab of the truck fell silent, and I let the empty bottle fall. My mind wandered, and I considered my dreams. I'd be falling back there soon, falling asleep, and if I was lucky, enjoying rest sans more memories. Memories played out on a projection screen, as if I sat in the dark, eating popcorn and licking warm butter from my fingertips.

"I loved my teacher, *I loved that bastard so much.* I've worked my *ass off* to forget his face, forget his voice, his touch, all of him. It hurt less that way. But, with Aubree, it was just easier to lie to myself, pretend that I *didn't love her."*

"Who's *Aubree?"* Rizwan spoke, softly.

"No one." I shook my head, not willing to confess my sins further, "Just a person. From the old days." Sleep was taking me, and I was grateful. "Jennifer, take a south-eastern route. We're heading to Utah."

WHITEHALL, PENNSYLVANIA. LONG PAST.

No, not *this dream*. Not Whitehall, not this place, not *this memory*.
Today was my 31st birthday. I don't believe that my teacher had forgotten, he *never* forgot, but he always enjoyed playing it off like he might have. In previous years, he'd pretended that he had to work on my birthday, or that he'd scheduled something monotonous, dull, dreary, for us to do. I fell for it every year, and each time he'd proven me wrong.

Last year was the exception, of course. We'd flown across America, on and off major highways, fleeing the worst of the Collapse as it spread east. *Last year* we were trying to save Crafton from the fires raging across Pittsburgh.

Today we were ranging for food, medical supplies, and water. A group of us twenty strong had traveled south to the Whitehall district. What were once upscale neighborhoods, suburbs of Pittsburgh, found themselves mostly abandoned, quiet, and unchecked. There was a large shopping center here, dozens of stores, and one particularly large grocery outlet. Large enough that even picked *mostly* clean, we could have hauled weeks of food back to Crafton with us.

I remembered it well, we knew a small raider group had dug in, fortified the parking lot with two overturned tractor trailers. Our scout, a quiet man named Matt, had watched the structure for a week. He was former Marine Recon, had a bad eye that wouldn't focus and scars on his forehead. He never conversed, but he followed orders, and his scout work was beyond reproach. There were supposed to be eight of them total, almost certainly civilians, with mid-grade weapons, nothing heavy.

I went with our team; I went with my teacher and Lorne, my son back home in Crafton, where it was safe. I didn't have the experience of the others, so I followed the front row with a shotgun; a 12-gauge pump.

The fight was over before it began. Lorne and his friend Jeffery Moss, also former Army took point, engaging the raiders in and out of cover across the parking lot. All of us had settled in for an extended siege, but without warning one of the raiders *charged* out of cover, at us, *screaming* that "they" were all over him. Jeffery clipped him in the knee, a second round cut him in the head, in seconds his limp body clad in winter coats and jeans lay on the parking lot. His skull was cracked open like a pumpkin thrown at a house, and red fluid tinted the ground. Blood and asphalt blended to create a strange mulberry color that existed nowhere else in nature, a color I had been intimately acquainted with since the fall of the Bay Area.

I remembered the next few seconds well. We heard *pop-pop-pop* from behind cover, followed by a shrill scream, panicked hyperventilation, then a second man raced from behind cover, he'd dropped his gun and tripped over himself trying to look behind him and hit the parking lot so hard, so fast, that he slid. My teacher was the one to deliver three lethal rounds this time. He looked back at me, eyes making contact with mine and I could *swear* I heard him speaking to me, in my mind.

Come up on my right, something is wrong.

I did as he told me, or as I *thought* he told me. The shotgun stock was nestled against my armpit, I was peering down the fluorescent green sites, on the move next to Alexander's father. I heard Jeffrey Marx stand to take his left, the three of us moving up the center. Past the initial cover of the overturned trucks, I spun right, sweeping the ground with care. I saw a third man in a plaid shirt with a long, gray, beard, sitting on the ground. His chest was a bloody mess, but he was still breathing, his hand holding a revolver near the crotch of his pants.

I didn't think, I simply unloaded a round into his face.

He was not the first man I had killed since the Bay Area, he was not the tenth, or the twentieth either. I had seen *enough* by the time his face exploded that I was not paused or shaken by the gore, I simply pumped another round into the firing chamber and swept up the undercarriage of the truck, looking for anyone else. Two more from our team came up from behind, following me down the back of the truck, where the belly of the trailer faced me.

Two men lay dead, not from our gun shots. One's throat was open, his green parka shiny with drying blood. The other man had a hunting knife sticking out of his sternum, directly in the middle of his chest. I glanced to my right and saw Matt, Matt and his eye that focused off on sights unknown. He shrugged at me, but said nothing.

From the front of the group I heard another firearm discharge, *pop-pop*, and then a third, fourth, and final fifth *pop*. I heard my teacher shout, "*Clear!*"

"How many was that?" I backed up slowly, toward the engine of the tractor, past the man whose face I'd shot off. Matt didn't answer me, Matt almost *never* answered me. I tried counting in my head, but Lorne beat me to it. I saw him come around from a burnt-out car, closer to the store front. He was wearing full gear, even his helmet. He held up gloved fingers, counting to *seven*. There was one man left.

I felt Matt's hand push me down at an angle, against a nook between the engine and the big, front tractor tire. He was making sure I have cover, there was *one more* combatant left unaccounted for. I nodded to him and settled in, pulling my knees up, shotgun at the ready. Matt was right, I didn't have the experience to play hunter.

From my vantage point I could see a half dozen ruined cars and then the face of the grocery store. Big windows had been boarded up and there was only one entrance now on the right-hand side. I saw Matt follow my teacher and two other men, as they swept up, past the cars, past the bent and battered parking lot lights. Lorne and Jeffrey remained back watching the rear perimeter with me.

"*Whoah! Whoah!* Barrels down, it's just a kid!" That voice was my teacher, I struggled to see him, and instead I only spot a child running toward the center entrance to the overturned tractor trailers. It's a little girl, and she's running for *me*. Lorne grabs her, almost toppling her over, face first into the ground. He searches her, even making her open her mouth. It wasn't *unheard of* to send children running, packed with explosives.

Lorne grabbed the girl roughly, saying nothing, pointed at his eyes, the girl's, and then back at me. He shoved her my way and she ran.

There wasn't much to her, she was a skeleton mostly, with eyes too big for head and a messy tangle of long, auburn hair, bunched up and matted at the back of her neck. She was wearing a coat too big for her, pajama pants, and her feet were bare.

"What's your name?" I ask her, offering a smile, knowing I needed to soften slightly for the child. Lorne and the other men knew I was a mother, *knew* I was inclined to be a little kinder.

"Margaret." She says to me, her voice a rasp. Something is strange about her, I can *feel her vibrating* with energy, a vibrant red glow behind my eyes.

"I'm Maggi. Stay here with me for a little while, yeah?" I ask her, glancing back to see my teacher, Matt, and two more men enter the single grocery entrance.

"They *shouldn't* go." Margaret pointed to the store face.

"They'll be fine." I didn't believe my own words at the time, and I didn't believe them now. The little girl was trying to warn me. "Where's your parents? Are they inside?"

"They're *dead*." As she speaks, Margaret's teeth chatter. It's cold, but it's not *that* cold. I reach my hand over and put a palm on her forehead, she's feverish. When I placed my hand there, our skin touched, and I got glimpses of her memories. It was the clearest I'd known the sensation to be, I could smell and taste what she'd seen. The smell of her parents burning on a pyre lit by the men who'd taken this grocery store, their laughter and humid breath close to her face. I jerked my hand away as the memories progressed.

I wasn't an idiot, eight men; one little girl. I had no desire to become intimate with that experience right now, through Margaret's mind *"Jesus fucking Christ, I'm sorry."* My breathing quickened, and I tried to calm myself, push the glimpses from my mind. I looked back the grocery store, watching it, with Lorne, and the others. How long had they been in there?

"They *shouldn't* go." Margaret pointed at the building.

125

"Why shouldn't they go, honey?" I ask her, my words nearly caught in my throat.

"They *knew* you were coming." She blinked big eyes at me, "They were afraid. I made them *more* afraid, I made them *all of the afraid*."

"You did, *didn't you?*" I remembered the two men that ran straight into our guns, straight into a kill-zone, terrified of the emptiness that chased them. Others had pulled knives, locked themselves in a bloody cavort, so afraid of each other that they willing to die, arm in arm. It all came together. How else could I have as quickly gleaned her memories on touch? More than any regular person. How else did she feel like she was vibrating, an intense glow of red next to me? Little Margaret with eyes too big for head was *just like me*.

"The boss," she points at the store, "he has dynamite."

"No." I turned to yell, to get Lorne's attention. I had seconds to react, what could I possibly have done? Could I pull myself to my feet, run for the grocery store, yell for them to get out while they could? Perhaps Lorne could relay a message? What would be faster?

I would never know. The store face exploded.

As I looked back now, watching it unfold, I was no longer consumed with regret. I'd blamed myself for many years, and even blamed Mayy when she was older. Why hadn't I listened to her? She was *trying* to warn me, she kept trying to tell me something was wrong, and I dismissed her, trying to comfort a child, ignoring the peril my teacher was in. I had been focused on a sick little girl with mangy hair. What if Margaret hadn't sewn terror in those men? Made them paranoid, convinced their leader to hold up with a pallet of dynamite in a grocery store? I *was* a mean drunk, I'd slapped a teenage Mayy in the face for that, a decade later.

The simple truth I'd come to after twenty years of walking through this memory, over and over again, was that there was nothing I could have done differently. None of us could have known, or suspected.

This was where he ended, the only man I ever loved. Alexander's father, and three of our best soldiers, died instantly as I watched.

My shotgun fell and my fingers clutched at my chest, clawing at my armor, at my fatigues, nails on my throat, rending at flesh. I was screaming, I was screaming so many words that they jumbled together in a miss-mash of language, a fetid soup of anger and loss. My face was salty and wet, snot and drool mixed on my face and all I could see were flames. Lorne rushed toward the blast, so did Jeffrey. Did they even hear me crying, wailing? Or had the explosion deafened them? Perhaps they simply didn't care. Back then, it wasn't *me* they bent their knee for, it was my teacher, *my lover.*

I knew he was dead. His existence, his energy, the glowing morsel that I could always feel no matter how far away he was, had been drowned. It didn't stop me from trying to stumble to my feet, pawing at pavement, and crawling to stand. I simply fell again.

I lay prone, face down. Margaret extended her hands and put them on my temples. As a young witch, she almost certainly saw plenty of my memories. What I *did* remember was a calm wash over me, the sense that I stood on a beach, listening to the waves at my toes and a breeze against my face.

The sorrow didn't subside, but my heart stopped racing, my breathing was easier. I was no longer choking on my own spittle and mucus. I lay on my back, looking up at a little girl with eyes too big for her head.

"I don't *have* to make people afraid. Sometimes I can make them peaceful."

"You can, *can't you.*" I whisper up at her. My eyes still wept, my heart was still bleeding. None of the pain had vanished, but she was right, she could make me *peaceful.*

"You loved him." Margaret nods to me, "But, you love your little boy, too."

"*I do.*"

"Your little boy needs you Maggi."

In her kindness, and in her genuine affection for me, Margaret reminded me that it wasn't the end of the world. She never told me what she saw of my mind when she touched me, but I suspect she knew what I *wanted.* I *wanted* to walk into those flames and burn with the man I loved, I wanted to die that day, for the first time in my life. Little Margaret knelt and hugged me then, arms around me, shivering in the morning air. I couldn't smell the smoke or flames, and I was grateful now, for that.

"Can I come home with you?" Margaret said after long minutes.

"Yeah, honey, you come back home with me. I'll take care of you."

Near Cedar Mesa, Utah. Present.

It was much harder than you'd think to read a map that had been burned into the flesh of your palm by an ancient desert demon.

We were out of Omaha but we'd been slowed down on and off by highways that had never been cleared of their dusty, wrecked, vehicular husks. Some had burned, *miles* of them had burned, while other sat pristine; as pristine as one would expect after two decades of scavenging. Their fuel tanks had long ago been siphoned, valuable parts stripped from their engines. Now we were southbound on a very empty, and *very lonely*, Highway 191, continuing up a grade that would eventually lead us to high desert, salted with islands of autumn snow. Much of the morning had passed by the time we crossed mountain ridges into southern Utah. I did my best to follow the roads, etched into my palm, running south, then west, then *north* again.

I had taken the wheel now, although I disliked driving. I would drive a truck or car, only if needed, only if pushed into it by mitigating circumstances. Rizwan was asleep next to me in the passenger seat while Jennifer sat in the back, watching quietly.

I drove maybe another ten miles and then came upon a wide, desolate turn off. Near us, a dozen or so cars had started rusting fifty years ago, next to rising stone cliffs. I parked the truck, got out, and leaned against the bed, listening to a gusty, cold wind whip at my loose hair. Jennifer followed me, also getting off the truck, leaning on the opposing side of the bed.

"Is this the place?" She asked me, and I struggled to hear her against the wind. Her hair was down, unlike mine, and washed over her face like leaves across an early fall snow. I studied her for a while, then the sky and the rocks and the land of this place, listening. Nothing here smelled, *felt* like Djinn, nothing so exotic or old. This place filled me with a peaceful grace, an old land that was comfortable with itself and happy to enfold me into that comfort.

"What do you feel?" I asked her. She shook her head, so I repeated myself, louder.

"It feels *peaceful*." Jennifer replied, yelling. I nodded to her, and went back to listening, straining to hear quiet in a quiet place. When I finally made *something* out, it was just an echo of a voice, words in the air, so distantly soft they could be any language, spoken by anyone. I had to focus, using all my talents, my experience, but I could pick out a direction.

"Jennifer," I spoke loudly now, not wanting to be misunderstood, "I have no idea what I'll find out there. Wait for me to return."

"How do you even know there's *something* out here?" Jennifer replied, tugging hair from her face.

"You'd rather not know, I *promise*." I stepped away from the truck and started heading toward the stone cliff faces.

Jennifer followed me, approaching, speaking softer this time. "Tell me."

"*Tell you?*" I laughed, "*Fine*. It was another Djinni, back in Nebraska, at the roadhouse."

"*Wait*," I stopped walking away from her and turned to smile, knowing what she would say, "you're chasing Djinn, to hunt and kill, and now you're taking advice from *another* Djinni?"

"*Yup*." I nodded.

"How do you know this isn't a trap?" Jennifer's face was one of worry, her brow furrowed and she flattened her lips. I'd seen her make this face before.

"I don't know that it isn't."

I spun and walked away. In my heart, in my soul, I knew that this was something I needed to do. Although it was *always* possible for a Djinni to lie just a little further, my gut told me that I wasn't walking into a fool's errand.

I walked higher into the canyon as the trail became more ragged and difficult to traverse. My hands were buried in my pockets, except when I needed to maintain my balance.

This place was *different*. It felt like one history had been carefully laid over another, as if someone had worked to bury the past. I found myself walking up a tight canyon with jutting rock walls and jagged stones all around me, painted in remarkable hues, pastel reds and oranges, painted against a layered cake, centuries of erosion showing different minerals and stone. Wind filled my ears, whispering as it moved across the canyon walls, up into the sky, then back down around me. No ghosts here, not even memories. I felt like I was ascending the stairs of an ancient cathedral, its stone steps eroded over millions of years.

The sun was setting by the time I reached the top. Distant thunder rolled back and forth in the sky and the air smelled like rain. I was high off the canyon floor and no longer anywhere near the road where my companions waited. Extending out before me was a narrow peninsula of rock, extruding out of the earth and rising at vertical angles. Severe drops, hundreds of feet, on either side. The echo of the voice I'd heard was louder here, words beyond my perception, just that pulled at me, *begged* for me to come closer, like a child with a broken toy.

I crossed the stone walkway. I did my best to forget my vertigo, reminding myself it was easier than crossing a bridge. As I neared the tip of the stone peninsula it started to rain, and a gust of wind pushes me forward. In the falling darkness, I found a series of old rocks, assembled like a wall, wrapped around the inside clefts. I ran my hands over them, standing on the precipice, overhang protecting me from what was now a deluge. This structure was older than *anything* I'd ever touched. It pulled me down close, and stopped being something that was simply *built*, it was now part of the world. This design told me it was a fortress, built to stop anyone, or *anything*.

I turned, took a deep breath, and walked inside, where the air seemed to muffle the wind beyond, the rain and thunder.

"*Welcome.*" I heard *her* voice, but I did not see anyone. I was not afraid, watching with my eyes, *behind* my eyes, searching for the presence.

"What's up?" I blinked hard, silently chiding myself. I was never good at these greetings.

Light expanded from the center of the bastion. The floor was dusty, and no flame burned, but the light itself remained constant as it shifted colors and danced across walls. Out of curiosity, I turned to see my shadow, and found none.

When I turned back, toward the light that didn't glow, the flame that didn't burn, I saw I was not alone in the *physical* world. A spider, *a spider the size of a human*, skittered up and around, out of the shadows, shifting and glimmering in light around us. Glossy black legs clicked and brushed against the ground, but dust remained undisturbed. The air shifted, as did the light, and she seemed to be an old woman moving unnaturally on all fours, her head moving about on a twitching neck. It was *both* forms, at once, without being either. Watching created more vertigo than the walk across the fortress peninsula, and I was disoriented by in-congruent images.

"I'll make it easier." She cocked her head, moved to sit, cross-legged, opposite from me. She swayed and became more *human*, her skin shifted colors from a dark brown to matte black, absorbing light. Thin black linens moved across her skin, constantly in motion. Her hair, too, weaved and wound about her as if caught in a breeze that I could not feel. The only constants were the obsidian eyes and two thick, viscous, and bloody streaks down the left side of her face. It was far easier to focus on her now. *"No one has gazed upon me in millennium."*

"I'm getting that," I exhaled hard and forced myself to the ground, "Who are you?

The sound she made was halfway between a screech and cry. It vented rage and raw anger directed, dropping the temperature of the room it was so intense. Her hair was blown back for a moment, palms dropped to the floor. I heard *cracks* and *snaps* in the stone around me as her force pushed out into the world.

"No one remembers, except the ones who called my children 'enemy.'"

"What is your name?" She glanced away from me, back down to the stone floor. Her fingers were long, thin, narrow things that looked like bones and moved like spiders, gesturing at me, at the walls, around the room. I could *feel* emotions wrenching out of her, caught in frozen time, shaking free dust and crawling inside my mind. The world was slowly beginning to bend around her. When she was sad, *the rocks were sad*. When she was angry, *the sky was angry*. She was no old spirit, left forgotten in a cave, she went beyond that. I remember, then, the words of the Djinni in Nebraska, *she considered herself a god*.

"I am mother. I was their mother. Now I am alone." Her voice cracked, like knuckle joints.

"What is your name?" I repeated my question. I repeated it partially because I was not sure how else to proceed, I had *no idea* who or what she was.

"*All my children. Gone.*" Forlorn eyes stared through me. I wondered whether she'd gone mad. She must have been in this place a very long time, just waiting and watching. Winters and summers rolled by along this place, forgotten, so far from the rest of civilization. "*You are a mother.*"

"Yes, I am." I nodded, slowly, now certain that she was mad, having forgotten her own name. She had nothing to offer me but sadness, a deep, complicated sadness that wrapped around the world and squeezed until it wept for her. I wept for her as well, but I couldn't bring her children back, no one could.

She looked at me with confidence, and said, "*I have not forgotten my name.*"

"Please, pardon me." She was in my mind, *also*. I had my defenses up, I'd had *all* my defenses up when I left the truck, hours ago, I'd never felt her walk through them, had never felt her in my mind, peering in or listening. No one should have been able to get in that easily.

"*If I have nothing to offer. Why stay?*"

"Respect, mother." I saw flashes of her children, but they were not *her* children, they were Alexander and Mayy. She was not only pulling thoughts from my head, but mixing her memories in with my own. How long would that last, I wondered?

"*Forever.*"

"What?" I blinked, shaken as our conversation was carried out on two tiers.

"*Little humans cannot fathom what I know.*"

"How did this happen?" I forced myself calm. There were a lot of questions that she wasn't answering and our connection only seemed to intensify.

"*You loved. Your child. Your mate.*" The room itself changed, it ceased to be. The stones faded into darkness and everything around became black until finally it was just us two together. Her face and form were illuminated by a fire that existed solely in her eyes. Around those unchanging eyes, her ever-changing form shifted and when she leaned in closer to me, the hues of her skin changed with her. "*Now we can speak, they can't hear us here.*"

"Who can't hear us?" I already knew, why did I bother asking her?

"*The ones who pursue you. How much would you pay to protect your son?*" She repeated the words of the Djinni, and I stiffened. She addressed my unspoken response as if I'd said it aloud. "*You would pay with your life, you would pay with a million lives to protect him.*"

"You know my heart, it seems." I licked my lips, stiff, now afraid of her. The words were my own, I had spoken them, but not sober. I wasn't prepared to answer for those words now.

"*Know me.*"

It wasn't that she commanded me to know her, she commanded the universe to bend its laws, to teach me. I found myself in a place where I *did* know her, in her time, and I saw what she had witnessed. In that moment, I *did*, in fact, know her. She was no mere *god*, she was one of the primordial beings that walked the Earth when volcanoes bled, when the seas boiled, and the continents formed. She had watched fire fall from the sky, bringing the land metal it had not before known. She was *young* and *small* among those titans and she was considered mad, even by their standards. She prowled the world even after the others went to slumber for a million years. She waited and watched as apes became human, learned to use tools, talked, and *walked across the world*.

All her suffering, loss, and pain became mine. Gods had knelt at her feet to court her favor. They offered her people, entire races, gifts on her altar so that they might show respect *for the ones who came first*. In the days before written words, when stories were just told around a fire, she brought awful suffering and devastation to anyone who harmed her children. In return for her favor and protection, they too brought terrible destruction to others in her name.

She didn't know why they went away. One day she was simply in the dark. There was no one left to love her and no one left to offer her blood. There was no one for her to watch over in the early hours of the morning, when it was still so dark and cold, when no one knew for sure if the sun *would* rise. No one needed her anymore, and that *hurt* her more than anything.

"You are primordial. You are titan."

"*Yes.*" Her voice rasped now, cool and soft in my ears, as though I had some acclimated to new sound that hadn't existed earlier. "*Would you die for him? I will die for you.*"

"You can't die."

Again, she was beyond my defenses and I *knew* her. She was consumed by an obsession with those little *monkeys* who were so young and so new to this planet. She isolated herself and lived for those tiny people. Now she was prepared to sacrifice her own immortality to walk among us. "*I can summon all that power. For moments. A second for me. Centuries for you, I can give you strength you could never imagine.*"

"That means you'll *cease* one day." The thought broke my heart, the tears that ran down my face were as real as when I watched my teacher die, whatever her name was, this *primordial* was a unique gem in the world, something spectacular and special. Knowing that she would someday *stop* was like bad news from a lover. I didn't want to believe it.

"*To give you what you want. To protect him.*"

I had no more words or defenses, my mind was laid bare. I couldn't deny what she'd said was true, I could neither run nor hide. In many ways, she and I were one entity, existing in the alternate world that she had created for us both. "You're right. I want to protect him."

"*You understand. I am no creature of mercy.*" Her voice raised to a hiss, shrill, penetrating my ears and eyes and inducing pain. "*I will spend my rage.*"

"I will spend mine." I smiled at her, or I *thought* I smiled at her. Perhaps it was simply how I felt, a common belief which I acknowledged.

"*You have no love for those who stand against your child.*"

"I would pay with my life. I would pay with a million lives to protect him." When I spoke, my voice was a hiss, just like hers. I could feel my voice penetrating the world, digging its claws in and proclaiming my sincerity. I now owned these words, I made them my own, and I sang them for a thousand ghosts and gods to hear.

"Then we have a bargain. You will sleep now. When you wake, you will continue your journey. You will end the creatures who haunt you for folly. When it is complete, I will show you the way. You will possess an eye that does not see. You will find a hole in the earth. In that hole, you will find tools. You will need to die to use those tools. I will be with you, you need not be afraid. You will live forever, or close to it."

Her words seemed timeless, stretching on forever. Each syllable lasted years and I aged where I sat with her. My eyes grew heavy, my body felt light, and I felt that I just needed a moment to close my eyes, to rest briefly. A short nap was all I needed, I told myself.

Near Cedar Mesa, Utah. Present.

Free of dreams, memories, and nightmares, I slept peacefully. Prior to my night in The Citadel, I did not believe I had ever known true rest, true respite. My mind felt clear, unburdened, and without the weight of my regrets and dereliction. It was not to say that I felt *absolved* of sin, rather that I was given a chance to exist in a vacuum, a place where I didn't *hate myself*.

My body, on the other hand, felt like I'd been beaten, inside and out.

I pulled myself up off the dusty stone floor, my face covered in dirt and drool, my neck stiff and unforgiving, my head pounding at the glimpses of sunlight. As I pulled myself up and stood, my lower back ached and my thighs felt weak and flimsy. It wasn't my age, I wasn't even *that* old. No, this was a mixture of a hangover, a morning-after beating, and a *harsh cocaine come-down*. I'd experienced all three in my life, but until this moment I'd never dreamed that they could be combined into one conglomerate of suffering.

I'd taken, in my mind, to calling the rock and earth peninsula 'The Citadel." Moving back down from The Citadel was a struggle. It was far less smooth. I had a hard time descending loose dirt and shale. Finally, I pulled the green and black shemagh off my neck and wrapped it around my right hand to protect my palm and knuckles from scrapes and bruising. The morning light was unforgiving, and standing water in the canyon floor slowly evaporated in the dry air. The rain from the night before was simply a distance memory.

By the time I reached the truck, I wanted to pass out again, sleep for *another* day. As I approached I saw Rizwan performing his morning prayers, kneeling on the small rug he kept with his pack, forehead prone to the ground. Judging by the fogged-up windows, Jennifer was asleep in the truck still.

I approached Rizwan loud enough for him to hear, neither wishing to startle him, nor disturb him. He was shirtless next to a shaving kit, a boar bristle brush, and other toiletries. We'd all been on this road trip for two weeks, without a shower. We found ways to keep ourselves clean, ways to keep from *stinking*.

When Rizwan was finished, he stood, looked at me, and squinted. "You are *changed*." He didn't recoil, but I saw a degree of shock at the edges of his expression.

"You don't mean that in a *chakra-tea* kind of way, do you?" Rizwan shook his head, so I shrugged, mostly for myself, and walked over to the truck a few yards away. I bent the passenger side mirror forward and looked at myself. I was filthy, covered in black dust, caked with dried spittle, dry leaves stuck in my hair. What shocked me was that my eyes were black. My pupil, iris, and sclera were all an indistinguishable orb of reflecting *black*.

"You didn't ask for that?" Rizwan pulled an undershirt over his muscular torso.

"I don't even know what *that* is." I stood up straight and opened the door to the truck's cab, looking for a towel, a cloth, something to wipe the grime from my face. Having spent the night in open air and starting my morning with a hike, I was unprepared for the strong odor of the cab. Jennifer needed to bathe, desperately.

"Perhaps you're one step closer, to being a demon."

I paused, looking for a towel, considering Rizwan's words. I turned to him and studied his features, his close-cut hair, his long lashes and thin lips. He regarded me seriously, and I was not entirely certain how I wanted to react. "Explain yourself, *Corporal*." I finally replied.

Rizwan laughed, pulling his fatigues on, lacing the breast over a narrow piece of chain mail that protected his chest. "You demand we disregard *rank*, speak *casually*, to each other. But the moment that you're not *drunk*, or flirting with Jennifer, and hear something you dislike," Rizwan shrugged, "It's back to ranks again."

I closed the cab door, glaring at him. "What do you mean, *flirting* with Jennifer?"

"*That* was what you drew offense for?" Rizwan raised his brows. I smelled a faint scent of fear on him, and although he was backing up, he knew he'd stepped too far.

"I don't flirt with Jennifer." I shook my head, biting at my lower lip then answered him with eyes averted. "Where I come from, that's not something you *ever get caught doing*. My parents would *disown me*."

"Where are your parents now?" Rizwan answered, then reached for his flak vest.

"Likely, they're *dead*. I haven't seen them since before the Collapse, since I was a child, back in Los Angeles." I don't feel immediately sad, but some of my familiar self-loathing returned, biting at my skull, tearing at my hair, wishing me ill. I tried to ignore it, push it back to the place that it had slept dormant since last night.

"So, why would you care *today*, what your parents felt?"

"*Respect*." I snapped back at Rizwan. He was speaking lightly, not nudging me too far, but he was pushing me in ways that either amused him, or piqued his curiosity. "Why are you *so* curious about me? What do *you* have to hide?"

"Easy," Rizwan held up both hands, palms to me, but didn't back away. "Do you know why I'm Captain Winslow's driver? Why she chose me for this hunt?" I watched his eyes, looking for a hint that he was playing a game with me.

Satisfied that he wasn't, I nodded for him to tell me. "Go on."

"In a fight, in a place like Claysville, I *only* know how to follow orders. But when it's calm, when people are just acting, or reacting, I can't help but ask questions no one *really* wants to answer." Rizwan shrugged and puts his hands down, "Cursed or blessed, Captain Winslow thinks I keep her *honest*. I think maybe she hoped I could keep *you* honest."

"A witch is many things," I wiped at my face with the rolled shemagh in my hand, "but we can never be honest. Too many secrets to keep."

"Answer me *one* thing honestly." Rizwan held up a finger, eyes focused on mine.

A second time I nodded for him. "Go on."

"When you decide to pay the piper for your sins, are you going to drag Jennifer and I with you in that bonfire of self-hatred?" I considered his words, turning them over in my heart, looking in all the details. Before I hiked up to The Citadel last night, I genuinely *hated* myself. I was a murderess at fourteen. I had betrayed and left a woman to die, who I *did love*. In the grief of my teacher's death I abandoned an *adopted daughter* who'd spent her lifetime begging for my affection. And most importantly, as Alexander had grown, I was the absentee mother who found more solace in blood lust then watching him become the man his father wanted him to be.

I answered *honestly*, though I wondered if he knew it, "I think I *did* hate myself when I climbed that rise," I gestured behind me with my thumb, "But now I know that nothing matters, so long as I *seek the elephant*."

"*What does that even mean?*" Rizwan scowled.

"It means we're going home. *California here we come*."

<hr />

PORT AMBRIDGE INDUSTRIAL PARK, PENNSYLVANIA. LONG PAST.

This dream, *this memory*, was my finest hour.

It didn't look like it, of course.

There was a dozen of us, the remains of a Company strong group who'd foraged north, towards warehouses, train tracks, and industrial yards up the Ohio River. Everyone else who'd followed me on this expedition was dead. We nestled ourselves on the distant side of sleeping iron, rail cars, far from the bloody fight we'd just *lost*.

"We *should* have brought the kid to fight." Jeffrey Moss shook his head, arms crossed, standing next to Lorne, in camo and gear, covered with blood, sooty face and hair disheveled from his helmet.

"*No,*" It was hard for me to talk, "she's too young." It was a small miracle that my jaw wasn't broken. At least four of my teeth were missing at the back of my mouth, and I *only* tasted copper.

"Then *why* did you bring her Maggi?" Jeffrey replied. The team, a mix of men and women in combat gear, wearing various injuries, nodded in agreement. "She could have scattered them before we went in, that's *more* useful than your fire trick and your *shit shotgun work*." *I didn't even have my shotgun now.* It'd been taken away from me; that was what had broken my teeth, the stock hitting me.

I glanced over to Lorne, and the small girl hiding behind him. I had no intention of humiliating her by explaining to a group former military and ex-cops that Margaret had night terrors and begged me to bring her along. I also had no intention of deploying her in a firefight.

140

"I made the call," I gestured, dismissing Jeffrey, "and that's *that*."

"Maybe you're not the one who should be making calls. Lorne is an experienced commander. With all due respect to your husband, I'm here for *Lorne*, not you Californians." Lorne looked mortified as Jeffrey spoke, but he wasn't alone in his words. I could feel their minds wander. I smelled doubt, mixed with the vomit that covered my plate carrier. We were losing them, *I was losing them*.

My teacher had been dead for less than four weeks. Food and resource runs since his demise had ceased, but Crafton was growing day by day, and whatever slapdash government we'd fabricated was bending, breaking under the strain. Not enough food, or medicine. Not enough metal, or lumber. Our infrastructure relied on this foraging party and my ability to not just *lead*, but also end a rival *witch*.

"This is *no time* to dissent," Lorne's goatee wasn't white back then, it was pepper dusted in salt. His blue eyes were brighter, and fewer lines crimped at his face, "We need to put together a plan to complete our retreat, get back to Crafton." He was doing a good job distracting them. Lorne's voice commanded respect, he had a clear and precise tone, and he spoke with respect to those around him. Like my teacher, he'd been a natural leader, and the two of them had convinced many to join in Crafton's defenses.

I was about to become an afterthought, however. I had failed these men and women; I had made calls that cost us lives. Although it was my teacher's desire that his son be a *King* one day, his partner lacked the ability to be *Queen Mother* up until this night.

My next words came hard and fast, like a tidal wave. They hit my mouth harder than the butt of my shotgun. "I'm not going back to Crafton." Lorne and Jeffrey halted, mid-conversation, and silence fell over the survivors. "You go, Lorne. Take Margaret with you, get her to safety. I'm going back; I'm putting this *bitch* and her mercenaries down. I'll get us the resources we need." I knew that my eyes were tearing up as I spoke, regardless of what I wanted.

"That's suicide." Jeffrey laughed at me, crossing his arms.

"Maybe so, but they're not expecting us to turn around and punch back, are they?"

Lorne held up a hand to Jeffrey, looking me over with concern and trepidation, "That's not a bad idea. We did a lot of damage, they're licking their wounds."

"They still have a witch." Jeffrey shook his head.

"I'll *end* Vix." *Why did we have to keep talking?* The pain was blinding.

"You couldn't before." Jeffrey answered. He wasn't wrong. I had broken fingers on my left hand and a face like a ripe plumb to prove my failure.

"*I'm going*," I whispered, looking directly at Jeffrey, then at the others. "You can come with me, or you can go back to Crafton."

The first person to replied, was the last person I expected. Our Marine Recon, Matt, the same Matt with a bad eye and no last name. The same Matt who *never spoke*, looked at me with a giant, ugly grin, "I'll go with you."

"Matt, *really?*" Jeffrey gestured to me, "you're going to get yourself killed."

"Sounds like some *shit* an Army boy would say." Matt stepped backward and came up to flank me, quietly, arms resting across the rifle draped on his chest. I had nothing more to say, I was not even sure I could still speak. There were no more theatrics left to play, only action. As I watched this dream unfold, I wondered how much of my bravery was real, and how much of it was a legitimate death wish. I turned then, and walked away from the team with Matt, my Marine, following me.

I heard Lorne call them to heel, from behind me. Even Jeffrey, so worried that I would get everyone killed, followed. He followed Lorne of course, but right now, it didn't matter where he laid his loyalty. We passed through steel boxcars, towards the river, barely visible behind a tower of reeds and tall grass. On this side of the tracks was a series of narrow warehouses. Each one was full of lumber or steel or copper, each one a key target. On the adjacent side, from where I approached were small storehouses, used as barracks, kitchens. There were also empty tractors, used for storage. *These* buildings were irrelevant to our needs.

As I approached the storehouse bungalows, I stretched my right hand out and wrapped my consciousness around the first wooden structure. I burrowed through it like a termite, losing my own vision for a second, and then whispered a single word.

"*Burn.*"

Lorne called me a *fire eater*. Since the Collapse, since the Veil ceased to exist, I could light cigarettes with a snap of my fingers, call fireballs into my palms, and *burn myself*. My fingernails were caramelized from constant practice. These were parlor tricks, however, and I needed to be much more dangerous. My teacher had used words to bend reality before the Collapse, not to this extent, not with this intense of a result, but he could force his will into fruition this way.

I only *suspected* it would work, and I was both surprised and thrilled when the first storehouse was consumed in bright orange and yellow flames. There were mercenaries inside, nameless, faceless men, who fled to the cool night, screaming. They'd assumed we'd left, we'd *lost* after all, why would we return? They wore cotton under shirts and boxers, unarmored, unprepared. Matt gunned them down with precision.

This was the first time I had displayed *real* power. I was no longer my teacher's *girlfriend*, I was no longer *the baby's mother*; at this moment, I ceased to be Maggi Lopez. It would be years before I earned the moniker, *The Bruja*, but that menace was born this night. That woman was created here, in this industrial park, as she lit building after building on fire using only her mind. My tendrils stretched across a field of dirt and grass, magic and essence, I was linking myself through a web of energy and dominating all I survey. It was here that I learned what it *felt like* to connect with the universe and have it *connect back*.

I was the walking embodiment of havoc, my mind barely connected with my body, listening and charting the field around me as it unfolded. I knew where *my people* would be, I stretched part of myself into the minds of Lorne, Jeffery, and Matt, feeling the impressions their bodies made against the world I was embracing. I also knew where *the enemy* would be, and I showed Lorne, Jeffery, and Matt, where to go, where to stand, and where to take cover.

In the middle of the slaughter, rifle to his cheek, Matt glanced over at me. He gave me a smile of pure joy, and although we had come from two very different worlds, we understood each other that night for the first time.

This was all *very impressive*, but I still needed to face another magic user. The woman stepping out of her aluminum cottage was short and lumpy with large breasts and beady eyes. Like myself, she was *Latina*, but she had softer features, darker skin and dusty brown hair pulled up in a bun. She didn't wear the body armor and gear I did; instead she was wrapped in denim pants, dark boots, and black linens. I could feel her, *see her in my head*; and like little Margaret, she vibrated with power, a constant chatter and whistle. She called herself Victoria Victrix. Everyone else called her *Vix*.

"You're back?" Her voice accused, spitting the words as if I was a sinner meant to repent at her feet. She lowered her hands and flames *near her* subsided. Her actions drew oxygen up and out of the air, her fingers extensions of meticulous energy, contacting every bit of air she desired, and tethered it as she wished. She could halt my fire on a whim; she had done so earlier. She had suffocated my soldiers with a glance. I watched men die, good men, writhing on the ground, clutching their throats, clawing at their faces, fighting for the breath she had stolen.

She could turn that on me at any time, and I had no idea how to defend myself.

"I'd like my shotgun back." I shouted to her, as loud as I could manage.

"Come take it, *two o'clock beauty queen*." Vix laughed at me, hands taunting me to come closer. I had few options. We stood about a dozen yards apart. The only thing I could command at this point was fire, and Vix understood the ebb and flow of magic better than me. I reached into one of my pockets and removed a balisong, one of two butterfly knives I wore. My left hand was useless, but not my right. I flipped it open, handles spinning end over end, locking in my fingers. I charged directly for her, blade against my palm, nestled on my wrist, dull edge kissing my flesh with cool steel.

I lost my breath as I closed the gap, but I wasn't merely suffocating, I was dropped to my knees, skidding in the sand and dirt, just a few yards from Vix. Arms held wide, her eyes locked on mine, shaking her head at me, lumpy features sneering down. I wanted to cut her face off; I wanted to pry those *beady eyes* out of her skull.

Instead I looked up at her, eating my own blood and slowly dying. Seconds drug on, one after another. I wouldn't reach for my throat, I wouldn't give her the satisfaction of clawing at my skin, trying breath. I was almost back on my feet when I felt something strange I'd never quite known. It reminded of woebegone dread, the intimate terror I remember from my childhood, the night in the liquor store.

My skin crawled, and an intense sense of paranoia set in. I wanted to scream but there was no breath. Intense fight or flight set in and I wanted to jump down on all fours, *look behind me*, for what was surely a primordial darkness hot on my heels, licking at my haunches.

This was no Djinni, this was the little girl who cried in her sleep. *Margaret*.

While I understood, what was happening, and could control it to some degree, Vix was utterly clueless. Her focus was shattered, fingers controlling oxygen around me released. She'd broken her attention; her connection to the magic was gone.

Margaret had infected us both, equally, with savage panic. I doubt she could have focused more effectively. It was in my heart, running through my veins. When I leapt those last few yards towards my foe, I was close to feral and Vix was close to madness.

My right hand slashed for Vix and she held an arm up to stop me. The balisong cut through linens and opened tendons. My hand snapped back and stabbed the blade through the center of her palm, forcing her wrist back and letting me crawl up to her, a hound mauling it's pray, jaws locked around a wild rabbit.

It was true that I couldn't beat her with magic, she *was* a better witch. But I wasn't a noble warrior, I wasn't chivalrous or honorable, I was a little *scrap* who grew up fighting. I was not obliged to meet the enemy on equal footing; I was only obliged to win. Matt understood that, and now I did too.

Even though my mind was starting to clear, I was *angry*; that desire I had to rip Vix's face off didn't yield with the primal fear of Margaret's magic, but rather burned hotter. We were a jumbled mess of body parts, legs kicking, elbows jabbing. A third cut bit the inside of her arm, gnawing into thick arteries. A fourth cut slid *into* her armpit, and she was a crippled doll in my arms. I was covered in her blood, and I *liked it*, I wanted *more of it*. My left elbow wrapped around her neck and I slammed my forehead into her skull, left leg bracing us, and my right knee in her rotund stomach, hard and fast.

We were locked together now, and I was holding Vix's lower lip in my teeth when I jabbed her the first time, under the chin with my butterfly knife.

She couldn't pull away, couldn't separate herself from me. She didn't scream; her throat exploded in a gurgling groan as I jabbed her a second, then a third, and a fourth time. I kept striking her under the chin and throat until I was holding her dead weight. The struggling subsided, her arms dropped down, and I was forced to let go of her.

The body of Victoria Victrix, the witch who'd broken my fingers and knocked my teeth out, toppled to the ground. I was covered in her cruor, thick and opulent against my skin. It stunk of rust and iron, broken bridges, forgotten highways, and empty cities. I wretched at the odor and then forced myself to inhale deeply. Her blood smelled of the apocalypse, and *I was now the daughter of the apocalypse.*

I turned slowly, looking back behind me. I saw Margaret. The little girl dashed toward me and slammed into my legs, hugging me. Part of me, the *proper part of me*, wanted to warn her away, chastise her, for following me into this fight. I wanted to scold her, yell at her, tell her she'd made a mess of herself, covered in Vix's blood. I was angry that she took the risk. I imagined a stray bullet penetrating her skull and finding her lifeless body after such a ferocious victory.

The fantasy turned my stomach and I was crying.

I didn't yell at her. I let her hug me. I decided that if the *tough little bitch* wanted to scrap with me, I'd teach her properly. Margaret became my student that night, and in a few years, she would begin to use her preferred moniker, *Mayy.*

Matt was smiling at me, his big ugly smile. He chewed at something that I couldn't quite see, maybe seeds, maybe nothing at all. Matt would never speak much more than he had that night, but he'd walk with me into a hundred battles like this one. It broke my heart when he was killed at New Castle.

Jeffery wasn't smiling, but he was accepting. He too would die at New Castle, many years later, but he never questioned me again after that night.

His friend Lorne *wasn't* smiling and I didn't know why at that time.

We would rule the Antecedent States together for nearly two decades, in the shadow of his affection for me, a woman who had only ever loved once before. His loyalty was unwavering, his wisdom was unquestionable. If I became a good leader in later decades it was due to what he'd taught me.

I was reborn that night, into something that couldn't exist before the Collapse. I was at the genesis of a new world, and for the first time in my life I wasn't a coward.

——————*

SANTA CRUZ, CALIFORNIA. PRESENT.

Since we had left Crafton, four weeks had passed.

Four weeks of tracking the Ifrit across America. Following whispers at the edge of my mind, a jitter in my spine, disjointed feelings. Four weeks, asking Jennifer to turn down a dusty highway, or chasing dreams of black dogs. Four weeks, and I'd met a third Djinni, as well as some kind of primordial being, deep in the Utah desert. Four weeks, and now I stood on the beach watching a grim, gray Pacific Ocean lurch in and out, waves and seagulls filling my ears and a heavy mist plastering hair to my face. The air was wet, salty, and I let it soak into my lungs.

I was crying, *bawling my eyes out.* Giggles climbed out of my throat as well. I was elated to be back here again in a place I so fervently loved. On this beach, down past The Boardwalk, my teacher and I had laid in the sand, late at night. He taught me about the stars, constellations, and planets that could be seen in the sky. A few miles away lay Evergreen Cemetery, where I first met Le Baron Samedi. There was a *very* good chance, that my son was conceived in one of the old beachfront hotels.

Yet, I stood here, alone. Though my teacher had long passed, I'd have liked to have shown Alexander this place, where his parents fell in love, or show Mayy where her teacher learned so much. It was too late, now, my *children* were thousands of miles away and I chewed sea salt, dreaming of my youth and all that had come before.

I crouched down, running my palms across the wet sand. I was extending aspects of myself and my energy into this place, spreading out and listening. There was no magic here to practice, there were no black

148

dogs to hunt, no enemies to fight. Rather, I was looking at the world with a different set of eyes. Enjoying the view with my gifts, feeling the world play against my mind, the ocean waves crashing back and forth against my soul, the wind kissing my heart. I had many more senses I could study the world with, devouring all its beauty and majesty.

Dig in the sand.

I was jarred from my wonder, coughing, looking around for the voice instinctively. I already knew that it was in my own mind. I opened my mouth to reply and thought better of it. I thought the words instead, wondering if it was the spider mother from The Citadel.

Yes. I am now a part of you, I see what you see, and much more. You don't plant your feet where you plant your feet by happenstance.

"I don't believe in random happenstance." I whispered aloud.

Dig in the sand.

In all my years, I'd never known a voice like hers. I heard it in my teeth, my fingers, my stomach; it infused every part of me. I wondered how deep our connection ran, and how much more complex the changes were, beyond my set of eyes.

You'll find out soon enough. Dig in the sand.

I was not used to taking orders. I finally began to dig at the sand where I knelt, fingers penetrating and shoveling at the moist alluvium. As I did so, the ocean swept in, further and further, finally filling my little trench and flooding my clothing and boots. That wasn't *me*, I'd never been able to interact with water the way I had fire. Flame, for me, was like a loyal dog, it watched over me when I slept, it whimpered when I was sad, and it barked when I was angry. My ability to summon it to my hands, fingers, was some sort of strange mix of genetic predisposition and magical connectivity that I'd never had a choice in. Water, on the other hand, was an element that treated me with difference, a preoccupied cat, as uninterested in me as I was in it.

I buried my bare arms past the elbows in seawater and sand, so close to the rising tide that my hair fell in the brine and I could taste the ocean on my lips. By the time my fingers wrapped around an unfamiliar item, I was drenched and filthy.

That's it.

What was it? I wondered, standing, pulling myself up. I cleaned off the object. It felt like glass under my fingertips, and as I examined it further I realized it was a *prosthetic eye*. It was shaped like a smooth stone, white, with a painted blue iris looking back at me. My relaxed sense of whimsy and wonder evaporated, and I heard the words in my mind, spoken by Her Lady of the Dry Arms; "*You will have two eyes, when you die. One of these eyes will not see as the other. I want that eye, one last gift.*"

I looked around me, expecting to find Her Lady of the Dry Arms standing next to me, as foolish as that idea was. My heart fluttered as I ran the words over in my mind. *You will have two eyes*, implied I'd *lose* one of my own eyes. That idea made me genuinely fearful. I'd been hurt, in my life, but that sort of injury turned my stomach.

I turned then, and walked away from the beach. The prosthetic eye was buried in my palm as I walked towards the parking lot. It was empty, save for our dirty, dusty 4x4 truck, Jennifer and Rizwan leaning against it, their arms crossed, watching as I approached.

"It's good that you don't pay us by the hour." Jennifer smiled, at my return, her tone jovial, but I can feel an edge of irritation in her voice. The two soldiers routinely waited for me, by the truck, when I wandered off to listen or seek out our prey.

"Touch this." I held up the oddly shaped piece of glass for Jennifer to touch as I approached her, and she did. Her fingertips briefly touched and for a moment I felt her irritation, mixed with relief. *Every time she walks away, I wonder if it'll be the last time*, the words recite, in my mind, like a book.

"Is that a glass eye?" Jennifer looked it over in her fingers, Rizwan leaning in to examine it also. "Is that what you walked out there to find?"

"No," I smiled, "I walked out there to enjoy the beach and some old memories, privately. I found *that* without looking."

"It feels, *strange*," Jennifer's mood shifted, and she looked at me, seriously, focusing on what she held in her fingers. "It feels like, I want to *wear it*." She lifted it up, closing her eyelids, pressing it against her face then dropped it back in my palm.

"It's *stranger* than you know," I flipped up my shemagh and place the glass eye in my cleavage, "I wondered if you could feel more than I could." My body armor was left in the backseat, now I only wore a tank top and my military jacket. It was easier to breathe that way and I could relax my back.

Rizwan was now the irritated one, however, "Did you find your *elephant?*" He asked me, not quite mocking, not quite joking.

"California *is* the elephant." I replied.

"I think what Rizwan meant was, are we back on the trail of your Djinn?" Jennifer's voice was kinder, but it felt *disingenuous* somehow. I glanced down, and she was wearing my 9mm, the combat pistol I'd kept for decades, the weapon my teacher had gifted to me. Normally I kept it holstered, but I'd known the beach would be wet.

"Why are you wearing my gun?" I asked, ignoring Jennifer's first question.

"*Your* gun is now our *only* gun." Rizwan answered before Jennifer. "Whatever weapons, money, and gear we could pawn or tradeoff for fuel in Bakersfield is now gone."

Jennifer withdrew the weapon and handed the firearm to me, fingers wrapped around the slide and receiver. "It's our *only* gun. It doesn't do much good sitting on your seat. When you wander off, we're left protecting the truck. The truck is worth *a lot* out here."

I *wanted* to be angry. The gun was one of the memories I kept from my teacher. He'd owned it before we met, he'd worn when we fled the fall of the Bay Area, and when he found a larger .45 ACP, he'd given it me. He taught me how to break it down, clean it, fire it, and handle it effectively and safely. Seeing it on Jennifer's hip was a slap in the face, but I couldn't argue her logic. Our 4x4 was worth more than *all* the guns we'd sold in Bakersfield. "No, you're right, you have the magazines?"

"Of course. Fifty-one rounds, total."

I nodded, then gestured for her to return the 9mm to its holster. "To answer your first question, *no*, I have no idea where the Djinn are." I pointed past the truck, up towards the heavily forested hills behind Jennifer and Rizwan, "I'm heading up *there* to find out what the residents know."

"Let me guess," Jennifer lips curled up, showing her front teeth and betraying a degree of amusement, "a cemetery?"

"If you already know all the answers, what are you asking me for?" I replied, bereft of joy, "Wait here. I want to *walk*."

"That'll take you *hours.*" Rizwan glared at me.

"*Hours* until the sun sets." Some laughter lurked into my voice, "don't worry Jennifer, you don't need to worry. *This* won't be the last time I wander away from you."

My two travel companions had become frustrated since we left Utah. The trail of our quarry had grown cold for weeks, and selling our weapons and ammunition sat on them terribly. I had needed to pull rank and *order them* to sell everything so we could buy fuel. Without it, this entire journey was for nothing. Even if they failed to understand the depth to which I desired to find and fight the Ifrit, my own motivation had not faltered.

The walk across Santa Cruz was a beautiful and surreal experience. Before the Collapse, this was a place that had floated between worlds, elements of the unseen always sneaking, peeking around the corners. It always felt like you were being watched as you walked the streets late at night. Eating your dinner or talking to a friend, there was a whisper in the air that you could never quite ignore.

It was the same in all the important ways, different in new ways. Gone were the vehicles, only a few were left to visibly rot, and decay, in the town's deliciously scented ocean air. The people had not changed much, many looked as though they could have walked out of my youth with their mohawks, tie-dye shirts, and guitar-strumming in the dimly lit alcoves.

I had no problems finding a liquor store, a large corner building, advertising itself. The shelves were mostly stocked with old canned food, locally grown crops, and trinkets of various merits. The lady tending her store was not cheap, however; I had to trade my favorite switchblade for a bottle of black rum. She wouldn't accept either of the smaller knives, the little flip-outs I'd worn, only the switchblade would do, the same knife I'd opened my palm with back in Pennsylvania. Unfortunately, she had no cigarettes to sell me.

It was dark when I found myself crossing the train tracks, heading toward the old, familiar cemetery, at the foot of a lush hill. Rain danced out of the sky, kissing me on the face and scalp, a friendly breeze caressed my cheek. I pulled the shemagh from my neck and used it to tie up my hair and protect my head a little from the sky. This also exposed my cleavage, something Le Baron Samedi had *always* enjoyed about me.

The ornate ironwork of the entrance hadn't changed at all, no rustier for the years. The cobblestone walkway that led uphill was overgrown now, weeds and native grasses spreading rampant, obscuring smaller graves and low walls. I climbed up, into the darkness, where no more ambient light could find me, toward a great mausoleum, belonging to the Heath family. Eight white marble headstones were set into the wall of the structure. That is where I stood, waiting, hands buried deep in my jacket pockets.

"Maggi. It's been a *long* time."

The air pulled against itself, forcing colors to appear, soft blues mixed with accents of gray and light red. I turned to watch the colors flicker and change. It was like watching an abstract painting come into focus until, after a few moments, a young woman stepped from thin air. I had dreaded her arrival almost as much as I missed her. Her dress was from a different era, long before my parents or grandparents were born. The neckline plunged and the color of her flesh was off, like a photo left in the sun to fade, for too many years.

I gave her a genuine smile, "Marie."

"Never thought we'd see you again," she mused in a thick accent, some flavor of England. "Don't suppose you have an oily rag?"

"Yeah, I got a *cigarette*." I pulled out the pack, only three remaining, and handed one of them to her. Our hands brush against each other, it felt like sweeping my hand through a bucket of ice water, almost frozen, but still slush, and my skin goose-pimpled.

She accepted, "*Right*, well, where is he?"

"He didn't visit you?" I answered, knowing *exactly* who she was talking about. I reached out to find a distant flame, borrowed it, and with a snap I ignited her cigarette. The quick burst of flame cast a strange, shadowed glow *through* her, she reflected and refracted light.

Her young face and tired eyes watched me with care, framed in dark locks of hair. "He's dead, is he?" She inhaled, somehow. The smoke just seemed to float lazily within her.

"He's been dead, twenty years now." I replied.

"And has he visited *you*? Even once?" Another puff.

I didn't want to answer honestly, it hurt me to do so and reminded me how much I missed him. "No, he hasn't." Marie and my teacher had known each other some years before I'd met him. In their own way, they'd been lovers. Although, that was a very inaccurate description for what the living and dead might share together. He had a complex relationship with Marie, just like Aubree, and that had angered me to blind rage when I was young. Ultimately, I realized that a dead woman was no threat to me.

"Right *bastard*," Marie barked, "Me, he'd not visit. I'm just his former, he's not thought a *peep* in decades. Can't rage on a man for that, right? You, on the other hand, he'd do well to visit you. Bastard loved you, he did." Her expression went from annoyed, to weary, her eyes more tired than before.

"I don't know *why* he didn't visit," I shrugged.

"A girl can be sad for what she ain't got, but a girl *can be content knowing he's happy*." I didn't really know how to respond to that, and she continued, "Besides, you always had an advantage over me. You were *warm* to the touch."

Besides our affinity for the same man, Marie Holmes and I had very little in common. She was a Victorian prostitute who'd come to Santa Cruz from England, and murdered herself one night by *quaffing carbolic acid*, as the gravestone explained. We were over a century apart, from two different worlds.

"How could he belong to me? He belonged only to himself, to his ego, to his *drive*." I said finally, admitting something I rarely discussed. I wasn't lying, and I wasn't regretful. His drive had attracted me to him, and we'd never disagreed on our dreams for Alexander.

"You speak *true*," Marie nodded.

The air around began to sink, heavy, bloated, pulled to the ground and wrenched open until the very laws of physics yielded. I reached for the shemagh and pulled it down, so that my hair could roam freely, no longer acknowledging gravity. *Le Baron* always loved my hair.

Cigar smoke and bourbon filled my nose as ice water ran down my spine. I knew that feeling well. As if it was the most natural thing,

Le Baron Samedi appeared next to us like the ringmaster of his own private circus, Marie and I his unwitting performers, each glowing in the adoration of his applause. Without the Veil, he was every bit physical, no glowing form, no ghost or goblin, he hammered himself into reality, standing no less real than Jennifer or Rizwan. His black, tailed tuxedo was immaculate, yet dusty, faded at parts, and crisp in others. His big, black, top hat was shiny from one angle, dull and dreary from another. His smoked lenses faded between, opaque pools that glimpse the world beyond our own. At his core, he was a skeleton, bleached bones grinding and articulating, clicking as he gesticulated and swept his arms about.

"*Now, how'd I ever find myself as lucky to be escorted to the dance by not one—no, not just one—but two of the finest big-tittied ladies this side of the goddamn Mississippi?*" He cooed at the two of us.

"I'll have you know, *we is mourning.*" Marie said matter-of-factly, holding up her hand for him to kiss. He did so with elegance and panache. Her form, with its washed-out colors, sharpened and brightened when he touched her. Color flowed back into her skin, and she flushed with ruby red lips. In the shadow of Samedi, Marie ceased to be a ghost and became a living girl once more.

The Baron's arm swept through the air as he spoke, "*Why mourn for the dead; they don't have to deal with the living anymore!*"

"Right! Always got the flesh and blood waggling about and showing off all they got. Should be unlawful." Marie turned to me, hands groping her bosom, jiggling her breasts in my direction as her words played through the air to a sing-song parody of her own design.

"*Miss Holmes, always a pleasure to see ya' here. England's Jewel, Lady of the Night!*" The Baron chuckled before turning to me. "*And of course, my favorite Spanish Harlot, Mary Magdalene, hair fit to bathe the feet of Jesus!*"

He made me laugh. I hated it, but he *always* made me laugh. I reached into my jacket and produced the bottle of black rum I'd traded for earlier. His gloved fingers never met mine, but as our hands grew closer, my head became light. With a flourish, he loosed the cap and it sailed into darkness. It was hard to describe what it looked like to see a skeleton knocking back a swig or three. "It's good to see you both, but I need help."

"Not a bit of small talk, eh? Straight to business." Marie reached out for the rum, and both held the bottle. She could drink the alcohol, as Samedi kept them both planted firmly in the living world. "Same old Maggi."

"Don't ya' worry, dahlin'. We'll hit the town later. Just you an' me."

"I need to find someone." I said, not trying to barrel through their conversation, but knowing full well that Samedi would neglect me quickly for a woman like Marie, a *dead* woman whom he could, and *would,* bed later.

"Don't we all, dahlin'?" he interrupted, with a mischievous grin. I sighed, accepting the rum from Marie this time, taking a swig of the freezing liquid. *"It's just tawdry! Back in the old days, your boy would come here and fetch my kindness with a gift. Here you show, rum in hand, ready to barter with me as though I was a common merchant man!"*

"Baron, there's nothing *common* about you." I smiled, flirting with him. "I thought *good girls* came, *gifts in hand* if they wanted a taste of your sweet favor." The sheer charisma of Samedi made it impossible not to love him. Men would share a cigar at his side, and women would share *a whole lot more.*

"Why Maggi Lopez, I had no idea your thirsts were compatible with my own."

I took another drink from the rum and then handed it back to him, "How many years have *we* known each other Baron? *Tobacco, booze, and bitches."*

Marie watched me quizzically for a moment, brow furrowed. I winked at her and Samedi busts out laughing; laughter so deep that it rattled my ribs, vibrating the stones beneath my boots and making a real smile spread across my face. *"How many questions da ya' think this bottle earns, Miss Holmes?"* Samedi turned toward Marie, pointing to the bottle.

"Two. No! Three questions." Marie answered, then he handed the rum over to her. The cigarette I'd given her was smoked down. He handed her the cigar, the same cigar he *always* smoked. Each puff made the embers burn bright, casting reflections off his smoked lenses.

"All right, the young lady seems to have a right mind for this sort of thing. You have three questions, and maybe a half question. I haven't decided yet."

I removed the prosthetic eye from my cleavage, *slowly*, so Samedi would enjoy the show. I held the eye up for him, "What is *this?*"

"*Mmmhm,*" The noise he made is low, bass, and again I feel it in my ribs, "*I know that eye, that is an eye which does not see. Let me guess, that little forest critter, Marinette Bras Cheche wants it?*"

"Her Lady of the Dry Arms, yes." I withdrew the eye, placing it back into my cleavage and taking extra time to resettle my bosom. "She asked me for it, after I *died.*"

"*Oh, after.*" Samedi nodded, making a sarcastic chuckle, "*that was the deal?*"

I nodded, saying nothing.

"*That eye was made for someone else, but it will serve you in the end. You will die in a dark place, you will die in the darkest of places, and when your body turns to maggot nibbles, Marinette will claim her prize.*" That mostly answered my question, or as well as The Baron ever answered a question.

"This is boring, this is." Marie took a drag off Samedi's cigar, then traded with him for the rum again. This time, without her hands *and* Samedi's on the bottle, the rum just splashed ineffectively on the cobblestones.

"*Yes dahlin', this is boring.*" Samedi favored me again, "*You don't even have a third question, do you? Just one more. I can feel it burning inside you, heating you up, making your skin red and angry like in the old days.*"

He wasn't wrong, and I answered him quickly, "Where can I can find the Ifrit I hunt?"

"*First a boring question, then a stupid question, dahlin'. Aren't witches supposed to grow wiser with age?*"

"Give me another hit of that." I accepted the rum from Marie, drinking more than I had the first time. I enjoyed the smooth burn and the sweet spices as they settled in my stomach. "I don't know where to go."

"*Maggi, you marvelous, meticulous, miscreant minx, you are one of the sharpest tools I have ever borrowed from the shed, and you waste a bottle of rum to ask me a question you already know the answer to?*"

He was right. The Djinn had warned me already, they'd practically invited me to seek them out. It fell into place, pieces colliding and chipping each other, and I completely understood. *If you wish to hunt us, you will suffer your past sins.* It wasn't a threat, they weren't trying to ward me away, they weren't *scared* of me, why would they be? I was a mortal witch, nothing more than a petulant insect for creatures made from smokeless fire. It was one more manipulation, one more plan they'd designed and directed for me.

"My *sins*, back in the Bay Area, where I left Aubree to die."

Samedi nodded, somberly. It was hard to imagine a skull and sunglasses being anything other than somber, but it was such a rare sense he radiated that I was filled with sorrow having witnessed it.

"Sweetie." Marie took the bottle back from me, "You're gonna *die*, you are. It's why I was so nice to you, I can see it."

"*Miss Holmes, here, is only half right. She's delirious with fever, clearly, and is in need of a gentleman and cunning linguist for an evening conversation.*" Marie giggled like a teenager, paying more attention to the cigar with her lips than was required. He tipped his head and motioned for the rum, grabbing it back with his left hand, then offered Marie his right arm. Marie slid her arm through his, posing like a proper couple. "*Ya' won't make it home. No, ma'am,*" he shook his head, "*But ya' ain't gonna die. In fact, ya' ain't never gonna die.*"

Samedi took back his cigar from Marie, and turned with her, starting to lead them both up the path, up the hill, into total darkness.

"Hey!" I shouted up at them.

He looked back over his shoulder at me. "*Yes, dahlin'?*"

"Thank you. Thank you *both*."

"Maggi," Marie turned, and smiled at me for the first time with genuine affection, "We never got on, did we? Doesn't much matter now; I think I'll miss you."

"I'll miss you too, Marie."

"*Be seein' ya' around, dahlin'.*" Samedi nodded. As the two of them ascended the hill in darkness, they were lost to the night. Samedi's black tuxedo was stitched from the very fabric that made a graveyard dark, and when he wanted, he simply washed away in the background scenery, like he'd never been to start with. Marie, on the other hand, faded back to the color of an old photo, wet paint smeared on the night, turning to sepia and then dull shades of dusk before simply ceasing to exist.

All I could hear was Samedi's echoing laughter.

I stepped forward, then, snapping both my fingers and borrowing a little flame in both my hands to light the night. I could see, if I looked carefully enough, the heart that had been laid out in a familiar pattern, when these cobblestones were first laid here. I walked over to that heart and stood in the middle, letting my flame die, my own body vanishing into the night.

This was the place my teacher and I had first kissed, almost a quarter century ago.

SAN FRANCISCO, CALIFORNIA. PRESENT.

Although Santa Cruz had propelled me forward with a familiar joy, the drive north was only dread and loathing.

We crossed the mountains on Highway 17 and entered the Bay Area. The northbound lanes were clear, empty, littered only by an occasional rock slide or overgrowth, while the southbound lanes were an endless carpet of rusting cars, sitting where they'd been abandoned.

The sky was filled with dawn light, orange and red on the horizon, fading into deep blues and purples. The morning illuminated life bustling across the South Bay, encampments and minor villages. The region had been too urban for any real farming, and resources were harder to appropriate here across long distances, so the populations were smaller.

By the time, we reached Highway 101, northbound, visible battle scarring from the Collapse escalated. I'd heard of continued shelling, pitched battles had been fought in the East Bay, and most of those cities had become a desolate wasteland. These were rumors, but my eyes now confirmed some of what I'd heard. The path was more difficult than expected. Memory got us by, despite an altered landscape. Wrecks, both military and civilian, obstructed our travel. What had once been suburbs were now empty fields being consumed by vibrant green grasses, young trees, and local shrubbery. In other places, the bay itself had begun reclaiming a century old land fill, in addition to consuming industrial neighborhoods and retaking sections of highway.

We drove across parking lots and sidewalks, trying to detour around the destruction. We never made it over ten or twenty miles an hour. It smelled like the Bay Area I remembered, rich ocean air and clear skies. Gone were the smoke and ash and a winter breeze nipped at the back of my neck when my hair fluttered loosely. Jennifer, who drove, peered out the open windows, "We just keep driving north?"

"Yup." I nodded from the passenger seat.

"*Now* you know where the elephant is?" Rizwan piped up from the backseat.

"Yup." I nodded a second time.

As best as I understood what Baron Samedi had told me, I would find the Ifrit here. If I hunted them, I would find them in a place that would force me to endure a hard gaze upon the selfish mistakes I'd made years ago. Driving up the Peninsula now reminded me of the horrors I witnessed *driving down it*. Knowing that Aubree had died in a hospital, somewhere here, her mind screaming for me to save her. If the Djinn wished to wreck my mind before they fought me, this was a good start.

"Is this, the end?" Jennifer asked and I nearly choked. When she realized what that sounded like, she shook her head and corrected herself. "I *mean*, is this the end of our trip?"

"It is if I kill the Ifrit."

"Why would they be *here*?" She replied.

"Because they know this place is important to me." I sighed, pulling a foldout blade from my jacket. I'd stitched a small pocket, under the chainmail lining. The blade was compact and fit in snugly. "Because they've known I was hunting them, because they *know me*."

"Djinn are manipulators," I heard from the backseat, "all what they speak, is a lie."

"Basically? *Correct*." I opened the knife and used it to cut open my hand, where the thumb met my index finger, the same hand with a map of scars on the palm. Several slices produce a momentary burst of cruor. Using my right thumb, I painted it across my forehead, down my eyes, my lips, and finally my throat. I whispered under my breath, words in a dead language, building defenses around myself, walls, barriers upon barriers, networked and connected, each one tapping into the world, the Bay Area, for strength. I could feel Rizwan's his eyes on me, watching, burrowing into me. None of his previous irritation seeped into the air, instead he felt *concern for me*, so did Jennifer. They were anxious, and if truth be told, *so was I*.

"Which of you is a good writer?" I asked, once my blood work was complete.

"Rizwan." Jennifer said, softly.

I turned, looking over my seat. His face seemed older today, as if he'd aged overnight, a decade of worth and experience played across his features. "Write about me, after I'm gone. Tell people about me, what I was like."

"What do you want me to tell them?" He asked, quietly.

"You're smart. You'll find the words."

"I'd like to tell them that you were a good person. You had a good heart." I smiled at him, suffocating a chuckle. I didn't wish to insult the boy.

It was noon when we reached San Francisco, a shamble of half-collapsed skyscrapers, burnt steel frames, crumbling roads, and a sea of ruined cars and trucks. Dead still littered this place, skeletons in their clothes, shoes and hats gripped steering wheels, or lay prone on the streets, as bodies stacked high on sidewalks. No one had cleaned up the city, whoever survived, had never returned. Each passing year left another layer of dust, a thicker growth of weeds and grass, and a few more cracks in the pavement.

Eventually we were forced to abandon the truck and continue on foot. We disconnected the truck's battery and lug nuts from the tires, hiding them nearby. Jennifer kept my 9mm, since I didn't plan on needing it, for this fight. After securing what items we could, we waded into the urban jungle that was once San Francisco.

The further we hiked, the more my defenses tingled, visible sparks snapped off my barriers once or twice. I glanced back at Jennifer, wondering if she felt the invasion. She only nodded at me, understanding my look completely. Somewhere in this city, *something* was watching us, pressing against us, attempting to learn our motives. I could keep it out of my mind, and perhaps Jennifer as well, but Rizwan's thoughts would be an open book. The Ifrit would know we were here and *why* we were here. I pushed back, listening, looking for anything.

I couldn't feel a single soul around us.

We began to hike east after a few hours, toward the bay. I noticed, at one point, as we passed a burnt-out grocery store, where *newer* bodies littered the ground. They'd rotted, for sure, but they weren't dressed like old world corpses. Instead they had mix and match fatigues, similar to Crafton's security forces, assorted weapons, and supplemental armor. They'd died here maybe a decade ago, not a year longer.

I was following a feeling, making a line for *something* I didn't understand. Behind my eyes this world was quiet, but the constant purr of my defenses being scrutinized lured in one specific direction. I realized, with bona fide delight, that my destination was The Wave Organ.

As my teacher had explained, after the earthquake and fire of 1906, all but a few graveyards had been removed from city limits, bodies relocated and the monuments demolished before being used as fill. Thousands of stones had been broken and deposited here, covered in sand, to form a small peninsula above the choppy surf. This peninsula truncated with a miniature, stone amphitheater; solely constructed from gravestones. Extruding downward, built inside, were PVC pipes that made their way into the surf, each at a different angle and height. The waves created echoes, in the amphitheater, resulting in random collection of long, subtle musical notes, reflecting watery reverberation.

Something waited for me, here, at The Wave Organ.

"Wait here." I didn't turn to Jennifer and Rizwan, but I didn't walk away immediately.

"And do *what?*" Jennifer asked.

"*Wait.* You're no good to me in a fight against Djinn," I paused, closing my eyes, "and I don't want either of you to get hurt. Just *wait* for me. If I don't return, run for the truck and get out of here. Doesn't matter where you go, just *leave* San Francisco."

"Something lives here. Doesn't it?" Jennifer said gingerly.

I nodded, then walked away, heading down to the bay.

The day was now overcast, chilly, and a biting wind from the bay cut through my jacket. Gone was the South Bay's warmth, replaced by a gray horizon and fermenting water. As I walked closer I could see silhouettes waiting for me, all the way out, standing on The Wave Organ itself.

One stood on a ledge of antique gravestones, a woman in hemmed skirts and a faded corset pulling her waist into an hourglass. Tall, with wide hips wrapped in heavy belts, she hunched over a bit and twisted her neck. She wore a wig made from deep red and dark gray fibers, pulled into long, thick dreadlocks, each one covered with bones. Where her eyes and cheeks ended, a black leather muzzle began, a salad of metal, chrome and rust, garnished with razors, and broken blades, extending out and down, arranged in an alloy smile.

She squinted at me. This was *not* Djinn "I speak for my mistress." The second woman, down in the sand, closer to where I stood, spoke. Her skin was darker, and her eyes narrow, *sad.* Her dark hair was pulled back and she wore a churlish dress that didn't flatter her. "I speak for The Dread Harvester."

"Who are you?" I asked the girl with sad eyes.

"I am the voice of The Dread Harvester." Her eyes closed and she dropped down to one knee. I glanced up at the bigger woman on the ledge and when the sad girl spoke again her voice had changed to an excoriated growl. *"You look good, Maggi."*

I took a step back. Could these two be the Ifrit? "You know me?"

"Maggi, you unrepentant cunt," The woman named *Dread Harvester,* jumped from her ledge, a five or six-foot drop. When she hit the ground, I saw her knee twist, slightly, and her eyes squint with pain. She shrugged it off, standing erect. *"You forgot me?"*

Maggi, you unrepentant cunt. I took another step back; my heart began to race and I felt my face flush. "Aubree?"

"Do not call me that!" The sad woman kneeling on the ground screamed at me. My defenses snapped and sparked, I could nearly taste her rage. *"That was his name for me. You didn't earn that when you were young, and you didn't earn that when you left me to die."*

So much of her face was obscured by the muzzle that I couldn't recognize her or tell her age. *"No!"* I answered, considering every trick a Djinni could play, "She *did* die when I left the Bay Area, she was in a coma! *In a hospital!"*

The Dread Harvester reached up, pulling off her wig, unpinning it, and tossing it to the sand. Long, red curls spilled out. It was partially gray now but I knew that hair, I could never *forget* that hair. *"You wouldn't recognize my face."* The sad girl spoke, spitting words out like sour candy. I didn't know what to say, I didn't know what to do. It never occurred to me that she would have survived the shelling, it never seemed possible.

"Aubriana," I used her proper name, *"Is that actually you? How did you survive?"*

Her surrogate voice laughed at me, *"I survived, hating you."*

If you wish to hunt us, you will suffer your past sins. It wasn't a threat, it wasn't a warning. The Ifrit didn't mean to subject me to introspective soul searching, no the Ifrit intended to lead me to Aubree, here in San Francisco. I would *suffer.*

I deployed my active barriers, above and beyond my static walls. Some were perceivable to the naked eye as flashing symbols, and dark red pulses. Others manifested as swirls of wind, churning dust at my feet and expanded in a hazy sphere around me.

"I don't want to do this." I spoke the words for *me* more than Aubriana.

The initial attack was blinding, dissolving against my barriers like waves. Followed by an audible crackling in the air as Aubree, *The Dread Harvester*, reached an arm out for me, fingers delicately playing a piano that didn't exist. I was forced to counter each attack, each cord of energy that hammered my defenses, spreading like a web through my barriers.

Twenty years of practiced *defensive* magic, penetrated like a prom queen in the football team's locker room. It took less than a minute. Before the Collapse, Aubree had been my *better*, my *teacher's* better. Today, she was still formidable.

Aubree charged me.

Feeling energy slap against my face, stings and burns at my ears and shoulders, I wasn't about to break and cower now. If she wanted to fight me, I'd oblige her, charging at her in return. As we drew near, I glimpsed the blade in her right hand, tucked along her forearm. She took a swift, high slash across my face. I deflected with my left forearm, and the edge sliced through fabric but slid harmlessly across my chain mail guard. Her return strike pierced my jacket above the left collarbone, almost sliding into my flesh. I twisted, using momentum to power my right arm into her chest. We grappled sideways, my fist hit her in the skull, quickly, two savage strikes on her temple, so I could disengage.

I reached for one of my butterfly knives, at the back of my pants. "You want to *fucking* dance, Aubree?" I shouted, steel balisong whipping out, no flashy moves, just speed and grace. I tossed it to my right palm, gripped the knife with white knuckles, and lunged for her. "Let's *fucking* dance!"

We were *both* skilled knife fighters. We'd both learned as young girls, for entirely different reasons. Aubree moved with talent and grace, dodging my first strike combo as I cut low. Her blade caught in on my jacket's chain mail, just above the wrist, for a second, and I used the leverage to yank her in close. My balisong swept in across her exposed inner elbow, slicing deep and severing muscle and tendon.

She was still in the fight, I hadn't hit a major artery, and I don't know that I *wanted to.*

She pulled back out of my grip. Our eyes met, and she lunged once more, throwing her wounded arm out as if to strike for me. I easily deflected her attack, but she had her free hand out, clamping onto my wrist, twisting, hyperextending the joint and causing me to lose my balisong.

Her hands were all over mine, digging into my elbows. She pulled me forward and I stumbled mid-stride before her forehead landed *in my face,* her skull slamming into mine. The impingement complete, she headbutted me twice more.

My blood was hot and I was dazed. I groped for her blade with both hands, fingers crawling along her wrist, elbow whipping at me. I brought a knee up high, into her gut. It did nothing to help, she was still in control of my balance, and in that moment, I reached for my second balisong, releasing her. My other hand, balled in a fist, landed two sharp strikes to her face above her razor maw. I felt the satisfying crunch as her nose broke, *finally* something forced her to lose balance. This time, as she stumbled, I kicked her again in the face, my boot shattering part of the muzzle and putting her into sand.

"*Stop!*" I was yelling, panting, blood hammering at my temples, "I don't want to hurt you."

Aubree pulled herself out the sand, back to me. The sad girl, Aubree's *voice,* who'd been so silent, burst out laughing, cackling madly.

When Aubree spun, she was lightning, moving so fast I could barely counter her strike. She'd retrieved *my balisong*, and now fought me, a blade in either fist. I couldn't counter her, she pushed me back and I took my eyes off her for a moment to glance at my footing. That was all she needed, and I felt the butterfly knife bite my face. I stumbled, my free hand grasping for *anything*, then slid into the pumping surf.

It took a half second, maybe a full second, before the pain hit, boiling oil simmering in my eye socket, scalding my nerves and eating away to the bone.

"Chinga su pinche puta madre!" I screamed. Aubree had just stabbed me in the eye. Kneeling in the water, drenched, I fell back on my posture with one hand fastened to my face, the other clawing at the air. *"Burn."*

Aubree's barriers burst into flame, licking the borders of an invisible orb around her. I was whispering words I didn't even understand, and I *didn't care to understand*, I let absolute rage overflow from my stomach, drowning my pain, cascading across the beach like a tidal current and pummeling her barriers *hard*, burning white hot.

I became faintly aware of a heat against my skin, on my forearms. I was so focused that I didn't realize what she was doing to *me*.

The cords of energy that had eaten into my barriers earlier had also wrapped around me, twisted up inside, running in my veins, my nerves, across my skin and clothes. The fire I was raining on her, she reflected into the metal I was wearing on my body. I had to disengage, my focus completely broken. If I hadn't been completely drenched in seawater, she'd have burned me alive. I tore my jacket off, trying to free myself, stumbling and falling again into the bay. My chainmail had burned hot enough to brand imprints into my forearms.

Before I could focus, Aubree was back, her full weight hitting me hard, one arm wrapping around my neck, pushing me down. I realized my second knife was *gone*, probably lost in the waves. I felt Aubree wrap my own lose hair around her hand, grappling my head to her palm.

Four times, in slow, methodical order, she brought her knee into my face, my own nose broken now, repayment for the savage blow I'd left her with moments ago.

I was addled, blinded, and disoriented. All I could do was reach for her, *some part of her,* and summon fire again. Just enough burning, just enough flame to get her off. If I stayed this close to the bigger woman, she'd very quickly crack my skull open.

I think I'd grabbed her thigh. I felt steam and heat hit my face, this close to her. It was exactly what I needed and she shoved me to the sand.

I crawled back, half rolling, half clawing at the beach around The Wave Organ, pulling myself back to my knees, one hand over my right eye. Rising, I withdrew my hands to see them covered in thick cruor and sand.

Blood was blood, and I could use anyone's to charge my magic. I squeezed my hand, absorbing the essence and channeled its energy. I thrust towards her, unleashing waves of kinetic energy that assaulted her defenses head on. This wasn't a single strike, or a *shove,* it was multiple impacts that looped back and cracked open her shields, assaulting from all sides. The force knocked her to the ground as she crawled from the ocean. I stepped forward as I continued to pour more into my attack. Her defenses were now collapsed, and I was thirsty for blood. I wanted to pay Aubree back for this pain.

"You fucking stabbed me in the fucking eye, you fucking bitch!" My words weren't angry enough, they weren't loud enough, my voice impotent to unleash the rage I felt. Raw emotion erupted out of my body swallowing Aubree in a hateful glow as flames licked skin, blistering her, igniting her clothes. The *only* reason she survived was because she was soaked, and I lost sight of her in a swarm of steam and smoke.

The quickest way to break a witch's focus was to break the witch. I was in so much pain now that my magic was sloppy, I wasn't paying attention, and I was making a lot of mistakes. Aubree was *on fire* and her focus wasn't broken. She remained dangerous.

Her tendrils of energy reached back towards me, following the connection between us, tying us together. Dark and sinewy, moving like snakes under my skin, coiling, then striking where I was weakest. She was siphoning off my attack and redirected it. That energy was in me now, spreading like cancer. I had never felt anything like this, I'd never *heard* of anything like this. My teacher had once told me, Aubree had experimented with necromancy. It was a sidelong comment, I'd barely paid attention. In all my years, I had never run across this kind of power, this kind of magic. I had no idea how to counter.

It entered my hands and crept up my arms, erupting through my skin, black with oozing pustules. I felt my bones ache and my muscles becoming unresponsive. I dropped to my knees, clutching at my chest, I couldn't *breathe*.

She was invading my internal organs with affliction, *shutting them down*.

When Aubree emerged from her own holocaust, I could smell burnt hair and skin, cotton and leather. She was a shamble of melted flesh and exposed bone, and possibly the most terrifying site I'd known my entire life. How she still stood, how she still worked *magic* was beyond what I could understand.

Her own knife was gone, but she still held my balisong, stumbling forward like a rabid animal. I had no more tricks left. I was gasping for air, and I felt death closing in, step by inescapable step. I assumed these were the last few seconds of my life.

Aubree slammed me into the ground with all her weight and I wrap my arms around her to control our fall. As ravaged as my hands were, she was in no better shape. I tussled with her, kicking, fighting, groping blindly until I had the knife. I swung out wildly and managed to break free of her hold, scrambling to my feet, fighting a bleak haze of blood loss and pain.

I had managed to cut her, just below the throat, under the broken muzzle. I looked at my left hand, holding my balisong. Her razors were protruding from my flesh.

Aubree was holding her throat, bleeding out. With no barriers left between us I could feel her panic as she realized what was happening to her.

When I came to San Francisco today, I never dreamed I'd be stabbed in the eye or that I would be forced to *murder my friend*. I had left her to die once, I had no desire to apologize for that sin by killing her. Now we were a wreck of meat and muscle, cut tendons and burned flesh.

There was no way to save her, not losing blood like that. I stumbled back towards her, gently. I was shaking, from pain or fear, I didn't know.

It didn't have to end this way, *none of this had to happen*.

"I'm sorry, Aubriana." My voice sounded like sand in a blender, I coughed and fell forward onto her prone body. My hand was resting on her chest, and her eyes locked on me. We watched each other and I could feel her chest rise and fall, hear ragged and caustic breathing through the leather mask. "*I'm sorry. I'm sorry I was a coward, twenty years ago, I'm sorry I left you to die.*"

It took me a moment, but I realized that the second woman was standing over me in her long black dress, watching me with her sad eyes. She made no move to strike me or attack.

"*Don't hurt this girl.*" The girl said, in Aubree's voice, "*She's my caretaker and student.*"

I turned back to Aubree and nodded. "If I could go back, I'd have *gone back. I was afraid Aubree, so fucking afraid.*"

"*I know. You were consumed with fear and pride. These are cardinal sins for anyone, but most especially a witch.*" The sad girl spoke clearly, no hint of Aubree's ruined body or cut throat, the words flowed distinctly.

"Alexander is a man grown now," I smiled, watching blood drip off my face, smacking at her muzzle, "You ought to see him. You'd be proud."

"*His father?*"

"Dead," I was heaving up a well of sorrow. It hurt more than the burns, cuts, or rotted flesh. "He died the first year, after we made it to Pennsylvania."

"*Everyone is dead now, but you Maggi,*" The girl standing over me, spoke, "*you must be so lonely.*"

"I am," I laughed now, "*fuck* this life, Aubriana."

If the Ifrit wanted to kill me, Aubree almost killed me. If the Ifrit wanted to cripple me, Aubree crippled me. And if the Ifrit wanted to dive into my chest, wrap their claws around my heart and rip out, *they had done that also.*

Watching Aubree's eyes, I felt when she passed, her body shutting down. She died in my arms, and I held her as close to me as I could, despite vomiting bile and blood on myself. If death did not come today, it would manifest soon.

Ultimately, Aubree had won. I had only beaten her through *random happenstance.* My knife had somehow clipped her throat, I'd struggled against her blindly, my victory strike was that I'd simply refused to give up.

"I don't believe in random happenstance," I whispered before I passed out from the pain.

Or the loss of blood. Or the exhaustion.

Or maybe, all three.

Act 3

MAGGI, IMMORTALIS

SAN FRANCISCO, CALIFORNIA.
OCTOBER 11ᵀᴴ, PRESENT.

My Maggi, my perfect Maggi, this is a gift for you.
The spider mother with a forgotten name whispered half-formed syllables and simmering vowels in my mind.

I was not sure exactly who I was. I was certain I had been Maggi Lopez, but I was drowning in the memories, sights, sounds, and pain of another. There was a crawling, hissing fear at the back of my neck, telling me that if I closed my eyes or laid down for rest, I would never wake again. I would be caught forever in a waking dream, comatose and trapped, in the hospital. I remembered the *smell* of an empty hospital and the *sound* of waves cracking at the Peninsula's northern tip. A boy's voice, reciting a sing-song rhyme, "Trespasser, trespasser, heed these words. Do not seek for her, for San Francisco is the home of The Dread Harvester."

I was eating a picnic lunch with a young woman who I did not recognize. We sat together in the Marin Headlands, tall, bright grasses billowing in a salty ocean breeze and the sun shining warm on my skin. The girl asked me if she could have a sandwich. Instead, I removed a hatchet from her picnic basket and chopped her legs off at the knee. Curiously, there was no blood, just skin ripping open and bone fragments shattering like broken china. I heard her screaming.

I willed myself to open my eyes, *my eyes*, not impressions of Aubree's dreams or nightmares; only my left eye complied. I was in a bed, I could feel the mattress under my back, and it was heaven. During the many weeks of sleeping in the truck, I'd yearned for this. The bed was a

175

four-post antique, carved from cherry wood and maintained lovingly despite a fine layer of dust. The pillows under my neck and head were firmer than I liked, perhaps stuffed with down, and they smelled of sweat and pus.

I could see a wall next to me, faded with age. Dingy paintings hung, smeared, visages of pastures or mansions in forgotten mountains. I turned slowly, favoring the right side of the room with my *left eye*.

Next to me, in a rocking chair, was the young woman from The Wave Organ. Our proximity allowed me to study the features of her face for the first time. She was a child, not yet twenty years old, with tan skin and sad, almond shaped eyes. I decided that she was probably Filipina. Her black hair draped across her face like a curtain, but she did not shy away from my eye contact.

"You haven't killed me." When I spoke, I sounded like a frog, my voice rough.

"My Mistress already killed you." Her voice was softer and deeper than when Aubree used her as a megaphone, with the hint of an accent teasing at the edge of her vowels.

"I feel very *alive*." My voice balanced better this time.

"That is because I'm easing your pain, Maggi." I glanced away from her eyes, down to her hands. She was still wearing the dour, morose dress. In her lap, she held one hand, palm up, while the opposite hand traced a pattern with her index finger. If I looked closely, I could see the soft, yellow glow of her magic.

I sighed. *"Another fucking witch.* Very few can do *that,"* I nodded towards her hands, "very few who command fire, or the power of death."

"My Mistress has said," the girl nodded to me slowly, never ceasing her hand gestures or taking her eyes off mine. "She said those who practice magic bend our world at their pleasure and the world bends back on them. Probability becomes skewed, and *random happenstance is* no longer so *random."*

I smiled, or tried to, my face felt *strange,* "What shall I call you, kid?"

"Aniceta." The girl replied, still with no emotion or change in her expression.

"Do you know who I am, Aniceta?" She tilted her head, breaking eye contact and looking over my body. I could feel an anxious rhythm rise in her energy. She was unsure how to answer.

"I know your name. I know that long ago, you left my Mistress to die. I know she hated you for that. I also know that she dreamed of your arrival."

"*Dreamed?*" I considering my own vivid dreams on the road west, my memories playing as manifest dramas where I was the star participant.

"I also know that you loved my Mistress. You didn't wish her death."

I wanted to reply. I opened my mouth, tried to speak, but nothing came out. "Maggi, my Mistress was dying. I was her student, her companion, and her caretaker. I had never seen her move so fast or so hard as she did with you. She suffered great pain, and walked with a cane."

"What happened to her face?" I asked softly, my voice almost completely returned.

"She was hurt in the Collapse," Aniceta's eyes closed, her voice remained steady, "an explosion during the shelling took her jaw, most of her teeth, burned her. I never saw anyone so badly hurt who kept breathing."

"Who kept fighting." I corrected. Aniceta nodded, and opened her eyes again. "That's why she couldn't use her own voice to speak. I'm in her bed, now, aren't I?" Again, Aniceta nodded.

I closed my eye, relaxing. More memories, *not my own*, flooded back. I looked through Aubree's eyes, perfectly calm when the third, and final, shell hit my front porch. I couldn't hear the ceramic tile and dishes shatter; the other explosions had deafened me. A quiet ballet of spinning shards, broken handles, and bent silverware. I watched the kitchen sink and all its contents as they were propelled upwards into my face, jaw, neckline, and chest. Aubree blacked out, then, and my vision of her past faded.

I didn't speak. Perhaps I fell asleep for a moment, perhaps no time at all passed. I opened my eye, when Aniceta spoke. "I've done all I can do, with your companion Rizwan. You will die soon without real medicine."

"I'll die, *regardless*." I sighed, remembering Aubree unleashing death across my body, feeling my organs slow and stop, the skin on my arms turning black. I looked down as best I could. There was a dark green blanket draped across me and outside of that blanket I could see my right arm wrapped to the elbow in beige, linen bandages, like a mummified corpse in an old monster movie.

"Yes, you will." The Djinn had taken me out of the game before the game was even started. They had never dreamt of allowing an arrogant, mortal witch hunt them. They had never considered the option of letting me and my forgotten primordial near them; instead they had laid the groundwork for me to suffer at the hands of my past sins. The Dread Harvester would render me impotent to fight them.

"*Fuck.*" It was really all I could imagine saying now. My victory against Aubree was bitter, and now the Black Dogs had free reign to act as they pleased, against me, *against my son.* Could Mayy protect him? My mind skipped across ideas, hope threatening to lick at my wounds and ease my passing from this world. Mayy was, without a doubt, *powerful.* Around her, *no one was* in control of their faculties. Perhaps even creatures made from smokeless fire might descend into a paranoid madness under her sway.

"Margaret could stop the Djinn, but she's too jealous of your son to save him. She will one day seek his throne for her own, seeing herself as your legitimate *daughter.*" Any haze that I had labored under until this point was lifted. My good eye focused on Aniceta and my mind swept out, clawing for her, pushing through her defenses; a mix of shock and horror filled my throat and spilled from my lips. As I broke her concentration, I also broke the magic she performed with her index finger and palm. Aniceta didn't need to force me away from her; as the pain flooded into my awareness, the agony my physical body suffered broke all focus needed for magic and kicked me to the curb, a stray dog, too weak to beg. "Don't distract me, Maggi."

Aniceta regained control of the pain, slowly hiding it behind layers of calm, hazy, numbness. That was all she was doing, concealing the discomfort. I wouldn't have dreamt of stopping her, and when I was finally in control of my thoughts and emotions, I asked her; "How do you know *any of that?*"

"My Mistress called me a 'cypher.'" Aniceta shrugged and the pattern she drew on her palm continued, much to my relief, "I can peer into a person's eyes, touch them, care for them, and I will know all of their secrets. All their lies, their secret loves. I knew The Harvester's name, I saw her childhood, her first kiss. I knew her better than she knew herself. Now, I know you."

I coughed, too tired and too unfocused to be angry, *"Fuck,* I just thought you were a nurse."

"That too." Aniceta smiled for the first time.

"Did Aubree teach you the three forms of magic?" Again, I coughed, instinctively moving to lift my hand, to cover my mouth. My arm didn't move at the elbow and when my shoulder rotated, it partially dragged my bandaged appendage across the blankets covering my chest.

"Magic can *divine a truth.* Magic can *obscure a truth."*

"Magic can *destroy."* I finished for her, looking at my arm. I attempted to move my fingers on either hand, but nothing happened. It didn't shock me as it should have, it felt so *normal.* No pain, no struggle, there was no effort. I simply couldn't move my fingers. "You're just obscuring the pain."

"Your fingers won't work again."

"Yeah." All I had to say was *yeah.* I bit down on my lower lip and felt my calm eroding and along with it went Aniceta's magic. If I focused too hard, became too emotional, if I broke out of the quiet place she helped me remain within, the physical discomfort came back. I stayed *aggravated* and a little *scared.* I wanted some of the haze in my mind to be burned off, I needed to think and consider.

"Your eye socket is infected. Your fingers, hands, and forearms have turned necrotic. My Mistress broke your nose, as well, but you're not in danger of that killing you," Aniceta's face was slowly beginning to relax. "You need a real doctor, you need the dead limbs amputated, and you need *antibiotics."*

I laughed at her, leaning my head back into the pillows. "Your Mistress was wise, kid, she taught me a lot too. But, while she hid in this city for twenty years, I was on the front lines of war." I smiled, closing my eyes, "I'm a *fucking battlewitch."*

Like so many puzzles I'd solved before, in the field, or with Lorne, there was a solution to be found here. Fire had always been my easiest gift, but another witch, like Vix, might feel most at home with *air.* Each of us had the potential to weaponize those talents, and although magic escaped rhyme or reason with how it affected us, the more powerful a witch, the more he or she could *learn.* Now, I found myself lying in the bed of a *very experienced witch,* all her hopes and dreams buried in these pillows I disliked. All of what she felt when she used her magic, when she looked beyond her four walls, listening at night, connected herself to pieces of the world through her nerves and veins.

Listening to, watching the emotions and thoughts of another witch play across your brain *and heart*, wallowing in everything that was once herself. It started off simply enough, illustrations scrawl across my vision, accompanied by smells and sounds. Before long, those sketches evolved into an oil painting, thick, dripping with reality. When Aubree knew fear, *I was her fear*. When Aubree was amused, *I was her laughter*. I wasn't merely a spectator watching the painting become more complex, I *was the very paint itself*. My colors mixed, darkening, or lightening as the scenes demanded. The odor of the canvas a ponderous idea in my nostrils; soon I was no longer sure who I was, or if I ever existed at all.

Aubree had once commanded *necromancy*. That word implied a degree of control over the dead, but that's not how Aubree would have worked. In death, there was a different kind of magic, a magic of deep centricity. As creatures moved across the Veil, they were unified by a common center of *rot and decay*. It wasn't merely entropy; it was the transitory state between an *ending and a beginning*.

I guessed that Aubree had survived the Collapse by controlling that transitory energy. She could have silenced her infections, kept her wounds from inflammation that way. This was no substitute for penicillin, of course, but it kept her alive for a long time. *No wonder you hurt so much, Aubriana*. Did I say that? Or did she say it to herself? The words were just abstract ideas drifting past, and I dismissed them, falling deeper into the world of The Dread Harvester.

I needed to learn her *necromancy*. Whether it took hours, days, or *weeks*, I would stay in the mind and dreams of a dead woman. I needed to halt the decay of my arms. I needed to command my fingers again, make them unwilling slaves. I still had two Djinn to kill.

———✳——

SAN FRANCISCO, CALIFORNIA.
OCTOBER 18TH, PRESENT.

Little in Aubree's apartment suggested who she'd once been. Her personal belongs were lost in the Collapse, and once she escaped abandoned San Francisco General, she'd simply taken possession of the city, reigning as The Dread Harvester. Aniceta explained, her health had allowed her few options, she could never have traveled. She could never have followed me east; she could never have hunted me down. Separated by two decades, the only way I would have met her again was by machinations of the Djinn.

"You can't be *serious*." Jennifer stood behind me as I faced out the front window of Aniceta's personal room, across from Aubree's. It allowed me to look down on the rusted and friable streets of Lower Haight. Aubree had located a beautiful two-story Victorian home that had long ago been converted into an apartment building, but that didn't detract from its elegance or the quiet pride of the neighborhood.

"Serious as a heart attack," I replied. It was hard to breathe. I no longer wore bandages across my nose, but the break forced me to mostly inhale or exhale from my mouth.

"Maggi, I saw your arms after the fight, they need to be amputated."

"Do they?" I turned away from the window and faced Jennifer. She was cleaned up more than she had been on the road; her hair wasn't greasy and she'd gotten enough sleep these last few weeks to cure the dark circles under her eyes.

"That's not possible." She pointed as I waved my bandaged hand

181

across my face, rolling my fingers. While I had lost a lot of my dexterity, my hands could grip a knife, a gun, or anything I wished.

"Your fingers were *black*; the flesh was falling away."

"My fingers are still black," I smiled at her. I was in pain, but I no longer needed Aniceta's obfuscation. A dull ache ran through my right eye socket and into my shoulders and upper arms where nerves still lived, my flesh caught in a state of suspended decay. Magic pulsed in my blood and bone marrow, acting much like the electrical rhythms that drove the heart to pump cruor through my veins. "I'm still dying of my injuries, just much slower than before."

"How much slower?" Jennifer pursed her lips and crossed her arms. I could see something on her face, an emotion I couldn't identify. She felt like fear and *sorrow*.

"A month, I think." I spoke softly, keenly aware now of what it was I spoke, "I'm not nearly as good at necromancy as The Dread Harvester was, but I learned all I could."

"You think you can hunt these Djinn down in a month?" She replied.

"You don't believe they exist." I grinned now, pushing past the subject of my own mortality. The weight of my own death hadn't fully settled in yet, and there were sadness's that I refused to share aloud. Aniceta knew, of course, she *knew everything*.

"I never saw the Ifrit, Maggi," Jennifer shook her head, "We followed you across the continent, through the desert and near the ocean. A thousand things you said would lead us to our enemy, and when we finally reached your Ifrit…" Jennifer's voice trailed off.

"It was just an old witch I'd betrayed in an old life."

"Yes." Jennifer whispered. I stepped closer to Jennifer, watching her out of my left eye alone. I reached for her with bandaged arms and fingers, but she stepped back. "You smell like death."

Much of what I had worn since Crafton was destroyed in the fight with Aubree. My armor, was gone, likewise my shemagh and other clothes. Though my fatigue trousers and boots had made it, Aniceta had helped pick through Aubree's clothes to find replacements. It had required some customization, Aubree was a larger woman than me. She wasn't just taller; her shoulders were wider, likewise her hips. Though, my bust was, and always had been, larger. The result was that I wore a sleeveless leather top lined with warm wool and a bustier style corset manufactured from black plate carriers. It wasn't as good as my previous protection, but Aubree and I had evolved in two very different worlds. She had favored aesthetic, while I favored protection.

"Jennifer," I squared away my shoulders and tilted my head back. I didn't feel that proud, but right at this second, I needed to be *The Bruja*. "For my entire life, these Djinn have haunted me. Made a chew toy out of me. When I pass, they will turn on *my son*, and *my son is* your General, *Captain Winslow*."

"Yes, sir." Jennifer stiffened. It was the first time in a long time that she'd been so formal. I reached once more for her arm, but she stepped back a second time. "There's one condition."

"Oh?" I answered.

"Aniceta says there's a city-state east of us, House Owens, with a bounty on The Harvester's head. We need to re-provision, re-fuel, and re-supply if you want to chase your Djinn further. They'll help us, with proof of The Harvester's death."

I nodded to her, "Of course. *Of course*, pack up the gear."

Jennifer saluted me and left. Her attitude was cold, her exterior walled against me. Not real walls, nothing I couldn't push through, but it would gain nothing. I already knew how she felt; I knew I'd broken our agreement to stay informal and taken away her illusion of control. Jennifer's only sin was believing that she had an equal voice with *me*.

Aniceta returned a few minutes later, still wearing her ugly, dour dress and studying me like a hawk where I stood. *"Yes?"* I smiled at her. It wasn't hard to keep my face stoic, half buried in bandages; smiling and glowering were still my two most expressive emotions.

"The Captain captivates you."

"Oh, for fucksake," I went to place my palm across my eyes, a mix of frustration and embarrassment in my words. Much to my horror, my hands *stank like death*. "Just because you know someone's secrets doesn't you should *discuss it with them*."

"She's not attracted to women." Aniceta, blinked seriously at me.

"I know." I'm repulsed by myself briefly, so I turn away from Aniceta and seat myself at the foot of her bed, "I knew that the moment I met her and got lost in her eyes."

"She sees you as her superior, as a *friend*. She will never see you the way that you see her."

"*Oh, my fucking gods, Aniceta.*" I hissed at the girl, "If I were to stab you in the gut, *wiggle at the knife*, how good of a time would that be?"

"It wouldn't." Aniceta's brows furrowed and she seemed confused.

"*Look,*" I sighed, regaining my composure, "I've spent my entire life keeping it a secret. Some *secrets are* best kept in the dark, where an old, one-eyed witch can die *peacefully.*"

"I'm sorry." Aniceta was apologizing to me and she meant every word, "I've been here many years. This is all new to me."

I felt guilty for snapping at her. "We can call you 'bubble girl.' Look, Aniceta, come with us. You'll be safe and you'll learn more than Aubree could teach."

"Aubree was wise," her voice faltered, eyes darting around me for a second, hesitant to speak, "but a poor teacher."

I laughed, softly, just a chuckle, "I know. My son's father said the same."

"Your son." Aniceta slowly stepped towards me, then seated herself on the bed to my left.

"Alexander," I nodded.

"I've never met him, but I'd like to. I've watched him in your memories. I can't forget him, the way he *smiles*, the way he walks, his absolute confidence."

I turned to study her. She was a pretty girl, despite the awful clothes and sad eyes. In her face, the color of her skin, the dusting of soft hair at her lips and long lashes I saw a world I'd grown up in, a world before the Collapse. It hit me with a tugging sense of nostalgia. It also occurred to me, as her cheeks flushed red a little, that she had found herself potentially attracted to someone for the first time. The fact that she was potentially attracted to *my son* left me as confused and uncomfortable as I'd been discussing *my own attractions*.

"I'm too Mexican for this *shit*, kid." I sighed, looking away, back at her barren walls.

"What does that mean?"

"It *means*," I stood, proceeding to walk out of Aniceta's room, "that you should come with us. I don't know where that'll lead you, but there's *a big fucking world* out there, if you want."

"*Alright.*" I heard her answer behind me, and I was uncertain if she meant that as an acknowledgment that *yes*, she'd come with us, or *yes*, she understood me.

"But get rid of that *ugly fucking dress*, kid. You're not Mormon."

I turned away and headed downstairs to find Jennifer and Rizwan.

———※———

STOCKTON, CALIFORNIA. OCTOBER 19ᵀᴴ, PRESENT.

As we left San Francisco, I wondered what kind of place it would become in the absence of my dead friend. She'd created a no-man's land for herself to rest peacefully, but that wasn't a city that could stay empty. Trade had only increased every year since the Collapse, and the world had happily marched forward in the ashes. I imagined that San Francisco would be a radiant jewel again one day, queen of the Bay Area, sovereign of all she surveyed. I wished, deeply at that moment that I could walk those streets again in a hundred years.

As we traveled back south again, we ventured through the soup of Alviso, wretched smelling swamps and mud, near the southern tip of the Bay, a place that smelled distinctly of sewage. We managed to find a road eastward across Mount Hamilton; a similar route to the one that my teacher and I had taken the night we fled the Bay Area. Now, of course, nothing remained familiar; the roads were overgrown and my memories were a distant, sooty haze of sorrow and terror.

Once we arrived in the Central Valley, we reached *House Owens*. This was not a city-state of the east coast, this was a fledgling empire like my Antecedent States. The borders were guarded with a loose series of watchtowers running north to south. Burgeoning agriculture spilled forth across the flat landscape as far as the eye could see. The deeper we drove, the more alive the land seemed: developing townships, micro-farms, and a web of trade that visibly layered itself onto the region. Here we were strangers in a strange land. Aniceta only knew this place by the memories she had gleaned from those unfortunate souls The

Dread Harvester had murdered. Jennifer and Rizwan could extrapolate theories based on what they understood of land and infrastructure; they could draw comparisons to our home and wonder how this place had grown over the last two decades.

The drive into Stockton herself was like nothing I imagined. As a young woman, I'd visited this place, driven through more than once, and even stayed a day or two. It was a maudlin metropolitan, hot and bleak on even its best day. No one wanted to visit Stockton, it was the kind of place you moved away from, to take English classes in the Bay Area.

Now, twenty years past the fall of civilization, it was a gleaming walled city, bright with an infinite variety of *paintings*. The walls that faced out to the farms and homes beyond were covered in *artwork*. Some of it showed a young woman, beautiful with brown hair and eyes, covered in jewelry, watching out across the land proudly. Words and characters standing twenty feet all announced her as *Lady Aurora Owens*, and the *Heart of House Owens*. Other artwork was sweeping epics of armies marching across plains or endless farmland.

It wasn't merely the city walls. All the old power lines, now devoid of their wires and cable, flew brightly dyed fabrics and textiles, waving in the wind. Some regions were marked in flowing red and orange hues, while others were cast in green or blue.

The interior of Stockton was a bustling madhouse that made Crafton look like a dull, rural, cattle-town. The flow of human traffic was a vibrating rhythm that painted scenes across my mind as colorful as those on the walls outside. This place wasn't a broken, fractured monument of the past, and it wasn't a struggling island either. In the hearts and minds of these people, merchants and laborers alike, I found a delicious new sort of idealism, a strange hybrid glow that was revolving around a *magic-ridden* and post-Collapse world.

This place didn't fear magic. It revered it.

I saw things on these streets, intersecting with the daily mechanics of man that I'd only heard whispered in books. Strange creatures I'd not ever known before, scurried in the gutters, unfettered wild things, keeping company with the rats, a mechanized task force bent on maintaining the cobble streets and sidewalks, keeping *horse shit and* sewage out of the thoroughfares. I'd heard tell of things *like* this, but not the same, in Crafton and a few other large cities. I could only assume this was yet another side effect of the Veil's descent.

While I'd been lost in a dark place, drowning in my own regret, since we left San Francisco, this world, House Owens and her shining capitol, brightened my spirits above and beyond what I imagined possible. If I had less than a month left to live, I would call myself lucky beyond description to have seen the mortar and stone of the new world rising, strong.

The four us were broke, hungry, and tired. Rizwan had broken his razor in San Francisco and now suffered a patchy, dark beard that threatened to obscure his face. Jennifer had lost weight from rationing our food; her face gaunt and drawn. Aniceta, who'd managed to produce an outfit slightly *less awful than* her *Mormon modesty gown* looked like a scared cat, eyes bouncing off her skull, mouth agape, nearly panting. I attempted to calm her as best as I could. This was a panic of her own design. She wasn't using the barriers, instead she was trying to *see it, hear it, and touch it all.*

Despite the heat here, I'd adorned myself in a black cloak from Aubree's closet, along with a collection of antique apparel and hand-made designs that hearkened back to subcultures from decades prior. Camouflage hadn't been in Aubree's vocabulary and someone had failed to tell her that *desert tan was* the new *black.* Regardless of my amusement, the cloak covered my face and arms effectively. Even in a place as richly rooted in magic as this, I wore a mutilated face and bandaged arms cast in shades of rot and dried blood. If all that was too much, my remaining eye of liquid midnight painted me as something unlike anyone else here.

You are unlike anyone alive.

The spider mother purred in my mind, responding to my own internal narrative, a peanut gallery unbidden by myself, a creature I had slowly begun to refer to as *the crazy cat lady of primordials.* The spider mother herself had never responded to *that.*

Within the center of Stockton was a former college, now a walled capitol campus surrounded with fortifications and commercial structures that had been converted into military motor pools and barracks. By now we'd been forced to leave the truck behind, parked in a merchant structure and guarded for a small toll. On foot, we'd crossed perhaps a mile of city, and in the central valley heat we baked. By the time we neared the former Delta College, fewer and fewer civilians were visibly doing their business. I chose two gate guards and proceeded forward. The walls surrounding the gate were a mix of polished aluminum and brick, sparsely decorated in trees and more vast murals of Lady Owens and the House Owens military. Near that gate was a tiny lodging, large enough for one person, occupied by a middle-age man with a sprinkling of hair across his bald skull and a brow full of sweat droplets. When he looked up at me, his dull eyes didn't register surprise, rather he merely recited a rote script, devoid of any passion.

"Entrance to the capitol is by appointment only. Do you have an appointment?"

"No," I pulled the hood on my cloak back. My hair was tied back in a loose braid and a slight breeze rustled over the back of my neck, providing instant relief. "I'm here to collect on a bounty."

"We don't handle bounties at the *capitol*."

"Not even for The Dread Harvester?" I smirked. The bald mad suddenly paid attention to me; life flashing through his eyes that was quickly followed by terror. He saw my face, lingering too long on my good eye; then I felt his heartrate increase. There was no need to be a student of magic to know that I'm *a witch*.

"Show me." He swallowed hard.

I obliged him, and, why wouldn't I? There was nothing to be gained by playing games. I pulled Aubree's muzzle from my cloak, two sets of leather buckles fell loose and the grin of broken blades smiled at the guard. How well was that muzzle known for a simple man to have recognized it?

I already knew the answer. *Someone else stepped* into the guardhouse; they'd watched behind his eyes, frittering about, hoping I wouldn't see them. It was another witch, male or female I couldn't tell, but I expected it.

"Hello." My smile widened, considering the guard's eyes, bright now.

"*Who are you?*" His voice hissed at me.

"Maggi Lopez, *The Bruja*." I gestured to Jennifer, Rizwan, and

Aniceta, "These are my travel companions. I seek no quarrel with House Owens, only to trade in a bounty."

The guard's face jerked, the man who'd been here earlier was fighting to take his body back. I could feel his confusion spill up from the background where he'd been forced by the other witch before being stifled a second later. I disliked *that*, because it was rank with slavery. This was a foreign land however; their ways weren't likely to be shared with me.

"What do you desire for this bounty?" The witch, wearing another man's face, looked at the muzzle and I could feel eyes on the accessory, devouring it, authenticating it, searching for traces that Aubree had left behind.

"*Re-provision, re-fuel, and re-supply,*" I repeated what Jennifer wanted, the conditions by which she had agreed to continue my hunt for the Djinn

The bald man stared at me with a focused expression he'd likely never made of his own volition. "Lady Owens wishes an audience with you."

The guard collapsed like a marionette, stumbled forward, head first into my breasts. I didn't have the dexterity I once commanded, but I could wrap my fingers around his arms, pull him upright, and keep him from hitting the pavement.

Rizwan helped me settle the man back into his little hut, then looked at me, behind dark eyes and patchy beard; "These people lack *compassion.*"

"No," I shook my head, glancing from Rizwan, to Jennifer, "That witch lacked compassion. I was meant to taste a cured wine, all I found was *arrogance.*"

We waited there at the gate, in the heat, until a dozen or so soldiers approached us. Their rifles were worn back on shoulders. They looked *relaxed*, but bubbled in my mind with fear, trepidation, and woe. Although they found me a bit frightening, something else shook them, something out of sight, out of mind, the presence of *their masters*.

They asked politely to take my gun from Jennifer and I agreed, but only after they promised to return it once we left the capitol palace. They struggled, awkwardly, attempting to balance a real need to keep security, but also generate no offense. As they searched the other three, I offered myself up, and they eyed one another, grimacing, then refused.

The campus was well kept and had obviously been gardened,

maintained, and watered in this heat. The interior of the capitol itself had been escalated beyond any academic roots it may have once held. The opulence was not hidden; House Owens had every intention of showing off their wealth to visitors.

The further we were escorted, up stairwells and down halls, the more I became aware that this place was spun in a complex web of subtle and sophisticated magic. I found myself impressed with how well it interconnected, security bindings, wards to keep secrets *a secret*, and the buzzing glamours that drew breaths and starts from marble pillars and floors. They were marvelous, certainly, but not that marvelous. This wasn't a single witch; this was a concerted effort by *many*. House Owens was almost certainly an aristocracy made up magic users of no small talent.

We stopped by two double doors not originally a part of this structure, hand carved wood enameled in sea-foam green and gold, latched by a huge bronze chain that served no purpose other than to inspire awe.

"No." One of the guards, a slim man with a triangular face, held a hand for Jennifer, Rizwan, and Aniceta. "We'll take you to a parlor. Her Lady Owens commands you dine at our pleasure, but you *are not welcome* for a private audience."

I looked over the slim man before wrapping my mind around him and I felt the tethers at his skull. He'd been taking orders this entire time and those orders had been quietly hidden in the background noise, the echo of footfalls, of breathing, the rattle of *swamp coolers and air conditioning*. It was clever and brought a smile to my face.

"Maggi?" Jennifer looked at me, lips thin, concerned, even a little worried.

"Go with them," I favored each of my companions with a look, exercising a little of my own glamours to inspire sincerity above and beyond what I felt. "They're not lying."

"Ma'am," The slim soldier favored me a stiff salute, old world military, the type I enjoyed back home in the Antecedent States, "Lady Owens extends full amnesty and safety to you and your companions while in her capitol."

I nodded to the slim man and removed my cloak, untying it at my throat before handing it back to Aniceta. My hair was pulled back in a loose braid, my clothes were filthy and my bandaged arms were a *horror show*, but this Lady Owens had extended me the respect of a noble. The respect I was accorded by my own little empire. I would greet her as another *Lady*, regardless of the ruin I had become.

"Present me," I nodded to the slim man, "I am Lady Lopez, *The Bruja*, battlewitch of the Antecedent States." I presented a grubby hand wrapped in filthy bandages.

"*Yes*, Lady." He accepted my hand, holding it at chest level a foot between us, and stomped his right foot twice on the floor. The *crack-crack* echoed in the hall and two of his other soldiers stepped forward and pulled open the immaculately decorated double door.

The slim man and I walked in, a half-dozen paces. The room was grand with high ceilings, artificially humid air, and vaulted windows allowing vast amounts of natural light in. This room was no mere post-civilization conversion; this was the labor of craftsmen, carpenters, metalworkers, and electricians. This was the throne room of an Empire. Walls were arrayed with artwork from *centuries past*: bronze sculptures and stone carvings. The black carpet was *so soft, so inviting that* I could have fallen to my knees then, falling asleep in its thick folds. The air smelled of bold incense, crisp flavors of perfume, and exotic spices I'd not known in twenty years.

"I present, Her Lady Lopez, *The Bruja*, battlewitch of the Antecedent States."

I released the slim man's hand, stepping forward. In the center of the room was a circular depression arrayed with dark red, wooden tables. Opposite from where I stood were two people. One, seated on a throne, was the brown-haired woman from the murals that adorned Stockton. She wore red silks, linens, and cottons draped across her arms and shoulders. Jewelry coated her neck like a thick, glistening slab of moss. Her features were older than I expected, we were likely the same age, and gray hair now peppered those earthen locks underneath a vertically spun crown of gold and silver. *Lady Owens.*

The second person, a man, sat across from her. His hair was short, neat, and nearly all silver. He had our age beat by perhaps a decade, lines creasing and folding around his dark green eyes mercilessly. He wore similar opulence, red and white robes, but no jewelry or crowns adorned him. He sat far enough from Lady Owens as not to be confused with anyone of *real importance*, but close enough to express his status above others.

"Slayer of *The Dread Harvester*." I released Aubree's muzzle from my belt and tossed it to the carpet in the center of the room. Lady Owens offered no expression, except a nod that told her male companion to heed her and fetch the leather collection of broken blades. He stood and did as he was bid, returning the mask to his queen.

He then turned and, with stiff accent, growled to the slim man next to me. "Thank you. You'll not be needed further." The slim man saluted before departing.

"*Come here.*" When Lady Owens spoke, her voice was augmented by a reverberation that I'd never heard before. I wasn't sure if it was a glamour or a habit, but I doubted she intended to do it; there was no purpose in *intimidating another witch.*

As I approached the depression and stepped down into the pit she occupied, I heard the big double doors slam shut behind me. Lady Owens raised a hand for me to stop.

"You stand before her Lady Owens, Queen and Protector, *The Sanguinary*."

"*The Sanguinary?*" I smiled, looking sidelong at the silver haired man.

"It means, *bloody*." He smirked at me.

"Thanks, *Captain Bootlicker*," I returned his smirk.

"*Behave*," Lady Owens, responded, "This is Lord Cuttersark, he is administrator of The Orders."

"The Orders," Cuttersark, replied, his voice just as condescending as it was a moment ago, "Is the noble regulatory of magic users, within House Owens. We believe that only those who enjoy *the gifts of the Veil are* fit to wrangle power."

"Oh, *you're a witch?*" I was careful to keep my eyes on him, not to show Owens any disrespect, "I could barely smell magic on you."

Cuttersark balked, *visibly rattled*, he stepped back a quarter inch, and the comedy of his body language is so cliché that I burst out in a giggle. "A wastelander should show more respect. Males can absolutely be witches as well."

"Oh, I know that," I attempted to cease my laughter, it was genuine and not at all appropriate for a verbal duel with *lord admiral fancy pants.*

"My teacher was also male. You're much more arrogant than him, and I'd bet not nearly so talented." I winked.

"*Enough.*" Lady Owen's voice reverberated across the room, "*Cuttersark, you'd do well to notice that our guest carries enough power as to command her own rotten limbs with necromancy.*" Cuttersark said nothing in reply, rather he stepped back another few inches from me.

"Lady Owens," I nodded to the bejeweled women, "I'm sorry that I come before you in rags, tired from the road, and wounded. The Antecedent States are distant lands." I had never been a sophisticate, but for short periods of time I could play the role as well as was required.

"*Lady Lopez,*" Owens smiled at me, showing me a sincere grin, "*It is I who should apologize for the poor manners of my subjects. They are foolish and set in their ways.*" Owens extended her right hand, covered in thick awkward rings. She snapped her fingers to Cuttersark, gesturing him out. I sneered at Cuttersark's back as he exited the grand visiting room, dismissed in a degree of disgrace. I didn't regret this; his behavior was foolish, no matter what level of rank he commanded in House Owens.

Owens reached up and clawed at her throat, growling a brief cough. "Come, sit next to me Maggi." The reverberation in her voice was gone, the stiffness, the certainty of the words; Lady Owens spoke to me in her real voice. I approached her slowly, taking care to sit on the carpeted steps near her, but not too close.

"What shall I call you?" I asked her softly.

"Ro, just call me Ro."

"Alright, *Ro.*" I folded my hands on my knees, continuing to move slowly, and spoke quietly. Aurora Owens was displaying numerous vulnerabilities to me and I was unsure how easily she would startle in that state.

"I made them call me *The Sanguinary*, you know," She smiled at me and I got a good look at the lines on her face. She was a few years younger than me, or maybe a few older. "After I came back from San Francisco they called me Aurora the Bloody, because I was covered in blood. *My own blood.*"

"The Harvester?" I inquired with care.

"Oh, yes." She nodded, eyes falling away from me and across her black carpet, "This was over a decade ago. I used to lead my soldiers into battle, back then. We entered the city, and that beast set forth on us. She massacred my team, and then came for me. She was a mad woman, dancing across the pavement as she spoke through the *lips of my dead soldiers*. She let me escape, but promised I would pay a price. She ate away at the marrow of my knees, and bones, detaching ligaments, and unhinging joints."

"You can't walk?" I was careful when I asked, then I glanced to the forearm crutches next to Aurora Owens, as she pointed. They were chrome, customized just for her, elegant, and lost in the sparking nobility that she projected.

"I can walk with *those*. I'll never run or jump. I'll never lead my troops into war." Owens smiled, sadly, and then locked her eyes back on mine. "The Harvester crippled me as a lesson that only she understood, and made me crawl home for *giggles*. Do you know what a person looks like after they drag themselves, face first, out of San Francisco?"

"I'd rather not imagine." I wasn't lying.

"Very bloody. Hence, Aurora the Bloody. I've fantasized about going back to San Francisco for over a decade and making that *cunt eat her own leather mask*." For the first time since I entered, I saw a carnality in Owens. She bared her teeth I could almost see loathing pour out of her mouth, a fountain caught in summer, beautiful and stone cold.

"I didn't make her eat that leather mask, but I did cut her throat." I closed my eyes and decided to be honest. Aurora Owens had lowered her voice of authority with me and met me as a peer. I found a connection in her eyes that I had not known in anyone since my teacher's death. She was another *witch like me*. "The thing you knew as The Dread Harvester was once a friend, a woman I cared for and *loved*. I abandoned her during the first days of the Collapse."

"Oh, *Maggi*. Come here." Owens waved me towards her. I moved a little more comfortably, until I was seated directly next to her. Owens reached out for my bandaged left hand, and though I could no longer feel her fingers pressed against mine with my own flesh, the energy from her was soothing, *calm*, something like a mother's kindness. "We both did things we regret, during the Collapse. Maybe you were wrong, and maybe you're a monster to abandon your friend, but these things are past now. She's dead, and you're *not. Not yet.*"

"I know," I felt one tear fall from my eye, then another. I wanted to wipe it away, but I didn't want my necrotic limbs anywhere near my face.

"You're dying Maggi. Your hands are putrid and you're blind in one eye. Are you halting the spread of infection? Decay? *Impressive.*"

"I'm not nearly as good at necromancy as The Harvester was. I figure I'll be dead in two weeks, bedridden in half that time."

"You smell like a corpse, Maggi," Owens smiled, "but you taste like a mother. Tell me of your children, a boy and girl?"

"Yes," I returned her smile, feeling oddly thrilled to gloat of my progeny, "the boy is my blood, the son of my teacher and me. His name is Alexander. He'll one-day command the Antecedent States."

"*Alexander,*" Owens nodded, looking off for a moment, "That name sounds familiar, like a man I know I'll meet one day. *Alexander of the East.*"

"The girl," I pretended not to hear her, not to see her eyes as they glazed over with dreams of distant visions, "is adopted, my student, a witch like me. Her name is Margaret."

"But they call her *Mayy,* don't they?" Owens closed her eyes and reached for my second hand. "You want to protect your children, don't you Maggi? My children, *my foolish children know* nothing of the nightmares I kept at bay, for their sake."

A connection had formed between us over the conversation. A connection that was implicitly born from our shared past and our shared magic. I wondered how much I had in common with Aurora? She smelled a little like burnt coal and cinders this close, a heat radiated off her face. Was she a fire eater, like me? Had she loved a man who died too early? Had she raised her children behind a curtain of sorrow?

"I have almost no time to hunt my quarry," I said finally, "two Djinn, Ifrit, stalk me. They've stalked me since I was a child, haunted my dreams, and led me to your Harvester so she'd *kill me.* I know as fact that they will hunt my son, my daughter, after I die. They tricked the Federals, they enslave their own kind, and command old world technology. They are smokeless fire and they are made of malice I cannot begin to understand."

"*Can you kill them?*" Aurora raised her right hand from my bandages and pressed her fingertips into the center of my chest.

"*Yes.*" I replied.

"You can kill them." Her voice was a whisper, dripping with incredulous awe and a hint of fear as her fingers were withdrawn. "Something *old* is living, in your center, Maggi."

"*Yes.*" I replied again.

"Something *old*, and powerful, like the gods who *our gods* once worshiped."

"*Yes.*" I replied once more. Aurora Owens studied me. There were secrets between us, she can't swim in my mind like Aniceta, but we had a clear understanding now that superseded anything I'd ever known with another. Our tether lacked the affection and desire of my teacher, it lacked the adoration of Mayy, or the burning love for my son, but it was a connection still and none cheaper for our lack of familiarity.

"Maggi Lopez, I owe you a debt of gratitude, for granting an old woman her vengeance. I know these Ifrit you stalk, my House has done business with them recently, and I know where they sleep. I will resupply your friends, as you asked. But for you, *old witch*, I will take you in the wings of my House. We will clean your wounds and armor you for one final battle. I will personally go with you. I will escort the noble Lady Lopez to her demise. I will make sure my scribes write epics in your name, such that you are never forgotten."

STOCKTON, CALIFORNIA. OCTOBER 20TH, PRESENT.

In addition to being a deeply arrogant witch, Lord Jeremy Cuttersark was also Doctor Cuttersark, an actual medical doctor from before the Collapse.

"I have no idea where you learned to do this," Cuttersark gestured to my bare arms. Gone were his opulent robes, replaced with light gray scrubs, a white apron, and rubber gloves. Narrow glasses framed his eyes, which he hadn't worn when we met. Those same green eyes weren't nearly as intense, either. "But, this will kill you, Lady Lopez."

"Maggi, please." I smiled slightly and looked down at my arms. They were *disgusting*, Aubree's parting gift to me. The flesh that had once been covered in colorfully faded ink was now puckered, black, twisted, and oozing either blood or pus. Although Cuttersark tried to clean them, the smell was repugnant. My teacher and I had once spent hours hiding in a meat locker, on our trip to the east coast, a meat locker with no power. This was a similar smell, only I couldn't walk outside and breathe fresh air and it was me who was rotting.

Cuttersark didn't cease looking at my arms and hands, "I've never seen necromancy used with such little restraint."

I chuckled now, "The Harvester really hated me."

"If I amputated your arms *now*, you might perhaps still survive this. By rights you should already be dead, but I know what power you use to slow the decay." Cuttersark crossed his hands and swallowed hard. For all the arrogance, he showed me on our first meeting, he now spoke to me with humility. "But you don't wish to survive. Do you?"

I shook my head slowly, keeping my smile. "I have two Ifrit to kill, before I'm done with this life." I remembered Aubree's words and the sadness that licked at my wounds was a tangible thing, like a puppy, greeting me. *Everyone is dead now, but you Maggi, you must be so lonely.*

"I rarely apologize, for anything, Lady Lopez. I will apologize for misjudging you so thoroughly the day we met." Cuttersark turned away from me to wash his hands *again*, and it was not lost on me that he can't offer redress while maintaining eye contact. "You are a singular witch, unlike any I've known, unlike myself, or even Lady Owens."

"I get that you Owens types love the titles, but I'm sitting in my bra, in a cold examination room. Just call me *Maggi*, please." I sighed, the apology only serving to raise my ire.

"This is just as much a time to call you *Lady*, as in the court of House Owens," Cuttersark turned away from the sink, drying his hands aggressively. "We are civilized men and women; we are superior to others, and must act accordingly in our nobility."

"*Jacking each other off isn't* 'noble,' *Doc*, it's arrogant. Arrogance is a good way to lose various limbs," I slowly raised my left arm, focusing my control over the dead tissue and bones, wrapping my fingers closed and pointing at my empty socket, "or an *eye*."

"As you please," Cuttersark shrugged, clenching his jaw a few times, "*Maggi*."

"Why do you think we're so *superior*, anyway?" I licked my lips, genuinely curious about what Cuttersark believed or even why he believed it. The idea that witches were better than others had never occurred to me or anyone else in the Antecedent States. We all fought, and we all fought in the ways we were skilled. Snipers, engineers, and magic users.

"It's simple," Cuttersark moved toward the metal table near me, picking up the glass eye I'd found in Santa Cruz and cleaning it. "Before the Collapse, some people dug ditches, and some studied academia. Some worked in consumer stores stocking shelves, and others, *like me*, labored in an ER, saving lives, solving the vast puzzles of a human body. What really separated us? Our intellect, our minds, a biological commodity based on genetic code. Some of us are just born superior to others."

"*Huh*," I watched as Cuttersark held the glass eye up towards the bright light to examine.

"It's simple, after that, really. The genetically superior have a duty to serve those who are inferior; they have a responsibility to help those weaker, slower, less intelligent. This development, *magic*, those of us who can use it, it's no happy accident."

"*Huh*," I said a second time, as I was even more curious what he would say next. "How do you figure it can be genetic? My teacher was a powerful witch, like me, and our son doesn't share the gift."

"Heterogeneous *Inheritance*," Cuttersark approached me, holding the glass eye, "You know your eye socket will heal quicker if I don't install this prosthetic now."

"My gut says I'll need it." I responded to him, bracing myself by placing my arms behind me and leaning away from him.

"It feels, *strange*, it feels like, I want to *wear it*." Cuttersark studied the misshapen thing.

"I've heard that before," I remembered what Jennifer said, "so *shove it in*, Doc."

Cuttersark sighed quietly then focused on my face. I felt his hands around my face, cool from the tap water, smelling strongly of disinfectants, pressing open my eye by pulling at the skin and pinching my brow, "Heterogeneous *Inheritance tells* us that traits, though likely, are not guaranteed. A mother and father with *brown eyes have* a twenty-five percent chance of producing a child with *blue eyes*. Magic hasn't existed long enough for us to learn the exact genetic likelihood of producing an heir with strong abilities." With that, I felt Cuttersark shove the prosthetic in. It felt cold, irritable, and strange in the wound where my own eyeball had once existed. As he pulled back I blinked several times, both eyes watering. "How does that feel?"

"*Shit*." I answered, looking up from the black and white tile of the examine room to focus my good eye on Cuttersark. I didn't know what I had expected, but nothing changed in my field of view as I used the eye. "It feels like *shit*."

"I'm sure, it'll probably itch too. Don't touch it with your hands."

"My rotten meat hands? I didn't plan to." I laughed, wrenching my jaw side to side and exhaling sharply as I came to terms with the awkward sensation.

"I don't know why your son can't practice magic, or connect to the world around him. Although, I'd wager a guess that it's based on his gender," Cuttersark turned to wash his hands again and tears blurred my good eye. "For some reason, males suffer a greatly reduced likelihood of commanding magic, although, it's not impossible. It's a variable we just don't understand yet."

"I wonder, Doc," I inhaled sharply, as the tears were now making my nose run, "Is that the kind of thing The Orders will research in depth, one day?"

"Of course," Cuttersark laughed, facing the sink, "The Orders have several major directives as an organization. Understanding the genetic likelihood of producing talented witches being one of them."

Cuttersark's words were so confident, so *friendly*, that I almost forgot what he was really saying. I considered arguing with him, however, I wondered briefly if he wasn't right. This was a new world we enjoyed, a world where hobgoblins cleaned the streets of Stockton, a world where we hunted Ifrit, where witches rode with armies, and people like Aniceta could act as a walking cypher able to unlock any secret at a glance. Perhaps we did need to understand how magic evolved in our blood, and control it even more effectively in the fullness of time.

"That doesn't sound like any future I want to be part of," I finally replied, as my tearing subsided. Cuttersark was collecting the thin, black leather strips that sat rolled up and coiled next to me on a rolling steel table. These were wrappings to protect my hands and forearms for the fight that was to come, less flammable than linen bandages, more durable. "So, you want to catalog, document, and alphabetize? That seems like you're binding magic, mechanizing it, taking away the wildness of it."

"Of course, we are, Maggi," Cuttersark smiled, as he unrolled some of the leather to wrap on my fingers and hands, the lines at his mouth creased, and I saw the intensity from our first meeting spread across his face, "We can't fully control magic, so long as it's wild."

"Maybe magic shouldn't be 'fully controlled.'" I shook my head, watching him take my right hand and begin his work. I couldn't feel the wrapping, I could only watch it.

"Nonsense. You say you hunt these Djinn for the health and happiness of your son? Imagine a world where your son was never at risk from such things."

I nodded, watching Cuttersark work, "That's easy for us to imagine Doc; we grew up in that world, not this one." I sighed, and closed my eyes, tilting my head back. "I was one of your *inferiors* in the old world. I used to *throw freight at* a big box retailer. I never even graduated high school."

Cuttersark didn't reply to me. I couldn't tell what he thought because whatever openness he had offered in his energy and personal self quickly closed, becoming a wall to me. Although his gloves kept us from really connecting, our skin brushed close enough more than once that I could smell his energy and he likely knew mine very well. Two witches, this close, were forced to have a better understanding of each other, no matter how many secrets they kept hidden.

"The old world is dead," He said finally, the leather wrap halfway up my forearm now. He was crisscrossing it like the grip of a knife, "I don't seek the mediocrity of my childhood. I only seek to hold witches of the future, *our blood*, as nobility. Nobility above the mediocre."

Not sure what else I could say to him, I said *nothing*. I didn't lie, I had no desire to be a part of his new world. By the end of the week that wish would be granted, I'd be dead.

—————*—————

STOCKTON, CALIFORNIA. OCTOBER 22ND, PRESENT.

I rested my hands on the hood of our battered 4x4, the truck that had so selflessly conveyed me and my companions across America, like modern day *49ers*, the dream of gold heavy in our stomachs and our eyes full of stars. We quested after monsters though, not the gold fields of the Sierra Nevada. We'd crossed rivers, valleys, and mountains, seen the ruins of a dusty age and dead civilization. We'd also seen the birth of a new world, dawn rising on an America reborn from the ashes and slowly waking to the new possibilities that came with *magic and gods*.

"We saw the Elephant, old friend." I spoke now, to the truck. My fingers, wrapped in leather strips, couldn't feel the metal under my palms, but the weight of the hood and engine below is something I could feel deep in my chest, her oil like blood, her fuel resting quiet, the beating heart of her engine waiting to be ignited. I would miss our truck.

"Maggi," I heard from behind me, Jennifer's voice, and I turned slowly. She looked healthier now, her face was full, colored, and her hair was combed and pulled back tightly. Rest and food had done her a world of good. Next to her sat her bags and a new rifle was slung at her shoulder.

"Captain Jennifer Winslow, I presume." I smiled with no effort.

"This is yours, I believe." Jennifer reached to unhook my 9mm and its holster from her belt, holding them out for me to accept.

"No," I shook my head, "I'd prefer you keep it."

Jennifer seemed hesitant, looking to the side for a second, "Shouldn't you keep it? You're going to fight the Djinn soon."

"Funny thing about Djinn, the ones I seek are made from smokeless

203

fire. Put a bullet in my head, no more Maggi. Put a bullet in *smokeless fire*, no more bullet." Jennifer nodded, pursed her lips and then withdrew the weapon, placing it on her belt. I winked at her and continued, "My son carries his father's big 1911, a good gun for a man, a man with big hands like Alexander. This is my gift to you. Wear it at your side, always."

"I will wear it, with pride," Jennifer's smile was weak, like a kite on a breeze barely strong enough to fly it, "Always."

"*Besides*, a witch wore that gun for two decades, and I was good shot. Maybe there's a little magic in the trigger and slide?"

"Maybe there is." Jennifer averted her eyes as she grabbed her bags and supplies, walking past me hurriedly. She blocked me to some degree, and I couldn't quite feel sadness on her, but at the edges of her eyes I thought I caught the reflection of tears.

I leaned back on the steel bumper and grill of the 4x4, watching Rizwan approach from the direction that Jennifer had walked. He was clean shaven now, fatter in the face and healthier looking in general. The wilderness had been more kind to him than Jennifer, but he cut a much better silhouette now, strutting towards me, new weapon shouldered, and bags in hand.

"*Maggi Lopez*," He delivered a quick salute for me and I laughed involuntarily. There was an unexpected affection in his voice as he declared, "It's been an honor."

"Has it?" I was still smiling, "Traveling with a sinner and *sorceress*, dragging the rest of you with me?"

"It has been an honor," Rizwan nodded, giving me a quirky little smile, "You're not an easy person to like Maggi, but you're not dishonest or cruel. Understanding you takes time, but after a while it's hard to dislike you."

"I can absolutely say *that* was the most shit compliment I've ever heard." Rizwan extended his hand to me, his bare hand. I wondered what I would know if I shook it with dead fingers, wrapped in leather? Slowly, I brought up my hand, controlling all the movements and joints with my mind, and accepted Rizwan's hand. I couldn't tell if my grip was firm or soft, but we made eye contact and I was lost briefly in the sights and sounds that pulled me into those eyes.

I saw Rizwan retelling stories of our adventures to other soldiers. Visions of his animated gestures, dramatic pauses, facial expressions, and *dramatic exaggerations*. He loved building me up like a legend, he loved watching people's eyes grow wide as he told my stories. When he wrote his memoirs he also published a second book called 'A Case Study of Maggi the Bruja.' For future generations, it would serve as historical testament to our time together, *seeking the elephant*. When asked, in private, why a devout Muslim would elevate an infidel to such stature, he would explain it simply; "A good heart is a good heart regardless of who she worships."

I let get go of his hand, gasping, weak in the knees. Rizwan lunged forward, an expression of concern on his face, but I waved him off. "I'm okay," I said, "just the sickness catching up with me."

Rizwan nodded, and I saw that he didn't quite believe me. I wanted to tell him what I had seen, but I was not quite sure how I had come to this glimpse at the future. Perhaps that was how my necrotic flesh now worked, allowing me to see how a person's life could unfold, rather than the true nature of their heart today. Magic was a tool, a tool none of us fully understood. You could cause destruction or harm with magic, you could obscure a truth, or uncover a lie. Visions of the future were part of that strangely unpredictable world power.

"Keep Jennifer safe in the years to come." I said finally, regaining my repose.

"I will. Take care of yourself, Maggi." Rizwan saluted me again and departed to the other side of the truck. I wondered if Jennifer would come back to say goodbye to me and I felt ridiculous for that, a young woman again, obsessing over foolish ideas and impossible ideas.

Last to arrive was Aniceta, finally wearing clothing that reminded me less of a black circus tent with square shoulders. Like Jennifer and Rizwan, she wore camouflage trousers tucked into her boots, but her short-sleeved top was made of knit wool and cotton, black with silver flecks and a design across her bosom that displayed cleavage. Her hair was cut, elegantly short in the back, long at the front, as befitted many women of House Owens. The eyes that peered back at me from serious brows seemed as sad as ever, but an honest smile seemed to tug at full lips.

"You clean up pretty nice, kid." I nodded at her, approving.

"So do you, kid." Aniceta flashed me a thumb up and I thought that she had *no idea what* that meant. I decided to say nothing in response.

"Do me a favor," I stepped forward, so I could speak a little softer, "I want you to look up my student, *Mayy*, when you return to the Antecedent States. She's a talented witch, a little older than you. She could help you, teach you, be a *friend*."

Aniceta smiled, "I've been alone most of my life Maggi, I don't need a friend."

"No, maybe you don't," I sighed, "But Mayy might. I adopted her when she was a little girl. I wasn't a very good mother to her."

"You'd like me to watch over her?" Aniceta seemed perplexed, tilting her head to one side, then suddenly nodding at me as her talents weeded about in my soul, finding the truth. "You feel guilty for abandoning her; you're hoping that I can alleviate that guilt now offering her some sort of personal friendship to help her forget about your death."

I blinked at Aniceta, again wondering what I should say, if anything, about the way she spoke. This time, I replied, "Ask Mayy if she can teach you how to talk to people."

"*Okay*," Aniceta nodded seriously.

"Also, don't tell the other two about my *death*," I gestured back towards the truck, "They are not like us, and it'll make them uncomfortable. We all know what's going to happen to me, but normal people like to talk about normal things."

"As you wish, Maggi." Aniceta nodded a second time, her brows furrowed. "I won't shake your hand, or hug you either. One who is half dead, like you or The Harvester, can glimpse the future of one they encounter."

"Huh," I shrugged, "maybe you can teach Mayy a thing or two."

"Maggi," Aniceta looked around and suddenly she seemed nervous to speak, "If you fight the Ifrit the way you fought My Mistress, you *will win*. Maggi as I know her will die, but I don't believe that's the end. I will tell your son this truth, one day, when the time is right."

I watched Aniceta and didn't answer right away. She was young, and there was a wealth of things that she needed to learn, but her gifts granted her wisdom that few others could have enjoyed. A great many things she understood beyond me and now her words touched on the warnings of others. The idea that somehow, I *would die* and yet would *not die*. We watched each other for a few minutes and, finally, I replied, "Tell my boy that I love him, tell him that I have loved him since before he was born. Tell him what I did for him, tell him the stories you've seen in my soul."

"Tell him how you betrayed your friend to keep him safe?" Aniceta asked.

I wiped moisture away from my good eye with the clean leather of my hands, "Tell him all of it, and tell him even this is for him."

"I can do that, Maggi." One last time, Aniceta nodded to me before turning to walk towards the truck. I considered telling her goodbye but Aniceta knew my heart and soul so well, it'd be a waste of words, it'd cheapen the moment and seem tawdry considering what we shared.

The 4x4's engine roared to life; oil and fuel flowing, pistons cranking, the heart began to beat, alive, breathing at my back. I leaned forward and walked toward the entrance door to the long, narrow garage. I was too sentimental to not turn around. Sunlight poured in from behind the truck, Rizwan sat shotgun, talking to Aniceta in the rear cab seat. Jennifer was watching me, both hands gripping the wheel. We watched each other for a moment and then I saw her shift the truck into park, open the door, and slide out.

As she approached me I saw anger in her eyes and felt a burning fury at the tip of my tongue.

"They're all okay with it," she spoke to me, loudly, over the truck's engine, "They're all okay with you *dying*. I'm not, *I'm not okay* saying goodbye to you and running away, back to the Antecedent States, forgetting you ever existed."

"You've been a good *friend*," I smiled at Jennifer.

"We're not friends. You don't have friends." Jennifer put her hands on her hips, still angry, "I will miss you regardless, Maggi. You're the bravest coward I ever met, and you've got a bigger heart than anyone I've ever known."

"Get on the road, Jennifer. Stay safe." Jennifer watched me, as I had watched Aniceta, her mind considering responses, and after a minute she dropped her hands, took another step forward, and leaned in to kiss me on the cheek. It was not romantic or friendly, but it was sweet, and a strange kindness that I had never expected. I doubted I'd ever know what lips against my flesh felt like again.

When our skin connected, I was jarred with another vision of the future, this time Jennifer's life unfolded in my mind for a brief second. She would be a general in a *civil war* that would one day tear apart the Antecedent States. She'd fight hard and, after peace was restored, would take command of the Antecedent State's internal defenses, garrisons, and oversight for mercenary units tasked with patrolling the ever-expanding frontier. Those who knew her and called her a friend said that she never married because she was already married to the service. Even in retirement, older than I was now, a head full of white hair, she cared for the very veterans she'd once fought alongside.

The vision faded as Jennifer turned and walked away from me. I watched as the 4x4 backed out of the empty garage, Rizwan waving to me, then it pulled away slowly. I stood there, watching the oily floor of the garage and the bright blue sky outside, in no hurry to leave. It surprised me how low my heart sank at the absence of my companions. It also surprised me how much Jennifer's words stung; I had considered them my friends.

CARBONDALE, CALIFORNIA. OCTOBER 30TH, THE DAY MAGGI LOPEZ DIES.

M y friends gone, my health as good as it would ever be, this was the
day that Aurora Owens would lead me to the place she claimed the
Ifrit slept.

I had slept better than I had in years during the prior night, neither
haunted by dreams nor nightmares. When I rose, I wasn't nervous, nor
was I afraid. I felt no trepidation, only a sense of normality, as if this day
were any other. Although I was not guaranteed to perish in the place
Aurora had called *the pit*, I doubted I would survive combat with two
ancient Djinn

I was okay with this.

We stood, in Aurora's personal wardrobe, separated in the palace
she had created for herself. Around us were tall mirrors, reflecting light
from the morning, as well as light bulbs and small candles. Aurora's
closets unfolded like a child's puzzle, one door leading to another and
another. Brightly colored dresses, skirts, and tops, separated by colors
and designer, endlessly filled racks and shelves; above cupboards filled
with shoes or boots.

"I admit," Aurora chuckled, "fashion was always my joy in life."
While she spoke of clothes and slowly limped around me on her forearm
crutches, I wondered what my joy had been? I'd always drank heavily,
I'd enjoyed *cocarina*, and a good scrap, but before my son was born I'd
never really been happy or content. Even my teacher was a distraction

from my edifice of disdain and discontent, for all that I loved him, and for all that I missed him.

"It's a remarkable collection, Lady." I replied, calmly, using her formal title. A young girl, an apprentice, and an old man fitted me for armor. They'd adjusted the waist and size of the long, woven crisscross skirt, slit up to my hip, manufactured from linens and leather, animal fats and adhesive, tiny steel plates between the woven pattern, allowing it to move with me, but offering protection. Whatever was left of my Catholic modesty made me dislike the long slits, but Aurora promised me that I'd be able to move just as fast as I could in trousers, with better protection, and the added measure of my opponent not seeing where my feet were placed for an attack. I had still protested that Ifrit would not be watching a mortal's footwork, until finally Aurora made it clear that this armor was not an option, "Dammit *Maggi*, this is a *gift*. This was my armor when I went to war, this was my armor when I went to San Francisco. I can't wear it anymore, I can't even fight. Someone should put it to good use."

"Funny thing," Aurora spoke philosophically now, "All the beautiful things you possess, and you can't take a single one of them with you, when you die."

I stood on a pedestal while the man and girl fitted and adjusted my chest armor. Also made from linen, leather, and fat, this torso piece was far more rigid than the skirt, painted white with red trim. I could see pockmarks and nicks across the breasts and wondered how many potentially lethal impacts this had protected Aurora from. "I never had much, I never wanted much. I knew love, love of a good man and my children."

"*Love*," Aurora stopped, watching me, "Love is such an overrated idea. My parents didn't love each other, I didn't love my husband, but we did what was needed, each of us."

"Your children?" I replied, not sure how to respond to her disdain. My one motivating factor for over two decades had been *love*. Love for my son's father, my son, and even the little girl I cared for after my teacher died.

"My children?" Aurora sneered, watching me. She wore an elaborate dress of black and yellow, a pattern of sequins and embroidery wrap up the left side, cross her chest, and then down toward her shoulder. The black looked like velvet; the yellow seemed like a faux silk. She didn't wear all the jewelry from when we first met, but she looked no less regal. "They're spoiled fools who will drive my House to ruin if I dare die before they've had a chance to show their mettle."

"Have you considered service?" I answered. I was holding my arms out, at my sides, and my shoulders had become weary, "My son, Alexander, served in our military since he was fourteen. He saw combat his first year."

"You didn't fear for your child?" Aurora arched an eyebrow.

"Of course, I did. I was there, watching over him. He didn't know of course, only my man Lorne knew. I didn't want him to be embarrassed by his mother, or his men to think of him as weak. But I was there, ready to rain fire on anyone who hurt him." I laughed, softly, at the memory. It had been a minor strike on a raider camp, two Companies of Antecedent soldiers striking a foe so disorganized they'd never bothered with sentries. Alexander had been in no real danger, but I had fretted like a mother hen for days prior.

"Not a bad idea," Aurora nodded to me before turning to limp on her crutches to a seat several yards from me. It was a red cushioned couch, thick, comfortable, and soft. As she seated herself, she grunted softly in pain. "My husband would never allow it, of course, he believes aristocracy shouldn't get their hands dirty or their boots muddy."

"Who is your husband?" I replied.

"Lord Cuttersark," Aurora laughed, "You didn't know?"

"I had no idea," I laughed with her, honestly stunned by the revelation. "He seems nothing like you; there was no affection between you both."

Aurora shook her head, then glared at me with a look of disappointment. "We didn't marry for affection, we married because he was the only man my equal, the only witch in California as powerful as me, as *smart as me.*"

"You wanted strong children?" I asked.

"Of course, Cuttersark believes the talent for magic is chosen genetically, and I'm not inclined to disagree. I wanted the best for my children. I wanted their health and strength; I wanted them to rule this new world." I realized then that Aurora, despite her dim views on love, was not so different from me. We were women of the old world, who'd had little of our own victories. After we learned that our talents set us apart, we'd both used those gifts to help our children. Aurora could speak ill of love all she wished, but we were no different. She would have died for her progeny, just as I planned to die for mine. "Do you know what the irony of all that is?"

"I can't imagine." I squinted at Aurora, grinning.

"Jeremy used to fight with me. Before we had a palace, before House Owens ruled these lands. He commanded air and wind, I could call fire. Together, the two of us would burn armies with *fire tornadoes.*"

"*'Fire eater,'*" I nodded, "is what we call it. I could smell it on you, when we met."

"Yourself, as well," Aurora shrugged and leaned back, "Jeremy and I may have loved each other back then, high on the heels of victory, blood singing in our ears, we didn't make love after battles, *we fucked each other.*"

"Lady," I chuckled, as the tailors finally allowed me to lower my arms and began to fasten and tie my armor tight, "I'm no expert, but you speak fondly of the man."

"It's no lie," Aurora crossed her arms, "I was fond of Jeremy, when he was Jeremy, our trauma medic and warrior."

"*Battlewitch,*" I replied, thankful I that could relax my shoulders.

"Yes, *battlewitch.* I was fond of him then, when he liked the feel of mud in his cot, when he was brave and ardent, when each day may have been our last. In the years that followed he created The Orders, decided he was better than everyone else." Aurora's face, cynical and icy, turned a shade of sorrowful then, her eyes distant and lips narrow. "Decided he was better than me too, a woman of low birth."

I didn't reply immediately, though I was surprised that she spoke of these things with her tailors nearby. It didn't matter, I supposed, it was her household, not my own. "I'm sorry, Lady."

"Don't be sorry," Aurora shook her head, replacing her gaze back to mine, "Never be sorry for having something more than another. I feel no guilt that my jewels are greater than yours, you shouldn't regret that I never knew love *like you did.*"

"Lady, I don't presume what love I had, or didn't have, compared to you."

"Ha!" Aurora barked a laugh at me, pointing now, "I appreciate the respect you offer me, *Maggi,* but don't lie to me. I am no fool. I can see your eyes shimmer and shake when I speak of my children, I feel you empathize, and contrast. You can't decide to pity me or be *jealous."*

The tailors completed armoring me and Aurora dismissed them, ordering me to seat myself across from her. While Aurora had used her real voice around those servants, she remained proud, aristocratic, only in our privacy did she speak with humility or sincerity.

"You're not wrong," I answered finally, sitting myself on the pedestal on which I'd been standing for nearly an hour.

Aurora nodded to me, laying her palms one on top of the other across her knees, "I don't know your stories, Maggi, I don't know who you lost or why you lost him, but that loss is tangible thing on you. It's like a stillborn Siamese twin, connected at your hip, you drag it around with you, tragic and forlorn."

"That might be the most disgusting description of my loneliness I've ever heard." I didn't know how to respond to her, other than being bluntly honest. *"But,* you're right. I lost my son's father nearly twenty years ago. Each day has been a day I felt incomplete, a part of me broken off and lost. I am *jealous* you can be so callous about Lord Cuttersark."

"We all respond differently to loss, Maggi, you chose to mourn your lover. I choose to hate mine." Aurora smiled sadly and just watched me for a long moment, or long minutes, I couldn't be sure. When she spoke again, she gestured her hand to the side, as if she'd dismissed the conversation itself, a servant she'd grown bored with, "Are you ready to leave?"

"As ready as I'll ever be," I supposed, nodding. I reached to the soft carpeting next to me, picking up the balisong I'd left to rest there, along with the clothes I'd borrowed from Aubree's bedroom before we left San Francisco. The twin to this knife had been lost in the surf when I had fought her, one more casualty in the wake of The Harvester. I carefully commanded my mind to control dead fingers, articulating delicately, to hold the small blade.

"You almost certainly ride to your death," Aurora narrowed her eyes, her voice serious, sympathetic, "Are you certain this is what you want?"

"Those Djinn, and I, go way back," I shrugged, slowly standing up, feeling the years and injuries in my hips and knees, "We have a dispute to settle, going back before the Collapse. If I don't end them today, they will toy with my children for decades to come."

"*Why is that?*" Aurora leaned in, her voice dropping to a whisper, as though we had begun to conspire against the gods.

"Why does a cat torture a spider before it kills it?" I answered.

"I suppose," Aurora nodded, pulling herself up carefully on crutches. She took a second to steady herself before approaching me. "You're doing me a fine favor. When the two Ifrit came here to trade, they walked in flesh-suits, dead farmers. *Owens farmers.* A few deaths mean little to me and my House, but demons like that will rest easy in a comfortable place like Xanthous Mine. I don't trust them, and I'd kill them myself if I could."

"You offered them sanctuary, didn't you?" I smiled at her, reading the expression on her face, the frustration and disdain in her voice.

"*Of course,* I'm no fool. You think I want to end up like *you?*"

I laughed, a real laugh that I couldn't dismiss for awkwardly long seconds. Aurora must have believed me crazy for it, but it no longer mattered. I was neither offended, nor was I angry, because she was *right*. "Lady Aurora, you've been a good friend to me and my companions since we arrived. I offer you this as a gift." I reached out my dead right hand slowly, palm up, my butterfly knife resting there easily.

Aurora offered her hand in return, laying a palm down on the weapon. She didn't take her eyes off mine, considering the gift with care, before she finally answered, "You killed The Harvester with this, didn't you?" I nodded, calmly closing my eyes but saying nothing. "That's not why you want me to have it. You love this knife."

"I don't want it to rust in a ditch, next to my skeleton," I said, after a second.

"I suppose," Aurora repeated herself, accepted the balisong and gripping it in her fist. "Not sure what another witch's blade will do for me. I'll mount it on display in a museum."

"If it's not buried with me," I shrugged.

Aurora was solemn then, watching, studying me. She didn't burrow in my mind but she saw through my flesh and bone, recognizing the soul that is really me, down deep inside. I returned the gaze, wondering what she was doing. When she finally spoke, she spoke in her conspiratorial whisper from earlier, "You know, one day, your son will come here, to my House with an army greater than my own. He will demand I bend my knee for him, and I will oblige for the safety of my House. When that day comes, do you wish I give him a message for you?"

Her words didn't shake me, nothing could shake me on the event of my own death, but I had not expected to answer such a thing now. "Tell him," I paused, swallowing hard, "*Tell Alexander*, that I loved him. I loved him, and I'm sorry I was never there as much as he needed me. Tell him that I died for him, for his father's dreams, and my own. Tell my boy, *I am proud of the man he became.*"

Tears fell from my good eye, rolling down my face, trickling off my chin and tickling my cheeks. It took a moment to see clearly again as I blinked back more weeping. "Do you want to know any of your future? I can see yours as easily as my own. Maybe it's the death, thick on you Maggi, but I see sights and sounds you cannot dream of."

"Dead women don't have a future," I wiped at my face now with leather bound wrists.

"Normally, I would agree with you, Maggi. But today when I gaze into your eyes, look at your soul, I see things I can't begin to understand. A great neon city by the sea, majestic like when *I* was a girl, watched over by a metal monster, *five hundred feet tall.*"

"Insanity." I replied, shaking my head.

"Perhaps," Aurora took her eyes off mine, licking her lips and shaking her head. "I don't understand these things, but the future seldom makes sense. I saw my defeat in San Francisco, but that vision was only useful after the fact. Prophecy is seldom the tool we wish."

I nodded to Aurora, not disinterested, but I had no desire to know what dreams or nightmares the future could hold. I only cared for the fight that was to come. "We should get going, Lady Owens. I'd hate to be late for my own death."

CARBONDALE, CALIFORNIA. OCTOBER 30TH, THE DAY MAGGI LOPEZ DIED.

X anthous Mine was a massive semi-circular open-pit, abandoned shortly before the Collapse. I'd heard some stories of its construction, although I'd never much paid attention. From the lip of the mine I could see down, what looked like hundreds of levels, each cut at a slight angle. Dirt slides had ruined many of the clean cuts and equipment was scattered across the inclines leading deeper. Near the bottom of the pit I could see the rusting husk of an enormous bucket-wheel excavator, larger than any vehicle I'd known in my life. My glass eye irritated the empty socket it rested in and I felt a quiver of energy as I watched.

"We've scavenged equipment from the lips of Xanthous, but our engineers will not go down deeper." The House Owens soldier next to me crossed his arm on the three-point rifle sling hanging from his chest. He was middle-aged with salty red hair, buzzed, and a single scar across his right temple. "No one goes into Xanthous. Except, perhaps, the insane."

"Or Djinn" I nodded.

"I can imagine no other creature that would live here," The man with salty red hair pointed out across benches of the mine. "During the Collapse, they dumped the dead at the lowest level. Some say a hundred thousand dead, from the Bay Area alone. Some say *millions* rest here."

"*Mhm*," I nodded, not taking my eyes off Xanthous. I could feel the background din, the vibration of the so many dead, more than any mass grave I'd seen on the east coast. It made the air colder, choked me slightly, pressed on my wards and barriers like thick, oily water. The

216

soldier's estimate of a *million dead* wasn't an exaggeration. "Why so much equipment? I see the trucks, for the mine, but there's so much more."

The House Owens soldier shrugged, "A year after the Collapse, a skeletal state government was formed. Some of the Federals tried to clear highways and cities. They hauled tractors, trailers, cars, trucks, buses out here by the thousands. Much of it they just dumped in the pit."

"What happened to that state government?" I turned back to the man. Part of me wondered if the lines I saw in his face, the white of his eyes and thick brows, were the last human face I'd know in this life. I'd always imagined saying goodbye to my son at my departure from this world. Part of me even assumed that I'd be looking at Jennifer or Rizwan, before the end. Realizing that a total stranger was now my last contact with humanity became a sobering notion.

"*House Owens happened*, ma'am." The man grinned widely at me.

The crazy cat lady spoke in my mind. *Go down. Into the pit.* I already knew that I must; I knew that was why I was brought here, to perform my final actions in life. My first response was to bristle slightly, but her insistence also made me wonder why she would be so driven now.

I gazed back into this earthen scar, this dismal pit, and began my descent, my emotions both heartbroken and furious at once. Level by level, I traversed down the spiral. Scattered about the rutted roadways were various earth movers, wrecked cars, and ruined vehicles by the thousand, destroyed by being rolled end over end down the pit decades before. Now they cluttered my landscape; I was an ant descending through the waste bin of a self-loathing artist, his attempts at greatness wadded up, crumpled, discarded hatefully.

The further down I went, the bones of the dead became more common. Most were indiscriminate, broken or crushed, tattered bits of clothing protruding from the loose earth. I talked to myself and argued with myself, swearing in Spanish and English, barking off insults at offending skulls or inconvenient rocks. The flowing moan of the dead became a sea of white noise, almost forgettable, in this place where even light struggled to reach.

At one of the last dry benches, I stopped, near the bottom of this upside-down layer cake. Xanthous had filled with rain water and had become a shallow, murky lake. Two decades of rain, elements, and rot, had made short work of the bodies here. While the dirt was covered in bleached bones, the swamp before me obscured any evidence of what must have once been *mountains* of bodies. I realized that the center of this mire was two more benches deep.

On dry ground, all before me were abandoned vehicles. Massive dump trucks with six wheels, each wheel larger than an armored tank. Earth movers with swing cranes that extended a hundred feet in the air and treads measuring a dozen feet across, along with bulldozers and blades large enough to level two-story buildings. These once brightly colored vehicles had faded into dusty, rusted hues of yellow or orange. In the center of all this was a tracked excavation vehicle, its extended scaffolding and support beams looming. Here, in the bowels of a forgotten mine, stood the metal ghost of a fallen god, a god of excavators, a god of the earth movers, blessed beyond all others, a man-made deity. As large as it was, nearly a quarter of its frame was submerged in water.

Nestled, somewhere under this monstrous numen were glowing embers.

I realized, I'd not been a fool to follow the *crazy cat lady's instruction* in Santa Cruz. The glass eye possessed a use, the magic it might allow a wearer to see the unseen. Before the Collapse such an eye would have been priceless, now such an eye would allow me to see the Ifrit when they did not want to be seen, showing me the truth of their form. I cupped a hand over my glass eye, watching the cartilaginous swamp for what it was, dull gray and green, groping at reeds or sickly yellow moss. When I removed that hand, the embers glowed again, two of them, side by side. Their dim light breathing, like the belly of a sleeping animal, rising and falling.

I was a single minded mad woman come upon this cursed place. I sought out two ancient demons who were likely immortal, and I intended to fight them. The third Djinni in Omaha had warned me I'd need help, directed me toward the *crazy cat lady*, and gave me the map to find her. He'd known that she alone could offer me the edge I so desperately needed.

They will soon be aware of us, my Maggi, my perfect Maggi.

I wasn't afraid to die here, in this place. At this moment, at the end of the road, where my journey had finally led me, I knew no fear at all.

Carbondale, California. October 30th, the day Maggi Lopez dies.

I leaned forward on dead hands, dead arms, kneeling in a crouch, my heart beating so fast and so loud that I could scarcely focus my energies.

While my surviving eye surveyed the pit, my glass eye saw nothing but trails and flashes left by former Veil creatures; the sharp, crisp, impressions left behind by those manufacturers of smokeless fire. The images superimposed on my field of view and I watched the Ifrit dart, hither, and leap across the fetid swamp at the bottom of Xanthous Mine,

They were faster than I could ever have dreamed.

"Sabah al-hayri, Magdalena. It's been a long time." I heard their voices in the air around me; they speak in unison, two unique sounds bombinating against my eardrums, laced with whispers and sizzles like meat grilling on a skillet. I'd never heard their true voices until this day; I'd never imagined what it would sound like, knocking around inside my skull and worming through my marrow. *"We can smell you from miles away."*

I looked down, struggling to see my ankles in the dim twilight. I watched the bound combat knives at my boots to command my dead fingers, grasping their handles. I forced my rotten bones to grip them hard and unsnapped catches with my thumbs. It was clumsy, *pathetic*, but I freed them and fell forward in a full kneeling position, settling each of my knees a few feet apart in the loose dirt so that my hips were exposed from the sides of my armored skirt. I glanced back up at the light show generated in my glass eye to see the Ifrit settling behind a titanic mining vehicle. "Aren't you tired of smelling my fear?" My laugh wasn't genuine.

"No," one Ifrit voice separated from the other, "*in all the world, in all history, nothing smells like you. You are a creature of dead cities and empty battlefields, vulgar in your cloying repugnance, an unparalleled idol of gruesome diamonds.*"

"You fucking Djinn," I laughed, this time in mirth, and then looked back down to poise my knives against my exposed flesh. "You really know how to sweet talk a girl." I cut myself. It was imprecise because I could no longer feel the pressure I was applying. I cut too deeply and shuddered in pain.

"*We are no mere Djinn! We are royalty, we are divinity, we are the manifest glory of this world, gods made mortal!*"

"Mortals can die," I drove both combat blades into the soft dirt at my anterior, and then pressed the palms of my wrapped leather bandages against bleeding cuts. "You're not *gods*, you're the *dogs of gods who* forgot about you. Fetch! Roll over!" I screamed, this time no longer restrained by my focus. Now my own rage was simmering to the surface.

"*How dare you.*" The Djinn spoke together again, and I could feel their hatred against my flesh, hot, and flowing, like boiling wax. They ceased their dance and converged separately. I could hear a mechanical groan, a steel howl, and I looked across the enormous vehicle that stood front and center in the pit, looking for movement. "*Which god will you call upon, Magdalena? Which one will you call upon to save you?*"

"None of them," I replied, forcing myself to breathe. I was sweating now; fever had set in. The Ifrit wanted to force me into a long conversation, force me to break my focus, force me to lose myself in rage. I couldn't lose that time; my injuries would force me to the ground by the end of the night, writhing in my own misery.

"*In ten thousand years, we never corrupted someone as well as we corrupted you. As a child, we introduced you to fear, and you became so fluent in the language of terror that you betrayed your friend to die.*" I didn't answer right away; instead I begin summoning the barriers and boundaries that would protect me. I knew what I was about to face and I needed every advantage I could muster. My walls were separated by layers of common barriers, more incantations and whispers to nullify various elements, slowdown impacts, and silence curses. Around me evolved a sphere of neon light in a thousand colors, melting into the shadows and gusting loose dirt away from me. *"We taught your wretched Federals how to enslave our kind, just to play with you. We lured you across a continent because we were amused at the idea of your scampering and scraping to reach us. Do not forget yourself, you are no more a threat to us than a fly, and we shall end you in suffering you can't imagine."*

With my hands coated in cruor, I reached forward and carefully forced my necrotic fingers to grip the handles of my knives again.

Speak my name. The crazy cat lady hisses in my mind. I don't know her name, I can't answer.

"Help me learn your name," I whispered. *"Introduce me to the primal forces of this world, show me the power that created mountains and valleys."*

The two Ifrit approached me from either side of the mining equipment; they were bound inside hulking suits of armor, jerking unnaturally, bending on hinged knees, belching heat and fire from their components. These were far more advanced than the exo-suits that those big dumb creatures in Claysville had worn. These were lost technology, pinnacle engineering, memories from a time that would be forgotten once my generation passed. Like their more brutish cousins, the Ifrit wore these suits like skin, no electricity, no batteries, no fuel. They powered their own armor, powered their weapons, powered their guns. This was an amalgamation of technology that allowed these creatures to interact with the world above and beyond their own talents.

They could have just killed you, the primordial spoke in my mind, *yet they play a game.*

"Arrogance," I replied, for the crazy cat lady, "we know a thing or two about arrogance, don't we?"

Yes, she replied.

These Djinn were devastating creatures, they could summon magic, outside of their suits they could cut me down like starving rat or they could end my life in a thousand different ways. My sole advantage this evening, my *one chance at* killing them, was capitalizing on their arrogance, their cruelty.

The primordial inside me was a gatekeeper, she could open doors closed to me for a million years. I hadn't lied to the Ifrit, I would call on no gods, but to the heart of the Earth herself and the burning fire that raged inside. I focused on the ancient elemental powers, the powers that formed the Earth, the powers that wrought life from raw destruction, the powers who knew the Djinn by their true names. I was no longer part of my own body; I was seeking heat from the first eternal spark, *true fire, real fire.*

"*Now you will die, Magdalena,*" the Ifrit voices separated again, no longer in unison, only one of them spoke. "*We will flay your flesh and use it as a carapace, excrement nascence from a million burning monkeys in a hundred ruined cities. You will be our slave until the sun grows dark!*"

It was almost time. My heart was a jackhammer and I could feel a trail of drool spill over my lower lip as my lips spread into a grin. "Blah, blah, blah," As I spoke slowly, my voice changed, a deep resound, and I could feel the primordial inside me speak, her voice manifesting outside of my mind for the first time. "You should have killed the little girl in the liquor store. You should have killed the young woman in Salt Lake City. And you should have helped Aubree end me in San Francisco."

The two powered suits, shifting loudly as armor plate and gears hammered into each other, stopped less than fifty meters away from me.

We were silent for one second, two seconds, *three seconds,* then finally the Ifrit both spoke as one, "*You are not alone.*"

"*How fucking stupid do you think we are?*" Did I say that? Or did the primordial? No, I definitely said it, but she was alive inside me, she was in my blood, my bone, my organs. She was a part of my genetic structure, living in both my good eye and glass eye; she crawled in my hair like lice and skittered across my skin like fleas.

I felt my hands again, or more accurately I could *feel her hands.*

"*You are not alone!*" The Ifrit screeched at me, a sound beyond words, a sound that could peel paint and shatter stone; a sound that created terror a million years ago.

I stood up at that moment, rising from my knee. I was no longer quite in my own body, I could see my leather and linen armor, black skirt, and reinforced top. My legs glistened with blood, and I was illuminated by orange fire. As I rose, my knives lifted from the earth, each one trailing thick strands of *belching, molten lava.* The very core of the planet had offered me her kiss, the smallest of gifts for an old friend, the primordial inside me.

Fingers wrapped in thin strips of leather glowed, barriers protecting me from the heat. I spun gracefully in the loose dirt, my whips of lava unwinding around me, vicious and sensual. I was grace personified, my body in motion. Ifrit, oldest of the old, must bow before the titanic powers of the planet. So, I stood, luminescent arms outstretched like a ballet dancer, flaming scourges of liquid rock spilling from my knife handles.

"I'm going to kill *the fucking shit out* of you both."

The devil himself would have flinched from my smile.

CARBONDALE, CALIFORNIA. OCTOBER 30ᵀᴴ, THE DAY MAGGI LOPEZ DIES.

The primordial, the *crazy cat lady inside* me, viewed the world in ways I'd never dreamed of. She was aware of *everything* and, while she didn't watch from fields afar, the perspective was a mix of bird's eye view and a brutally intimate frame of reference. I could taste the oil leaking from the Ifrit's suits; I could feel their prickly energy cut into my skin like the thorns of a rose. All the while we fought them.

We fought them.

I could not have done this without her. She protected me from the lava, though my leather wrappings still caught aflame. She gave me the strength I needed to heft the sheer weight of the whips. She guided my hands, my arms, and my body through a pirouetting ballet, winding viscous stone around me like coiling snakes, snapping out, biting chunks of hardened metals. This was no talent I possessed, I had none so grave. Maggi Lopez, in her flesh and heart, was a brawler; the elegance that the *crazy cat lady* allowed me was beyond my fantasies.

The powered suits were identical in their rattle and clatter, moving fast, but unnaturally. Each one stood roughly fifteen feet tall at their *heads*, a collection of sensors and cameras, jittering as they snapped about and peered back on me and the pit we fought. Differing shades of green and tan camouflage streaked the suits, joints bulbous and plated, fingers articulating like giant metal spiders, empty engines crying loud as their occupants forced the artifices above and beyond any design specification.

One of them often took lead, an alpha role, while the second fell back to support it, unleashing bright tracers from a mini gun across the dirt and mire from deeper in the pit. When the beta opened fire on me, I had to fall back and keep moving. The suits were not meant to track or engage a single, fast woman on foot and the Ifrit had no comprehension of how to make their weapons work for them. Before long, alpha's mini gun ammunition belt had jammed and beta had exhausted all its available ammunition chasing me.

Unable to keep me away from them, they closed range and the fight became a desperate melee. Alpha charged me, *again*, one arm's fingers clenched into a sloppy mechanical fist. We ignited the air around me into a boiling storm of fire as I spun to dodge. One whip sliced through the arm, super heating the metal and cauterizing the wound as the hand flew toward the ground, uselessly. The second whip crossed alpha's breastplate on a white Federal star, opening its armor like a gutted pig, exposing the vulnerable internal structure. I savaged the suit as it turned to follow me and I brought both whips down, slashing through its shoulder joints. In a shower of sparks, both arms amputated.

I was showered in sparks, shrapnel, and molten slag. My barriers protected me to some degree, as did the armor gifted to me by Lady Owens, but I still felt sharp burns across my face and upper shoulders. I still choked on the dust and smoke, I still fought to keep my breath, and to separate my mind from the carnage, to stay focused on the connection I maintained with my *crazy cat lady*, my magic, and my defenses.

Reduced to a walking torso, the alpha could be ignored for a time. I knew the second Ifrit was nearby, trying to outflank me, taking advantage of my blind side. It had no clue that my *glass eye could* see the ancient imprints of such a creature, crawling and squirming on the inside of its armor.

I turned about quickly, catching the beta as it charged in. I extended my arm, a molten whip lashed out to decapitate the suit. I succeeded, but the Ifrit won the gambit, sacrificing the suit to add momentum for a swing.

Part of the hardened steel arm hit me.

Disconnected as I was, bound to the *crazy cat lady*, I could not feel the pain, but I was affectionately aware of the damage done to my body, as though I watched a lover stretch out next to me in bed. Every bone below my right shoulder shattered as the hulking artifice tore at my elbow, breaking my dead forearm away. It was not a cut, nor was it clean. I felt every tug as muscles and blood veins were ripped out of my body.

Although my dead hand still gripped the knife handle, the lava whip tumbled to the sand, uncoiled, and fell into the swampy mire one more level down into the pit. A wall of steam rose fast and one of my weapons was gone.

I felt an assault against the barriers on my flank as the alpha Djinn's magic, no longer fully contained by the suits, began to leak through and make itself known. Ancient incantations in mother tongues echoed, tunneling through my protections, seeking to petrify me. I resisted, using energy that was freed by the loss of my whip, and conjured searing flame to exploit breaches in the alpha's armor.

I ignored my injury. I couldn't feel pain and I wasn't sure I could feel the loss of a limb right now; we were still fighting. I snapped my remaining whip like a lion tamer toward beta, forcing it back. We danced around each other, beta and I attempting to brawl now. Each crack of the whip further debilitated it, my punishment for daring to assault me. Although the *crazy cat lady* and I shared a body now, I was *The Bruja* and instead of simply cracking open my foe, I was going to smash the suit to pieces, *angry, outraged,* now that the beta would not submit.

The armor, caught in my wrath, began to glow and melt, waterfalls of molten materials cascading to the pit floor. The beta, built by clever men, was reduced to base components in the wake of my fury. A dozen yards away the alpha stood still, armless, a steel torso cracked open like a busted melon, hiccupping flame and sparks, disgorging black smoke so thick it seemed like fluid clay to be twisted into physical objects.

We watched through *crazy cat lady's* senses and my glass eye, watched as the two Ifrit freed themselves, wrenching their energy, tendrils of fire, from the armor. They were somewhat wounded, but strong. I could hear them cursing me in Arabic, or some language dead before history was ever written. Free now, they were fast and unlimited in their power.

They were angry. This was no longer about my *enslavement*, I was no longer an amusing toy for them to chew on. This fight had become very real for them.

Tossing aside the second lava whip, I clutched my burning left hand to my bloody and ragged arm stump. *Crazy cat lady* informed me that this would cauterize the wound, stop the bleeding, I still have a few more minutes of fight left in me.

I only laughed and bared teeth soaked in blood, mouth thick with copper and hate.

"Round two."

CARBONDALE, CALIFORNIA. OCTOBER 30TH, THE DAY MAGGI LOPEZ DIES.

I was no longer certain what part of me was *Maggi*, and what part of me was the *crazy cat lady*. I grew annoyed with that nickname now, frustrated that I couldn't remember my own name. How many times had they cried my name in blood, how many times had they whispered my name in begging? How was it that I should forget *my own name?*

But, I knew my name, I was *Maggi*. Or perhaps she was Maggi?

The Ifrit were invisible to all senses when they wished it. They could vanish from view, oily and opaque, shunting heat for a second and rippling the air in a brief mirage. I couldn't sense them or hear them in my mind, their howls silent, and the air whipping past my face, merely dead.

One of them knew my name.

Panting, I shuddered, my thoughts a mix of two minds. I was merely form connected to this world through a narrow thread of ashen awareness. The glass eye filling my blind socket showed me the Ifrit. There, lurking at the edges of the shallow pool of rainwater collected in the pit. They moved behind the enormous mining vehicle near me as they crawled up the sides of this colossal ditch. They resembled something akin to spiders, a collection of fiery, bright tentacles, lashing onto whatever they please, choking on their own bleeding energy. We had been careful to not tip our hand, we knew they had no idea that my glass eye provided the ability to see them; we planned to wait, lure one in, *and kill it.*

As much as I did not feel pain now, I also felt no fear. Rather, I only felt the vibration of my flowing blood and the indomitable passion of our rage.

"You know these demons, don't you?" I whispered the words, or did I even speak? I was no longer clear on that, but *crazy cat lady and I* separated briefly enough that I must speak aloud to her. I felt her withdrawing, crawling deeper inside me, away from the surface.

I know the male, they are mates. I will take my name from him before they die.

As *crazy cat lady* retracted further, I was aware of the world again. I was standing knee deep in black mire, water reflecting ambient fires and moonlight. I could smell the fallow murk, could feel the cold against my legs and the pain of my *missing arm* grips me so deeply that I fought to keep from passing out. The Ifrit ceased their circle, pausing, watching as I stood alone.

Did I even have barriers up now? I realized my magic has been shattered. I was defenseless.

Maybe I had learned something of *crazy cat lady as* our minds mingled or maybe I had just been a tactician for too many years. Either way, I knew what she was planning.

The smaller Ifrit charged me head on.

Watching as it covered ground quickly was like watching a dust devil twist across an empty parking lot. As the Ifrit unwound on top of me, it also fell back into the physical world. I could feel the heat of its tentacles; could smell Baharat, cumin, and other spices thick in the air. There were no sounds as the Ifrit hit me, only the dull silence of pain and the cold shock of being tossed into the water.

As the smaller Ifrit attempted to rip me limb from limb, I felt her flood back into me full force, deeper, more intensely than before. I could feel her in my bones and the pain vanished. We pulled ourselves out of the mire as the Ifrit lost grip on our body. It took a second to regain *our feet* and I realized the Ifrit is trapped before *us.*

My name is Maggi. Her name is *crazy cat lady.*

The mire, the bottom of the pit, was reaching up to restrain the Ifrit. I could see bones and equipment fall away from the mud, as it turned pitch black and spindles. Flames dimmed, steam off the water, flash bright. There were *pops* and sizzling noises as something like oil weaved and crossed around both my body and the demon. It smelled of decay, old basements, stale rain and moldy caverns. The oil pulled like taffy, stretching and molding, running across my flesh and armor, finally accumulating at my truncated arm. It solidified, then loosened, sculpting a new limb with long, narrow digits and claws.

I reached out with my surviving hand, tattered and black with burnt leather. The Ifrit was now summoning all its power to burn the black oil, the *liquid death*, off itself. Just as I had commanded fire to ignite, I now commanded the flame to die in my presence.

"Extinguish."

It didn't quite work; parts of the Ifrit flashed hot as raw Djinn energy was diverted into the water and it flash boiled. The silence collapsed in the wake of *screams*, screams like nothing I'd known in this world. Somewhere between a haboob howl and a dying animal's death throes, there was a noise that gave birth to this auditory abomination.

The thick, freezing oil covered me, licking across every inch of my skin, wrapping me tight until I feared I would slip into death. As I stepped forward, my magic couldn't subdue the demon flame and we were roasted in a heat made of rage and fear, but we did not burn. We reached forward with a hand manufactured from death, fingers outstretched, then dove into the very heart of the Ifrit.

Perhaps a million souls lay at uneasy rest in this pit. I had felt their rage, their loathing, their unadulterated anger when I came here. *Crazy cat lady now* tapped into all of them, calling forth a power I had never dreamed possible. The necromancy I had learned from Aubree is nothing compared to this, parlor tricks, games for children, animating my own dead fingers. This was tapping into death, into the souls of the departed and creating a viscous material of it. It flowed through me and into the Ifrit, pulling, rending and tearing.

In all the amarantine glory that this creature had existed within, death was an alien idea, unfathomable, unimaginable. We were introducing a blind man to spring. We were allowing the deaf to hear *all the symphonies at* once, an all-inclusive horror so beautiful that I would have wept to hear, *if* I could have wept.

In the Ifrit's final moments, I saw lands and strange cities that existed in no history books. I saw the *court of Djinn*, the mountains of *paradise*, the frozen glaciers of *hell*, the castles and cathedrals of a thousand *gods*. Then, as though the Ifrit never was, it was over.

Flesh and blood, I stood at the bottom of Xanthous Mine, covered in crumbling ash and moist mud, my new arm pulsed, alive, slithering and mischievous.

"*You killed her.*" The surviving Ifrit slowly unfolded from its phantom world, perhaps five hundred feet away from me, on dryer levels of the pit. "*Ifrit do not perish, not since the Earth was young and the primordial gods walked these lands.*"

"Do you remember me?" I spoke those words, with my lips, my throat, but those were not *my words*. "Before we kill you, Ifrit, you will tell *me, my name.*"

Laughter filled the pit. So deep that the water vibrated, so loud that loose sand slipped down path and brim, into the crater. The laugh was long, a rolling melody of emotions and images, cruel pressure and revived disdain became things that I could have touched.

"*Before you kill us? Before you die from your own fragility, whore. Even with the primordial's help, you're too small and weak.*"

The Ifrit's words were perhaps their own form of magic, or maybe I was just a little too curious. I glanced down and saw half a dozen sharp scintillas of shrapnel extending from my chest. They had forced through my back, through organs, bones, and blood, to shatter my woven armor. When the smaller Ifrit had slammed into me, I must have landed in a pile of wreckage.

The suffuse wounds were not bleeding and I felt no pain, thanks to the connection between *crazy cat lady* and I, but it didn't matter. The Ifrit was right. My body couldn't withstand this.

I looked up, back to the Djinni, numb except for the chill. I felt *nothing*, no rage, no sadness, or regret. "I came here expecting I would die. Did you?"

"*I am Abu Abdallah Sa'id, one of seven Ifrit Kings. I am so old that I knew your primordial when she was young. Shall we die, together, here, in this fallow place?*"

I forced my lips to part and my teeth to open. I was smiling, arms wide, covered in a curdled mixture of blood, mud, and *death*. The *crazy cat lady* uncoiled in my skin and soul, and we both spoke; *"We shall die, together, here, in this fallow place."*

Carbondale, California. October 30TH, THE DAY MAGGI LOPEZ DIES.

I was sitting against part of a mine bench, my shoulders against the dirt, my midsection at an angle so I didn't put pressure on the shards extruding from my chest.

The air was chilly down here, but I was *shivering*, my teeth rattling. I had watched enough men die to know that shock had set in. Without the *crazy cat lady* to keep my body functioning, to keep my injuries in stasis, my body was shutting down. I was drooling blood that gathered at my chin and fell onto my armor, where other wounds glistened in the bright firelight that surrounded me. *I was in such pain*, but the pain was so abstract now, so disconnected from my reality that it was just one more inconvenience.

If I were to guess based on my experience, I would be dead in less than ten minutes.

Above, an atramentous sky calmly glistened with a million stars to match the million souls who surrounded me. Hundreds of fires burned and I could not remember why. Was it from the power armor that we had destroyed? Or was it from the remains of an Ifrit King, his body rent apart in the wake of an angry primordial, torturing the demon for the name she sought so passionately.

My *crazy cat lady* was no longer inside of me, no longer coiled around my spine or clutching my soul. Had she forsaken me, here at the end? It was incredibly difficult to invest trust in an ancient primordial when you lay dying at the bottom of a graveyard mine, listening to the cacophony

233

of dead around you. I wondered now, something I hadn't thought of earlier-would my fate be to rest for eternity with these unquiet dead? Those who'd died in the shelling of the Bay Area, those who'd been shot by Federal troops, or starved in their homes? There was an irony to that; my flight from California was to escape the fate of these poor souls, only to be reunited with them at the very end.

I held up my remaining hand, and studied it. The leather was charred, curled, and cracked, melted to my dead bones. I worked those fingers now, slowly, carefully, using what may have been the last of my magical reserves to amuse myself.

One hand was all I had left, and one eye to watch it. I remembered holding my son with those hands, my fingers soft and forgiving for him, my palms warm. I cradled him in these arms, against my chest where rusted and broken steel now protruded. He slept against my breasts and I had lain down with him, my chin at his forehead, as I listened to him breathe.

Those same hands had reached up, clutching my *lover's face*, that of my son's father. With two good eyes, I had studied his features, his rough stubble and thick brows, the smirk he always kept just for me, when no one else looked. I had stood on my tiptoes to kiss him, but he had always needed to crane his shoulders down to meet me. How many times had I wrapped my arms around him tightly so that he could stand up straight and lift me off the ground?

At the end of my life, choking on my own blood and shivering in the chill, I only studied fingers that looked like burnt steak left on the grill too long. My glass eye offered no more vision here, no insights or wisdom. There were no clever epiphanies, no realizations that changed my views of the world, nothing that made this *okay*.

My *crazy cat lady* was right. At this moment, at the end of the road, where my journey had finally led me, I was filled with *fear*, my heart boiled with terror, and I was gripped with a burning panic. *I did not wish to die.*

Holding my hand up, cradling a swaddled child who was now a man grown, I sang to myself. "*Hush, little baby, don't say a word. Mama's gonna buy you a mockingbird. And if that mockingbird won't sing, mama's gonna buy you a diamond ring."* My song was interrupted when I coughed on my blood, choking and barely regaining my breath, *"Shit."* I cursed.

The murky lake was disrupted as I pulled myself up, trying to breathe *a little better.* The water hadn't been water since we arrived here; during the fight it had transformed into some sort of manifested death energy, thick, black, and oily. That same greasy fluid now rose out of the pit by its own volition, coiling up vertically at first, one little tower, then a second. Side by side two legs and torso were formed, dripping and oozing; two arms and a head came next. The form was a woman, wide in the hip and bosom, narrow in the shoulders. The oil rippled and pulled, making slapping sounds, reforming repeatedly until the details of the body had formed themselves precisely.

Human bones from the pit erupted from the oily edifice, clean and bleached, like exploded abscesses, churning in the liquid flesh, turning to align themselves correctly. The bones wrapped and sculpted, giving the body form, skulls laughing at me from where the figure's breasts ought to have been and a hundred finger bones and teeth formed a fully articulated face. Thousands of spinal vertebrae extended from her shoulders and lower back, fluid like whips, then suddenly bent into monstrous *spider legs* a yard or two long, around her. The figure was perhaps twice the size of an ordinary human, bent at the knee, limbs and neck jerking as if dueling with the very air.

"My crazy cat lady." I smiled, before coughing up blood again.

"Maggi," the spider lady stepped from the lake, walking on nothing at all before her slender feet rest on the loose dirt around me. *"My Maggi."*

"Did he tell you? Your name?" I coughed again, almost unable to speak.

"Yes." With her reply, I nodded to her, holding my charred hand to my mouth. It did nothing to stop the blood and I began to feel light in the head. *"You're almost dead Maggi. You have minutes left, perhaps less."*

I nodded a second time, withdrawing my hand and looking at it. I was struck by how much my fingers looked like burnt pork ribs, covered in a deep red chipotle sauce. Who would possibly think such a thing? The dying, I supposed.

I forced the words out, gasping, "I don't want to die."

The crazy cat lady, in all her majesty, knelt next to me. She placed a hand on my chest; the black oil of her form separating and giving way to the protruding metal. I felt the pressure of *her* but my pain eased, and it became a little easier to breathe. She was dripping all over me, oil running down my hips and legs before puddling at my hind in the dirt.

"I could not have fought Abu Abdallah Sa'id, or learned my name without you." Her voice was a succulent whisper, the sound of sucking the marrow from a peach, or a kiss goodnight on a warm summer evening. So close to me I could hear the oily lips form vowels and syllables as she spoke.

"I could not have killed my monsters, without you." She had alleviated my cough. I breathed easier, spoke easier. I was grateful.

"My Maggi, would you hear an offer? A deal, between us both?"

I laughed a throaty cackle, "You hold me, alive, at the edge of death, and wonder if you can bargain with me? *Of course,* you can bargain with me."

"Maggi," She came closer and placed her lips next to my ear, cold and moist, the words not just rolling off her tongue but manifested in my heart as well, *"I cannot exist in this world yet. I need to heal and build my strength. I need to sleep, for perhaps a century, dormant and safe. If I take you with me, you will awaken when I do."*

I considered her words, her voice, all of her. I realized as we spoke that her liquid form has flowed across my body. I glanced down, watching the broken shards of steel be forced from my chest. I felt her inside my wounds, my veins, crawling along my marrow. I glanced back to her eyes, empty, dark pools, "What's the price, crazy cat lady?"

"You live as long as I live, we cannot separate."

"Offer the dying woman immortality?" This time when I laughed, I didn't gurgle or choke, "Threaten me with a good time."

"I will construct a beast made from bones and blood, I will even make sure our might protects the hopes and dreams of your son." As she spoke, her lips and face merged with my own, and I could no longer see the fires of the pit or fathom my own flesh and heartbeat. She already knew my answer, she'd already begun whatever ancient methodology of magic she commanded.

"He doesn't need his mama anymore. He's got the world now." I replied. "I'm ready."

Speak my name. Her voice wasn't in the world around me anymore, it spoke as a part of me, combined with the rhythm of my breathing and the pace of my heart.

My mind stretched out as far as possible, I let the universe unfold before me like an ancient map and listened to the heartbeat of time itself. There was a flash in my soul and I became aware of her presence moving like a distant whisper across the land a hundred miles away. In that ancient place, forgotten by men many years ago, was a collection of massive stones erected and arranged in her honor. Only her presence recalled the echoes of songs sung and chanted for her. At the court of a primordial goddess, an elemental queen, the regal lord of the Ifrit visited, one of Seven Kings who ruled lands across a young Earth. They crouched in respect and intertwined each other in acceptance, speaking each other's name, recognizing their own glory and might.

The thought came to me like a single teardrop hitting a still pool and, in that moment, I knew her. She had torn this memory from the Ifrit King in his final seconds of existence.

"*Anapu Weita*," I whispered.

Lightning flashed in my soul, or perhaps overhead. I wasn't sure anymore what I saw with my eyes, I was no longer quite human now.

Call to them! Gather them! Make this place whole!

Slowly, masses moved within my realm, a realm that superseded anything I could understand in life, creating eddy currents as they began to shift. The masses collected more of the surrounding energy, pulling it along and pushing other masses in a single direction. The pit mine was now a strange kind of womb, bloody and visceral, I was but a tiny embryonic form with my primordial. I felt her presence within me, her limbs extending into me and from me, filling me and enveloping me with her energy. I heard her murmuring a forgotten lullaby as she strengthened me and comforted me. As we synced, I breathed and hummed along to her song.

My voice became her voice and her voice became my voice, added to the growing symphony that inhabited this pit. The cries of the dead were embraced in our song, a cacophony vibrating the very bedrock. It was a catalyst that threatened to crack open the husk of earth and let lose the soul of a planet.

No weapon forged shall break us. No magic conjured shall dispel us. Somewhere between the words and song, the melody of death, and a memory so old that its very form was a blight across the new world, my body ceased to be. The little girl named Mary Magdalena Lopez had grown to become a woman, a mother, and a witch. Her flesh and bones became mortar and the pit became pestle. *For a century, shall we be manifest in this form.*

In that terrifying hurricane of raw energy, I died.

CARBONDALE, CALIFORNIA. OCTOBER 31ST, AFTER MAGGI LOPEZ'S DEATH.

There was little that Aurora Owens could do but watch the battle unfold. Standing at the lip of Xanthous Mine with her soldiers, half a dozen LAVs, 4x4s, and an old Federal MRAP, Aurora watched as Maggi descended into the pit. It took her time to find good footing, and she wasn't a young woman, but eventually at the lake that sat full of rot and decay, Aurora had fallen silent for long minutes.

When the fight began in earnest, it was *loud*, machine gun chatter, explosions, bright flashes of light, and the *screams*. The screams did not belong to Maggi, but to something much older and less acquainted with the world Aurora had grown up in.

As it all unfolded, Aurora was forced to steady her troops. The howls of angry Djinn were not for the faint of heart; even strong men would be inclined to flee with terror. Along the edge, those soldiers paced, speaking softly among themselves as Aurora leaned uncomfortably on crutches and listened to the mayhem ensue.

Although she knew there was a presence nestled deep inside Maggi, something *old*, and powerful, one of the gods that gods had worshiped before man walked this world, Aurora was unsure how that entity would support Maggi in this battle. With energy and eye, spirit and mind stretched out to see as much as possible, the answer to that question came after dark.

One of the two Ifrit had perished, evaporated and consumed with death, eaten away like bowl of sugar cubes tossed to into water, boiling froth and angry steam making an imperfect and impermanent grave marker to a creature who had watched mountains rise and fall. Aurora was an educated, worldly woman, but in her decades, she'd never known that kind of death for anyone, least of all those who might be considered *deathless*.

When the fight between Maggi, her elder god, and the last Ifrit unfolded, it was the manifestation of unholy terror. Flames swept the pit of Xanthous Mine, bright, throwing shadows across many hundreds of benches and the pit wall itself. For a second the shadow of a giant spider was cast, a spider large enough to eat Aurora's personal MRAP whole. House Owens soldiers either dropped to their knees as they shivered and prayed or cast their weapons to shoulder and neck, circling their Lady, ready to die. The men would not flee her side, all were veterans and well trained, they'd all seen the unthinkable.

Tonight, the unthinkable cowered.

Only Aurora knew what she saw, what she *felt*, only Aurora could have described the fight in detail, but instead she stayed silent, wrists and shoulders supporting her weight on crutches, exhausted and unable to turn away.

When the flames died down, when the screams of a dying Ifrit were silenced, when the black lake receded and calmed, Aurora could feel Maggi at the end. Part of her cried out to rush down into the pit to comfort the old witch in her dying moments, but a pair of ruined legs would never have allowed it. Aurora hated this, and quietly, alone, tears ran down her face.

Aurora Owens had not cried in many years. Oh, she had cried leaving San Francisco, but no mortal subjected to that degree of pain could have avoided it. No, the tears that fell on her face now, cold in the frigid night air, were the kind she'd not known in nearly two decades. Although she had two fine, strong children today, Aurora had miscarried her first child. The death of that child in her, reminded her of this moment. She was unable to *stop it*, all the magic and power in the world, for naught. She was unable to *comfort it*, she was unable to *share it*. She couldn't stop Maggi's death either, or hold her close, offering friendship during her last breaths.

Separated by countless yards, burning Djinn, and caustic smoke, Aurora and Maggi were again connected, this time in sorrow.

"Bring her body here," Aurora turned to one of her men, a middle-aged man with salty red hair. "Be careful to fetch me her glass eye."

The soldier looked at her, pausing, realizing that Aurora spoke in a normal voice, not her usual reverberating authority. He considered questioning her on it, he considered *saying anything other* than an acquiescence to her demand, but in the end, all he said was, "Yes, Lady."

Aurora turned to walk away from the lip of Xanthous Mine then, no longer wishing to subject herself to the grief, the loss of her *friend*.

A few yards away, limping on her crutches, sore and exhausted from standing, a jarring metallic crackling sound jolted her to a pause. It sounded as if a car or some other vehicle had been twisted, rent, pulled like taffy, and *popped apart*. A second sound, distant, an echo of steel and rock grinding against one another.

"Lady!" One of her soldiers shouted after her. "Something is happening."

Aurora looked over her shoulder, as a strange feeling crept up her into her stomach. Uncertain if it was fear, or worse, Aurora took precautions. *"What do you mean something is happening?"*

"Lady," Another Owens soldier responded, "The junk down there is *moving*."

Aurora squinted, then turned on her crutches. She balanced her weight and pivoted herself, quickly, quicker than she ever moved nowadays. Throwing herself forward, tossing her weight into a flurry and swinging across perhaps yards of dirt at a time. She was at the lip of the mine again in a heartbeat.

The soldier wasn't exaggerating. The wrecks that had lain up and down the mine benches were rolling end over end, spinning and whipping about. They didn't fall into the pit; however, rather they were pulled into the air above Xanthous Mine, sailing through the night in a clockwise circle.

While her men stood agog at the site, Aurora questioned how much danger could they be in? What if the last Ifrit had survived? Or, more likely, and just as terrifying, *what if the ancient primordial inside Maggi had survived.*

The very ground lurched, once, then twice. Sand and dirt collapsed into the mine further away. The Owens soldier with salty red hair, the one Aurora had sent to fetch Maggi's corpse, saw how close his Lady was to the edge and rushed to pull her away. A third violent heave tossed Aurora sideways off her crutches. The man with salty red hair only barely caught her, dragging her back, away from the pit.

Aurora barely noticed this, her eyes so focused on the site that was unfolding. The contents of Xanthous Mine were being pulled into a tidal hurricane, a swirling mass of flashing energy and oily black water from the lake at the lowest level. The wind just kept whipping faster, sand kicked up and rocks spun by. In the center of the typhoon were the largest of the mining excavators, *numerous machines*, turning slowly, metal bending, breaking, cracking.

Sounds erupted from the pit unlike anything Aurora had ever heard. An avalanche of metal and stone fell in torrential downpour, bent and molded by a million edifice parts, and symphony forced it's away from the cruel aural maw.

As Owens soldiers fell to the ground, holding their ears tight, the man with salty red hair crawled with Lady Owens away from the pit, her crutches long gone, desperately trying to protect her.

The very heavens above answered this madness, bolts of electricity crossed the ground, striking the center of the store, illuminating liquid black skin and oily muscle sinew, a humanoid form that must have stood *hundreds of feet tall*. The lightning sparked and spit off steel, iron and aluminum grew bright and molten, a monstrosity molded from alloy, stone, water, and the dripping, leaking, *sorrowful howls of death*.

As the Owens soldier with his salty red hair pulled Aurora away from the increasingly violent melee and behind her own MRAP, Aurora stretched her mind and heart across the tempest. The very power of gods was rending open the natural world, clawing at the laws of physics, commanding the impossible, terrible powers no mortal had seen in ten thousand years.

The dirt and stone under Aurora and her most loyal man turned liquid from the vibration, sand and grit tore apart the MRAP's enamel. Aurora's soldiers tumbled through the air, blood and sand mixing, clothing ripped and tattered. The men were already dead as they burst into flames.

Titanic forces vomiting forth raw havoc from Xanthous Mine were summoning the tidal power of an infant planet. This was the crux of creation, manifest in the big bang; the *death throes* of the old world. Nothing recorded in human history compared to this expulsion of *creation*.

Aurora wasn't afraid and though no human eyes could have gazed upon this site, she was a very talented witch. She watched in her mind, she felt with her mind, she could taste what it was like for the universe to accept *change*. Somewhere, in all the chaos and cacophony, Aurora thought she heard the words in her ear, *I love you*. It wasn't ghosts or spirits, it absolutely wasn't gods, and it most definitely wasn't Maggi. A soldier had pulled her from the edge of Xanthous Mine, had it been *him?*

Hours passed and when the first rays of morning light cast themselves across the landscape, the sounds of steel and stone battering each other to oblivion finally ceased. The howling winds quieted, and the air grew still.

Aurora had never eased her attention from the pit, and now that she could safely turn back, she did so, pulling herself across the Owens soldier, crawling on elbows, she clutched at the ground, clawing to pull herself forward, just as she had leaving San Francisco. She was not *afraid*. This time she was not in *pain* and she definitely had not been *defeated*.

This time Aurora was a giddy child again, eager to see what sort of strange new creature was born into existence in the wake of the supernova she'd survived.

The soldier, realizing that she'd fled to see more, arrived to help her off the ground. She allowed him to pull her up, helping her to her feet, supporting her weight on dead legs. Their skin touched, bare hands on wrists, forearms brushing, Aurora was aware of the soldier's energy, his heart, and his mind, but she couldn't focus on anything but *the beast before* her.

The horror was beautiful beyond conception, generated neither by logical thought, nor by human mind. This was a glimpse into the oldest stories, passed on from generation to generation, stories told around fires before anyone knew how to read, to write; these were the stories of carnal power, gods dreamed of by the most primal hindbrain,

The mine *burned*, white hot, spitting magma and fire, and silhouetted against those flames, it stood perhaps *five hundred feet* tall, partially humanoid, lurching and jerking forward on misshapen legs that crouched. It pulled itself free from the mine, each step on the earth shook Aurora's ribs and made her gulp back the drool that gathered at her lips as she forgot to swallow or even breathe.

On the head that erupted unnaturally from a broad metal torso, narrow eyes burned white like magnesium, belching black smoke. It sneered with an inhuman maw of jagged scrap, shredded automobiles, impaled on thousands of extruding lengths of rebar and mixed with varied shards of heavier I-bar. In its entirety, it was a senseless amalgamation of scrap. It defied the eyes; it was impossible to single out one item in the grand mess, only to view the whole creature, a ball of clay, *mechanical clay*, molded into some sort of childhood boogieman, complete with sinister eyes and portentous expression. Massive hands swept side to side as it lurched forward, leaving the burning womb that birthed it; arms and fingers moved like a broken puppet, something that didn't know how a person ought to behave.

There was no way to build an educated understanding of this creature, the power of the gods made manifest in a whole unnatural entity, made up of nothing but the cast-off debris, dead husks, and garbage of a dead world.

"I saw this metal monster," Aurora whispered, "In Maggi's future."

"Lady, we need to get you to safety." The soldier spoke to her as Aurora tried to claw away from him and chase after the beast. She forgot that her legs no longer worked, she was angry at him for a second, before remembering.

"Maggi?" Aurora cried out after the glorious newborn monstrosity, a golem of wreckage, ruin, a million dead souls and their bodies, held together by a burning heart of lava.

If the beast heard her, it did not care, it did not react. It lurched, jerked, and shuffled its way east, toward the rising sun.

"Maggi." Aurora repeated, quieter now, her ears ringing, and her flesh pimpled with sweat as heat washed out from the pit.

"Maggi is dead, Lady." Aurora's protector spoke to her.

"Did you say you *loved me last* night?" Aurora glanced up at the man.

His features were dirty and dusty, his eyes red and teary from the sand, his armor tattered, but he did not flinch when she asked him this question.

"I may have Lady. I believed we'd die." He nodded.

"What's your name, soldier?" Aurora leaned against him, aware again that she was crippled, she could never run after the beast, never run through the grass and sea ever again.

"Cyrus, Lady. Captain Cyrus Johnson."

"*Cyrus*," Aurora rolled the name around her mouth, repeating it again, "Cyrus, did you mean that? You love *me?*"

"Lady, I have served in your personal guard for over a decade. I've been at your side through war and peace, watched you sorrowful alone and fake your joy at court." Aurora had no idea what to say to this man. She'd seen him before of course, though for how long she couldn't remember. How could she answer him? She didn't love him, and even if she did, she was married to Lord Cuttersark. Regardless of that, in this moment, her heart was aglow.

This day Aurora had bid her friend farewell, watched the death of ancient demons, and saw the birth of a beast so titanic in scope that her mind refused to accept or understand. Now she stood, her crutches gone and a soldier holding her off the dirt, a man who proclaimed his love for her.

Aurora had not felt this way in *two decades*.

One last time the Lady Aurora Owens turned to see the silhouette of the beast, shrinking in the distance. Was this a final parting gift? Was this something Maggi shared with her?

She spun back to Cyrus and his buzz cut of salty red hair, "Take me home, back to Stockton."

"Yes, Lady." He replied.

"And Cyrus?" Aurora leaned close now, wondering if it was a mistake, when she whispered, "When we're alone, call me *Ro*, please."

STOCKTON, CALIFORNIA. EIGHTEEN YEARS AFTER THE DEATH OF MAGGI LOPEZ.

In the decades that followed the death of Maggi Lopez, Aurora rarely considered her.

It was not that Maggi hadn't been important or that Aurora didn't value her friendship. It was simply the fact that Aurora refused to accept *sorrow*. In life, Maggi had been fueled by sorrow, her smile had been a bittersweet one but she had known who she was.

Aurora Owens was never that person. She'd spent a lifetime avoiding things she *disliked*, and she had no intention of changing that now. Such as it was, she felt awkward telling the last story in the tale of Maggi and her deeds, but she'd made a promise, and she was a woman of her word.

The court of Aurora the Elder was a grand room with high ceilings and vaulted windows. It had changed little since a dirty and disheveled Bruja had come before Aurora, almost two decades before. Now there was more artwork on the walls, much of it trophies from museums in San Francisco. Aurora had also ordered the collection of Auguste Rodin's bronze sculptures at Stanford to be brought here, watching over her when she accepted visitors; behind her throne stood *La Porte de l'Enfer*, one of only seven in existence before the Collapse.

A few years prior she had ordered the black carpet replaced with ornately carved black tile, each piece of the floor a separate image from the early days of House Owens. If one followed the floor, they'd see a story unfold. Maggi had her own section, depicting the day she held the muzzle of The Dread Harvester as barter.

Next to her stood Cyrus, still Aurora's guard after all those years. His face had aged and his red hair wasn't red *at all anymore*, a short-buzzed mane of white as thick as the day he'd saved her from her own wonder at Xanthous Mine. He glanced down, asking for permission to adjust Aurora's formal ribbons, the heraldry worn at times like these. She nodded to the soldier, allowing him to affix the decoration on her left breast accordingly. When he turned away, his fingers brushed the top of her head, *physical contact*, and quietly, every so quietly, she could hear his mind whisper, *you look radiant*.

Cyrus, lowborn and without a magically talented bone in his body, knew more about nobility than Aurora's fool of a husband ever had. Quietly he'd nursed a burning desire for her, serving as her personal guard, ready to sacrifice himself at moment's notice. He might have loved her *first* but she had reciprocated his feelings equally over time. She did not divorce Lord Cuttersark, but before Jeremy died she'd done her best to keep it a secret. Jeremy likely knew; he was a *witch* and a clever man for all his stupidity, be he never seemed to care.

On the right, a few yards away was the oldest Owens child, Aurora the Younger. Daughter, Magnate of The Orders since her father's death. She wore a black dress, tight on her fat hips, covered in tiny plates of enameled metal. Like her father, she labored under the idea that witches *did not need* to wear the uniform of the House. This had always disappointed Aurora the Elder, who now glanced to the left at her son holding his head high.

Eric Owens was named for Aurora's father. He was one of House Owens' four Generals now. As a sickly boy, he had been spoiled by his parent's good graces. Maggi had been wise in her advice, recommending that Eric be sent to service. He'd lost his baby fat, lost his whine, and lost his stutter. He'd gained some scars and a bad limp, but considering that his mother had been a cripple for decades, she figured he'd do just fine. He'd do *more than fine*, Aurora the Elder favored his shrewd and successful leadership in the army, and favored him as a successor.

On *this day*, on *this morning*, Aurora Owens could have used the council of her old friend. It was, after all, *her* son that the Matriarch was about to meet.

The double doors of court cracked open, lurching slowly at first, before swinging wide. Several guards stepped into the room, weapons at shoulders. Time had changed Owens uniforms, protocols, and procedures.

"I present, Emperor Alexander Lopez, Lord of the East, Ruler of the *Antecedent Empire.*"

The announcer was far too eager, far too thrilled for Aurora's preference. She decided to have him fired from his post later.

Although she'd seen this day in a vision, she had not seen all the details. A glimpse at the future wasn't always as simple as opening a page in your favorite book and reading.

To Maggi's credit, she had produced a beautiful child. Alexander was *tall*, probably a foot and a half taller than his mother, if memory served Aurora. His skin was a lighter shade of brown than Maggi's and his shoulders were squared away as if he'd been carved from marble. There was a dimple on his strong chin, jaw clean shaven, and a dour look about him, too serious for his own good.

"You are your mother's son," Aurora whispered, only to herself.

Alexander's armor was a combination of dark fabrics inlaid with silver embroidery with plate steel on his chest and shoulders that reflected light like chrome. The second man who flanked him, a few paces back and to the right, wore a black woolen uniform, sans the polished metal. He was wide in the shoulders, a brawler if Aurora had ever met one, with a bald skull and mustache that dominated his face the way a mountain owned a horizon.

It was the woman, on the left, who drew Aurora's eye from the Lopez boy, however. This one was a witch, *a battlewitch* as Maggi has called them. Her energy flowing vibrant and red, illuminating the Owens court and even warming Aurora's tired flesh in her gaze. She was tiny, unnaturally so, and slim with dark eyes *too big for* her face, lips too narrow, and a face *far too young* for the tomes of history her eyes spoke. Her auburn locks were braided and pulled up around her face in an elaborate knotwork pattern into which was layered curving bits of metal that reflected light like Alexander's chrome plate. Her gown was a vibrant red, made of deeply intoxicating fabrics, and patterns. She walked next to Alexander, *not at his flank.* She smelled like *terror and lust,* and there was a tempered edge of kindness that ran parallel to her more extreme components.

When the three Antecedent officers stopped a few yards from Aurora's throne, she nodded to a guard further against a side wall and the main doors were closed.

"*Emperor Lopez, I've heard much about you.*" Aurora spoke, using the voice of command, less because she wanted to intimidate her guest, more because this was the formal procedure at court.

"Lady," The blazing red witch, so small, a miniature person next to Alexander, raised her hand, "We have no use of parlor tricks. You will speak to the Emperor with a voice to which you were born, or no voice at all."

Aurora didn't answer, only turned to the lady and watched her. She flowed with energy, it poured off her like a waterfall, flooding the court and wetting Aurora's lips with the memory of youth. She simply nodded to the small witch and turned back to the tallest of the officers, nodding to him, "Apologies, Emperor, I am an old woman, set in my ways."

"It's my pleasure, Lady Owens," Alexander leaned in, deeply to Aurora, speaking no further of the voice she'd used, "Allow me to introduce my envoy."

"Of course," Aurora leaned back, placing her palms on the edges of her throne.

"This is Lieutenant General Townsend, commander of our advanced recon forces here in California as well as my personal escort." Townsend saluted smartly, and Aurora accepted the respect from him. "This is my advisor, *Lady Mayhem,* lead battlewitch of the Antecedent Empire." Mayhem curtsied smartly, shooting a look of mischievous joy. Aurora considered scratching at her defenses, just to rattle her, reaching out with her mind and pushing back a little. She thought better of it, but nodded again, accepting her faux respect.

"Impressive, you do me honor to bring such fine examples of the Empire with you." Aurora smiled, eyes returning to Alexander, and then drew her hands up so she could gesture to both children who flanked her, "These are my heirs, Aurora the Younger and Eric. Aurora the Younger is Magnate of The Orders, *assistant* battlewitch to the House Owens."

"I see that the Empire also favors an *informal formality for* their witches, mother." Aurora's daughter returned Mayhem's curtsy, but Mayhem showed as much disdain for the child as she had for Aurora Owens herself. The younger's comments at court on *this day*, rubbed her mother the wrong way. It was a purposeful jape at the elder's expense.

"An honor to meet such regal officers," Eric, however, made his mother proud *again*, smartly answering the guests of House Owens as if they were *his* guests.

"Emperor," Aurora the Elder focused on Alexander again, "We'll perform the appropriate ceremonies this evening, publicly, but I would like to take this moment to offer my acquiescence to the Antecedent Empire. The lands, the army, and the resources of House Owens shall be at your pleasure by morning."

"I appreciate your openness, Lady," Alexander's voice was deep and, despite his serious expression, there was a degree of mirth at the edges of his syllables, "Not all city-states have joined us so cordially."

"We're not a city-state," Aurora smiled, drawing hands up to meet over her lap, "House Owens was born from the Collapse. We never *raided*, we accord ourselves conduct above the *rabble*." Jeremy would have been proud of the self-importance and pride which Aurora beamed. She was not about to hand this man much of California without him paying *some damned respect*.

"Of course," Alexander nodded, "House Owens is well known across the land."

"House Owens gives you the key to the Pacific Ocean, Emperor," Aurora the Elder leaned forward, letting a little venom slip into her voice, "Have you any idea how much trade runs up and down the coast? San Francisco is the jewel of the west, for a thousand miles in either direction."

"Lady," Alexander held up his palms, flashing her a smile that was difficult to dislike, "We mean no disrespect, House Owens is a powerful nation, and their decision to join the Empire is one we accept the deepest of respect and reverence."

"Not much of a decision," Aurora the Younger answered curtly, "The

Antecedent Empire doesn't knock twice, and marches with an army of one-hundred thousand."

"One-hundred and *thirty* thousand." The previously quiet Townsend corrected the Owens daughter, no hint of a smile on his lips, though Aurora the Elder could taste ego bursting from his chest at the opportunity to remind others of their inferior military.

"It's easy to conquer the world when The Beast spent a decade slaughtering the remains of Federal bases and bastions." This time Eric Owens answered.

"*Enough,*" Aurora the Elder held up her hand, "Alexander and I will work out the details in private, but House Owens will still retain a modicum of independence."

"More than other states could dream of." Alexander's voice dropped from charismatic and jovial to a lean, threatening growl. Rather than accept her offer to end the dissension, he forced her to submit to him in front of his officers and her children. Aurora could have replied with a snappy retort, a one-liner befitting the fearless Maggi Lopez, but nothing could be gained.

Instead, Aurora the Elder decided to neutralize his demand, "Alexander, I'd planned to speak to you in private, but I think this is as good of a time as any. I was once, many years ago, given a message to offer up the day we met."

"For *me?*" Alexander was perplexed, the edge on his voice gone, "From *who?*"

"Emperor, I'm sure your companions must have told you; your mother came to my court two decades ago now, seeking my kindness."

"Yes," Alexander nodded, slowly at first, then quicker, "Yes, I do remember. My wife, Aniceta, told me that they'd stopped here, they'd refueled and resupplied."

"But, your mother didn't return home with them." Aurora the Elder said, careful to not appear malicious or cruel as she spoke.

"Lady," Alexander smiled a very narrow smile, "My mother rarely returned home from anything. I knew when she passed, years ago, and I slowly came to accept it."

"*Regardless,*" Aurora drew her syllables out, matching eyes to his, aware that Mayhem was also following this conversation with keen interest, "Your mother and I knew each other briefly, but I called her my friend."

"Maggi had no friends," replied Mayhem, clipped and cool, cutting off her Emperor.

"Untrue, Lady," Aurora smiled sincerely, "Not a day goes by that I don't miss her." Those words dug into the tiny woman, Aurora felt her energy shift, watched her oversized eyes blink too many times.

"Lady Owens, my mother was an enigmatic witch. *The Bruja* knew many people, but few people knew her." Alexander sighed, and Aurora wondered if he was bored with this conversation. Did he disdain Maggi so much or was he working to maintain the upper hand in front of his officers?

"*Regardless,*" Aurora drew her syllables out, a second time, "The last morning Maggi and I spoke together, she asked me to give you a message. '*Tell Alexander,* that I loved him. I loved him, and I'm sorry I was never there as much as he needed me. Tell him that I died for him, for his father's dreams, and my own. Tell my boy, *I am proud of the man he became.*'" Aurora Owens quoted Maggi's words from memory. Her inflections, the words she leaned into, she had replayed that message in her mind a million times. The stories Maggi regaled her with of her boy, they had painted him as tender, sweet, and dashing. Maybe the decades of war, conquest, and strife had changed him.

Or perhaps he was just like his mother: monomaniacal and driven.

Aurora's message seemed to impact Alexander. She watched his eyes shift and his shoulders slope ever so slightly. He wouldn't drop his head or tear up, he hadn't become an Emperor by showing weakness like that, but she could sense a change in his heart, in what made him function. Likewise, she detected a prickle from his witch and she wasn't hiding it well. Mayhem felt like a child, jumping up and down, demanding answers to a thousand questions at once. Her face was serene, but Aurora made note and decided she'd throw the dice in a moment and see if her suspicions were *right*.

"Did you," Alexander paused, correcting himself. "*Were you* there, when she died?"

"Yes." Aurora the Elder nodded, but offered up no more words. She waited for Alexander to come to her, to ask, to beg her for something she had which he wanted. It took a moment of percolation, but finally he gave in and questioned further.

"How did she die?" He asked.

"She fought like a hero and she died like a mother, *Alexander*." It was then then Aurora rolled the dice and made her bet. "Maggi died for you, for you and *your sister both*." It was at this moment, with such an innocent phrase that Aurora Owens laid the foundation for her nation's independence. She was listening closely to the tiny lady in red, watching her mind as her eyes danced with Alexander's, the two locked in a moment of real connection. Despite his ego, despite his desire to break an old woman in her own court, Alexander *was his mother's son*.

"Sister?" Alexander turned to Mayhem then back to Aurora the Elder, laughing, "Oh, we're not *brother and sister*."

"Isn't this the little girl, named *Mayy*, with *two y's*?" Aurora glanced from Alexander to Mayhem, feigning a look of concern, playing confused. After losing her House, Aurora Owens *must be losing her mind*.

"Mayhem was my mother's *apprentice*, her student," Alexander shook his head, laughing at the *foolish old lady*. "I'm the only true-born Lopez child my mother birthed."

"My mistake, Emperor," Aurora smiled. The damage was done. Aurora the Elder's chest vibrated under the simmering rage that Mayhem was exuding, anger rolling off her, heating the court and choking the air with pungent emotion. This was the thumbscrew she had desired, this was the weakness she'd searched for during the meeting. Mayhem, somewhat physically deformed, *yes*, walked at Alexander's his *side not at his flank*, showing how much the position meant to her. Maggi had talked endlessly of her *boy*, but only loosely mentioned the girl she'd adopted, an orphan witch named *Mayy*. It wasn't hard to figure out that the woman who became Mayhem *did* consider Alexander her brother and hated playing second fiddle to his *conquering hero*. "As I was saying, Maggi died for you, *Alexander*, she fought the Ifrit who'd plagued her, who threatened to plague you as well. She sacrificed her life, all that she was, to keep you safe."

In those words, Aurora did not lie or manipulate. She told Alexander the truth, as she had promised Maggi that she would.

"My mother was a difficult woman," The Emperor sighed, finally showing a hint of emotion, the sorrow at the edge of his words, the longing, "But I never loved her any less for it. Thank you, Lady Owens. For delivering this message and for receiving my mother with such compassion."

Aurora the Elder smiled and let real sadness seep through, "Maggi *was* my friend."

"Lady Owens," Alexander stood up straighter now, squaring his shoulders away and dismissing any further suggestion of sorrow. He was a good Emperor, a good leader. Unfortunately, he wanted Aurora's House and she had no interest in letting Alexander walk away with *her* prize, unmolested. "We have taken up too much of your time. My officers and I will depart for breakfast. You and I shall meet this afternoon, in private, to go over the formalities of House Owen's *surrender*."

He just couldn't let it go. Aurora the Elder closed her eyes, the single, unique word pressing a dagger into her heart. It was just for an instant. She shook it off quickly, separating her hands and showing respect to Alexander and his officers.

"Alexander," Mayhem called the Emperor by his first name, a familiarity perhaps inspired by Aurora's needling, "I'll stay to speak with the Lady Owens, if it pleases."

"Of course, but don't take too much of her time. The elderly tire easily."

You little fucking bastard, Aurora Owens nearly spat, her lips parted from teeth. The memory of Maggi Lopez had been a bad influence on her.

Instead, she only smiled at the two of them, a *kind and generous old woman*.

With that, Emperor Alexander Lopez and his General spun on their boot heels, clicking as they walked, strutting out of Aurora's court like lions with oversized manes. Once the two departed the room, Aurora's guards swung closed the large double doors and Mayhem was alone with Aurora the Elder and her two children, who were quickly dismissed.

Lady Mayhem stepped closer to Aurora's throne, lips pulled tight and eyes aflame. This time she hid nothing and a look of disdain spread across her cheeks. "My brother will not acknowledge me publicly, but I changed that bastard's diapers while Maggi sobbed into a bottle of tequila."

Aurora the Elder was surprised at how quickly she gave in to informality. She could hear the frustration on her; fists held so tightly that her knuckles cracked. Aurora decided then that she would not lie to this girl. She was being open, and although she had yet to show her respects, Aurora knew that she would eventually. "Your brother reeks of arrogance," Aurora spoke honestly, of the man she would kneel for later that same day, "If I recall correctly, Maggi hated arrogance."

"Maggi believed arrogance the greatest sin a witch could commit." Mayhem shrugged.

"Oh, *true*," Aurora nodded, gesturing her closer, "But your brother is no magic user, and you are. I don't know that *you* smell any humbler."

"Humility is a crime for Alexander, punished by indifference. His Generals, his other witches, the court he keeps, all *swing their dicks like a pack of rabid baboons.*"

Again, Aurora the Elder was taken back. Alexander spoke with none of his mother's coarseness but Mayhem reminded her so thoroughly of her friend, she wondered how this girl could *not* have been birthed from Maggi's own womb. "Mayhem," as she came closer Aurora realized she was not even five feet tall, "I wonder now why you *need* your brother."

"He's my *brother*," Mayhem shook her head, "I love him even if he's a fool. His daughters are my family, *and* my students."

"Alexander has *daughters?*" Aurora asked, further intrigued.

"Yes," Mayhem nodded, her rage slowly easing off, "Twins, actually." Aurora's mind raced through the possibilities. An illegitimate sister whose discontent was a palpable thing, a layer cake of woven complexities sweet in Aurora's mouth and endlessly promising in potential. An illegitimate sister who also had close ties to the true-blood daughters of Alexander Lopez? Old and crippled as she was, Aurora the Elder was not slow of mind. There was much she could make of this; much she could do to change the future of her House.

Maggi Lopez had died to protect her children from a future she didn't wish for them. Aurora Owens was no different.

"Lady Owens," Mayhem delivered a real smile, "I understand that The Beast rests in your borders, that it's been asleep for a decade?"

"Yes," Aurora nodded to Mayhem, "The Beast stands watch over San Francisco, at the tip of the Bay Area Reach, and golden heart of House Owens. Would you like to see it?"

"What *was* The Beast, Lady?" Mayhem squinted, her voice hushing, sultry in its conspiracy.

As Aurora the Elder spoke, she felt her own face light up, "When your *mother* died she managed to summon a great golem to wreck suffering on the enemies of her son. After a decade of carnage, The Beast came home to San Francisco to sleep."

If Mayhem had worn a collar, it would be now that she handed the attached leash to Aurora Owens. Aurora would see no harm come to her, she *liked* her. She would, *however*, ensure that Mayhem would kneel before an Owens heir in the fullness of time.

-END-

The world of Maggi Lopez and the Collapse will return!

*"MAYHEM"–A SEQUEL BY MICHAEL
MOLISANI–DUE 2018*

ABOUT THE AUTHOR

Michael Molisani has had a mind full of terrible horror and bewildering beauty. Unable to exorcise these visions of worlds that do not exist, he set out to become a writer. Having had no idea what a terrible decision this was, and he soon went mad, burrowing into the unspoken mysteries of how to tell a story in a style that would be worth reading.

When he's not hard at work writing, Michael Molisani can be found falling backward in time on the sidewalks of Virginia City, Nevada; or exploring the remote mysteries of The Great Basin. Michael and his wife, Kim Molisani, reside in Northern Nevada. With their cat. Their cat is, however, a jerk.

Printed in the United States
By Bookmasters